GAMBLE'S RUN

By

DAVID F GRAY

David F. Gray

**A HellBound Books LLC
Publication**
Copyright © 2018 by HellBound Books Publishing LLC
All Rights Reserved

Cover and art design by Andrew Post: for HellBound Books
Publishing LLC

www.hellboundbookspublishing.com

Printed in the United States of America

Also by David F Gray –

One Perfect Moment, Fangoria's Frightful Fiction, 2001
Mamaw's Beast, Whispers From The Past: Fright & Fear, North 2 South Press, 2014
The Abomination Of St. Jude, Urban Temples Of Cthulhu, 2016
The Stars Denied, Shattered Space, Tacitus Publishing, 2017
The Cypress Wood Terror, Shopping List, HellBound Books, 2017
Wade Flick, Shopping List 2, HellBound Books, 2017
Mark Is Still Missing, First Hand Accounts, Siren's Call Press, Upcoming

David F. Gray

Acknowledgements:

My deepest thanks to James Longmore and the entire HellBound Books family for taking on Gamble's Run. Their hard work, support and encouragement had been amazing. It has been a genuine pleasure working with them.

Also, a heartfelt thanks to Andrew Post for his extraordinary cover art. It not only depicts a key scene in the story, but also manages to capture the essence of the entire novel.

Dedication:

For Heidi
Constant friend and loving companion.
Thank You

David F. Gray

GAMBLE'S RUN

David F. Gray

Chapter 1
The Hungry Earth

Garrett Webb awoke with a start, his heart pounding. He wiped away the thin sheen of sweat that covered his forehead as he struggled to regain full awareness. The nightmare that had been tormenting him vanished in a dark puff of dream smoke, leaving him with nothing more than a fading impression of being slowly smothered.

The only light came from the glowing red numbers of the small clock perched on the nightstand beside his queen-sized bed. He barely had time to see that it was 4:05 a.m. before they winked out. An instant later, his bed lurched sideways and slammed into the wall. His left shoulder struck the wall at an awkward angle, causing him to cry out in both pain and shock. Instinctively, he reached out for the woman sleeping next to him.

"Mel? MEL!" An instant later, his wife Melody cried out as she too was brutally dragged back into consciousness. Her arm flailed out, slapping him hard on his stomach. He was shirtless, and her fingernails scraped along his ribs, leaving four thin, bloody scratches. The bed lurched again.

"MOLLY," she screamed. Of course her first thought was for their ten-month-old daughter. On cue, Molly started crying. Husband and wife struggled to get out of bed, but suddenly the floor tilted. The bed slid along the wall, away from Molly's bedroom, and stopped under the window that overlooked the lake just outside their petite home. The lake had dried up during the long drought that gripped central Florida, and all that was left was a hard, cracked bed.

"MOLLY," screamed Melody again. The house answered them with another groan, and suddenly the window shattered. Shards of glass pummeled them. If they had been looking up, they would have been blinded. As it was, they sustained dozens of painful, shallow cuts.

"Garrett! What's happening?" Garrett opened his mouth to say that he had no idea, but suddenly a wall of dirt followed the glass. He covered his eyes and mouth and rolled sideways as the dirt piled onto the bed. Melody screamed again. She scrambled off the bed and fell to the floor. Then she began to crawl toward the bedroom door.

"MEL! WAIT!"

"MOLLY!" Melody's only thought now was for her daughter. In the next bedroom, Molly's cries became screams. The tiny wood frame house shook as dirt continued to pour through the bedroom window.

We are going to die, thought Garrett. For a moment, he was more amazed than afraid. How could a perfectly normal night transform into this kind of insanity?

Melody had put Molly down early. He had ordered pizza, and the two of them had eaten while they watched television. Afterward, there had been long, slow lovemaking.

Garrett was not due at work until nine the next morning, and they had stayed up late, talking about their plans for their new life. Both had been born and raised in Kentucky, but Gainesville was now their home. They were rapidly falling in love with the Florida city. It had been a plain and simple night…the best kind of night.

"No." He spat out the word, along with a mouthful of dirt. "We are not going to die like this." He was two-thirds right.

Melody was almost to the door, but it was an uphill climb. She scrambled against the hard wood floor until she reached the door frame. She grabbed it and held tight. Molly's screams were frantic now. Garrett knew that they had seconds to get to her. He crab crawled across the bed. He was wearing only night shorts, and shards of glass sliced into his hands, knees and feet. He ignored the stabbing pain and lunged forward, falling to the floor. Something ripped deep inside his calf. He screamed but kept moving forward.

He could see everything, even though the bathroom light at the end of the hall was off. It was the only light they had left on. He wasted a moment to wonder how seeing in the dead of night was possible. Then he glanced up and got his answer. Both ceiling and roof were split down the length of the house. Directly overhead, a full moon shone down, bathing everything in a harsh gray glow.

The wooden floor buckled and broke. Dust flew up, and he coughed again. Molly continued to scream, but now that they were almost to the hall, Garrett dared hope that they might be able to save her.

Their rented house was small…barely eleven hundred square feet…with only two bedrooms and a single bath. The bedrooms were within a few feet of each other. Like many older Florida houses, it was built on concrete blocks with no real foundation.

"Molly! Mommy's coming, baby!" Melody pushed through the door, and for the first time, Garrett saw the dark stains on the wood beneath her. Like him, she was barely dressed…panties and a nightgown that came to mid-thigh. The shattered glass had done its work on her lovely legs.

The house groaned again, only this time it was even louder than before. The splintered floor lurched beneath them. To their right, the entire structure fell away. Only jagged wood was left of what used to be a kitchen and living room.

"GARRETT! HELP ME!" Melody was almost to Molly's door. Another few feet, and she would be at her crib. He lurched forward, grabbed Melody by the ankles, and pushed her toward his daughter's bedroom.

"Come on, come on, come on," he muttered. The stench of shattered wood and plaster stung his nostrils. Tears squirted from his eyes as the pain in his leg multiplied a hundred fold. He knew that he was probably doing irreparable damage to the torn muscle, but it didn't matter. All that mattered was getting his wife and daughter out of the house.

The floor buckled. Garrett was thrown against the wall, but Melody was forced back toward their bed. She screamed, only now it was the mindless scream of a wounded animal. He tried to grab her, but she was beyond reason. With a feral snarl, she ignored his outstretched hand and clawed her way to the door.

A dark plume of smoke exploded from Molly's room, and her screams were suddenly cut off. *My daughter just died,* thought Garrett. Immediately, another part of his mind rejected the thought. *No. I can still get to her. I can...*

The roof over Molly's room gave way. The door, once a portal to saving a terrified child, disappeared. All that was left was a hideous pile of wreckage that seconds ago had been a warm and safe nursery. Garrett grabbed a loose piece of wood and threw it aside...a futile gesture. He clawed at the rubble, climbing over the pile until suddenly he was above the destruction. He saw the terrible truth. The house was gone. Half of it had broken away, disappearing down an incline that did not exist just moments ago. The other half was flat. The only part still standing was the master bedroom and half of the hall. There was no sign of his daughter's bedroom.

My daughter is dead, he thought. This time, his heart could not dispute the fact. Molly was buried under several feet of wood and plaster. He might have screamed then, but now the second half of the house was sliding into the earth. Behind him, Melody scrabbled up the pile of rubble, heedless of her many cuts and bruises.

"MOLLY! I'm here, baby. Mommy's here." Garrett sobbed. He wanted to shout 'she's gone' but lacked the strength. Instead, he grabbed his wife's arm and started dragging her across the collapsed roof. In the unforgiving moonlight, he could see that the entire structure was a good three feet below the ground. In seconds, they would be swallowed whole.

"LET…ME…GO!" She tried to pull away, but Garrett held on with maniacal strength. He struggled forward. Something else tore in his leg, and he felt it wrench in a direction that it was never meant to go. Bone splintered, and when he tried to put his weight against it, the pain nearly knocked him into unconsciousness.

We're going to die, said that damnable voice in his head…the same voice that had informed him of his daughter's fate. Suddenly, that did not seem so bad. He did not think that he could live with the knowledge that he had failed his baby girl.

But his will to survive was strong, and the thought of being buried alive terrified him. The image of tons of earth closing over his head and pounding him into oblivion spurred him forward. He kept his hold on Melody despite her struggles to get free and crawled across the roof. The ground at the edge of the roof was now four feet above his head. He had no idea how he was going to climb it, let alone how he was going to get Melody out, but it did not matter.

One foot at a time, he did it. Melody's thrashing weakened. She was spent. His strength was nearly gone as well. At twenty-seven, he was still in fairly decent shape, but marriage and fatherhood had made sure that his once frequent trips to the gym had dwindled.

Just to the edge of the roof. Just let me get us to the edge of the roof, and then we can rest. We can rest forever. It might have been a prayer, but neither he nor Melody really believed in any kind of deity.

The house lurched and continued its death slide into the earth. Now the roof was at least six feet below the surface. The loose dirt rolled toward them, a miniature avalanche that would bury them with their daughter.

A narrow beam of light stabbed down from above. Garrett squinted into it.

"Here! Over here!" The shout, like the light, came from above them. "Get that ladder over here NOW!" The house continued to sink. The wall of earth now towered ten feet above them.

"H-h-h-h-hellllp." He tried to scream, but his mouth was clogged with dirt. Melody was still trying to pull away, using her nails to tear at his arm. He blocked the pain and held on. He spat out the dirt. "Pleeease! Help us!" He could barely manage a whisper, but it did not matter. A shadow moved in front of the light, and suddenly he saw the end of an aluminum ladder descending toward him. It hit the roof with a dull thud. He tried to crawl toward it, but his strength was gone.

"Hang on, buddy," said another voice. "Just hang on!" The ladder vibrated as two enormous shadows descended toward him. They reached the bottom and resolved into paramedics with heavy ropes looped around their waists. He reached up, and one of the paramedics grabbed his hand.

"All right, all right, we've got you. Now stop moving. We have to do this fast."

"My daughter," screamed Melody, although her voice, like Garrett's, was barely audible. "Please help my daughter."

"Where is she?"

"SHE'S...UNDER...THE...ROOF," Garrett hissed. The paramedic surveyed the devastated house. Then he looked at Garrett and squeezed his hand tighter.

"I'm sorry," he said in a low voice. "I am truly sorry." He motioned to his comrades above, and seconds later the end of another rope landed next to him. The man started to loop it around Garrett's shoulders, but he tried to push it away.

"Get...my wife," he rasped.

"We're getting both of you out of here now," said the man. "It's not over yet. This beast is still hungry." Garrett looked at Melody and saw that the other man was tending to her. He allowed the rope to be tied around his chest.

"You're leg," said the man.

"I…know," said Garrett. "It's bad."

"Yeah, it usually is when you can see the bone peeking out. There's nothing I can do about it. It's going to hurt like a sonofabitch when we pull you up. Brace yourself." He gave the knot on Garrett's chest a tug and then waved at his friends above.

"Go, go, go," he shouted. The rope grew taut, and Garrett started to rise. Pain exploded in his leg again, and he sobbed. He looked down and saw that his knee was twisted at an obscene angle. Then a gray haze began to cover his sight as shock set in.

Wow, he thought distractedly, *I really can see the bone.* He swiveled, and that same leg banged against the wall of dirt. The pain intensified, but the haze deepened. He did not lapse into unconsciousness…not entirely at least. He knew that he was being pulled out of the ground, and he knew that he was badly injured. *I won't ever walk right again,* he thought dully. *And that's okay. I let Molly die.* He waited for the overwhelming grief that he was supposed to feel, but there was nothing, just an angry black hole where his heart used to be.

He reached the top, and strong hands grabbed him and pulled him over the edge. He landed on his back, staring at the night sky. The moon blazed directly above, and he had to squint just to look at it. A memory flashed bright and clear; he and Melody, lying next to each other by a tranquil lake. They had taken a camping trip to Indiana, and instead of using their tent, they had slept under the stars. The moon that night had been brilliant, and they snuggled together and watched it arc slowly across the sky.

That's the moon, he thought. *I'm under that moon, holding Melody. We've only been married a month. When I turn my head, I'll see her lying next to me. I'll look into her eyes, and she'll smile that incredible smile of hers. Molly will come along in a year or so, but we won't move to Florida. I watch my little girl grow up, get married, and make me a grandfather. We'll have more kids…a lot more…and they'll all come home for Christmas and drive us crazy. We'll…*

There was a shout, and something heavy hit the ground to his left. Garrett turned his head and almost screamed with joy. Melody was there, lying next to him. Her eyes were open, and she was staring straight at him. All that was missing was her smile.

For the briefest of moments, Garrett lived in a perfect world. He and Mel were safe and sound. Then cruel reality shoved its way into his muddled thoughts. He blinked, and Mel's beautiful body sprouted countless cuts and scrapes. Her dark face was covered in blood, and a deep gash ran across her left cheek.

She'll carry a scar for the rest of her life, he thought. Her eyes were still open, but they were devoid of any life or light. He tried to reach out to her, but even the smallest movement caused searing pain. He moved his lips, but his throat had turned into sandpaper. He started to cough and could not stop. Something dark flew out of his mouth, but in the moonlight he could not tell if it was blood or mud.

"Here, buddy." The voice came from his right. A hand slipped under his neck and raised him a few inches above the ground. Something cold and wet pressed against his lips. He opened his mouth and gulped down the offered water. "Easy. Just a little." Garrett took in the water, coughed up some more dark stuff, and drank a little more. The man…in the moonlight, he could see that he was yet another paramedic…eased his head back down to the ground. "We're going to get you to a hospital as fast as we can," he said, "but it might be a little while. We're not even close to being prepared for this."

"W-w-what," gasped Garrett.

"Damned if I know," said the paramedic. "They look like sinkholes; four of them in this neighborhood alone. We've got reports of at least a dozen across three counties, but I've never heard of this many opening up at the same time…or this fast. It's the damned drought, I guess. The underground springs are drying up, and the earth is caving in. We've already pulled twelve people out, but that's taken every ambulance we have, so just hang tight." He held up a small white paper packet, ripped it open and pulled out a syringe. Then he dabbed Garrett's arm with something wet and plunged the needle into his exposed skin. Garrett did not even feel it.

"I…I think my wife's hurt bad," he rasped.

"You're both in shock," said the paramedic. "But you're going to live. I can promise you that much. Now rest easy. I've got to tend to the others. I've given you something for the pain, but I don't want to try and move that leg until the ambulance gets here." And then he was gone.

Straining, Garrett turned his head so that he could see his wife. Her eyes were still open. For the first time, he became aware of a multitude of shouts and screams. They seemed to be coming from everywhere. Again he tried to reach out to her, and this time he managed to move his arm. He brushed the top of her forehead with his fingertips.

"Mel…" There was no response. She did not even blink. "Melody," he rasped. He ran his hand over her matted hair. Suddenly, she jerked away. Her eyes were wild with rage.

"Don't you touch me," she spat. "Don't…you…dare touch me."

"Mel…"

"You...let her die. You let Molly die."

"Mel," said Garrett, his voice breaking. "Don't say that. Please…" Melody reached up and slapped his hand away.

"Don't…don't ever touch me again." Her eyes flashed with an unearthly light. It was a vivid, sickening green, and it transformed her face into something inhuman. Garrett gasped and yanked his hand back in shock. The light faded. Melody rolled over and turned her back to him.

His body, already pushed well beyond the breaking point, started to go numb. The paramedic's injection was taking effect. The raging pain in his leg dulled. It did not go away, but the drug enabled Garrett not to mind it so much. He understood that he was hallucinating. There was no light in Melody's eyes, just anger and yes, hatred. Maybe both would fade in time, but he was suddenly certain that his marriage was now as much a wreck as his rented house.

It's not fair, he thought as his world faded to black. *I tried. Oh God, I tried.* He knew that it was true, just as he knew that Melody would never forgive him for not doing more. *Oh, Molly!* In his heart, the black hole that had swallowed his feelings continued to expand, leaving his soul as numb as his body. He looked at Melody's back.

"I'm sorry," he whispered. Melody did not answer.

Chapter 2

*T*he First Visitation

"Melinda?"

"What do you want?"

"Just let me talk to Melody. Please."

"No."

"Look, it's been over a year. I just need to talk to her. I won't make trouble."

"No, and don't you call here again."

"You're her mother, Melinda," pleaded Garrett. "We were family. Can't you just…"

"You were *never* family," spat Melinda. "*She* is my family. My two boys and their wives are my family. My five grandsons are my family. You stole my daughter, and look where it led."

"Melinda…"

"I warned her about a mixed marriage. I told her from the time she was old enough to understand. Never marry someone who's not your own kind. So what does she do? The minute she goes off to school, she lets some slick white boy steal her away from me."

"That's not fair, Melinda. We loved each other. You have to know that."

"You have no place in her life. Your own family knew this. Have you spoken to them lately?"

"You know I haven't," said Garrett. His frustration suddenly gave way to anger. "They disowned me, just like you disowned Melody. They're as mean and hateful as you are."

"That's enough," snapped Melinda. "Stay away from her, or I'll sic my boys on you. They've wanted to take you apart ever since she brought you home. They hate your guts, Garrett Webb, and so do I. Now leave us alone." There was a click, and the line went dead. Garrett stared at the cell phone in his hand, his lips pressed together in a hard, thin line. His finger hovered over the redial button for a moment. Then he turned it off and stuffed it back into his jeans pocket.

"Let it go," he lectured himself as he leaned back into his recliner and closed his eyes. The anger slowly faded and was replaced with the dull ache that he had lived with for over a year. "The divorce was final six months ago. She's not coming back, so just let it go." It was sound advice, but advice that he was incapable of taking. He was still very much in love with Melody Webb. "Chance," he corrected himself aloud. "She got rid of my name. She's Melody Chance again." It was a bitter truth.

He opened his eyes and sighted in on the framed picture he kept on the table next to his chair. In it, Garrett and Melody were dressed in white shirts and blue jeans, while Molly wore a tiny white sundress with blue flowers. They were at Daytona Beach. Behind them, the greenish brown waves of the Atlantic Ocean were frozen in time. The sky was a vivid blue.

Garrett stared at his former wife and daughter. Molly's skin was light brown, accenting perfectly Garrett's pale complexion and Melody's dark chocolate tone. Molly had inherited his nose, along with his fiery red hair, but otherwise was a clone of her mother. He had always been grateful for that. Melody was the single most beautiful woman he had ever seen. He had loved her the minute they met at college. He loved her still.

He looked away from the picture and closed his eyes again. His mind flashed back to the day the judge granted the divorce. It was the last time he had seen her. Melody could not even look at him. She had walked out of the courtroom, but when he tried to speak to her, Melinda's two sons barred his way. Melinda had not been lying when she said that they hated him. Arvin and Darrin Chance were not much bigger than he was, but together they made an impressive team. Darrin shook his head.

"Leave her alone. It's over."

"And don't you come sniffing around our house either," warned Arvin. "I see you, and I send you to the hospital…if you're lucky." Something broke inside of Garrett. All of the anger and frustration over the divorce came to a head.

"You're welcome to try," he snarled. "But you'd better bring more help than this waste of skin." He jabbed a finger at Darrin. He was ready and willing to take on Melody's brothers, despite the fact that he could barely walk. He clenched one hand into a tight fist and gripped his cane with the other. The Chance brothers squared off. Then, before it could get ugly, two uniformed officers stepped between them. They had had a lot of practice with divorce cases.

"None of that now," said the first. "You two," he pointed at Arvin and Darrin, "go with your family. And you," he said to Garrett, "go the other way, and all three of you, do yourselves a favor. Don't push this. If you do, then sooner or later one of you will do something you can't take back." The Chance brothers seemed ready to argue the point, but after a moment they backed off. With a parting glare, they turned and followed Melody and Melinda out of the courtroom. Garrett watched as Melinda put an arm around her daughter and led her away. Just before they disappeared through the door, Melinda looked back. The venomous look she gave him was half-naked triumph, half-seething hatred.

You didn't even know Molly, he thought, glaring at Melinda's retreating back. *You didn't care about your granddaughter. All you cared about was breaking our family apart. Well, you got what you wanted. I hope you choke on it.*

The divorce had been granted in Kentucky. Melody had left Florida and moved in with her family the week after Molly's funeral. They had buried her in a small graveyard not far from their devastated neighborhood. Garrett spent two months trying to rehabilitate his knee. It was supposed to be a six-month program, but he could not bear living so far away from his wife. He followed her, hoping to somehow win her back. It had been a futile effort.

Neither he nor Melody had many friends, and most of those had purposefully stayed away after they were married. The few of Melody's friends that would talk to him had no idea where she worked or even if she ever left her house. He did not dare show up at Melody's house. He had no doubt that the Chance brothers would make good their threat.

His parents were worse. His father hated...*hated*...African Americans in general and the Chance family in particular. It was a hatred that had been instilled in him by his own father and had been handed down through generations of Webbs. Garrett well remembered the first time he had seen a black man. He had been all of nine. An older man had been sitting in his car outside a Burger King. He had jet black skin and an almost pure white beard. Little Garrett was fascinated.

"Daddy? Look at that man," he said. "Why is he so dark?"

"That's just a nigger, son," replied the elder Webb.

Given his upbringing, Garrett should have turned out as bigoted as Harold Webb...or Melinda Chance, for that matter. Indeed, for a time he had embraced his father's racism, but gradually he had changed. Maybe he decided that he did not have to be his father. Maybe he became disgusted at the idea of hating someone just because they looked or believed differently. Maybe he just grew up. He did not change overnight, but he did change.

By the time he left for college, he and his father were barely on speaking terms. Harold considered his son spoiled and ungrateful, while Garrett saw his father as a hateful, bigoted jerk. He actually enjoyed writing to his parents about Melody; enjoyed it so much, in fact, that Melody accused him of dating her just to hurt them. It had taken him weeks to convince her otherwise.

Harold's reply was exactly what he expected; short and to the point. Don't come home...ever. It was one of the few times he was happy to obey his father. He had arranged for his own school loans and was not receiving any help from his parents. The university was barely thirty minutes away from his home by car, but he never went back.

The only other time Garrett had written was to tell them of Molly's birth. He had sent them a picture of the Webb's new granddaughter, cradled in the arms of a very happy Melody. He did not expect it to make a difference, and he was not disappointed. The envelope arrived a week later. Inside were the remnants of the picture. It had been cut into tiny precise squares. Garrett pictured his father sitting at the kitchen table, scissors in hand, methodically mulching the photograph of his daughter-in-law and granddaughter.

Like the Chances, the Webbs also lived in northern Kentucky. A week or so after Molly's death, Garrett had phoned them. His father refused to speak to him, so he had told his mother. She listened and then told him she had to go. Harold had never laid a hand on either his wife or only child, but there are other forms of abuse. He had an acid tongue that he used to great effect, especially on Alice. Garrett was deeply ashamed that he had never defended his mother, but like many sons, he had a healthy fear of his father.

With an angry grunt, he forced his mind back into the present. He grabbed the recliner's lever and slammed it down. The big overstuffed chair rocked forward. He grabbed his cane and struggled to stand. Even after a year of rehab, his leg still hurt. On good days, it was a dull throb that he could ignore, at least for a while. On bad days, it was a study in agony. On this particular day, it fell somewhere between searing and throbbing. He had pain pills but only used them on the really bad nights. The last thing he needed was an addiction to Vicodin.

He managed to get to his feet, putting most of his weight on the cane. He rocked a little. Then, when he was certain that he wasn't going to fall back into the recliner, he hobbled over to the window of his small apartment.

He had opted to live in northern Kentucky, like his parents, but they were far enough across town that he was reasonably certain he would never bump into then. He had landed a decent job at a small architecture firm. His monthly expenses were low, and over the past year he had managed to build a respectable savings account.

It was early September, and the leaves were beginning to change color. His apartment was on the second floor. Not particularly smart with his leg, he knew, but he wanted to look out his window and see more than the parking lot. His living room window offered a respectable view of the Kentucky hills. Soon those hills would be on fire with autumn colors. Now they were just pale shades of the coming grandeur.

Daylight Savings Time was still in effect, so it was not getting dark until well after seven. Garrett glanced at his watch and saw that it was only six. He leaned against the window, putting his forehead against the cool glass.

"What are you doing, Mel?" he whispered. "Do you even think about me anymore?" He pushed away from the window and took a few steps toward the kitchen. Then he realized that he wasn't hungry. "Screw it," he muttered and eased back into the recliner. He pulled the lever back and with a grimace lifted both legs onto the footrest. He stared at his right leg…he could see its deformity even through his jeans…with a mixture of self-pity and loathing. Then he fished out the remote from under the cushion and turned on the small television that sat against the wall in front of him.

Ten minutes later, he gave it up. He tossed the remote onto the table. It landed next to the picture, and for a moment he was horrified that its momentum would send it crashing into the photograph. It missed by less than an inch, and he let out a silent 'whew.' He settled back into his chair and swiveled it until he could see out his window. He watched as the fading sun traced shadows across the hills, and as the light faded, so did he. The pain in his leg eased, and he fell into a light doze. As darkness slid across the living room, that doze became a deep, fitful sleep.

* * *

The house split down the middle with a deafening *CRACK*. Garrett screamed as he was dragged back into consciousness. Beside him, the glowing red numbers of the alarm clock read 4:05 a.m. Garrett struggled to get out of bed. Beside him, Melody screamed and sat up.

"Garrett? What's happening?"

"Sinkhole," snapped Garrett. He was already rolling off the bed. "We've got to get out of here now." As if on cue, Molly began to cry.

"MOLLY," shouted Melody. "I'm here, baby! Mommy's coming."

"We'll get her," said Garrett. He was halfway to the door, but the house lurched at an impossible angle. He lunged toward the door frame, grabbed it and held on. Then he reached behind him and grabbed Melody's outstretched hand. He pulled her to him and then threw himself at Molly's door. Again the house lurched, but he was ready. He steadied himself and managed to make it into Molly's room. Melody was right behind him.

"Get Molly," he ordered. Melody did not have to be told twice. She grabbed on to her crib and pulled herself up. Then she scooped up the screaming Molly.

28

"Garrett? What now?"

"Now we get out of here," said Garrett. "Come on." He stumbled over to the window in Molly's room and threw it open. "You first." He steadied Melody as she climbed through the window, Molly held tight to her breast. Then he followed. The instant his bare feet hit the ground, the house shuddered. It reared up into the night sky like the Titanic and then split down the middle. Bruised, battered but alive, the Webb family staggered away from the wreckage and fell to the ground. They watched as the sinkhole devoured their home.

"You got us out, Garrett," whispered Melody. "You saved us." She put an arm around his waist and rested her head against his shoulders. Molly stopped crying and snuggled into her parents, satisfied that all was right with the world. Garrett closed his eyes, relieved beyond words that his family was safe and sound…

…and opened them again…and groaned. The dream was always the same, and it came nearly every night. Something tickled his right cheek. He reached up and batted the tear away. The apartment was dark, with only the amber lights from the parking lot outside providing any illumination. He thumbed a button on his watch, and his heart skipped a beat. It was 4:05 a.m.

"That's just not fair," he whispered. He released the button and debated hobbling to the bedroom and spending the rest of the night in his bed. It was Saturday, and he had nothing to do but sleep in. He mulled it over and then decided that it was a good idea. Maybe he would dream of Melody and Molly again. Waking up was always devastating, but for a few brief moments, in some distant reality, he would be reunited with the only two people he truly loved. He reached down, grabbed the recliner's lever and pulled it forward. The footrest slid down, and his feet touched the floor. He grabbed his cane and made to stand...

...and froze.

His apartment was small; a cramped living room, kitchen, bathroom and bedroom. The bathroom was off the bedroom, and the kitchen was to the right of the front...and only... door. There was not much furniture; just his chair, a cheap couch and a couple of end tables. A small dinette set was placed next to the wall that separated the kitchen from the living room. He could easily see the front door and just as easily see the human shaped silhouette standing there. His heart slammed against his chest as he realized that he was not alone.

I'm being robbed, he thought wildly. He gripped his cane, knowing that with his bad leg, he was defenseless against a determined attack. He opened his mouth...whether to scream in terror or challenge, he would never know...but all that came out was a raspy hiss. His throat was bone dry.

The dark figure did not move. Neither did Garrett. *I'm dreaming,* he thought, trying desperately to believe it. *Of course I'm still dreaming.* He concentrated, trying to bring himself to full consciousness. Nothing changed. His aching leg throbbed in time with his heart. That was enough to tell him that he was awake.

And still the dark figure did not move. Garrett knew that whoever it was could certainly see him. The glow from the parking lot was dim but adequate. The seconds ticked away. Finally, he managed to speak.

"I don't have much," he said, his voice barely above a whisper. "Just take what you want and go. Please." His voice was weak and shaky, and he winced in shame. He took a deep breath. "Just get out." He glanced at the table and then remembered that his cell phone was in his jeans pocket. He eased his left hand toward it, but suddenly the figure moved and Garrett had to gulp down a scream. It did not come forward or step backward or even sideways. It *shifted.* Garrett suddenly got the insane idea that it had stayed in the same place while the entire universe moved past it.

"Please," Garrett pleaded. Something was very wrong with this intruder. "What do you want?"

He did not see them move. One second the figure's arms were hanging loosely at its side, the next they were stretched out toward him. *It's come for me,* Garrett thought wildly. A sudden urge to hurl himself through the window came over him. He would be cut to pieces and no doubt fall to his death, but that was far better than whatever this dark intruder held in store for him. *It tried to swallow me with a sinkhole, and now it's come back to finish the job.* He had no idea how his terrified mind could make a connection between this silhouette and the sinkhole, but it did not matter. It felt horribly right. Suddenly, the window seemed like a perfectly acceptable option.

Garrett.

Now he did cry out, only this time in pain. Everything seemed to go green. It only lasted for a second, but then violent purple and green spots exploded before his eyes. The light show was followed immediately by the sensation of razor thin needles stabbing into his forehead.

Garrett. You have to concentrate. I...don't have a lot of time.

The green flash came again, followed on its heels by the searing pain, although now both seemed to fade a little faster. He realized two things; the voice was in his mind, and it was not his own.

"Wh-a-at?" It was all he could manage.

Help me, Garrett. Please help me.

"Who…who are…" Then he managed to match the voice in his mind with one in his memory. "Melody? Mel, is that you?" He superimposed his memory of Melody's shape over the dark figure. It was a perfect match. His terror fled, replaced by pure joy. His wife had come home! He struggled to get out of the chair. "Oh God, Mel, I've missed you so much!" Something pressed hard against his chest and forced him back.

Garrett, find me. He's…he's eating me alive. Please, help me! The flash and the pain came again, but now Garrett barely noticed. He struggled against the unseen force that was holding him down.

"Melody," he gasped. "What's happening?"

Oh God, he's here. There was panic in the voice now, and terror. *Find me, Garrett. Please, if you ever loved me, find me!* The scream echoed through his mind, once again accompanied by both light and pain. He grabbed his head and screamed as well. Through the hurricane of agony came Melody's final message. *Gamble! John…Gamble!*

"MELODY!" His vision cleared, and he looked toward the door. The figure…Melody…was writhing in agony. She jerked back and forth, held in the invisible grip of something both powerful and terrible. Her arms were flung outward, as if she was trying to grab the door to keep from being dragged away. Garrett lunged forward, struggling to get out of the chair. "MELODY!" The force that was pinning him to his chair pushed him back, hard. He wheezed, trying to gulp in another breath.

"STAY." This voice did not come from inside his head, and it did not belong to Melody. It was loud and male and vile. The picture on the table went flying across the room. It crashed into the wall, shattering both frame and glass.

"STAY." Garrett had no choice. Whatever was holding him down was relentless. He heard Melody scream again, only this time she seemed impossibly far away.

"M-m-mel…" It was all he could manage. Incredibly the weight increased. It forced the air from his lungs. He did not have the strength to take another breath.

"STAY." He gagged. He thrashed about in the chair, fighting to get free, but it was useless.

"STAY." He could not even scream as he tumbled into a deep, dark sinkhole that led straight to oblivion.

Chapter 3

Interlude

*H*e was in a nightmare from which he could not escape. Great waves of boiling darkness closed in on all sides, dragging him down into oblivion. A tiny part of Garrett's mind understood that he was unconscious. He fought against the darkness that imprisoned him, tearing at it. Finally, a dim light flared in his mind. He reached for it, knowing that it was his only way out of the darkness. He grabbed the light with his mind and squeezed. Slowly, the darkness receded. It was a long, painful process, but finally he managed to open his eyes.

He was still reclined in his chair, only now the late evening sunlight poured through the living room window, forcing him to squint. He glanced at his watch and saw that it was just after six. He had been out for at least an entire day. The sun's warm autumn glow mocked him. He felt dirty...defiled.

"Mellllllllll." He could barely manage a raw hiss. His throat was parched, and his dry tongue felt as if it had doubled in size. He moved it around in his mouth, trying to get his saliva flowing. After a few seconds, he succeeded. He tried to turn his head, but his neck was stiff and sore. Every muscle in his body ached. He groaned and tried to sit up, but suddenly his damaged leg made itself known.

"Arrrrrrgh." Tears squirted from his eyes. It felt as if molten metal was being injected straight into his knee. Suddenly he began to weep, and in an instant he lost all control. He sobbed, gulping in the air and expelling it almost immediately.

It wasn't the physical pain. He had dealt with that for over a year and had its measure. His *spirit* was in torment. A raging darkness, much like the darkness of his dream, had somehow rooted itself deep inside of him. He could feel it gnawing at his soul, or life force, or whatever it was that made him a unique being.

In the course of a single night, Garrett's world had been turned inside out. He had encountered something that was not only beyond his experience but beyond his belief. He had never been able to acknowledge the existence of anything beyond the limits of his physical senses. In an instant, that belief had been turned into a pile of rubble that now lay at his metaphysical feet.

Far worse was the shattering knowledge that he was no match for the power that had held him in its grip. He had never felt so helpless. Less than a day ago, the entity that had assaulted him was something that he could never admit existed, but now...

He's eating me alive. Melody's words formed a loop inside his mind. They played over and over, driving him to despair.

"Oh Mel, what have you done?" he groaned. That last night's visitation might be a dream did not even cross his mind. The shattered picture frame lying on the floor provided physical evidence, but he did not need such trite assurances. The darkness growing inside him was all the proof he needed. It was the same darkness that in some insane way was tormenting his wife. *And she is my wife,* he thought. *I don't care what the courts say, and I don't care what Melinda and her two idiot sons say. I don't even care what Melody says.*

The weeping subsided, and he managed to get his body under control. As he did, he was suddenly aware that, among his other aches and pains, his chest was tingling. He pulled up his T-shirt and gasped. The mark was the color of dark fire. It was seared into his chest in the shape of a large man's hand. He stared at it, and the only thing he could think was, *I've been branded.* He tugged his shirt down and closed his eyes.

Is she dead?

It was the one question he could not bring himself to ask, and it was the one question he could not ignore. It had been sneaking around in the back of his mind since he regained consciousness. Now he was forced to confront it.

"Are you dead, Mel?" he whispered. "Was that your ghost I saw?" He thought about it and then decided to give himself at least a tiny bit of hope. *He's eating me alive, she said...alive.* He tried to latch on to that, but the darkness raging in his soul was both real and potent. It took his barely glowing ember of hope and quashed it into nothingness. *What am I supposed to do, Mel? How am I supposed to find you?*

He thought of Melinda Chance. Would she know anything? Maybe, but judging from their previous conversation, she almost certainly would not help him. She had been vintage Melinda… cold, biting and hateful. Then something clicked. A memory lit up in his mind. His eyes snapped open. Melody had shouted a name.

"Gamble," he said aloud. "John Gamble." As far as he could remember, there was no one in his own past by that name. That left Melody. He was certain that she had never mentioned him. Would Melinda know? Would she tell him if she did?

"Fat chance," he muttered. His throat dried up again, and he started to cough. *Dear God, what did that thing do to me?* The fit lasted several seconds and left him shaking. His cane was lying in the chair next to him, and he grabbed it. Then, knowing that it was probably a bad idea, he brought the chair forward and struggled to stand. It took a couple of tries, but to his surprise he managed to get up. The room spun for a few seconds and then settled down.

He could see the picture lying next to the wall. It had been thrown out of its frame by the force of the impact. There was glass everywhere, and his feet were bare. He skirted the opposite edge of the living room until he got to the bedroom entrance. There, close to the bathroom, was a tiny utility closet where he kept a few cleaning supplies. He pulled out a broom and, using his free hand, swept the glass aside.

Every step was agony, but he made it to where the picture lay crumpled. When he knelt down to pick it up, the room started to spin again. Gritting his teeth, he grabbed the picture and managed…barely…to stand. He smoothed it out and stared at it. Both Melody's and Molly's face were burned and unrecognizable. His own likeness was untouched.

"You vicious bastard," he muttered, gripping the ruined picture in his fist. He stuffed it into his pocket. Another wave of dizziness hit him. He made his way to the refrigerator. Every step seemed to jab red hot needles into his knee, but he kept at it. When he got there, he jerked open the door and grabbed the gallon jug of distilled water he kept on hand. Not bothering with a glass, he pulled off the plastic top and started to gulp.

Drinking the cold water was like drinking life itself. It poured down his throat and seemed to seep into every cell of his body. He took it in, heedless of how it dribbled out of the corners of his mouth and trickled onto his shirt. The jug was half-full, and he finished it off in a matter of seconds. Then he threw it into the sink, opened an upper cabinet and took out another gallon. This time he used a green plastic tumbler that said TGI Fridays on one side and Coca-Cola on the other. He had found it lying in the restaurant's parking lot a few months ago and decided that it would be his lucky cup. He filled it to the brim, drank it down, and filled it again. Then, tumbler in hand, he hobbled back into the living room.

He felt stronger. The darkness was still there, but he managed to ignore it. He did not want to think about what might happen to him if he could not find some way to rid himself of it.

"John Gamble," he said again. At least this time there was no fit of coughing. He ran the name through his memory and again came up blank. He thought about calling Melinda, but even if she knew who Mr. Gamble might be, she would not tell him. She hated him that much. That left Melody's friends. He doubted that they would be of any help, but he had to try. He pulled his cell phone out of his pocket and made his way back to his easy chair. Setting the tumbler on the table, he started making calls.

Twenty minutes later, he gave it up. Of the seven of Melody's friends he still kept in his phone's memory, four actually bothered to talk to him. None of them claimed to know anything about John Gamble. If they were lying, there was nothing he could do about it.

Frustrated, he stuffed his phone back into his pocket. His eyes roamed the living room, coming to rest on his satchel. He had laid it on the dinette table late Friday when he had returned from work. Among other things, it held his laptop. With a 'why the heck not?' shrug, he struggled up again and hobbled over to it. Pulling it out of the satchel, he eased down into one of the dinette's two chairs, pulled out the laptop, and turned it on. The apartment came equipped with wi-fi, and in a few seconds he was Googling the name John Gamble.

His initial search resulted in over fifty-three thousand hits. Frustrated, he closed the laptop and stuffed it back into his satchel. Glancing toward his window, he saw that it was nearly dark. With a savage swipe, he reached behind him and hit the switch for the overhead light.

He was suddenly hit with an almost overwhelming urge to stuff his few belongings into a duffle bag, get in his car and start driving. He had money…enough to last for a while at any rate. He could run fast and far, but he knew that he could never outrun the darkness within him. And he had a sinking feeling that the entity could find him wherever he went. Not that it mattered. Melody was in trouble, and he would not abandon her.

"No," he said aloud. "I won't let you have her. She's my wife…my *wife,* do you hear. I don't know who or what you are, but I promise you this; I am going to find her and take her away from you."

There was no warning. In a single heartbeat, the mark on his chest blazed with searing heat. He gasped and doubled over, clinging to the edge of the table. *Dear God, it heard me.* He clawed at his chest, gasping for breath. Then, as suddenly as it came, the pain vanished. Garrett leaned against the table, shaking. The message was clear. *Back off.*

We're linked, he thought, his heart sinking at the realization. *I'm not just marked. Somehow, that thing is connected to me. It knows when I'm talking to it, and if it doesn't like what it hears...*

"It's got me on a leash," he said aloud. He sat up and put his head in his hands. How could he fight this thing? "Why?" he muttered, rubbing his eyes. "Why me? And why Mel? What's she done to deserve this?"

Suddenly, his stomach rumbled. He realized that he had not eaten since late the previous day. He did not want to eat now. It felt wrong, as if he was somehow betraying Melody. Still, if he was to have any chance at finding her, he had to keep up his strength.

He started to get up, but a whiff of body odor made him cringe. He had also not showered since the previous day. Resigned that he was going to have to serve the needs of his body before anything else, he went back into the kitchen and threw a frozen beans-and-rice meal into the microwave. While it was heating, he took a quick shower. The hot water stung the mark on his chest, but he endured the pain. He emerged from the bathroom naked and went into the bedroom. Throwing his dirty clothes into the laundry hamper, he shrugged on some boxers, another T-shirt and the sweat pants that served as his nightclothes. Then he limped back into the kitchen and pulled out his meal.

Eating helped more than he would have thought possible. He was beginning to understand that his encounter with both Melody and her tormentor had had a devastating impact on him physically. The entity had stolen something from him.

"Life," he muttered as he ate. "It sucked life out of me." He shook his head. Just twenty-four hours earlier, he would have laughed at the idea. Now it was all too real. The entity had invaded him on a level so deep that he could not wrap his mind around it. The seed of darkness growing inside was proof enough of the damage it…*he*…had caused.

"Rape," he whispered. It was an ugly word, a devastating word, but it was the only word that fit. His spirit had been raped, and he feared that he would carry the wound for the rest of his life. Still, the food helped. By the time he threw the disposable plate away and made his way to the bedroom, he felt considerably better.

He was also exhausted. He had been unconscious most of the day, but it had not been true rest. He desperately needed to sleep. Could the life the entity had stolen from him be replenished? A body could heal…sometimes. Could a soul? Since he had never really believed in a soul, he had no idea.

He pulled down the bedspread and slipped under the sheets. A glance at the clock on his nightstand told him that it was barely eight o'clock, but it did not matter. He was already fading. He started to turn out the light but then decided to leave it on. He could do nothing about the darkness raging within him, but at least he could sleep in the light. He closed his eyes and within minutes had slipped into a deep sleep. His last thought was a prayer to a God he did not believe in. *Please, just let me get through the night.*

#

He opened his eyes in darkness. It took him a few seconds to remember that he had left the light on. The air was heavy and inexplicably cold. He shivered once, hard. *It's happening again,* he thought, despairing. Not daring to move, he strained his ears, trying to detect any sign of the entity. The bedroom was silent…unnaturally silent in fact. Usually, he could hear the sounds of the night through the bedroom window; cars driving on Dixie Highway just a few hundred yards away, crickets chirping, and more often than not, the heavy thud of someone's surround sound system being played way too loud. Now, there was nothing.

He already knew, but he had to look. Slowly, he turned his head. The sound of his hair rubbing against his pillow was deafening. The red lights of the clock on his nightstand came into view… 4:05 a.m. *Then do it,* he thought. *Get it over with.* He waited. Now that he was fully awake, he could easily sense the entity's presence in the room, but there was no deafening voice ordering him to stay and no unyielding weight crushing him down into his bed. There was only silence. The seconds ticked by.

"Meeeew." The barely audible cry came from the other side of the bedroom. It was a high-pitched whine, and for a moment he thought that a cat had somehow slipped into the apartment. The complex was practically overrun with them, so it was not beyond the realm of possibility. "Meeeew." This time, the cry sounded as if it was inches from the back of his head. It was all he could do not to jump up and scramble out of bed. "Ah!

Ah-iee. Da! Da!" His mind re-evaluated the sound, matching it up with noises that he was all too familiar with. It was not a cat. It was a baby.

No, Garrett groaned. *You can't be that cruel.* His sheet moved. "Eeee-aaaa. De-de." Something warm brushed against the back of his neck. He knew that he could no longer ignore the presence behind him. He could not even run. Where could he hide from a creature that could sense everything he said…maybe even everything he thought? *God help me,* he prayed, aware of his hypocrisy. He rolled over.

There, lying just inches away was the silhouette of an infant. He knew immediately that it would be Molly's likeness. The dark shape wiggled, waving its hands and feet. Garrett swallowed hard. Suddenly he was angry, and for a brief moment that anger overrode his terror.

"You're not her," he said in a low voice. "My daughter is dead. She died over a year ago. It took the workers over two days to dig her body out of the ground." The baby beside him did not respond. It continued to make happy nonsense noises, kicking and waving as if all was right with its world.

"Stop it," growled Garrett. "Just…stop it. If you want to have another go at me, then do it and get it over with, but stop your stupid games." His chest started to tingle and then burn. He understood that the entity was going to do exactly that. Behind him, the bedroom light snapped on.

Chapter 4

The Second Visitation

*T*he likeness was dead on, although this version of Garrett's daughter was maybe six weeks old, rather than the ten months she had been at the time of her death. The baby (he would not dignify the apparition with her name) grinned with her toothless mouth. Her eyes fastened on Garrett's, and she wiggled her arms and legs in glee.

"Da! Ki ki awww aie!"

"Is that the best you can do?" he screamed, his voice still raspy. A feral rage welled up inside of him, complimented by the darkness that the entity had planted within his spirit. It was exceeded only by the deep, gnawing grief that he dealt with every waking moment of his life...grief that now threatened to consume him. Even though he knew beyond doubt that the thing in his bed was not his daughter, seeing her alive and happy shook him to his core. He desperately wanted to scoop her up and cradle her in his arms. The mark on his chest flared with red heat, and he gasped. He felt rather than heard the reply.

Of course not.

The entity lashed out at him, but this time he was ready. Over the past year, he had come to understand exactly what the human body could endure. He rode the wave of pain like a surfer, controlling his breathing and concentrating on the entity. He could feel its presence, but it was not emanating from the baby. It seemed to be coming from the foot of the bed.

"So you're not it," he said to the baby. "You're some kind of what? Manifestation? Illusion?" He tore his eyes away from her and looked toward where he felt the presence was at its most potent. "Is that it? Did you manufacture this just for me?" He could not help but be amazed at the situation. He was locked in a spiritual wrestling match with something that could not exist. Then another wave of pain hit him, and he had to ride it out again. The baby stared at him, quiet now.

"Come on," Garrett grunted through clenched teeth. "Quit kidding around. Bring on the real stuff." The entity obliged, and the pain increased. Every nerve in his body lit up with invisible fire. He grabbed his chest and held on tight, waiting for the entity to ease off. Then he felt something wet, and when he pulled his hands away, he saw red. Fighting thorough the pain, he was now literally sweating blood. His chest was slick with it. The white sheets of his bed were stained, and the stain was growing. Through it all, the baby watched, unblinking.

But Garrett possessed another line of defense. He thought of Molly. Then he took his mind to a place where she was still alive. It was a trick he had learned during his time in rehabilitation. His nurse, Marty, had coached him on it.

"When the pain becomes too much to bear, go somewhere else," she said. "Find a place in your heart and mind when you were happy and go there. See it in detail. Feel it. Smell it. It takes a lot of practice, but you will be amazed at how well it can work."

Initially skeptical, Garrett nevertheless tried it. In time, he taught himself to escape to that peaceful night in Indiana. There, Melody was waiting for him, and together they would watch the stars wheel across the sky. In time he added Molly, and the three of them lay together under a blazing sky of stars.

It had saved him. The pain during his rehab pushed him to his physical limits, but it had also taught him just how powerful a tool he possessed with his mind. In time, he was even able to hear the gentle lapping of the lake and smell the honeysuckle that tinged the air.

Now, with every inch of his body on fire, he cast his mind back to that same place by the lake. He envisioned a tunnel leading out of his lonely bedroom. It bored through time and even reality itself, leading to his safe place. As soon as it formed in his mind, he fled through it and emerged into the starry night.

It was all there, just as he imagined it. He could still feel the pain, but it was far away and unimportant. He took a deep breath and tasted the moisture in the night air. The ground under his feet was spongy with thick grass. A few yards to his right was the tent he and Melody, after several comic efforts, had managed to pitch. Everything was exactly where it was supposed to be, except...

"Mel? Melody?" She was not there. The campsite was deserted. Garrett felt the pain surge but fought it down. The darkness was there as well. He could feel it trying to break through his defenses and into his sanctuary. He focused his will and managed to hold it at bay. "Mel! Where are you, babe?" Something was not right. Had the entity managed to not only pluck Melody out of his life, but out of his mind as well? "Melody!"

"She's not here, Dad." The soft voice came from behind him. He whirled and came face to face with a beautiful young woman. Her skin was the color of creamed coffee. Her brown eyes were wide and piercing, and her shoulder length fiery red hair accented her flowing white dress. She was young, perhaps in her early twenties, but she moved with the grace and confidence of a much older woman. She smiled and raised her right hand. Garrett cried out and stumbled backward, barely managing to stay upright. He recognized the young woman immediately. How could he not? Other than her hair and lighter skin, she was the spitting image of his wife.

"You're not her," he gasped. "You're from him." The woman shook her head.

"No, I'm not," she said. "And you need to believe that, Dad. It's me…it's Molly."

"Molly's dead," Garrett growled. "I heard her die. I felt her die. I *buried* her."

"I know," said the woman. "And I know how hard this is for you, but I need you to see with your real eyes, Dad. I need you need to see me for who I am."

"Molly's dead," Garrett repeated.

"Yes I am," said the woman. "And no, I'm not."

"Stop playing games," snapped Garrett. "What do you want? Why are you tormenting Melody?" Exasperation mixed with impatience crossed the woman's face.

"We're not safe," she said. "It's amazing that you managed to get here. You're strong…very strong, in fact…but you can't stay. Sooner or later, he is going to break through."

"What do you want?" repeated Garrett.

"I want to save you," said the woman, raising her voice, "because you have to save mom. You're the only one who can."

"Oh, I'll save her, all right. You can count on that." Garrett was gasping now. Despite his efforts, the pain was seeping through into his safe place. Worse, the darkness was hot on its heels.

"Dad! It's me, Molly!"

"STOP IT," screamed Garrett.

"NO!" screamed the woman right back at him. "You have to see me. You have to know me." Before he could react, she took two quick steps toward him. She reached out and laid a warm hand against his chest. For the first time since he arrived, he realized that he was naked.

"No…" he groaned. He tried to pull away, but he was paralyzed.

"It's the darkness in you," said the woman, almost whispering. "It's why you can't see me." She closed her eyes. Garrett tried to pull away again, but he was held tight. "I can't take it away, Dad," said the woman. "I don't even know if it *can* be taken away, but I can at least do this."

Suddenly, the campsite was engulfed in a blazing white light. Garrett screamed, but for the first time in what seemed like forever, it was not a scream of terror. It was a shout of triumph. The light was pure, beautiful and perfect. If the darkness within him was anti-light, then the light was anti-darkness. It was life. He felt it surround him. It began to seep into his spirit, and he welcomed it. Everything he wanted to be was contained in that wondrous light. He wanted to merge with it. He wanted to become it.

Then the light met the darkness that infested his soul. Opposites collided. There was a brief, violent struggle, but the darkness was stronger. It expelled the light.

"No!" He reached out and tried to grab it, to hold on to it, but it slipped through his fingers like quicksilver. It started to fade, and he sobbed. For a brief instant in time, he had possessed something wonderful, only to have it ripped away by the darkness that was consuming him. Then, just before the light faded completely, a tiny, needle thin beam shot out. It pierced the darkness like a doctor's scalpel and sliced straight into Garrett's innermost being.

"Look at me, Dad. See me for who I really am." The woman still stood before him, her hand on his chest. The beam sank deep into Garrett's spirit, and as it did, it formed a bridge between the two of them. He looked into her eyes...

...and saw his daughter.

"Molly?" Relief flooded her face.

"Yes," Molly whispered. "It's me, but our time is almost gone." Garrett struggled to keep himself under control.

"You're...you're alive," he gasped. The implications crashed into his mind. "There's life after death. There is, isn't there?"

"Oh Dad, you have no idea," said Molly.

"Are we...do we..." Garrett could not form the words, but with the link between them, words were unnecessary.

"Everything that matters, we take with us; our memories, our feelings, our *love*. It's a long journey, but we *never* forget." Her eyes looked past him, as if she was seeing something unimaginably far away. "It's a journey that I am going to have to take soon, but not just yet. I've been given this little slice of time. I have to help you free Mom."

"Molly…" The link wavered. Garrett could feel the darkness pushing in from all sides.

"There's no time, Dad," said Molly. "He's got her, and he's not going to let her go. You're going to have to take her away from him."

"Who? Who has her?"

"He used to be John Gamble," said Molly. Again the link wavered, and for an instant Garrett was certain that it was going to wink out. Then it firmed up, although now he could see that it was only a matter of (seconds?) before the darkness destroyed it.

"Who is he?" demanded Garrett and then shook his head. "No, *where* is he? Where can I find him?"

"You have to…" The link disappeared, and Molly screamed. Suddenly, the darkness broke though the flimsy barrier Garrett had managed to erect. It smashed into the light, obliterating it.

"Molly!" He was still at the campsite, but he was now alone. NO!" For a terrible moment, he thought that his daughter had been destroyed. Then, from unimaginably far away, he heard her call out to him.

Come back to me, she cried, only now her voice barely registered in his mind. *Come back to me, and you'll find Mom.* Then the darkness overrode everything. Garrett felt his carefully constructed tunnel start to crumble. Suddenly, he was taken by something vile. It felt as if slimy tentacles, soft and yet as strong as steel, had wrapped themselves around him. With a jolt, he was dragged back through the dissolving tunnel. Then he was back in his bed, lying next to the thing that was pretending to be Molly Webb.

The pain consumed him. He curled into a fetal position and screamed. His sheets were now soaked with blood. Dimly, he wondered just how much more he could afford to lose. Desperately, he tried to form his tunnel again. He started to picture his safe place but could not call it up out of his memory. *It's...the pain. I...can't think.* In his mind, the entity sent a reply.

Guess again. Garrett groaned and tried to remember...what? His mind went blank. He knew that he had a safe place, and he knew that both Melody and Molly were supposed to be there, but he could not form the picture in his mind. He felt amusement emanating from the entity.

"What...what have you done?" he gasped.

"I took it," said the baby. "Kiki dada doo." Garrett focused his attention on the infant, trying to fight through the pain. It stared at him with eyes that were now solid black. It was still grinning at him, only now that grin was both malicious and very much aware.

"Wh-what?"

"I took it, Daddy," said the baby in its high-pitched baby's voice. "I don't want you going anywhere without me. That would be bad, Daddy. That would be very, very bad. Aie! Babababababa!" The baby waved its arms and legs again.

"You...can't..."

"Oh yes, I can," giggled the baby. Despite its lack of teeth, its enunciation was perfect. "And I did. It's gone forever. And if you don't want me to take any more, you will behave yourself. Be a nice Daddy! Kay ba ba!" As suddenly as it had come, the pain evaporated. Garrett pitched forward onto the soggy sheet, gasping. "I can make the bad pain go away, Daddy," said the baby. "All you have to do is be good. Can you be good, Daddy? Can you?"

"What do you want?" gasped Garrett.

"Leave me and Mommy alone," said the baby. "She doesn't like you anymore. Just leave her alone and let us be together forever and ever."

"Why? Why her?"

"Because she's my mommy and I love her," said the baby. Garrett pushed himself up so that he could look at the thing pretending to be his daughter. He had lost his safe place, but he still remembered the beautiful young woman. He knew that his daughter was somewhere impossibly far away, but she was alive…perhaps more alive than she had ever been in this life. The baby grinned.

"No," whispered Garrett. "I won't let her go, you bastard. I won't let you have her." The pain crashed into him again. Incredibly, it was even worse than before. He did not even have the breath to scream.

"Bad Daddy," cried the baby. "Bad, bad Daddy!" The room started to grow dark, and Garrett understood that it was his vision that was fading. "Go away, Daddy," said the baby. "I'll come back tomorrow. You can change your mind then. Okay?" Garrett groaned, knowing that the entity meant what it said. It would come back tomorrow, and this scene would be repeated. Then if he did not agree, it would return again and again and again. He would never know rest or peace or…

"No!" he growled. He struggled up and forced his mind to focus. For just a moment, his eyesight cleared. He could feel the darkness closing in, but for a few precious seconds he was awake and aware. "No!" His right arm shot out, and he grabbed the baby by the neck.

Touching the thing's skin was like touching millions of stinging wasps. His palm burned with red fire, and he was certain that his skin was going to burn away. The baby hissed, and for just an instant Garrett saw two distinct emotions crawl across its dead face; surprise…and fear. He clenched his jaw and squeezed.

"Stop!" The baby gasped and wheezed. "Stop."

"No," Garrett growled. The pain soared to new heights. His mind screamed, and a red haze covered his sight. And still he squeezed. The baby's mouth opened impossibly wide as it tried to gulp in the air.

"Daaaaaadeeeeee," it hissed. "Pleeeeeaseeee stop hurrrrrtinnng meeeee."

"Give her back," growled Garrett. The darkness was closing in again. His mind had reached its limit and was shutting down. It could only endure so much. He focused every ounce of his dying will on the thing writhing in his grasp. "Give…her…back. Give…her…"

And the baby was gone. His hand was suddenly clenching the blood-soaked sheet. The pain vanished. His mind cleared, and his heart rate slowed to some semblance of normal. He felt his knee throbbing with the year-old pain that he had grown accustomed to and welcomed it. Compared with what he had just endured, it was a very small thing.

From the foot of the bed, he felt the entity. It was still there, watching him, but he could feel something else as well. The thing was weaker. Whatever power it had used to torture him had taken a toll. Garrett could also feel something else …uncertainty.

"Get out," he gasped. "You can't scare me anymore. I took your best shot, and you know it." From somewhere…else…he heard the reply.

I have barely begun to hurt you, sent the entity.

"I know you now," said Garrett, still gripping the sheet. "I know your name…John Gamble."

You know nothing.

"I know that I can take everything you have to give. And I know that I can take Melody away from you." He pointed at empty air. "I'm coming for you, John Gamble. Do you hear me? I'm coming for you, and I'm coming for Melody."

It will cost you everything. You only have so much to give. You have no idea how to use what is yours.

"I don't care."

Where is your safe place, Garrett Webb?

"It doesn't matter. Nothing matters, except my wife."

Stay.

"No."

Stay.

"No. I won't…" But the entity was gone. Garrett stared at the foot of the bed, still trying to process what had happened. The pain was gone, but it was still very much alive in his memory. He wondered dully if he could endure it a second time, even if it meant saving Melody. He fell back into the bed and winced. The sheets were damp with blood and sweat.

He nearly passed out trying to sit up, but he managed to get his feet on the floor. His night clothes were soaked, and his bare arms were streaked with blood. In addition, his head was throbbing, and his mouth was dry. He barely noticed. He had a feeling that from that moment on he would never have any difficulty enduring physical discomfort. Not after what the entity (John Gamble) had inflicted on him. He grabbed his cane and shuffled to the bathroom. On the way, he peeled off his nightclothes. He resolved to shower and spend the rest of the night in his recliner. He stepped into the bathroom, turned on the light, looked into the mirror, and groaned.

You only have so much to give, the entity had said. Garrett understood now. He had gone to bed as a twenty-seven-year-old man who, despite a bad knee, had been in moderately good shape. Now, staring back at him from the mirror, under a shock of pure white hair was the haggard face of a man of at least fifty.

Chapter 5

Confrontations

*I*t took him a week to recover. After the encounter, he lay unconscious in his chair for over forty-eight hours. Then he ate, slept, and ate some more.

The days were bad; the nights worse. The image of Melody in the grip of the entity haunted him. He would dream of her lying alone; tortured, abused…probably raped. He would wake up screaming her name. He had to find her. He had to save her, but his body refused to cooperate. The entity…he still could not think of it as a man who may or may not have carried the name of John Gamble…had left him physically devastated.

When he finally regained consciousness two days later, he could barely move. Every muscle in his body was on fire. It was several hours before he could even get out of his chair. He managed one trip to the kitchen...he was badly dehydrated again…and then slept for another twelve hours. When he awoke, it was still dark. He thumbed the light on his watch and saw that it was 5:38. He groaned in relief. There was no sign of the entity.

As it turned out, it did not return. Garrett could only hope that their second confrontation had weakened it as much as it had weakened him. He doubted it, but he had managed to get his licks in. Maybe that would be enough to keep it away long enough for him to recover.

At the end of a week, he was nearly back to his old strength, although his hair remained white and he still looked like a man who had seen the back side of fifty.

The wounds inflicted on his spirit were not so easily healed. Try as he might, he could not remember his safe place. He knew that he had one, or at least he used to have one, but he could no longer see it in his mind. The entity had stripped it away.

The darkness was still there as well, growing like a cancer. He did his best to ignore it. For the most part, he was successful, but it was slowly gaining strength with each passing day. He did not know how long he had before it overwhelmed him, and he had no idea what would happen to him when it did, but he did know that his time was short. Every minute that his weakness kept him in his chair was another minute that he was not looking for Melody.

You only have so much to give. He understood the entity's words all too well. Their fight had cost him maybe twenty years of his life. He had a sinking feeling that those years were gone forever.

That led him to a single devastating conclusion. The next time would more than likely kill him. Could he do that? Before his last encounter, he would have said yes without hesitation. Now, in the deepest place in his heart, he was ashamed to admit that he was not so sure. Even if he knew for certain that he could save Melody, he honestly did not know if he could endure that kind of agony again.

More than once, he toyed with the idea of obeying the entity. He could stay away. He would have to live with the grief and shame of abandoning his wife, but at least he would never have to endure that kind of pain again.

Each time he was tempted, he would shove the thought away, angry that he had even considered it, but it would always return. Each time, the urge to do nothing was just a little stronger. *She abandoned you. She walked away, arm in arm with that shrew of a mother. Let her save herself.* He tried to tell himself that the thoughts were not his own; that it was somehow the entity planting them into his mind in the same way it had planted the darkness into his heart. He did not believe it. The thoughts were his and his alone. In the end, he did the only thing he could. He stopped thinking about it and concentrated on healing.

The first thing he did as soon as he was able was quit his job. He did not dare go into the office. His appearance would spark too many questions. Donald Devers, his immediate supervisor, took it badly. Donald had a mean streak that kept the office in a state of constant tension. He refused to call anyone by their given names. Instead he made up nicknames that were just short of being cruel. Julie Scott was Scott On The Rocks, and Ross Daniels was, of course, Jack Daniels. He had christened Garrett 'Webhead'. During their brief phone conversation, Garrett took a perverse pleasure in listening to Donald go from angry to enraged in what had to be record time.

"You're going to quit without so much as a two-week notice?"

"I don't have a choice, Don. My wife…"

"I don't give a rat's ass about your wife, Webhead. You've got three projects pending, all of them with unbreakable deadlines. Do you have any idea what's going to happen to this company if we don't meet them?"

"To your job, you mean," said Garrett. "You couldn't care less about the company."

"That's enough. Get your ass back in here now, and I'll forget this conversation ever happened."

"Liar," said Garrett calmly. Now that he was committed, he felt quite free. "You'll get what you need out of me and then fire me."

"Shut up," snapped Donald. "Get in here now."

"No."

"Then you'd better understand this, buddy boy. I will personally call every firm in this area and tell them not to hire you. You won't work here again. I promise you that." Garrett could hear the panic peeking through the anger in Donald's voice. Not surprising, since his head would undoubtedly be on the chopping block when the deadlines came up short.

"I don't plan on working here again," said Garrett. "I'm leaving the state." In his mind's eye, he could see Donald pacing back and forth in his office.

"Look, Garrett," said Donald, reining in his temper. That made him smile. Donald never called him Garrett. He was getting desperate. "You can't run out on us like this. What about Julie? What about Ross? Are you going to leave them hanging? Do you know what this will do to them?"

"It will put a lot more on their plate," said Garrett. "But they'll handle it. They're good…better than you've ever given them credit for. The only job on the line will be yours."

"I won't let you quit," said Donald, raising his voice. His temper was getting the better of him. "I'll put it in your record that you were fired. You won't be able to get work anywhere in the country, much less this city."

"Whatever," said Garrett. "I've got better things to do. Goodbye." He broke the connection before Donald had a chance to reply. He stared at his cell phone. *I've just flushed my career down the toilet,* he thought. Then he decided that he honestly did not care.

He spent the rest of his convalescence playing detective. Molly's visit had provided him with a starting point. *Come back to me,* she said. That could only mean one thing. He had to go back to where she was buried.

It was not a pleasant thought. Neither he nor Melody had been able to bring themselves to hold any kind of funeral. They had purchased a simple plot in a secluded cemetery not far from their shattered house. Both of them had signed the proper papers, and both of them had been there when the tiny casket was lowered into the ground. It was the last time they had stood together as husband and wife.

So what do I do? Find Molly's grave and hold some kind of half-baked séance? That did not feel right, and he was learning to trust his feelings. He was certain that Molly's visitation had been real. He was also certain that his daughter was not in her grave. Oh, her tiny body might be resting there, but her soul, or spirit, or essence, or whatever it was called was somewhere else. Visiting her grave would be useless.

There was also the question of exactly where Melody might be. Was she still close by, maybe living with her mother? He did not think so. Why else would Molly send him to Florida? That meant that she had to be somewhere near Gainesville. Still, just how was he supposed to find her? Gainesville might be a small college city, but one person could hide there forever if they were so inclined.

Seven days after the attack, he stuffed a handful of clothes into a worn red, green and blue Tommy Hilfiger duffel bag. He still did not know just how far he could follow Melody's trail, but he had to at least make a start, and as much as he hated the idea, that trail began with Melinda Chance.

He shouldered the duffel, grabbed his cane and opened the door. He glanced back at his apartment. There was nothing, he realized, to indicate that the unique individual known as Garrett Webb had lived there. The apartment was sterile, and as he gave it one last look, he realized that he really had never lived in it. He had merely existed in it for a short time. He shook his head, closed the door and walked away.

On the way to the Chance home, he stopped by the bank and withdrew a thousand dollars in cash. He debated closing his accounts but then decided that it would not be a good idea to lug so much cash around.

He had his VISA checking card, as well as an American Express. That would be more than enough to get him to Florida and sustain him for quite a while.

Twenty minutes later, he arrived at the Chance home. It was in an older middle class neighborhood, the kind where every house pretty much looked the same as its neighbors. He stared at the house, a single story red brick model. It was small but tidy. Melody's husband had left long ago, just after Darrin was born. Melinda had worked two and sometimes three jobs to keep her family afloat. She had poured her life into her children, determined that they would have better lives than the one fate had dealt her.

She succeeded. Both Darrin and Arvin made it through college and were moderately successful in the business world. She was tough, determined and resourceful. She was also mean and bigoted, not just against white men, but against men in general. No man would ever be good enough for her baby girl.

Neither of her sons lived at home, but both of them owned houses close by, and Darrin worked in an office less than five minutes away. A single phone call, and he would come running.

Garrett sat in his car for almost an hour before he got up the nerve to get out and ring the doorbell. He heard it buzz and waited. His knee was throbbing, and he tried to put as much weight on his cane as he could. After several seconds and no response, he rang again. He could almost feel Melinda peering out through the peephole. He was just about to ring a third time when the door flew open. Melinda Chance stood there with fire in her eyes and a wicked looking baseball bat in her hands.

"How dare you," she began, but then she took a good look at him. Her eyes grew wide with shock. "What happened to…?" Garrett was ready.

"John Gamble," he said, wondering if the name could possibly have any meaning for her. It did. Melinda flinched as if she had been slapped. Her free hand came up as if to ward off a blow. Her mouth opened, closed and opened again. The bat wavered and then lowered. Garrett's shot had not only hit its target, it had driven deep.

"What do you know…?" Her voice was a harsh rasp.

"I know that he did this to me," said Garrett, not giving her a chance to finish. "I know that Melody's in trouble, and I know that John Gamble is that trouble." Melinda stared at him some more.

"How could you know that name?" she demanded. From the moment Garrett had decided to see her, he had been wondering what he would say if she asked him that question. Now, seeing her reaction to the name, he decided on the simple truth.

"I've met him," he said. Melinda's eyes grew wide.

"You lie," she snapped.

"You know better," said Garrett. "I can see it in your eyes."

"You need to leave."

"Where's Melody?"

"Get out. Get out before…"

"Before what? You call the police? One of your useless sons comes running? I'm sure you've already called Darrin. He's probably on his way here now, but I couldn't care less. Where's Melody, Melinda?" He could see the hatred and loathing in her eyes, but he could also see the fear. She was terrified. He reined in his anger. "Her spirit came to me," he said, lowering his voice. "It wasn't a dream, Melinda. It was real. She came to me, and she begged me to save her."

"That's…that's impossible. She wouldn't…she couldn't…"

"He came as well…John Gamble, or something Melody called John Gamble. He did this to me, and he took Melody's spirit away. He's got her somewhere, and I think you know where. Tell me, Melinda. For her sake, tell me." His former mother-in-law took a step backward. For a moment, Garrett was sure that she was going to use her bat. Then he saw the unthinkable. He saw a single tear roll down Melinda's cheek. She did not have to say anything. He understood.

"You don't know," he said. She shook her head.

"She left almost four weeks ago," she said. "She wouldn't tell any of us where she was going." For a moment, her face grew hard and her hatred resurfaced. "We thought that she might be going back to you. My boys took turns watching your place, but she never showed." Garrett could only shake his head.

"Who is John Gamble?" he asked. "*What* is he, and what does he have to do with Melody?"

"That's not your business," snapped Melinda. "It's family, and you aren't family."

"Tell it to Melody," replied Garrett. "She came to *me*." Melinda looked away, but Garrett could still see her shame. His insight flared.

"She came to you too," he said flatly. "She begged you to help her." Melinda flinched again, and again Garrett saw the truth. "You can't," he said. "Whatever has her has some kind of hold on you too."

"What do you know?" she hissed, whirling back to face him. "What do you know about anything?"

"I know that Melody needs my help," said Garrett. "I know that whoever or whatever John Gamble is, he stole a big chunk of my life." He met Melinda's eyes and suddenly realized that he had just made his decision. "And I know that I'm going to get her back. I don't care what it costs me, Melinda. I'm going to save her." Melinda looked away again. Garrett pressed his advantage.

"Who is John Gamble? I know how much you hate me, but you must know that I'm going to do everything I can to save her. Who is he, Melinda?" Melinda gripped the bat until her fingers went white. Garrett could see that her hatred of him was going toe-to-toe with her fear for her daughter. He waited, but before she could answer, a black Volvo came screeching to a halt behind him. He turned, knowing exactly what he would see. Sure enough, Darrin Chance was climbing out of his car. His eyes were blazing, and his mouth was etched into a feral snarl. He slammed his door shut and stormed toward him.

"I warned you," he shouted, pointing at Garrett. "Now I'm going to take you apart. Mom, go inside."

"Stay where you are, boy!" Darrin jerked to a stop.

"Get inside, Mom," he said again.

"You stay right there," ordered Melinda. "I mean it now. Don't you come any closer."

"Mom…"

"Hush," snapped Melinda. She turned her attention back to Garrett.

"You save my baby," she said in a low, dangerous voice. "You give me your word."

"I'll save her," said Garrett. "Not for you, and not for me, but for her. I love her. I always have, and I always will."

"LIAR!" This was from Darrin.

"Shut up, boy," snapped Melinda. She turned back to Garrett.

"You'll have to go back to Florida," she said, "back to where you were." Garrett nodded. He knew as much.

"Why? What's down there?"

"Our past," whispered Melinda. Garrett could see that she was struggling with the words. It was as if something was fighting her. "And our future. I thought that when she came back, she might…but now…"

"I don't understand."

"You will," said Melinda. "When you get there, look for…Gamble's Run." Sweat was starting to bead on her forehead.

"'Gamble's Run'? As in John Gamble?" Melinda nodded, and then winced. She rubbed her chest. "Are you all right?"

"Gamble's Run. Do you understand? Find…Gamble's Run." She backed away, gasping for breath. "That's…all I can tell you. Now get out of here, and don't you ever come back." Garrett opened his mouth, but Melinda had already shut the door. He stared after her for long seconds. Then he turned to leave. Darrin was still there, and he was still angry. Garrett eased down the porch steps, hoping that the oldest Chance son would have the good sense to leave him alone. Of course, he did not. As Garrett made to pass him, he grabbed his arm.

"My turn," he growled. His other hand curled into a fist, and he pulled it back, ready to strike.

What happened next would haunt Garrett for the rest of his life. The instant Darrin touched him, he felt the darkness seethe. It boiled up, triggering a kind of anger that he had never known. Then a small part of it flew out of him. He could almost see it as lanced away and flew straight into Darrin. Part of him was horrified, but another part was grimly satisfied. He felt his mouth curl into a sneer.

"Don't you ever touch me again," he rasped. Darrin probably did not even hear him. He released his grip on Garrett's arm and stumbled away, his hands clawing at his chest.

"What did you do to me?" he screamed. "Dear God, what did you do?" At that instant, the door flew open. Melinda stood there, only now instead of a bat, she was holding a shotgun. She pointed it straight at him.

"You leave him be," she shouted. "Get out now, or I will kill you. I swear it on my daughter's life, Garrett Webb. I will kill you!" Garrett did not have to be told twice. He got into his car and drove off. He glanced in the rear-view mirror as he drove away and saw Melinda coming down to help her son. Then he turned a corner, and they were gone.

"Gamble's Run," he whispered. It was a start, but that knowledge had been bought with a price. He now knew a terrible truth about the darkness. He could force it into others, just as the entity had forced it into him. Far worse was the fact that it was now weaker inside of him. He could only wonder if he could get rid of all of it by doing the same thing to others. The idea made him sick to his stomach.

"You bastard," he whispered, rubbing his eyes. "You knew this would happen, didn't you?" The entity did not answer, and Garrett was fairly certain that it did not hear him. Maybe it was still nursing its wounds.

There was nothing left for him to do. He had severed every tie. The only thing that mattered now was finding

Melody. He made his way to the interstate and set his course due south.

Chapter 6

Dead Neighborhood

*T*hree days later, he stood silent before a vacant lot. The ground was barren, the only exception being a single scraggly dandelion that had somehow managed to take root in the far corner. Its wilted leaves lay flat on the ground, and its stalk was bent double, as if bowing in unconditional surrender. Life it seemed, even in the form of the heartiest of weeds, was forbidden to flourish in this place.

The sink hole was gone, filled in with tons of dirt. A waist-high chain link fence guarded the parameter. A bright yellow sign, bolted to a small gate, warned anyone who might want to do a little unofficial exploring that this place was forbidden. Nothing beyond the fence hinted at the tragic events of over a year ago.

The destruction that night had been catastrophic. The grim tally; four houses swallowed whole and fifteen people, including one beautiful little girl, dead. The rescue workers managed to pull twelve others out of the wreckage. The entire neighborhood had been condemned and evacuated. The surviving families would be battling with their respective insurance companies for years.

The tragedy had made national news. FOX, CNN and MSNBC had spent days replaying video from that night. Experts had tried to explain how so many sinkholes could open so quickly, but in the end it had baffled everyone. The odds of such an event happening even once were beyond astronomic. A team of geologists from the University of Florida had set up shop in one of the empty houses. They were conducting an intensive study of the entire area, trying to figure out just how such a disaster could happen and maybe prevent it from happening again.

It was early, just a few minutes past nine, but the Florida heat and humidity were already in full swing. Silence, heavy and unnatural, hung over the deserted neighborhood. During their brief stay, both Garrett and Melody had constantly argued with the trio of students that rented the house across the street. They were coming and going at all hours of the night, and their cars were constantly blasting whatever heavy metal song that happened to be called up on their iPods.

A handful of children used to live nearby, some with one parent, some with both. They were a constant but pleasant nuisance, riding their bicycles up and down the street, playing tag or hide-n-seek, or just running and screaming for no apparent reason. It added up to a very active, very loud neighborhood.

Now the houses stood vacant. The cracked driveways were empty, as were the backyard playgrounds. Mailboxes hung open, empty mouths hungry for letters that would never arrive. There was no music playing or engines revving. In a single night, this neighborhood had died in agony.

The silence was oppressive. It shrouded each and every house, as if preparing them for burial. Even the geology team was nowhere to be seen. Garrett stared at the lot, trying to sort through the cascade of feelings and memories that threatened to overwhelm him. He could see a grinning Molly running naked across the small front yard, chased by an exasperated Melody. He could see himself turning into the driveway, his two favorite girls waiting at the front door, ready to welcome him home. He could see…

"Excuse me, sir." Startled out of his memories, Garrett jumped. The voice came from behind him. He turned and came face to face with a pretty young woman of about twenty. She was short, barely topping five feet, and her straight brown hair fell to her shoulders. She was wearing jeans and a blue denim work shirt. She held a clipboard in her right hand and a pen in her left. On her right ear was a blue tooth attachment for a cell phone. A tiny blue light on its side blinked at regular intervals. Garrett realized that she was undoubtedly a member of the geology team from the university. Realizing that she had startled him, she took a step back.

"Sorry," she said, smiling. "I didn't mean to frighten you." Garrett managed a weak smile.

"No problem," he said. "I guess I was lost in my thoughts."

"It's just that you're not supposed to be here," said the young woman. "This entire neighborhood is off limits."

"I know," said Garrett. "I just needed to see it again." The woman's eyes widened.

"You were here, weren't you?" she said. "The night it happened, I mean." Garrett nodded.

"That used to be my home," he said, pointing at the lot. The young woman bit her lip and looked down at her clipboard. After she leafed through a few pages, she looked back up at him.

"Are you Mr. Webb?" Again, Garrett nodded. The woman frowned and checked her information again.

"There must be some mistake," she said. "I have here that Garrett Webb was twenty-seven years old." She looked at him, her eyes asking the question. Garrett shrugged.

"You're dead on," he said. "I'm Garrett Webb, I'm twenty-seven...twenty-eight now...and I really did live here. If it helps, I'm younger than I look. That night took a lot out of me." He looked down, hoping that the lie was convincing enough. The woman's face mirrored her doubts, but she nodded sympathetically.

"I'm sorry," she said. Then she held out her right hand. "I'm Jean," she said. "Jean Francis." Garrett took her hand automatically, shook it once and let it go. Jean glanced over at the lot. "It must have been terrible," she said.

"Yes, it was," replied Garrett. Jean consulted her clipboard again. Garrett heard her draw a sharp breath.

"Your daughter was Marlene Webb?" He had been expecting the question, but it still hit him like a runaway truck. To hear his daughter's name coming from the lips of a stranger was almost more than he could bear.

"Yeah," he whispered, "but we called her Molly." Jean saw his pain and looked away.

"I'm sorry," she said again. "I didn't mean to sound so calloused about it." She managed an uncomfortable smile. "I can't imagine what you must be feeling right now."

"Forget it," said Garrett. "I just needed to see this place again. I thought…"

"What?" asked Jean.

"Nothing," said Garrett, giving the lot one last glance. "There's nothing here for me. I probably shouldn't have come. I'm sorry to have troubled you." He brushed past Jean and limped toward his car.

"No trouble," she said. "I hope your wife is all right." Something in the way she said 'wife' brought Garrett up short. He turned back to her.

"Do you know Melody?" he asked. Jean shook her head.

"I only met her once, a few weeks ago when she stopped by. Some of the other residents have come here; not many, but a few. I guess they're like you. They just need to see the place again."

"When?" demanded Garrett, taking a step toward the young woman. "When was she here?" Jean's eyes widened, and she backed away. Realizing that he had just frightened her, Garrett held up both hands, palms out. "I'm sorry," he said. "I don't mean any harm. I just need to find Melody. You said she was here?" Jean nodded uncertainly.

"Two weeks ago," she said. "My team and I were doing soundings." Garrett shook his head. "We set off small seismic charges and record the results with ultrasound. It lets us see deep into the earth." Garrett nodded.

"She came here, to look at the lot?" he asked.

"We let her stay for a bit," she said. "We couldn't bear to send her away. I stayed with her." She eyed

Garrett. "I'm sorry. I just thought that you would have…"

"We've been separated for over a year," he said flatly, then shrugged. "For that matter, we've been separated since that night. Did she seem all right to you?" Jean hesitated. "I promise that I'm not trying to cause her any more grief," he said. "She disappeared and didn't tell anyone where she was going. If I can just let her family know that she's all right, I'll leave her alone." That was a blatant lie, but he thought he sounded sincere enough. Jean seemed to buy it, at any rate. She cocked her head, giving Garrett an appraising look.

"No," she said after a moment, "she really didn't seem all that well." Garrett nodded.

"How so?" he asked.

"Well, for starters, she looked exhausted," said Jean. "More than exhausted, in fact; like she was about to keel over. And she was nervous. She kept looking around. It was almost as if she thought she was being watched."

"Anything else?" asked Garrett. Jean thought some more.

"She…" She shook her head.

"Please," said Garrett softly. "I need to know."

"She looked scared," said Jean after a moment. "In fact, she looked downright terrified." Her eyes narrowed. "She wouldn't have been afraid of you, now would she?" It took Garrett a moment to realize what she was implying.

"No! Oh God, no," he said, taking a step back. "I swear to you, I would never hurt her. I…"

"You still love her," finished Jean. "Yeah, I get it." She eyed him carefully and then decided to give him the benefit of the doubt. "Okay," she said. "I guess I believe you."

"Thanks," said Garrett. He heard the sarcasm in his voice and tried to smile. Judging from the way Jean was eyeing him again, he did not quite pull it off. "I'm really sorry," he said. "It's been a bad year." Jean nodded, softening. "Did Mel say anything at all about where she might be heading?"

"No," said Jean. "In fact, she hardly spoke at all. She just said she wanted to visit the place where her daughter died. I tried to talk to her, but…no, she didn't say anything about where she was going." Garrett nodded. It was a long shot, but he was still disappointed.

"Jean! Hey, Jean!" The shout came from behind them. Both Garrett and Jean turned in time to see a tall, well-built man in his mid-thirties emerge from behind one of the nearby houses. If everything about Jean said 'student', then everything about the newcomer screamed 'professor'. He was wearing khaki work pants and a matching shirt. On his head was a blue cap featuring an orange 'F' and an angry alligator on the front…the mascot of the University of Florida.

Jean waved him over. Garrett could not help but notice how her body language changed as he drew closer. It was subtle but obvious. *Looks like the professor and Mary Ann here have been doing a little more than digging,* he thought. Then he blushed and looked away. It was none of his business.

"Hey, Bob," Jean called as the man drew near. "This is Garrett Webb. He used to live in the house on that lot. Mr. Webb, this is my boss, Professor Robert Davies." Davies held out a calloused hand, and Garrett took it.

"Good to meet you," said Davies.

"You remember his wife," said Jean. "She came by a few weeks ago." Davies nodded.

"Of course," he said. "I'm very sorry for what happened to you." Garrett nodded his thanks, although he could see that Davies was just being polite. The professor turned his attention to Jean.

"Linda needs you," he said. "They're ready to set off another charge." Jean nodded.

"It was good to meet you," she said to Garrett. "I hope your wife's okay." With a wave and a nod, she trotted off, disappearing around the corner of the nearest house.

"I'm afraid that I'm going to have to ask you to leave," said Davies. "This entire area still isn't stable. The last time we set off a charge, we caused another sinkhole; a small one, and it didn't do any damage, but the way this place is, you never know."

"Has anything like this ever happened before?" asked Garrett. Davies shook his head.

"Never," he said. "We still don't know what caused it."

"The drought…"

"That was only a part of it," said Davies, interrupting. "The water table was low, but it's been lower. This should never have happened."

"I didn't live in Florida long," said Garrett. "What's the water table?"

"The underground water level," said Davies. Garrett noted the way the professor leaned forward as he spoke. He seemed to have forgotten that moments ago he had ordered Garrett off the property. Here was a man who was deeply in love with his work. "The entire state is honeycombed with underground rivers," he continued. "We've had cave divers go down in one spring and come up miles away." Garrett shuddered. He had seen documentaries on cave diving. The idea of crawling through narrow underwater passages made for good nightmares. Davies noticed his discomfort and smiled. This time it was genuine.

"You wouldn't catch me doing it either," he said, "although we had a lot of fun following them. They wore transponders that we could track on the surface. We followed their trail through back yards, gas stations and even a Sonny's Barbeque. I think we made a few people uncomfortable. They didn't like the idea that someone was swimming a hundred feet beneath their feet."

"I can understand that," muttered Garrett. He looked down at the ground, half-expecting one of the divers to come bursting through the dirt. Davies nodded and waved an arm at the neighborhood.

"We think we walk on solid ground," he said, "but underneath there's a lot of empty space…well, empty space and water." He glanced at his watch. "Listen," he said, "I hate to do this to you, but you really do need to leave. If the board finds out that I let someone in here while we were doing soundings, they'll have my head, not to mention my funding."

"No problem," said Garrett. "I saw what I came to see." He offered his hand, and Davies took it. Then the two men started off in opposite directions, but suddenly Garrett stopped. It was a shot in the dark, he knew, but at the moment, it was the only shot he had.

"Hey Professor," he called to the retreating Davies. Davies stopped and turned. Both his irritation and impatience were evident.

"Mr. Webb…" he began.

"Just a quick question," said Garrett, limping over to him. "Please." Davies frowned but nodded.

"Have you ever heard of anything called Gamble's Run?" Davies frowned.

"Gamble's Run? No, I don't think so. Is it a street or something?" Garrett shrugged.

"I have no idea," he said. "Melody mentioned it to her mother, but neither of us has any idea what she was talking about."

"Sorry," said Davies. "But I've never heard of it."

"How about John Gamble?" asked Garrett. "Does that name mean anything to you?" Davies' eyes widened.

"Of course," he said. "John Gamble is something of a local legend. He was responsible for the Slave Canal." He pursed his lips. "That could be what you mean. I don't think I've ever heard it called 'Gamble's Run' before, but the name fits." Garrett felt his heart do a double thump. Had he actually struck pay dirt?

"The Slave Canal?" he asked.

"It was dug in the 1800s," said Davies, "Just before the Civil War. Like Gamble, it's a bit of a legend around here, except that it still exists."

"What's…"

"I'm really sorry, Mr. Webb," said Davies impatiently, "but my team is waiting for me. I have to get to work, and you really need to leave." He started off but then relented. "You can probably Google it if you want," he called over his shoulder. "It's not well known, but the locals love it, and I hear that it's a great place to canoe."

"Thanks," called Garrett. "I really appreciate it. You've been an incredible help." His sincerity softened Davies' attitude. The professor smiled and waved a farewell. Then he trotted away. Garrett watched him, envying the casual way he ran.

"Forget it," he huffed and headed back to his car. His running days were gone forever. Melody was gone too, but maybe not forever. There was still a chance he could get her back. For the first time, he had a lead. "Just hang on, Mel," he muttered as he slid behind the wheel. "Whatever it takes, just hang on." He drove out of the neighborhood, knowing in his heart that he would never return. "The Slave Canal," he said aloud. As soon as he got back to his motel room, he would take Davies' suggestion and 'Google' it. Then, if he needed to know more, he would head to the university.

His heart raged at the delay. Somewhere, if she was still alive, his wife was being brutalized by something so vile that his mind could not comprehend it. She could be dying. She could be dead. He had to find her, but he needed to know where to look. Like it or not, he was going to have to do some serious research.

"The Slave Canal," he said again as he turned onto the main highway. "What the heck is the Slave Canal, and what the heck do it and John Gamble mean to Melody?" He did not have the answer, but at least he had a starting point. His next stop would be the university. "I've got work to do," he whispered. "The question is, do I have time to do it?"

Chapter 7

Visions and Patterns

Surfing the Internet provided Garrett with plenty of information but little insight. After he left Davies and company, he found the nearest Starbucks, set up shop in a booth in the back and got to work. Two hours later, he closed his laptop and finished off his third latté. His eyes were glazed and his head was buzzing, courtesy of the heavy doses of caffeine.

Davies had been right. The information was sparse, but it was there to anyone who bothered to look for it. The Slave Canal was one of those well kept secrets known to the local residents, geologists from the university and a handful of out-of-town nature lovers.

The naturalists loved it because it was a stunning place to travel via canoe. The locals loved it because of its historical significance. The geologists loved it because the remains of a far older civilization they named the Paleo could be found there. Artifacts thousands of years old had been unearthed. Expeditions were mounted every year, and it seemed that every year they came away with a new discovery. Some of the geologists had nicknamed the canal 'Florida's Lost Atlantis'.

Garrett was able to dig up enough information so that he now understood how and why the canal was created. There was, unfortunately, absolutely nothing on the various websites that provided any clue as to the relationship between it and Melody. He sat back and rubbed his tired eyes.

The facts were straightforward. John Gamble had been a wealthy cotton grower living in central Florida in the 1800s. He was a part of a loose consortium of landowners and businessmen who needed a faster way to get their cotton to the Gulf of Mexico. Poor roads made transportation difficult and often impossible. The Wacissia, the nearest river, had a bad habit of disappearing underground for several miles at a stretch. It ended in a mazelike swamp that the locals called, charmingly enough, The Warriors.

Gamble commissioned the canal in 1831. The plan was to link the Wacissia with the Aucilla River, which flowed unobstructed to the Gulf. The canal would be about two and a half miles long and deep enough to allow the barges to pass. They could then make the run to the gulf in record time.

It was a devastating failure. The canal had to be dug by hand, and that meant that it had to be dug by slaves. The idea made Garrett shudder. The temperature that day had spiked at ninety-five, and the humidity had made being outdoors nearly unbearable. What must those poor men have endured while digging the canal? How many of them died in the process, laboring in the disease infested swamps?

From the beginning, the canal did not work. It had been dug too shallow. During the dry season, the water level sank so low that it was next to impossible to get the barges through. They kept getting hung up on the canal bed, not to mention the constantly falling branches from the trees that lined both banks.

Then, not long after the canal was finished, the railroad appeared and took over the transportation duties. A few decades later, the Civil War broke out, and that took care of the slaves. The canal was abandoned, left to stand as a silent indictment of John Gamble's folly.

Garrett found a portrait of the man himself on the website of a local newspaper. He seemed unremarkable in every way. Soft, almost effeminate features accompanied by a gentle smile gave him a friendly, caring look. His nose had just a hint of a hook, and his brown hair was cropped short. In the portrait, he wore a white scarf and a dark, high collared coat. He seemed in every way to be a typical country gentleman of the 1800s. Garrett could easily picture him hosting a gala at his mansion, inviting the local belles to attend in their finest apparel. There was no hint of a man who casually sent hundreds of slaves into a hellish environment just to get his cotton to market a little faster. Garrett had stared at the picture.

Is it you? Are you the monster who stole twenty years of my life? It did not feel right. He could not match the man on his screen with the creature that had invaded his apartment.

He could find no mention of Gamble's Run. None of the websites used that name, although it certainly seemed to fit. There had been an effort some time back by a few low level bureaucrats at the state capital to change the name from the Slave Canal to the Cotton Run Canal. The term Slave Canal was deemed racist and labeled as hate speech. The idea had been vehemently opposed by the local residents, both black and white. They considered the Slave Canal an important part of their heritage, something that should be remembered for what it was and what it represented. The proposal quickly died.

Garrett's next step was the local Kinkos, where he printed out every scrap of relevant material off the 'Web, including a map of the entire area. It all added up to a stack of over thirty pages. By the time he got back to his motel, it was dark. He spread the pages out over the bed and got to work.

The canal joined the Wacissia and the Aucilla rivers close to Nutall Rise. As far as he could tell, Nutall Rise was a tiny hill, a pimple on the mostly flat Florida countryside. Day trippers used it as an embarkation point where they launched their canoes.

Frustration was setting in. He had learned a great deal, but was no closer to finding Melody. He tossed the printouts on the floor and flopped back into the lumpy motel bed. The sheets smelled of dust and age. He stared at the ceiling, trying to make sense of the mound of information he had ingested. The caffeine was washing out of his system. His thoughts were becoming muddy, and he could feel the beginnings of a first class headache coming on.

"What am I missing?" he said aloud. "The Slave Canal, Gamble's Run, John Gamble, and Melody. What's the connection?" There was none that he could see. Melody had never spoken of her family line. It was possible that she was a descendant of one of the slaves who dug the canal, but if so, then why was the Gamble entity targeting her? There must be hundreds, perhaps thousands of descendants of those slaves. Were they all being tormented?

"What am I missing?" he asked again, closing his eyes. The events of the day, coupled with his long trip, caught up to him. His mind grew fuzzy, and he fell into a deep sleep.

# # #

The demolished house slid into the gaping maw that was the sinkhole. The wood shattered with a series of loud pops as the entire structure was sucked into the earth. Garrett and Melody watched in horror as the most precious thing in their lives was swallowed as well. Garrett screamed and tried to crawl toward the hole, but one of the rescue workers held him back.

"Let me go," he cried. "Please, you've got to let me save Molly."

"Too late," said the worker. "She's gone."

"No! I can still save her." He tried again. "Get...off...me!" He kicked and punched but could not break free. Bruised and bloody, Melody began crawling toward the hole.

"Melody", he cried out. "Wait! You can't...I can't lose you too!" He lunged forward, but again the worker pulled him back. "Please," he whimpered. "Save her. Save my wife."

"I can't," said the worker. "The hole's got her now."

"NO!" Garrett lunged forward again, and this time he managed to get loose. He fell to the ground and scrambled toward Melody, who had now reached the edge of the sinkhole.

"It'll get you too," shouted the worker, but Garrett ignored him. He clawed his way forward. "Wait for me, Mel," he shouted. "Just...wait!"

Light exploded all around him. He slammed his eyes shut. So intense was the light that for a terrifying moment he was certain that he had been blinded. He buried his head in his arms, his nose pressed against the dry ground. Angry purple flashes exploded against his eyelids, but after a moment they subsided. He managed to open his eyes. He looked in the direction of the sinkhole and screamed.

The light shot into the night sky, emanating from deep within the earth. It was green; mean, disease-ridden green. Garrett squeezed his eyes shut again. He knew that if he looked at the light too long, it would stab into his eyes, invade his body, and eat him alive.

Then a wonderful thing happened. Garrett's conscious mind decided that enough was enough. A different kind of light flared. It did not begin to match the intensity of the vile green glow that vomited out of the sinkhole, nor could it compete with the darkness that was eating away at his soul, but in its own way, it was powerful. It surrounded him, seeping over him like a second skin. He felt it bathe him in its warm embrace. Then it hardened, and Garrett realized that it was now a shield…a shield strong enough to repel the sinkhole light because…

Because I'm dreaming, he thought. Then he paused, uncertain. Everything felt far too real. He could hear the screams of those being pulled from the sinkholes by the rescue workers. He could feel the ground beneath him and smell its arid dryness. *Am I dreaming?* he wondered. It was a reasonable question. He had experienced lucid dreaming only once in his life. Then, he had devised a simple test. *If I'm dreaming, then I can fly,* he thought. *I'll open my eyes, and I'll be floating above the ground.*

He opened his eyes.

He was floating an inch above the bare earth, his arms stretched out to either side. *Yes!* He grabbed on to his courage and again looked at the sinkhole. Now, with his shield…his reality shield…he was able to gaze straight into the heart of the light. A dark silhouette lay on the ground, inching toward the edge of the hole. *Not this time.*

It's too late, said a still, small voice. It was not the voice of the rescuers. Nor was it Molly's voice, the entity, or even Melody. It was his voice. *Melody's not there, and Molly's dead. You know this. There's nothing you can do.* His vision wavered. The shield grew brighter, and suddenly he was glowing like a miniature sun. He could feel his mind expanding. He was waking up. *None of that,* he growled. He was not quite sure how he did it, but he managed to reign in his shield. His vision stabilized. He was still asleep, and still in command of his dream.

Pulling his arms back, he shot forward, flying just inches above the ground. When he got to the edge of the sinkhole, Melody was already tottering. In seconds, she would be over the edge. *Not this time,* he thought again. *Molly's dead. Maybe Melody is as well, but right here, right now, I can still save them.* He reached the edge and flinched. The sheer force coming from the malignant green light forced him back. He snarled at it and again pushed forward.

I've seen it before, but where? It was a fleeting thought, and it vanished immediately. The light fought him, but his shield held and he managed to reach Melody. She was lying face down on the ground, her head and shoulders hanging over the edge of the hole.

He grabbed her outstretched arm and rolled her over. Her eyes were closed, and she seemed to be sleeping.

Mel! Wake up! he shouted or tried to shout. His voice was thin and empty. He tried again but could barely manage a whisper. He shook her hard, but she did not respond. *Let her go, you bastard,* he growled. He planted his feet on the ground, got his arms under her and scooped her up. She weighed nothing at all. Then he turned and faced the green light. *My dream,* he thought. *My rules.*

Cradling Mel in his arms like Superman might cradle Lois Lane, he shot into the night sky. *Up, up and away,* he thought, giggling. The light faded, and he felt its power fade with it. *It has a range,* he thought. *Somehow, it's tied to the earth. It can't reach me up here.*

He stopped his ascent, hovering in the black velvet sky. There were stars everywhere. They blazed with a brilliance and glory that he had never seen and could never have imagined. Their light was like a soothing balm. He felt it wash over him, bringing peace and healing. He reveled in it. *You may be strong,* he thought, looking down at the now dim green glow, *but you're not all powerful. There are greater things than you...things that you will never be able to touch or defile.* The knowledge comforted and strengthened him.

Given a choice, he might have remained there forever, but he was not yet done with his work. Dream or not, he still had one more person to save. Gathering his courage, he held Melody close, feeling her warm skin against his. Then he dove straight into the light.

The instant he penetrated it, he knew that it was aware. He could feel its rage at the intrusion, and it put forth all its considerable might to repel him. His shield shrank, but it continued to hold. He plunged down into the sinkhole. The lip of the hole flashed past, and then he was flying deep underground. *I'm taking them both,* he said to something that might or might not be listening.

His shattered house came into view. Now it was split into four equal parts. He could easily see what remained of Molly's bedroom. There was her crib, still intact. He swooped down to it but found it empty. *Molly! Where are you, baby? Daddy's here. Daddy's come to save you!*

I'm not here, Dad. The voice came from behind him. Still floating, he turned and saw his daughter, not as an infant, but as the full grown woman he had met in his safe place. She was looking at him with what could only be described as exasperated love.

Molly! His voice was still impossibly thin. *Come on, baby. Let's get out of here.* Molly shook her head.

You're going the wrong way, Dad. You've got to go up again. You need to see the big picture.

Molly?

Dad, listen to me. Get back into the sky. You've got to go up now. You need to see the pattern. She pointed to the sky. *Go, Dad! Go now!*

But...

Dad! Go! So strong was the command that he obeyed immediately. Clutching Melody, he shot up through the shaft of light. The edge of the hole flashed by, but he ignored it. Maybe it was his own mind calling out to him, or maybe it really was Molly somehow communicating through his dream. It did not matter. Something was demanding his attention, and he knew with the certainty that only comes in dreams that whatever it was, it was vitally important.

The light faded as he gained altitude until it disappeared entirely. He was back in the sky, floating among the brilliant stars. He slowed, stopped and looked down. *Dear God.* He was floating high above the Earth, so high that he could easily its curve.

The Florida peninsula sprawled out below him. He could see several cities shining in the night, complimented by dozens of lesser glows that also indicated a human presence. There was the Gulf of Mexico and the Atlantic Ocean, both shimmering under a brilliant moon. *Moon?* He glanced up and saw that there was now a full moon. He looked down again, wondering just what he was supposed to see. *What the…?*

The cities were gone, extinguished, as were the smaller towns. He squinted, trying to make out any kind of detail, but he could see nothing. The more he stared, the more uncomfortable he became. He could trace the outline of the state but nothing more. He suddenly felt as if he was staring at a Florida-shaped black hole.

There was a flash of light. It was faint, but it was there. He glanced in its direction, but it disappeared, leaving nothing but the inky blackness. *Imagination?* He shook his head. *No way. Not here, and not now.* He looked over at the gulf, letting his mind wonder. The light flashed, but when he looked again, it was gone. *Got it.*

He relaxed his eyes, letting them slide out of focus. The instant he did, the light returned. This time, he did not look directly at it. He kept staring at the gulf, watching with his peripheral vision. It was a pinpoint, but it was there. It flared, followed almost immediately by another, and another, and another. They spread out across the state, winking like tiny Christmas lights, although there was nothing festive about them. They all glowed with the same sick green light that filled the sinkhole.

You need to see the pattern. Molly's voice echoed in his mind, guiding him. The dots continued to flash, and he realized what he was seeing. Each and every dot was a sinkhole, and each was infected with the same diseased light. *The big picture.* He understood now. There was a pattern. There was…

Melody stirred in his arms. He looked down at her and saw that she was regaining consciousness.

"Easy, baby," he whispered. "I've got you." Melody moaned. Suddenly, she began to struggle. Surprised, Garrett tightened his grip. "Melody, I've got you. You're safe." She moaned again. Her arms flailed. One of them caught Garrett's temple in a glancing blow. Dream or not, the blow staggered him, and he nearly lost his grip. "Melody! Calm down!" He tried to pull her close, but she pushed away. Then her eyes opened. Light blazed out of them, the same light that infested the sinkhole.

"Let…me…go!" Garrett gasped. He knew that voice. It did not belong to Melody. It belonged to the entity that had taken her. The circuits in his mind connected, and his memory flashed.

That's where I've seen it before, he thought, meaning the green light. Even in his dream state, he suddenly felt sick. He remembered the night of the sinkhole. He remembered trying to console Melody, and he remembered how, for just a moment, her eyes had flashed green. *Even then,* he thought. *He had a hold on her even then.* There was a blur of motion. He did not even see Melody's fist until it had already collided with his cheek. Stunned, he fell backward. Melody shoved against him, and this time he was unable to hold on.

"NO!" It was too late. Melody floated free. She snarled at him. Then something big, powerful, and invisible grabbed her. Garrett felt rather than saw a great hand, connected to an impossibly long arm, reach up out of the sinkhole and drag her down. She disappeared into the gaping hole far below. "NO!" he screamed again. He aimed himself straight at the sinkhole, but before he could move, he felt another presence.

Dad! Stop!

Not now, Molly! He's got her.

Yes, he does, said Molly. *And you're not going to get her back his way. The time will come when you will fight for her, but now is not that time.*

Shut up, snarled Garrett. *I've had enough of this.*

The pattern is real, Dad. Remember...

Suddenly, his shield blazed with brilliant white light.

No! Don't do this, Molly! He tried to stop it, but this time he lacked the power. The light grew, and the world beneath him faded.

The battle is not in here, Dad. The battle is out there.

And you need to hurry.

Please wait, Garrett sobbed, but it was too late. The light suddenly blazed with the strength of a sun as he regained consciousness. His dream was finished. He had failed.

Chapter Eight

Family Tree

*G*arrett awoke well before eight the next morning. Sunlight peeked between the slits of the heavy curtains that covered the motel window. He shivered and realized that he had left the air conditioning on high. He sat up with a groan, sending a few pages of his research floating to the floor. He had slept above the covers, and now his body was stiff and sore. He massaged his aching knee with a grimace.

The intensity of his dream, like most dreams, was fading. Unlike most dreams, however, the details remained vivid. He remembered everything, from the hellish green light to floating among the stars to diving deep into the sinkhole. He also remembered Molly.

"See the pattern," he muttered. His stomach growled, and he winced. The three lattes were the sum total of his nutritional intake since the previous afternoon. He could feel another headache lurking close by. Before he did anything else, he needed to eat.

The motel boasted a café that featured a small breakfast buffet. Garrett took a quick shower, slipped into fresh clothes, and made his way across the parking lot. The café was a standard motel restaurant, outfitted in muted red, browns and yellows. The smell of scrambled eggs, bacon and pancakes made his stomach growl again. The hostess, an older woman of maybe sixty, led him to a booth. Her name tag read Sarah.

"Coffee?" she asked.

"Just orange juice," he replied with a grimace.

"Help yourself to the buffet," said Sarah. "We've got maple and boysenberry syrup for the pancakes." A memory poked through the layers of time in Garrett's mind. He saw his father, sitting in a roadside café somewhere in Tennessee, pouring boysenberry syrup on a huge stack of pancakes.

He searched and found the proper slot for the memory. He was maybe eight or nine, and they were on vacation. His parents had taken him out of school early, and they had spent a few weeks exploring the mountains. The restaurant had been an early morning discovery, nestled behind a thick tree line somewhere near Gatlinburg. They had almost missed the faded wooden sign announcing that the Mountaineer was open for business. It turned out to be one of those hidden treasures that dotted the winding mountain roads, providing what both his mother and father proclaimed to be the best breakfast ever. It was a good memory, one that had faded thanks to Garrett's ongoing feud with his father. He shook himself back into the present and smiled at Sarah.

"Boysenberry," he said. Sarah disappeared and moments later returned with a small carafe of honest to goodness boysenberry syrup. She set it down, started to leave and then hesitated.

"We're having a get-together tonight over at the armory," she said. "If you're staying the night, you're welcome to come."

"Excuse me?" he asked. Had this woman just asked him on a date?

"It's a combination dance and pot luck dinner," replied Sarah. "The armory gives us a senior citizens discount, and all we ask is that everyone chip in five dollars." She smiled shyly. "You can be my guest if you want." He straightened his shoulders, realizing at that moment that he had been slumping. It was an old man's slump. Between that, his cane, his white hair, and the fact that he was not wearing his ring, it was little wonder that Sarah thought that they were close to the same age. He felt the now familiar bitterness rise in his gullet and forced it down.

"I'm afraid that I'm spoken for," he said, smiling tightly. Sarah raised her eyes, and he could see that she was not buying it…or at least she did not want to buy it. She shrugged and let it drop.

"I leave here at six if you change your mind," she said and started to walk away.

"Do you know the Slave Canal?" He had asked on impulse and was rewarded when she turned and nodded.

"Sure," she said. "It's maybe fifteen or twenty miles from here. Is that where you're headed?"

"I don't know," said Garrett. "Maybe. I hear it's a great place to canoe."

"It is," said Sarah. "Or at least it was when I was there. My husband and I went…well, I guess it's been over twenty years now. We made a day out of it." Her eyes got that far away look that was common to anyone who had stored and catalogued several decades of memories. "We went in April, in the spring. It was so beautiful. Ned was always finding out-of-the-way places like that for us to visit." There was a sad wistfulness in her voice that made Ned's fate obvious.

"How long?" he said softly. She blinked and quickly dabbed the corner of one eye.

"Five years," she said. "Cancer took him."

"I'm sorry," he said, suddenly uncomfortable. She waved his concern away.

"Hey, none of us are young anymore, are we?" she said. "It's life, that's all...just life."

"Just life," muttered Garrett.

"Believe it or not, you're the first man I've asked out since Ned passed," said Sarah. "You can take that as a compliment." That made Garrett smile for real.

"I will," he said. "Thanks."

"Do you know where you're going?" asked Sarah. He started at the question. It hit too close to home. Then he realized that she was still talking about the canal.

"I have no idea," he said, well aware of the double meaning.

"Just take 98 West," she said, "and as soon as you cross the Aucilla, turn north onto the first graded road."

"Graded?" Sarah smiled.

"City boy, eh? It's just a dirt road, although they may have paved it by now. Take it to the end. There used to be a place to rent canoes there. Maybe it's still around."

"I hope so," he said. Another question popped into his mind. "Have you ever heard of anyone calling it Gamble's Run?"

"You meant the canal?" she asked, and Garrett nodded. She gave it some thought. "No, I never heard it called that before, but really, the only time I was ever there was that one time with Ned. Sorry."

"Don't be," said Garrett. "You helped me a lot, and I really appreciate it." Sarah gave him a wistful look and seemed about to say something else, but at that moment a young couple, accompanied by three very noisy children, arrived. She hurried over to greet them. Relieved, Garrett finished his breakfast, left a healthy tip, and went back to his room.

Since the motel did not provide Internet access, he called the front desk to let them know that he would be staying at least one more night. Then he stuffed his research into his satchel along with his laptop and headed back to Starbucks. He winced when he stepped through the main entrance and smelled the brewing coffee, but he managed to hold off the nausea. He ordered another orange juice and managed to snag his booth from the day before. Logging on, he got to work.

This time, he was able to find what he was looking for almost immediately. A brief search led him to a site called Florida Wetland Conservation that kept meticulous records of every sinkhole over the past several years. The instant he called up a map that marked the sinkholes according to their dates, he knew that he had struck pay dirt.

"The big picture," he whispered, staring at the map. The pattern was not easy to see, at least to anyone not looking for it, but it was there. If he traced the sinkholes and cross-referenced them with their dates, he could easily see a long, winding arc. It started maybe forty miles south and gradually worked its way toward the canal. Not surprisingly, his former neighborhood sat well within the arc. Not every sinkhole fit into the pattern, but most did. He could only guess that the holes outside the circle were natural. The ones in the pattern…

"What the hell?" he muttered. "Just what the freaking hell?" The only real conclusion had to be that the sinkholes within that circle were not made by natural causes. He shivered at the implications. *That night was not a natural event*, he thought. *Something attacked us. Did it want Mel and Molly? Was that whole disaster caused for them?* Just thinking about it made him feel sick.

The data only went back five years, but if he took the arc represented by the sinkholes and extrapolated a circle, he could see that it eventually began exactly where it ended…at the Slave Canal. Something was happening deep under the ground, and it had little to do with the drought.

Just how long has this been going on? He pushed the laptop away and pulled out his stack of research. The copies were not double-sided, so he had plenty of scrap paper. He turned one of the sheets over and began writing out the dates on the screen.

Thirty minutes later, he had his answer. If he projected the dates backward, using the length of time between the sinkholes that had occurred over the past five years, the first sinkhole in the pattern would have happened somewhere in the late 1800s. *Definitely John Gamble's era,* he thought. He had not been able to find a date of death for the cotton grower, but it did not matter now. He had unraveled Molly's clue. He had found the pattern.

"So what do I do with it?" he muttered. It was a good question. "Come on, Molly," he said, staring at the map on his screen. "Help me out here." In the booth next to him, a young couple…students, most likely…glanced in his direction, but he ignored them. He knew plenty about the Slave Canal and its creator but was no closer to finding the connection between them and Melody Webb.

"Melinda knows," he said aloud. The couple glanced at him again. He gave them a 'so what' glance, and they quickly looked away. A moment later, they gathered their things and left. *They think I'm a crazy old man*, he thought glumly. He realized that he was slumping again and straightened his shoulders. His back cracked, and he rubbed it absently.

Maybe I am, he thought. *I'm down here chasing what ...ghosts? Demons? I have no idea, and I'm no closer to finding Mel.* He thought of Melinda. He could not believe that she would keep anything from him. She might hate him, but Melody was her only daughter. She would do anything to save her, even if it meant enlisting his help. And yet…

She's hiding something, he thought, *and whatever it is runs deep; maybe so deep that even her sons don't know about it...so deep that she wouldn't even tell me, even if it meant helping Mel.* He shook his head. That made no sense. If she knew something, she would tell him, plain and simple. Unless…

Unless she couldn't tell me...unless something was stopping her from telling me. Somewhere deep in his mind, the synapses were firing. He could feel an answer…or at least a part of an answer…lurking nearby. He drummed his fingers on the table.

"What?" he said aloud. The booths around him were empty, so at least no one was staring. "What are you hiding, Mrs. Chance? What's your connection with John Gamble?"

The instant he said Gamble's name, he saw it. His heart rate doubled, and his breath caught in his throat. *Oh my God,* he thought. *It can't be.* He closed the screen on his laptop. He felt dizzy, as if he was peering over the edge of an impossibly high cliff. *John Gamble. Melinda Chance. That's her maiden name. She took it back when her husband walked out. I must have been blind not to have seen it before.*

He was never good at history, but he did know that slave owners often had sexual relations with their female slaves. These liaisons resulted in biracial children that were almost never acknowledged by their fathers/owners.

"Chance…Gamble," he muttered. "I'll bet that old bastard gave them the name himself, probably as a joke. Either that, or they took it on after they were freed, maybe as a symbol of defiance." Either way, it all added up to one undeniable fact. Melody Webb, formerly Melody Chance, was almost certainly a direct descendant of John Gamble. It was a guess, he knew, but there was one sure way to confirm it.

He did not remember jamming his hand into his pocket and pulling out his cell phone, but he did remember calling up Melinda's number out of his directory. Melinda picked up on the third ring.

"Hello?"

"He's you're, what…great-great-great grandfather?" Melinda drew a harsh breath.

"What did you do to my boy?" she demanded. Her voice shook. Garrett could tell that she was trying to collect herself.

"Why didn't you tell me?" snapped Garrett. "How can Gamble still be around after all this time? What's he got on your family? Why is he tormenting Melody? Is it just because she's his great-whatever-great granddaughter?"

"He doesn't do anything," said Melinda, still speaking about Darrin. "He quit his job, doesn't even leave his house anymore. What did you do to him?"

"No more than what he was trying to do to me," replied Garrett. "He would have put me in the hospital."

"You've got the devil in you, Webb," said Melinda. "And now you put the devil in him."

"Good," hissed Garrett. He could feel the darkness writhing inside him, and a part of him welcomed it. "Now tell me the truth. John Gamble is your ancestor. He is, isn't he?"

"My…leave me alone!"

"No, Melinda, not this time. Tell me the truth."

"I…can't!"

"Tell me!"

"Arvin lit out of here yesterday," said Melinda. "He's coming for you. He knows where you went. Sooner or later he'll find you, and when he does…"

"When he does, I'll give him some of what I gave Darrin," hissed Garrett. The darkness bubbled up. Suddenly, he felt as if it was going to explode out of him. He took a deep breath and forced himself to calm down. "Just tell me what I need to know, Melinda," he said. "Tell me, and I won't bother you again." Melinda was breathing heavily now. Her breath came out in harsh gasps.

"I…can't…" Suddenly, Garrett realized that his initial hunch had been right. Whatever had taken Melody had its claws in Melinda as well. It – *he* - was literally stopping her from answering him. *And that's an answer in itself,* he thought. *Is he doing it now, at this moment, or did he plant some kind of block in her mind?*

His thought process revved into high gear. Melinda might be prevented from telling him about her family tree, but maybe he could come at it from another angle.

"Your family came from Florida, didn't they? They came from this area, in fact."

"Y…yes," said Melinda. She was panting now, and although he could not see her, Garrett was certain that she was sweating.

"Your line runs deep here," said Garrett. "Generations, I would guess."

"Many…generations," said Melinda. "All the way back before the war."

"The Civil War," said Garrett.

"Y…yes," replied Melinda. She seemed barely able to speak, but to her credit, she was trying. Garrett kept going.

"Your people were slaves here," he said. "They worked the cotton plantations."

"That…and other things," said Melinda. *Bingo*, thought Garrett. Despite their mutual loathing, he felt a grudging respect for Melody's mother. The same unforgiving determination that had raised three children as a single mother was now working for him. Melinda was fighting tooth and nail whatever hold Gamble had on her. For the moment, at least, she was winning.

"That's where it started," said Garrett. "With the 'other things'."

"Ye…yes." Garrett thought furiously. What did he need to know that he had not already figured out? An idea flared in his mind.

"Were you an only child?" he asked.

"I…had a sister," said Melinda. "She died years ago."

"How?"

"She…I…can't…"

"Never mind," said Garrett. The answer was obvious. Gamble had taken her sister, just as he had taken Melody.

"And your mother?" he asked. "What about her family?"

"My aunt died when she was twenty-five," said Melinda. Was that approval in her voice? Garrett couldn't have cared less. The last thing he needed was Melinda's approval.

"You moved to Kentucky not long after Melody was born," he said. "You moved to protect her. You tried to get away." Melinda's only answer was her heavy breathing. *Too direct,* he thought. He tried again.

"It doesn't make sense," he said. "Why did Melody agree to go back to Florida with me? Why did she encourage me to take that job? Why…oh dear God!" The implication hit him full force. His throat went try, and he gulped down a few mouthfuls of orange juice. "Was I manipulated?" he asked. "My job, our move, all of it; was it to get Melody down here?" The idea was absurd, but the instant he said it, it *felt* right.

"The waters…run…deep," gasped Melinda. "They…reach out to everyone, especially to those whose family lines go…way back."

"What? What's that mean, Melinda?" The only answer Melinda gave him…*could* give him…was her now desperate panting. *The waters,* he thought. *Gamble? Just how much influence does he have here?*

His former boss, Anthony Tope, used to boast about how his family had lived in the area for generations. Garrett flashed back to how he had landed the Florida job. A corporate headhunter had contacted him. The offer had been more than generous, and Melody had encouraged him to take it. The nausea he had been fighting since he arrived at Starbucks made a curtain call. Now he was the one taking deep breaths, trying to prevent Sarah's pancakes from splashing all over the table. Had John Gamble somehow influenced Anthony to hire him?

"The waters run deep," he muttered.

"Yes," breathed Melinda.

"But why did Melody…" and the answer hit him. "She didn't know," he said.

"N…no."

"And you couldn't tell her," said Garrett. "You were *stopped* from telling her." Silence. "He had his finger on her," he said. "He probably had his finger on her from birth." More silence. His questions were too direct now, but he no longer cared.

"How do I stop him, Melinda? *Can* I stop him?"

"You…you've got to try!"

"How? How do I fight him? How do I get Melody back?"

"I DON"T KNOW," screamed Melinda. "I DON'T…aaaiiiiieeee!" Garrett jerked the phone away from his head. Melinda's scream had nearly shattered his eardrum. He held it back to his ear, but the connection was broken.

"No," he hissed, thumbing the redial button, but before the call could go through, the phone's screen flashed once, then twice. "What the…" The screen went dark. Garrett hit the 'ON' button over and over again, but nothing happened. His phone was dead. He shook it and tried again, but nothing happened.

"Damn you," he growled, staring at the phone. The screen flared to life, only now it glowed with a disease ridden green light that he knew all too well. In the midst of that light, two black words appeared.

STAY AWAY

Seconds later, the glow faded. Garrett tapped a few buttons, but the phone was dead, this time for good. With a snarl, he stuffed his computer and papers into his satchel and headed for the exit. On the way out, he threw his phone into the trash.

Despite the encounter, a glimmer of hope now shone through the darkness in his soul. Melinda had confirmed his guess about Melody's lineage, and the incident with the phone suggested that he might be heading in the right direction.

Unfortunately, time was still against him. Both Melinda's sister and aunt had been taken by the creature they called John Gamble. Now it had Melody, and if he could not act fast enough, Gamble would destroy her as well.

He drove away from the Starbucks, heading back to his motel. There was no more time for research, no more time to try to piece together the mystery that was Gamble's Run. He was going to have to make the journey to the Slave Canal and pierce whatever mysteries awaited him within its depths.

Chapter 9

Sam's Bait and Tackle

*G*arrett found a small sporting goods store where he purchased a knapsack and a pair of sturdy hiking boots. To this he added several foil bags of dried food and a large thermos. The clerk rang up his sale with a cocked eyebrow, taking in his frail appearance. Garrett swallowed his pride and allowed the clerk to carry his purchases to his car. By the time he left the store, it was late in the afternoon. He decided to spend one more night at the motel.

He set out the next morning at daybreak. Less than an hour later, he crossed the Aucilla River. He found the dirt road, although it was little more than a wilderness trail, barely wide enough for a single car. There was a narrow grass strip on the right. Beyond that was a thick line of trees and brush. On the other side, the tree line bordered the edge of the road. If he met an oncoming car, there would be just enough room to ease over into the grass and inch past. Judging from the weeds growing in the center, it was not heavily traveled.

He swung onto the road and started forward, but almost immediately he had to stop. The drought from the previous year had returned in force. Dirt from the surface flew up in every direction, completely obscuring his vision. He skidded to a halt, waiting for the dust cloud to dissipate. After several minutes, he was able to see again. He started forward, inching along so as not to create another cloud.

There were no signs along the way, and as he crept deeper into the country, he began to get worried. If this barely navigable road suddenly ended, would there be enough room to turn around? It was a very real concern. Without his cell phone, he was effectively cut off from the rest of the world. If his car got stuck, he would have to hoof it back to civilization, and with his bad knee, his chances of success were questionable at best.

He bounced along, aware that he was probably doing serious harm to the suspension of his car. There were deep potholes, and more than once he heard the underside of his car scrape against the loose dirt.

Thirty minutes later, the road emptied out into a small clearing. He breathed a sigh of relief when he saw a wooden shack about the size and shape of a convenience store. It sat at the far end of the clearing, maybe twenty yards away. Two vehicles were parked in front...a fairly new white Chevrolet SUV and an older, battered red Ford pickup truck. Both were covered with dust.

The paint on the building was cracked and faded and might have once been yellow. Two feet tall letters running across the top of the structure told him that he had just found Sam's Bait and Tackle Shop. A sign next to a battered screened door announced that the place was open, although given its remote location, Garrett could not figure out how the place stayed in business.

Underneath the first sign was another one with big red letters that read 'Canoe Rentals Here!' Next to the door was a large picture window. Painted on it was an impressive fish…Garrett had no idea what kind…that was about to bite into a hook disguised as a smaller fish.

"It's a start," he muttered as he eased his car up to the shop. He shut off the engine, grabbed his cane and got out, grimacing as the pain in his knee flared. Scenes from a dozen horror movies…the kind that featured a masked killer slicing his way through a swarm of screaming teenagers at summer camp…flashed through his mind. He shoved them aside and headed toward the entrance. The back of his neck itched, and he had to resist the urge to hunch his shoulders. He felt as if someone was staring at him from beyond the tree line. He stopped and turned, scanning the forest. No one was in sight. Of course, they could be easily hidden in the dense brush. He stared at the forest a moment longer, trying to pinpoint the source of his unease. Finally, it hit him.

As Sarah had deduced, Garrett was a city boy at heart. The everyday background noises common to a large group of people living in relatively close quarters were deeply ingrained into his psyche. Now, those noises were missing. There were no cars buzzing by on a nearby highway, and no one was playing a stereo too loud. Instead, a single bird was chirping in the distance. A gentle breeze rustled the leaves of the nearby trees. There was nothing else.

I guess that appeals to some people, he thought as he started toward the door again, *But I don't think I like it.*

He shrugged off his unease, pushed the door open and stepped inside.

A half-dozen overlapping odors hit him as he entered. The most powerful was the somewhat nauseating smell of live bait. He could see several waist high metal troughs off to his left against the wall, where the offered bait…most probably minnows or some other breed of tiny fish…was kept. A low hum, accompanied by the sound of bubbling water, told him that the filtration system was working. He wondered where the power was coming from, as there were no visible power lines outside. *Probably a generator out back*, he thought.

Two large fans, hanging from the ceiling, rotated slowly, moving the warm air back and forth. The morning was still young, but the temperature outside was well into the eighties. The store had no air conditioning, but it was marginally cooler inside, thanks to the fans. Garrett felt a tiny drip of sweat trickle down his forehead and wiped it away absently.

To his right, at least two dozen fishing rods were lined up on a high shelf, leaning against the wall like tired soldiers. They came in all shapes, sizes and colors. A few even had reels attached. In the center of the store were two rows of chest-high free standing shelves that held assorted tackle, lures and other fishing paraphernalia. Immediately to his left was a low shelf that ran under the front window. It held canteens, knapsacks and other camping supplies.

Directly in front of him, about fifteen feet away, was a waist high glass counter. Displayed within it were fishing reels, probably of the more expensive sort. A cash register sat at one end of the counter. Behind that was a refrigeration unit, placed against the back wall.

Through the frosted glass doors he could see sodas, bottled water and beer. The floor was made of wood, darkened with age, which creaked with every step.

Garrett stepped all the way inside. The screen door swung gently shut behind him. The place was empty. There was no buzzer or bell hanging over the door to warn whoever might be on duty that a potential customer had arrived.

"Hello," he called out…not very loud. There was a sleepy silence about the place that seemed to discourage unnecessary noise. The only sound was coming from the bait tanks and the fans. He stepped across the shop to the glass case. To the right of the refrigeration unit was an open door that led to what was probably a small stock room. He could see daylight streaming through and guessed that the back door was standing open. "Hello," he called out, just a little louder.

"Just a second," came a male voice from beyond the door. Garrett jumped. Although he knew that someone was nearby…the dusty truck and SUV had told him as much…he had not really expected an answer. He heard a thump, as if something heavy had fallen, followed by muted cursing. Then a shadow fell across the door behind a counter. A second later, the owner of the voice stepped through.

Garrett blinked. He had been expecting a grizzled, older outdoorsy type…the kind of man who loved to entertain his guests around a campfire with ghost stories or who chopped up unsuspecting teenagers. Instead, he found himself face to face with a younger man, somewhere in his mid-thirties. His dark hair was cut short, and his bright blue eyes accented his broad, friendly face. He was slouching, but Garrett guessed that if he stood up straight, he might top six feet with an inch or two left over. He was wearing jeans and a plain white T-shirt, but Garrett could have just as easily placed him in a conservative business suit.

"Hey there," he called out in a cheery voice. "How can I help you?"

"Are you Sam?" Garrett asked. The man shook his head.

"Nope," he said. "Sam was my grandfather. He started this business over eighty years ago, and as you can see, I have taken it and molded it into the financial empire that it is today." Garrett chuckled at the joke. Somewhere in the back of his mind, a masked killer vanished in a puff of smoke. The man held out a hand. "I'm Kyle Masterson," he said, "owner, clerk, stock boy and all around great guy." Garrett took the proffered hand and shook it. Kyle's grip was firm and strong.

"Garrett," he said. "Garrett Webb."

"Good to meet you," said Kyle. "So how can I help you on this fine day?"

"I want to rent a canoe," said Garrett. "They're available here, right?" For the first time, Kyle frowned. He glanced down at Garrett's knee and cane.

"Sure," he said. "Mind if I ask where you want to go?"

"The Slave Canal," said Garrett. "Someone told me that this where I start." Kyle nodded.

"It is," said Kyle. "One of a few places in the area, at least. There's Dusty's…that's a few miles north of here, and Sally Blaine's place down closer to Nutall Rise, but yeah, you can get to the canal from here."

"That's where I want to go," said Garrett.

"Alone?" asked Kyle. Garrett nodded.

"Is that a problem?" he asked. Kyle hesitated. Garrett could see that he did not want to offend a potential customer.

"It is, actually," he said after a moment. "You take the Wacissia…that's a few miles from here…and it will lead you straight to the canal. Once you get in, you can follow it all the way to Nutall Rise. That's where most folk end their trip."

"So what's the problem?"

"Well," said Kyle, "the current's not all that bad, and the river flows in the direction of the canal. The problem is getting back. Five miles against even a weak current can beat a strong man." He glanced pointedly at Garrett's cane, his meaning obvious. Garrett said nothing. "Most of the day trippers come in groups and park at least one car at Nutall Rise," continued Kyle. "I leave a couple of trailers there so they can bring the canoes back. Either that or I charge them extra to go pick them up."

"What happens if they decide to steal them?" asked Garrett. Kyle chuckled at the question.

"The deposit," he said. "It's more than the canoe is worth, so if they want it, they can have it." Garrett nodded.

"I'd be willing to pay you extra to come and get me along with the canoe," he said. Kyle shook his head.

"You ever been through the canal before?" he asked.

"First time," said Garrett.

"Then you can't go alone," said Kyle. His tone allowed for no argument. "Even folks who have made the trip sometimes have a problem finding the entrance, and if you miss it, you'll end up in the Warriors. That's…"

"I've read about the Warriors," said Garrett.

"Then you know that they're a maze," said Kyle. "And they're dangerous. They're not all that deep, but they come equipped with gators and assorted snakes, a few of which are poisonous. Add to that the fact that it's easy to get lost in there, and you could have a real problem. That happened to a young couple just last year. It took a police helicopter over an hour to find them. I had to go get them myself." He smiled at the memory. "That was one humiliated couple." He looked at Garrett's cane again. "I'm sorry, Mr. Webb, but I just can't rent you a canoe. To be blunt, you don't look up to the trip. If anything happened to you, I'd be responsible." Garrett's mind shifted into high gear.

I'll buy a canoe, he thought. *According to the maps, there's a lot of open country around here. I'll find a place to launch and get to the canal, one way or the other.*

"...if you're willing, that is. How about it?" Garrett blinked and realized that Kyle had not stopped talking.

"Sorry," he said, embarrassed. "My mind was wandering." Kyle pursed his lips, and Garrett was suddenly certain that the store owner knew exactly what he had been considering.

"I said that I just rented a couple of canoes to some day trippers. They're regular customers…come up here once or twice a year, so they know what they're doing. They left here on foot about ten minutes ago. It's about a mile hike to the shed where I keep the canoes, so I doubt that they're at the river yet. The path winds something fierce. If you want to see if you can tag along with them, we can take my truck. We'll swing around on the road and meet them at the river. You can ask them yourself. How about that?" Garrett took a few seconds to mull it over and then nodded.

"I'd really appreciate it," he said. He meant it. If finding the entrance to the canal was as difficult as Kyle said, he was going to need the help. Kyle smiled.

"Come on, then," he said, heading toward the screen door. "We'll have to hurry, but I think we can catch them." He led the way outside to the pickup.

"Why is this place so far away from the river...or the main road, for that matter?" Garrett asked as he retrieved his knapsack from the trunk of his car.

"My grandfather used to own all of the land between here and the river," replied Kyle, opening the rider's door of his truck. "But he had to sell it to pay some debts. It belongs to the state of Florida now. Granddad built this place not long after he sold the land, and my dad and I managed to make it work...local customers mostly." He took Garrett's knapsack and threw it into the bed of the truck. He waited as Garrett climbed into the cab. Then he swung his door shut, trotted over to the other side and got in behind the wheel. "So why the canal?" he said, starting the engine, "if you don't mind my asking, that is."

Actually, I mind a lot, thought Garrett.

"I'm a Civil War buff," he said aloud. "I didn't even know it existed until I ran across a reference to it while I was doing some other research. It's not really well known." Kyle nodded. He turned the truck around. A moment later, they were bouncing along the same dirt road Garrett had followed earlier. He had not noticed that it continued on the far side of the clearing. The dust swirled around them, but Kyle ignored it. The lack of visibility made Garrett nervous, but he decided to trust that his guide knew what he was doing.

"We like it like that," Kyle said. "The lack of attention, I mean. We don't mind a few day trippers coming through…most of them are nice enough. Once or twice a year, an expedition from the university comes by. They're good people, and they don't make a fuss. Sometimes they find some interesting things from the people who lived here a long time ago."

"That would be the Paleo," said Garrett. Kyle glanced at him, his eyebrows raised in surprise.

"You *have* done your research," he said. "Yeah, them. They dive the canal….the scientists I mean, not the Paleo." Garrett smiled.

"I thought it was only a few feet deep?" he said.

"Most of it is," said Kyle, "But the water has worn it deeper in a few places. Anyway, the scientists dive the canal and excavate the mounds."

"Mounds?"

"There's a few of them in the vicinity of the canal, although they predate it. One of the professors told me that they were made maybe thousands of years ago. He said that there wasn't even a river here then."

"Only springs and sinkholes," muttered Garrett. Kyle gave him a sideways glance.

"Yeah," he said. "The river came later, and of course the canal itself is only a hundred and fifty or so years old." Garrett nodded. "Anyway," continued Kyle, "we get some fishermen, a few day trippers, and the occasional scientist. Not many others. Like I said, we like it like that. We really don't want our canal turned into some kind of half-assed shrine."

"Our canal?" asked Garrett. Kyle nodded firmly.

"*Our* canal," he said. "We might not own the property, but it's ours."

"You mean the locals?"

"The natives," corrected Kyle, "the folks who have lived here for generations. You'd be surprised how many descendants of the slaves who dug the canal still live around here."

"Really," said Garrett, fascinated.

"Oh yeah," said Kyle. "There's the Foreman family near Nutall Rise. The Coates family lives a little further south. A few others are scattered about the area. They're all good friends." His tone changed slightly when he said friends, and Garrett picked up on it immediately. He had lived with racism from both his and Melody's family long enough to recognize it, even in its subtlest form. The unease he had felt outside of Kyle's store returned.

"As for the rest of us," Kyle continued. "Well, the Gamble family died out a generation ago. My family runs back to before the Civil War. A lot of families around here can trace their line back that far…some even further." Garrett started to ask Kyle if he knew the Chance family but bit the question back at the last second. Kyle's racism aside, he did not want to draw attention to the real reason for his visit.

"I read that someone in the government tried to rename it a while back," he said instead. Kyle snorted.

"Tried…and failed. Cotton Run Canal, my ass. It's the Slave Canal. It's going to stay the Slave Canal, no matter what some low level bureaucrat says."

"Have you ever heard it called Gamble's Run?" It felt like a safe enough question, but the instant he asked it, Garrett knew that he had made a serious mistake. He looked at Kyle, expecting nothing more than a mild denial. Instead, Kyle tightened his grip on the steering wheel. His eyes narrowed, and he glanced sideways at Garrett.

"Gamble's Run?" he said, and Garrett heard the strain in his voice. "Where did you hear that?" Garrett's unease suddenly grew into full blown fear.

"It just came up in my research," he lied, trying his best to sound nonchalant. "One of the locals I interviewed called it that. It wasn't in any of the written documentation I found, so I was just curious. Is it a local name?" Kyle gripped the wheel even tighter and looked away.

"Never heard it called that," he muttered, and Garrett knew immediately that he was lying. They rode in uncomfortable silence for a few seconds. "Hey," said Kyle finally. He seemed to have reverted back to his original friendliness, but Garrett could see that he was forcing it. "I almost forgot. I don't take credit cards. If you can go with this group, they may need to rent another canoe. Do you have cash?" Garrett nodded.

"Yeah, I got enough," he said. Kyle smiled, but there was no longer any real warmth behind it.

"Good," he said. With that, he launched into a story of how his grandfather had cleared the road they were following, chronicling his battles the local government in order to complete it. Garrett only half-listened. In his mind, he was replaying his conversation with Melinda Chance from the day before.

"The waters run deep," she said. "They reach out to everyone."

Everyone, thought Garrett. *From Anthony Tope, who hired me sight unseen, to Mister Bait And Tackle shop here. Dear God, just how deep do the waters run? How much control does Gamble...whatever he is...have here?* He stared out the windshield, watching the dust swirl around the truck as they made their way toward the river. What awaited him there, he could not even guess.

He was alone, a spy deep in what could only be described as enemy territory, and he had a bad feeling that he had just blown his cover.

Chapter 10

Day Trippers

*K*yle finished the story about his grandfather and fell into a sullen silence. He kept his gaze forward, pretending to concentrate on the dirt road. Garrett was not fooled. His question had both surprised and angered the man. *Whatever is going on here, he's a part of it.* He thought of Melinda Chance. *The waters run deep.*

The crazed killer made a curtain call in Garrett's mind, only now he wore Kyle Masterson's face. With each passing second, he was growing more and more certain that Kyle was going to kill him. He would stop the truck, yank him out of the cab and beat him to death. Then he would bury his body where it would never be found. Garrett gripped his cane, knowing that it was a futile gesture. He might get in a few licks, but if Kyle wanted to kill him, there was no way he would be able to prevent it.

He desperately tried to concoct some course of action. Jumping out of the truck was not an option. With his bad knee, he certainly could not outrun the man.

Could he catch him by surprise? If he moved fast enough, he might get in a clean shot. Even if he just stunned him, another blow from the cane might be enough to knock him out. Garrett could then take the truck, get back to the store, grab his car and get away. The more he thought about it, the more the idea appealed to him. He gripped his cane even harder, visualizing his initial blow.

One quick jab, straight to the temple, he thought. *It should be enough to knock him out.* His eyes narrowed until they were barely open slits. He hunched forward, now gripping his cane with both hands. He could feel the darkness Gamble had planted deep in his soul. It was throbbing like a diseased heart, growing stronger by the second.

In his mind, it had already happened. He could see himself as he jabbed his cane straight at Kyle's head. He put all his weight behind it, knowing that he would only get one chance. He saw Kyle's head snap to the side as the cane impacted directly on his temple. The force of the blow drove his head into the window and cracked the glass. Blood spurted from Kyle's nose and mouth. He did not even have the time to cry out.

He fell forward onto the steering wheel. Garrett was ready. He reached over, grabbed the keys and shut off the engine. The truck ploughed off the road and ran headlong into a good-sized tree. Garrett was thrown forward, but his seat belt held. Kyle was already unconscious.

Garrett threw open the door and scrambled out. He limped over to the driver's door and yanked it open.

Kyle did not move. Garrett grabbed the latch to his seat belt and opened it. Then he grabbed Kyle by the arm and pulled him out of the cab. Kyle hit the dusty ground with a sickening thud. Blood was now pouring from his ears, nose and mouth.

I'm in it now. When he wakes up, I'm a dead man. He had no choice. He took the cane, raised it high over his head and brought it down as hard as he could. The solid wood hit Kyle's head with a sickening thud. Kyle grunted but did not move. Garrett raised the cane and brought it down again, and again, and again. On the fourth blow, the skull gave way with a wet CRAAAAK. Kyle's head caved in. His eyes flew out of their sockets. Blood splattered Garrett from head to toe.

Not this time, thought Garrett, staring at the body. *I beat you, you bastard. You thought you had me, but I beat you.* He began to laugh. It started as a barely audible titter, but soon he was cackling uncontrollably.

"You all right?" Garrett jerked around.

"Wh-what?" he gasped.

"You sounded like you were in real pain," said Kyle. He was still alive and still driving. "The way you groaned, I thought you might be getting sick or something." Garrett looked away, trying to get himself under control. His grizzly vision faded.

It tricked me, he thought, dismayed. His stomach churned as the impact of his murderous vision hit him. *It wants me to kill. What if it can make me kill?*

"Mr. Webb?" Garrett shook his head.

"I'm fine," he lied, patting his knee. "Some days it hurts worse than others." Kyle grunted and turned his attention back to the road.

"We're almost there," he said. Garrett did not reply. The darkness writhed and boiled. He could feel it, demanding to be released. Far worse, he wanted to let it out. He *needed* to let it out. He knew that if he did, the scenario he had just envisioned would play itself out, but he did not care. He wanted to see Kyle's face slam against the window. He wanted to drag him out of the cab and smash his skull into tiny bits of bone, blood and brain.

No, he thought, clenching his jaw. *I won't.* From somewhere unimaginably far away, he might have heard a reply.

You will...sooner or later.

Shut...up. He felt rather than heard a gleeful laugh that faded into nothingness. He concentrated on the dark power within him. After a moment, it oozed down into the deepest reaches of his soul, defeated but not banished.

"Here we are," said Kyle, easing the truck to a stop. For the second time, Garrett snapped back into reality. He peered through the windshield, trying to pierce the dust cloud that swirled around the truck like a baby tornado. It slowly subsided, and he saw that they were in a clearing that ran along the river bank for about fifty yards. The river itself wasn't all that impressive; maybe thirty or forty yards wide with a slow, barely discernible current. Kyle had parked the truck a few feet away from the water.

Directly in front of them was a small wooden dock where an impressive looking airboat was moored. Garrett had seen them before, in documentaries dealing with the Florida Everglades. Light and fast, it was essentially a shallow draft skiff with an airplane engine and propeller bolted onto the back. This particular model was a two-seater, with a passenger in front and the pilot in the back. Kyle saw Garrett eyeing the boat.

"That's what I used to get that couple out of the Warriors," he said. "It's mostly swampland, and the only craft that can get through are canoes and airboats."

"It looks fast," said Garrett. Kyle laughed, although he was still forcing it.

"Oh yeah," he said. "Sally Blaine's got one, but mine's faster." He pointed off to his left. "There they are." Garrett leaned forward and looked past Kyle. A stone's throw away was a group of four people sliding a pair of gun metal gray canoes into the water. Kyle opened his door and got out.

"You coming?" Garrett nodded, desperately trying to collect himself. The vision of Kyle's murder was far too real. For a moment, he was certain that he was standing over Kyle's mutilated corpse, waving his bloody cane and laughing uncontrollably. The living Kyle, the river, and the group of people gathered around the canoes were merely an illusion, created by his mind because it could not accept the fact that he had just become a murderer. In a moment, it would all disappear.

Kyle stepped to the front of the truck and turned. He held his hands out in a 'what are you waiting for' gesture. Not wanting to further irritate the man, and still half-certain that he was going to disappear at any moment, Garrett opened his door and eased down out of the cab. Kyle gave him a curt nod and turned his attention back to the group.

"Greg," he called. "Hey Greg, wait up!" One of them turned and waved. Garrett blinked in surprise. For some reason, he had envisioned an elderly group of four or five people, out for a leisurely trip down the river. Instead, he saw a powerfully built man barely into middle age, a striking woman who was maybe a few years younger, and two teenagers.

They were also African-American, and for an instant Garrett hesitated. Melinda's scowling face flashed into his mind. Her voice reverberated through his memory. *I told her not to bring home no white boy.* The darkness within him flared in response.

I'm not going with any niggers, it said, only now it used his voice. His vision dimmed, and his fists clenched. Then, at the last possible second, he realized what was happening.

Oh dear God. It was like a malignant weed, sinking roots deep into his soul and pushing out feelers into his waking mind. For a moment, he despaired. Sooner or later, the darkness would overwhelm him and get free. He glanced at the family.

If they let me come, they'll be in real danger. Can I do that to them...even to save Mel? He watched as Kyle trotted over to the group. He spoke to the man for a moment and then pointed to Garrett. *This is probably a special day for them. They won't want me along.* He started to get back into the truck, but at that moment Kyle waved him over. His resolve wavered. *Just shake your head and get into the truck,* he thought. *Get back to the store, and then get back to the motel. Find another way.*

It seemed like good advice, and he almost took it. Then he thought of Melody being tormented by something that might or might not be a man called John Gamble. He thought of his baby daughter, crushed under a ton of rubble that used to be a home. *I'll be careful,* he thought. *I'm the only chance Mel has. I can control it. For Mel's sake, I've got to try.* Kyle waved at him again. Garrett shoved his fears aside and limped over to meet the family.

"Garrett Webb," said Kyle as he reached the group, "this is the Powell family. This is Greg, and that beautiful woman behind him is his wife Andie. The young man is Sean, and the lovely young lady is Erica. As you can see, she is a clone of her mother." Garrett nodded at the two teenagers and received cautious nods in return. Kyle was right. Erica was maybe sixteen and a near match for her mother, while Sean, a couple of years younger from the look of it, took after his father.

Kyle turned to face Garrett. "Get acquainted. I'll be right back." With a nod to the Powells, he jogged to the truck. Greg smiled.

"Pleased to meet you," he said in a deep, gravelly voice. Now that they were face to face, Garrett could see tiny shoots of gray sprinkled through the rest of his close cropped black hair. He revised his earlier estimate and put his age at fifty. Andie could have passed for thirty, but he guessed that she was in her mid-forties. "Kyle tells me that you want to hitch a ride."

"Well, yeah," said Garrett, "but I don't want to intrude."

"Hmmm," said Greg. "Are you for slavery or against it?" The question caught Garrett completely off guard. From somewhere far away, he heard a faint voice. *Hell yeah, put 'em all in chains!* He cut the voice off and struggled to answer the question.

"I…uh…against, of course…I guess…huh?"

"I said, sir, are you for slavery or against…"

"Greg!" The woman…Andie…brought him up short. "Stop that. He thinks you're serious!"

"I am serious," said Greg, only now his eyes were glinting mischievously. Garrett realized that he was being teased. "We need to know if he serves our white masters, or if he is willing to fight for our freedom." He drew himself up, and Garrett saw that they were about the same height. "Well, sir, what of it? Where do you stand on the issue of slavery? What about state rights? Is the war a war of Northern aggression or a battle to free the oppressed? What say you, sir?"

"I knew that letting you watch the Civil War marathon on the History Channel was a bad idea," growled Andie. "Next thing I know, you'll be signing up for one of those re-enactments. For the record, I will *not* sew you a uniform."

"Give 'em hell, 54," shouted Greg. Garrett blinked. For just a moment, he managed to forget about the malignancy festering in his soul.

"Hey, I know that," he said. "That's from that movie; the one about the black unit that served in the Civil War."

"Glory!" said Greg. "Glory Hallelujah!"

"Greg!"

"Sorry," said Greg, relenting. He held out his hand. "Good to meet you, Garrett." Garrett took the offered hand. It was firm and strong.

"Nice to meet you," he said. "Look, I really don't want to impose. If this is a family day or something…"

"If we are off in search of our roots, you mean," said Greg, raising an eyebrow. "To see where our enslaved ancestors worked and died for their evil white masters."

"Well, yeah, I guess," stuttered Garrett. "I mean…"

"Please don't take my husband seriously," sighed Andie. "I never do."

"Ouch," cried Greg. Both Sean and Erica snickered. Garrett cracked a tentative smile. He suddenly discovered something wonderful. He liked the Powell family. The darkness rebelled at that, but for the moment, at least, he was stronger.

"Relax, Garrett," said Andie. "May we call you Garrett?"

"Of course."

"We're not on any kind of quest," said Andie. "My daughter is an aspiring photographer, and she needs some nature pictures for her blog. The river and the canal are absolutely beautiful this time of year, so we all made the trip."

"And you are welcome to come with us," said Greg. "That is, if you have the time. We're going to put in at Nutall Rise, but we probably won't get there until late this afternoon."

"That's fine," said Garrett. "I really appreciate it."

"Not a problem," said Greg. "It will give Andie and me someone our own age to talk to. It seems that the older our children get, the less intelligent we become."

"Dad!" This was from Erica. Garrett smiled again, trying to hide a wince. By his estimate, he was a good twenty years younger than Greg.

"Sorry," said Greg. "I should have said, 'The less cool we become.'"

"Can't argue with that," quipped Sean. Erica grinned while Andie rolled her eyes.

"Did you bring any supplies?" asked Greg. "You're welcome to share what we have, of course."

"Oh yeah," said Garrett. "I've got a…"

"Here you go," said Kyle. Startled, Garret turned and saw that Kyle had retrieved his knapsack from the truck.

"Uh…thanks," he muttered. He took it and slung it over his shoulder.

"No problem," said Kyle. "Well, is this going to work?"

"I believe it will," said Greg. "How about it, Garrett? Will you join us?"

"Yeah," said Garrett. "Thanks. I really appreciate it." Greg grinned at Kyle.

"There you have it."

"Good," said Kyle. "You can leave the canoes at the Rise. I'll have your SUV there shortly. You guys need anything else?"

"Nope," said Greg. He held out a hand, and Kyle shook it. "If we don't see you before we leave, we'll see you the next time."

"Sounds good," said Kyle. "Take care." He turned to go, but as he turned away from the Powell family, he glanced over at Garrett. Garrett kept his eyes on his new companions, but he could see in his peripheral vision that the look Kyle shot him was both hostile and threatening. He pretended not to notice, glad to be rid of the man. Then his heart sank when he remembered that he had left his car outside of Kyle's store.

"Hey Kyle," he called. Kyle swung around, hanging another fake smile on his face.

"Yeah?"

"Can you get my car to Nutall Rise? I'll pay the extra charge." Kyle nodded.

"Sure," he replied, his voice neutral. "I'll need your keys."

Crap, Garrett thought. *I should have seen that.* It was the last thing he wanted to do, but now that he had asked, there was no way to get around it. He glanced over at Greg, hoping that his new friend would offer to bring him back, but he was busy loading one of the canoes. He was effectively trapped. Walking back was out of the question, and even if it wasn't, the idea of returning to Kyle's store after dark did not sit well with him. He fished his keys out of his pocket and handed them over.

"That's an extra twenty bucks," said Kyle. "It's usually ten, but I'm alone today. My help called in sick. I'll have to drive your car to the Rise and use my bike to get back. Sorry."

"No problem," said Garrett. He pulled a twenty dollar bill out of his wallet and gave it to Kyle.

"It'll be there," said Kyle. Garrett watched as he jogged back to his truck. A moment later, he was gone in a cloud of dust.

"Hey Garrett," called Greg. "Daylight's a wasting!"

"Coming," said Garrett. He stepped over to the nearest canoe and handed Greg his knapsack. Greg placed it under the center seat.

"Shall we place the lady in the center and handle the paddling ourselves?" Andie snorted.

"You mean like the last time, when you dropped your paddle into the river…twice?"

"We don't speak of that," replied Greg with mock severity. He turned and gave Garrett a quick appraisal. "Do you do much canoeing?" Garrett was tempted to lie. He did not want to appear weak, and after all, how hard could it be to paddle a canoe? Then his common sense kicked in.

"None at all," he replied truthfully. "The only time I've ever been on a boat was back in Kentucky. My wife and I took an overnight cruise on the Delta Queen just after we were married."

"That's a riverboat…I think," said Andie. Garrett smiled.

"One of maybe two or three still in existence," he said. "It used to sail up and down the Ohio River before they retired it."

"And where is your wife now?" asked Greg. His voice was casual, but the question brought Garrett up short. Greg immediately saw his discomfort.

"I'm sorry," he said, and Garrett could see that he meant it. "I didn't mean to pry." Garrett shook his head.

"It's all right," he said. "We've been divorced for over a year." Greg smiled sympathetically.

"Again, I'm sorry." He glanced at the now fully loaded canoes. "Well, why don't you ride with us?" I'll take the back. Andie will be in front, and you can sit in the center. Later, we can change if you want to take a shot at paddling. It's not hard, but there is some skill involved." Garrett nodded his thanks.

Sean and Erica were already in the water, holding position. Garrett eased himself down onto the center seat of the other canoe. Once settled, he slid his cane down next to his knapsack. Andie hopped in nimbly, and Greg shoved the canoe into the water. Then he heaved himself over the side.

"And we're off," he cried. Andie gave a half-sarcastic 'yea' as they pulled away from the bank. Garrett tried not to squirm. Now that he was actually on the water, he felt distinctly uncomfortable. It seemed that every move he made was amplified by the canoe. He had a brief vision of losing his balance and sending the three of them into the river. Greg and Sean pointed the canoes southward, and in moments they were moving with the slow current.

"Next stop, the Slave Canal," Greg said jovially. Those simple words nearly stopped Garrett's heart. Somewhere ahead was a relic left behind by a vile man who lived in a vile time. As incredible as it seemed, that man might still be around…a part of him at least…haunting the place where his slaves had worked and died.

Now that Garrett was on the water, he was growing more and more certain of one simple fact. There was evil ahead. He could feel it growing stronger with each stroke of Greg's paddle. He could also feel the dark power within him, reaching out to that evil. He was going to have to be very, very careful.

Chapter 11

The Last Leg

*T*hey started out in a dead heat, but Sean and Erica slowly pulled ahead. Greg seemed content to let them lead the way while he and Andie settled into a slow, steady pace. They paddled in perfect sync, matching each other stroke for stroke.

"You're pretty good at this," said Garrett after they had been underway for a few minutes.

"We've had some practice," said Greg. "We usually come here once a year. It's a great family time for us."

"How long have you been married?" asked Garrett, more to break the ice than anything else.

"Just a little over twenty-seven years," said Andie.

"That's a good run," said Garrett appreciatively.

"And it's getting better," said Greg. Garrett glanced at Erica and Sean and did some quick arithmetic.

"You must have waited a while before you had kids," he said. It was barely perceptible, but Garrett saw

Andie's shoulders tense for just a moment. Then she relaxed and continued to paddle.

"We lost our first child a few weeks after birth," said Greg softly. "After that, we had a series of miscarriages. For a long while, we were pretty sure that we would never have children. It still hurts to think about it." Garrett glanced over his shoulder at Greg.

"Sorry," he said apologetically. "I didn't mean to pry." Greg smiled and nodded at Sean and Erica.

"It's all right. Those two are certified miracles."

"Except when they're arguing, which seems to be all the time these days," said Andie with a sigh.

"Kids are gonna do what kids are gonna do," said Greg philosophically. Both he and Andie chuckled, and the mood lightened.

They fell silent, and Garrett took a moment to appreciate the beauty that was slowly rolling past them. The drought was in full force, and the river was a good two feet lower than normal. Even so, the lush green foliage that lined both sides of the river was stunning. Blue green Spanish moss hung in long, graceful strands from the trees, and wild flowers dotted the underbrush with splashes of yellow, red and violet. At times, the river narrowed enough so that the boughs of the trees interlocked overhead. The sun filtered through the leaves, painting the clear water with a glowing, golden haze.

Garrett took a deep breath of the moisture tinted air and felt the pain in his soul ease. Even the dark power that resided there seemed to cower, as if intimidated by the intense beauty.

It probably hasn't changed all that much, he thought. *Gamble and his slaves would have seen it almost exactly like this.* The thought of the slave owner shattered his peaceful mood. His moment of tranquility disappeared in a puff of mental smoke as the real world reasserted itself. Suddenly uncomfortable with the silence, he tried to think of a way to restart the conversation.

"So what exactly do you guys do, if you don't mind my asking?" he asked at last.

"I don't mind at all," said Greg. "I'm a pastor. I have a small church down in Tampa; been there for over fifteen years." That caught Garrett off guard.

"Really," he said, his voice betraying his incredulity. Greg didn't seem to be the religious type.

"Is it that so hard to believe?" asked Greg. He sounded genuinely wounded. Garrett shook his head.

"No," he said. "I didn't mean it that way. It's just that, the only preachers I've seen lately are on television. Compared to them you seem so…normal."

"Thanks," said Greg dryly. "I think."

"Tell us about you, Garrett," said Andie. "What do you do, and what brings you to the Slave Canal?" Garrett thought about lying to his new friends but decided against it. If the Gamble entity had a hold on them, then they certainly knew what he was doing. If not, then it did not matter.

"My wife…my ex-wife, I mean, is a direct descendent of John Gamble," he said.

"Wow," said Andie. "I thought the Gamble family died out decades ago." Garrett started to answer but then decided that a picture could explain things a lot faster. Moving slowly so as not to rock the canoe, he pulled out his wallet and found the small family picture he kept there. He glanced at the three happy people in the photograph. They were at a small park not far from where their house used to be. He leaned forward and handed the picture to Andie. She looked at it and nodded.

"I see," she said. "That's your daughter?"

"Molly," said Garrett. His voice nearly broke, and he suddenly realized that it was the first time he had spoken her name out loud in months. "Her mother's name is Melody. I always called her Mel."

"Your daughter is with your ex-wife, then?"

"She died over a year ago," said Garrett.

"I'm so sorry, Garrett," said Andie. Her voice was sad and gentle. "She was a beautiful child." She glanced at the picture again. "This must have been taken years ago. Do you have a more recent picture?" Garrett opened his mouth to say something to the order of 'What the hell are you talking about?' but remembered his aged appearance at the last moment.

"Not on me," he muttered. Andie studied the picture, frowning.

"She would have been in her twenties when she died," she said.

No, he thought. *She was just ten months old. She wasn't allowed even a single year of life.* He choked back the words and nodded instead. Andie glanced back at him, her brow furrowed. Then she handed him the picture. He felt the canoe rock and looked back to see Greg reaching out. He started to hand him the picture, but as he did, he noticed Melody's handwriting on the back. He had to suppress a groan when he realized that she had dated the picture. Had Andie seen? Did it matter? She said nothing as he passed it back to Greg.

"So Mel is a descendant of one of Gamble's slaves," said Greg.

"Yeah," said Garrett. "But we have reason to believe that she's also related to John Gamble as well."

"Not surprising," said Greg. "It wasn't uncommon for a slave owner to use a female slave that way." He handed the picture back to Garrett. "A mixed marriage is difficult in the best of circumstances. I have two in my church. Their families give them a great deal of grief."

"So did mine," said Garrett. "So did hers." He flinched at the venom in his voice.

"I see," said Greg. "So you're coming here on her behalf?"

"Something like that," said Garrett. Greg waited, but Garrett was no longer in the mood to talk. *What else is there to say? My ex-wife is being held prisoner by her great-great-great grandfather's ghost?*

"Well," said Greg, "whatever the reason, I hope you are able to do whatever it is you have set out to do."

"Me too," whispered Garrett. A sudden shout drew their attention to the other canoe. It seemed that Sean had just splashed his sister with a healthy dose of water. Erica was busy preparing a vicious counterattack.

"Hey!" Greg's deep, booming shout brought them both up short. At the same time, a few hefty strokes from both Greg and Andie brought them even with their offspring. "That digital camera of yours cost eight hundred dollars, and it does not react well to water. If you want to spend the next few years giving us every cent you earn to pay for it, then by all means continue." Garrett envied not only the easy authority in Greg's voice, but the way his children reacted to it. Both of them muttered apologies and, after a couple of well-placed glares, started paddling again. He briefly wondered if he could have ever managed that tone with Molly.

Then he remembered that he never would. His daughter was dead. Anger and bitterness surged inside him. The darkness writhed, demanding to be released. He had the sudden urge to grab Andie's paddle and use it to pound her head into a bloody mess. How dare she have two healthy happy children when he was denied even one?!

Do it, said that same far away voice he had heard in Kyle's truck, only now it sounded much closer. *First the wife, then the husband. Save the two whelps for last.*

Get…out…of…my…mind. Beads of sweat popped out on Garrett's forehead, and he gripped the sides of the canoe. *This was a mistake*, he thought, despairing. *I've put this family in terrible danger.*

Too late, said the voice. *You should have listened to me, Garrett. You should have stayed away. Now, everything that happens is going to be your fault.*

Give me back my wife.

She's not your wife anymore. She's my whore, and she'll be my whore forever…just like that tasty bit of dark meat over there. What's her name? Oh yes…Erica. I think I'll enjoy taking her; after you kill her family, of course.

Never! Vile laughter answered him. It sounded as if it was coming from right over his shoulder. He jerked around, rocking the canoe in the process.

"Easy, Garrett," said Greg. "I don't want to go swimming. What's the matter?" Garrett blinked as the laughter faded. He mopped his damp forehead and wiped away the heavy drops of sweat that were running down his cheeks. Greg watched him with growing concern. "You okay?"

Shut up, nigger. Horrified, he grabbed the thought and crushed it into a tiny ball. Once again the darkness receded, only this time it did sink as deep as before. He could feel it waiting, just below the surface of his conscious mind.

"I'm fine," he said aloud. "Something buzzed my ear, that's all."

"Got to love the Florida insect life," said Greg. Garrett only nodded.

Thirty minutes slid by as the two canoes made their way slowly down the Aucilla River. Garrett kept quiet, focusing every ounce of his will on the darkness, trying to contain it. It was a losing battle. He knew the instant he lowered his guard, it would rise again.

I've got to ditch this family, he thought. *The only way I can protect them is to get away from them.* Of course, there was no easy way to do that. He was effectively trapped in the canoe. Even if he jumped overboard and swam to the nearest bank, Greg could probably catch him, if he had a mind to. *Maybe when we get into the canal, he thought. Maybe I can…*

"And here we are," said Greg. Garrett snapped out of his desperate thoughts and saw that they had stopped paddling. He scanned the river in front of him but could detect nothing that indicated any kind of canal.

"I don't…"

"That's why you don't try this alone," said Greg. "You have to know what you're looking for." Garrett glanced at Greg and saw that he was staring straight ahead. Garrett followed his gaze. He could see that the river curved off to the left, but other than that, there was nothing. "If you keep following the Aucilla here," continued Greg, "you'll find yourself in the Gulf of Mexico."

"It's the reason Gamble built the canal," said Andie. "His plantation was near the Wacissia River, which is at the other end of the canal. That leads to the Warriors. We checked them out once."

"What happened?" asked Garrett.

"It's insidious, really," said Andie. "For a while it just feels as if the river is getting narrower. Then you cross a small lake; after that…well, there's an opening that looks like the continuation of the river, but a little way in, it forks, and then forks again. You suddenly realize that there's a real danger of getting lost."

"I still don't see the canal," said Garrett, although his heart was pounding. It was close. He could feel it, just as he could feel the presence of the entity that had been tormenting him for weeks. It hovered over the entire area like a malignant cloud. He could almost see the darkness covering the sky, blotting out the sun. It was everywhere, but it had an origin, and that origin was just ahead. He closed his eyes.

There, he thought. The river sprang into vivid relief in his mind. He could even see the heavy foliage lining either bank. It was as if he had been suddenly gifted with some sort of third eye, although the darkness within him stained the edges of his vision. *It's right there.* He opened his eyes and looked. On the right bank, a small stretch of the undergrowth seemed less dense. Sure enough, Greg and Andie were now paddling in that direction.

Garrett hunched forward. He wanted to lie down on the bottom of the canoe and curl onto a tight, fetal shaped ball. The darkness behind the foliage seemed to throb in a distinct, irregular rhythm, like a gigantic diseased heart. He could feel it in the back of his mind…thud THUD. Thud Thud THUD. Thud…Thud THUD. The barrier of foliage drew closer.

Sean and Erica went through first. Just before they reached the foliage, they dug their paddles into the water and pulled hard. They hit the foliage at full speed. Garret heard it scraping the sides of their canoe. Their forward progress was slowed, but they kept going. In Garrett's mind, he saw the cloud of darkness reach out to them, surrounding them as they pushed forward.

Wait, he wanted to scream. *Don't go in there. It's your death to go in there! No, it's worse than death!* He tried to open his mouth, but something that was both real and not real lashed out of darkness. He gasped as it grabbed him. He could almost see it…a thick, throbbing tentacle that wrapped itself around his chest and neck. His jaw clenched, and his tongue latched itself to the roof of his mouth. Suddenly, he could neither move nor speak. *Let…me…go!*

It's much too late for that, came the reply. Sean and Erica were in plain sight. His physical eyes could easily see them. They were paddling hard, forcing their way through the water-choked foliage, but it no longer mattered. He could see, with the same third eye that had allowed him to see the entrance to the canal, that the cloud of darkness had already engulfed them. *They're already lost*, he thought, despairing.

Rage boiled up inside of him, a fitting companion to the darkness that infested his soul. He grabbed on to both of them, trying to use them…rage and darkness…as weapons against the power that was holding him mute. He heard the entity's maniacal laughter. *That's my power, fool! You can't use it against me.* He felt the darkness within him try to break free again and barely managed to rein it in. Greg and Andie, oblivious to his struggle, dug their paddles into the water. Again Garrett tried to scream a warning, but the tentacle-that-was-not-a-tentacle held him tight.

"Hang on," said Greg. They hit the foliage at full speed. The canoe barreled forward like a car skidding on ice. The dark cloud descended upon them, and again Garrett tried to scream, this time in agony.

"Greg?" Andie's voice trembled. Suddenly, she stopped paddling. Her shoulders hunched forward, and her head bowed.

She can feel it, thought Garrett.

"Almost there," grunted Greg, still paddling hard.

"We've…got…to…" Andie reached up and grabbed her head with both hands.

"Babe? What's wrong?" Concerned, Greg pulled his paddle out of the water. The canoe slowed, and then stopped. They were stalled in the middle of the foliage, the river behind them, the canal ahead.

"Something's…not…" Andie's voice was weak and trembling. Suddenly, she jerked upright. "LEAVE HER ALONE!" Her shout rang in Garrett's ears, but the trees, heavy brush, and possibly something else muted it immediately.

"Andie! For the love of God, what's…"

"GOD ISN'T HERE," screamed Andie. "IT is, and it has my baby!" She seized her paddle and dug it into the choked water. "Take your filthy hands off her, you monster!" She paddled hard, splashing both Garret and Greg with stagnant water.

"ANDIE," Greg shouted again, but his wife was beyond reason. She attacked the water with the paddle, and slowly the canoe began to move forward again. Ahead, Sean and Erica were floating in open water, waiting. Both brother and sister seemed oblivious to their mother's distress.

"Help me," snarled Andie. Her skin glowed with sweat as she pushed harder.

"But…"

"Do it," snapped Garrett. He looked back at Greg. "You can feel it. I know you can. If you love your children, help her!" Greg's eyes glazed over. A shadow descended onto his face. His features disappeared into darkness, leaving only a vague outline silhouetted against the backdrop of the river. *It's marked him,* Garrett thought. *It's marked us all. I don't think we're getting out of here.*

Then, as quickly as it had appeared, the shadow left. It did not disappear, but rather it lifted off Greg's face. In Garrett's mind, it floated up and rejoined the cloud of darkness that covered everything. Greg's eyes cleared. He gripped his paddle and went to work. Slowly they moved forward, inch by grudging inch. Garrett could feel something within the cloud watching them as they struggled the last few feet toward the canal. For a moment, he was certain that they would never get through. Then, with a last desperate effort, they shot into the open. The canoe caromed forward. Greg had to use his paddle as a rudder to keep from ramming Sean and Erica.

Garrett felt the warm sun on his face as they broke into the clearing, but he also felt the darkness congeal behind them. Now, it was no longer a cloud. It was a solid wall; an impenetrable barrier, rearing up into the sky and blocking the way home. He looked behind him. His physical eyes could see the foliage and the river beyond. It should be a simple matter to go back, but he already knew better.

They would not be getting out.

Chapter 12

The Slave Canal

*A*ndie's eyes darted back and forth between water and land. Her face gleamed with sweat, and her breath came in short, harsh bursts. She held her paddle in front of her, wide end up, gripping it the way a samurai gripped his sword. Something was threatening her family, and she was ready for battle.

Greg stared at his wife, dazed and confused. Garrett sat between them, shoulders slumped. Sean edged his canoe over until it bumped gently against his parents' craft. Erica reached out and gently touched Andie's arm.

"Mom?" Her voice wavered. "What was…"

"Quiet," hissed Andie. "Turn around and get back to the river…now."

"Andie?" This was from Greg.

"Just do it," she snapped. Garrett flinched at the sheer loathing in her voice. He wondered what she would do if she realized that this was his fault.

Nobody was inclined to argue. Sean and Erica pushed off and turned their canoe around until they were facing the river. Using quick, deft strokes, Greg followed suit. Andie did not help. She kept her eyes moving, searching for the danger her eyes could not see.

Greg edged the canoe past his children. They reached the foliage. With a grunt, he dug his paddle into the water and pulled hard. Garrett closed his eyes. He wanted to scream as they entered the dark barrier. Andie felt it as well. He could see it in the way she shrank in on herself. It settled over them like rancid fog. Pain that did not exist and yet was as real as the water beneath them exploded in his chest. The entity's hand-shaped brand burned white hot. The canoe slid forward for a few feet. Then there was a dull thud and the sound of earth scraping against the bottom and they came to a complete stop.

"What the…" Garrett turned to see Greg peering over the canoe's edge. "We hit land," he said, unbelieving. "That…can't be right." He scanned the area. "We must have missed it." Trying to ignore the pain, Garrett looked past Andie. He could easily see the river through the trees. It was maybe a dozen yards ahead, though it might as well have been a light year. The barrier of dark power blocked their way.

Garrett's mind reeled. The pain from the brand throbbed in rhythm with his heart. His natural eyes betrayed him. They told him that they were floating in the entrance to the canal. They also told him that the canoe was now beached on solid ground. Nausea swelled up in his gut.

"Greg." Andie's voice was now barely above a whisper.

"Hang on," replied Greg. He jammed the paddle into the ground that both was and was not there and pushed.

"No," whispered Andie, "please don't." But Greg was not listening. Slowly the canoe edged back into the canal. It bumped into Sean and Erica, causing them to swerve to the right. When Greg finally managed to get his canoe pointed toward the foliage, he took a deep breath and started paddling again. They hit the same spot, and again the canoe bumped to a halt. Both Garrett and Andie moaned in pain.

Garrett's physical senses dulled, and his agony doubled. Conversely, his newer senses…the senses that allowed him to sense the barrier…revved into high gear. He looked at Andie and nearly screamed, only now his scream would have been one of savage joy.

She was glowing. Something deep inside of her was shining out through her physical form, and it was both terrible and beautiful. It was the light of life itself; wild, untamed and free. It pushed against the darkness, and the darkness actually retreated. Andie's glow intensified, and for a moment to brief to be measured, she became something far more than her physical body.

This is who we really are, he thought, staring at the luminous being in front of him. *This is who we were always meant to be.* He watched in awe as the darkness recoiled. *She's going to do it*, he thought. *She's going to shatter the barrier. We're getting out of here!*

She almost made it. The barrier bowed and weakened, but then, just when it might have given way, its power increased. *No*, thought Garrett. *Please, no.* The entity answered.

Fool! This is my land. He felt a rush of dark power flow

into the barrier. It quickly reformed around them. Then Garrett saw something reach out of the darkness. It was the same kind of tendril that had silenced him before, only now it made straight for Andie. This time, it did not wrap itself around her mouth. This time, it reached *into* her. Helpless, Garrett watched as Andie's light dimmed. The tentacle scooped a part of it out of her and then retreated back into the barrier.

Hmmm, said the voice. *Tastes good!*

Stop it, he screamed silently. The voice only laughed.

Just a small taste, it said. *She won't even miss it. The feast comes later.* Behind him, oblivious to the battle that had just been lost, Greg growled.

"Damn it." The curse sounded strange coming out of the preacher's mouth. Again he pushed off and floated back into the canal. Andie clutched her paddle. Even though she had been weakened, she was still ready to defend her family against all comers.

Except I think that you're way out of your league, thought Garrett. He realized something else. *You don't even know what just happened,* he thought. *You don't realize that you've just lost a part of your life.* From somewhere in the back of his mind, or perhaps from deep in the darkness that seethed within him, he felt rather than heard an amused grunt of agreement. Behind him, Greg pulled his paddle out of the water and laid it across his lap, staring at what should have been the way out.

"Dad?" There was real fear in Sean's voice. "What's going on?" Garret glanced over his shoulder and saw Greg staring at the foliage.

"What do you see?" said the preacher. Garrett opened his mouth to reply but then realized that Greg was speaking to his son. The young man stared, trying to describe something that his rational mind was telling him was impossible.

"I…I see the entrance," he said at last. "There's the river…I think." He closed his eyes and shook his head. "It's there, but…not…really."

"Erica?"

"I don' feel so good," she said. Her voice was weak, and her hands were trembling. Suddenly, she leaned over the edge of her canoe and heaved. Her last meal splattered into the clear water. It floated between the two canoes, a tiny island of half-digested food. It was an effective trigger for Garrett. His stomach heaved, and a few seconds later his own lumpy island was floating next to Erica's. Mercifully, the pain in his chest faded.

"Oh God," squeaked Sean, his voice a good octave above normal. He gulped hard but at least for the moment seemed to be controlling his own nausea.

"Greg." Andie's voice was weak, barely above a whisper. "We've got to get out of here. It…wants us."

"What wants us?" demanded Greg. "What's going on, Andie? What do you see?"

"I…I don't…just get us of here." Greg started to argue and then thought the better of it.

"Hang on, then," he said. The water swirled around his paddle as he pushed against the water…a tiny whirlpool that rocked the two vomit islands. The canoe edged forward.

"No," pleaded Andie. "Not that way." But Greg did not hear her. He plunged ahead, this time veering to the right. They hit the foliage at full speed, but once again the canoe hit the non-existent land and stopped short. Impossibly, the barrier thickened. It pressed in on them.

Through his renewed pain, Garrett could feel the darkness within him reaching out to it, welcoming it.

"This is ridiculous," snapped Greg. "Come on, then. We're getting out of here, if we have to walk or swim." He made to stand, but Andie's scream sounded out an instant before Garrett's.

"NO! Don't get into the water! That's what it wants!" Garrett added his silent agreement. The dark power rose into the air, but it seemed to emanate from under the water. He flashed back to the night of Molly's death. That attack…and it was an attack, he knew that now…had also come from beneath.

"Who?" shouted Greg. "Who's doing this, Andie? For the love of God, what's going on?"

"It's old," whimpered Andie. She lowered her paddle and bowed her head. "I…can…" She faltered. "Get us back into the canal, Greg. Please. It *hurts*."

"What…"

"Do it," snapped Garrett. "Get us out of here." He looked over his shoulder at the preacher. "Now." Greg saw the look in his eyes. He pushed off against the real/not real land one final time. Seconds later, they were back in the canal.

Garrett stared at Andie. She seemed to be at war with herself. He certainly understood. Her mind was screaming at her, telling her that this could not possibly be happening. Her heart, or maybe her soul, was telling her to flee. Garrett had a hunch that Andie was the kind of woman who led with her heart. A nasty thought presented itself.

She can hear him, he thought. Suddenly, he was terrified…not of the entity infesting the canal, but of the half-mad woman sitting in front of him. *He's going to tell her that it's my fault.*

Of course, said that distant-but-near voice, *but not until it's too late.* It laughed its mad laugh again, but Garrett wasn't listening. Now that they were free from the barrier, the pain from the brand was gone and his mind was clear. It revved into high gear, and he played back what the entity's last words.

You just made a mistake, he thought. Suddenly, he had the urge to laugh. *You're not infallible after all.* The canoe lurched. Greg was making another run for the river.

"We're going through," he growled. "Hang on, Andie. We're getting out of here."

"NO!" This time, Andie screamed. "Not again, Greg! Stop! For God's sake, stop!" The sheer terror in Andie's stopped Greg cold. He pulled his paddle out of the water, and the canoe slid to a stop.

Garrett took advantage of the lull and closed his eyes. He reached out with his newborn senses. There was the wall of dark power, rooted deep in the water. They would not get through it. He could see that, but now he could see something else as well. He turned his attention toward the canal.

Gotcha, he thought. For the first time since they had entered the canal, he dared hope that this innocent family might be saved. The darkness hovered like a malignant fog over both water and land. Garrett could not tell if it was clouding their senses, making them think that the way back to the river was blocked, or if it was somehow actually transmuting water to earth. It did not matter because further into the canal, the cloud *thinned.* He could see dark tendrils shooting down the length of the canal, both in the water and above it, but they seemed to fade with the distance.

He doesn't control it all, thought Garrett. *Maybe he doesn't even control any of it.*

Wanna bet? The voice was mocking, but Garrett was no longer intimidated.

Yeah, I do, he thought. *'Until it's too late,' you said. That means it's not too late. I can get them out.* The entity did not reply, but Garrett thought he might have heard a faint growl of rage. Behind him, Greg dipped his paddle into the water again.

"One more time, Andie," he said, showing a streak of stubbornness that no doubt served him well with his congregation.

"No," said Garret, looking over his shoulder.

"What? What do you mean 'no'?" There was real anger in his voice. "What do you know about this?" Andie swiveled in her seat. Her eyes were on fire. They sighted in on him like twin lasers.

"Is this your fault?" she demanded. "It is. I can feel it." She raised her paddle higher, ready to unleash the full force of her wrath against her passenger. Garrett thought about lying but decided against it. She was right, after all.

"I came here to find my wife," he said. "I think that she's…trapped here somehow."

"What do you mean, 'trapped'?" Andie's voice was low and dangerous. Garrett knew that she was a hair's breadth away from slamming the paddle down across his head. He closed his eyes. His resolve wavered and then firmed up.

"I think that the spirit of John Gamble has taken her and somehow brought her here," he said, trying not to wince. To actually hear the words coming out of his mouth made him feel like a fool.

"That's the most insane thing I've ever…" Greg began, but Garrett cut him off.

"You know I'm telling the truth," said Garrett, speaking to Andie. "You can feel his presence, can't you? Maybe you can even hear him." Andie raised her paddle higher.

"What I feel is…it's obscene," she hissed.

"Andie, you can't be serious," stuttered Greg. Frustrated, Garrett waved at the visible/invisible exit. Even as he spoke, he could feel the dark cloud expanding down the canal.

"You see what's happening," he snapped. "And you can feel it too." He waved at Sean and Erica. "They can. Don't tell me you can't." Greg shook his head.

"This is impossible," he said in a low voice.

"Do you believe in God?" Garrett demanded. Greg jerked as if he had been slapped. His eyes narrowed.

"Of course I believe in God," he answered indignantly. "It's my job to believe in God."

"And what about the devil?" asked Garrett. "Do you believe in Satan? I mean, a literal devil?" Greg nodded once.

"Yeah, I believe in the devil too."

"Then consider Gamble one of his demons," said Garrett. "Who knows, maybe he is. He's real, he's here, and he wants you and your family." He looked back at Andie. "Yeah, it's my fault," he said. "I had to get here, and you were the only way. I'm truly sorry. I never meant for this to happen, but it has." He waved back toward the exit. "We're not getting out that way, either by boat or on foot. We have to go down the canal. His power gets weaker further in." He nodded at Andie. "You can feel him. You must be able to feel that too." Andie stared at him, and Garrett could see that she was still considering using her oar on his head. She wavered, and then lowered her paddle.

"Yeah, I can," she said. She looked at Greg. "We go through the canal and make for Nutall Rise. If we can get that far, I think we'll be okay." She looked back to Garrett. Her eyes grabbed his, holding them in a grip tighter than steel. "And when this is over, you and I are going to have a long talk. Nobody puts my family in danger...nobody." Garrett nodded slowly. Greg stared at the two of them for a moment.

"All right," he said finally. "We go through the canal." He glanced at his children. "You two ready?"

"Let's just get out of here," said Erica in a weak voice. "I never want to come back."

"Yeah, me too," seconded Sean. He looked at his father, and Garrett could see that he was ashamed. "I'm scared, Dad."

"You're not alone," said Greg. "Come on. God willing, we'll laugh about this later."

Not a chance, thought Garrett. They swung the canoes around, and a few moments later they were paddling through the canal. For the first time, Garrett had a chance to really see it. He could feel the entity's dark power dogging them, nipping at their heels; but even so, he was impressed by the natural beauty of the place.

It was narrow...ranging between twenty and forty feet wide. There was color everywhere. Shrubs and bushes lined both sides, along with the ever present oak and pine trees. Several of the larger trees had split near the ground, sending thick branches out in every direction. Many of them interlaced overhead. The sun shone through them, creating shadows that danced on the water's clear surface.

The heavy undergrowth made it impossible to see beyond either bank. There were no wild flowers, but the rich, vivid greens and browns of the trees and foliage, coupled with the clear water and deep blue sky, combined to form a magnificent beauty that rivaled anything in Garrett's experience. A pile of a dozen large moss covered rocks on the right bank drew his attention. Even to his untrained eye, it was obvious that the pile was artificial.

"Those are limestone slabs," Greg said in a tight voice. "The slaves digging here would occasionally run across a limestone ridge and have to dig it out. That's where they piled the rocks." Garrett nodded.

The last time they were moved was when the canal was being dug, he thought in awe. *Some poor slave, maybe no older than Sean, had to break them apart and haul them out of the ground.* The Florida heat was in full force. He felt a trickle of sweat wind its way down his forehead, making for his left eye. He wiped it away, thinking of the men and women who had been forced to dig the canal in the summer furnace. How many of them had died here?

"You said your wife was trapped," said Greg as the limestone pile slid past and disappeared behind them, "by a man long dead. How can you possibly believe that?"

"Talk, Garrett," prodded Andie. "What's happening here? Why have you put my family in danger?" Andie's tone left no room for refusal or compromise.

"It's a long story," he said. He saw Andie open her mouth, undoubtedly to give the tried and true reply, 'we seem to have plenty of time.' That was debatable, of course, but Garrett was not about to argue. He owed them an explanation. "I'll tell you as much as I know, but you have to believe that I had no intention of harming you. I was desperate."

"Fine," said Andie. She was not even close to forgiving him.

"I told you that my daughter died in a freak accident," said Garrett. "Do you remember the sinkhole story from last year?"

"Sure," said Greg. "It was all over the news." He paused a moment. "Do you mean to tell me that she…"

"Was killed when one of those holes ate our house," said Garrett. "That picture I showed you was taken just a few months before that. She was just ten months old when she died."

"That picture showed a young man, not yet thirty," said Greg.

"I'm twenty-seven," said Garrett flatly.

"You're lying," snapped Andie.

"I wish to God I was," said Garrett. "Do you want the whole story?" Andie did not answer.

"All right, Garrett," said Greg. "Tell us."

He did. Sean and Erica edged their canoe in closer so that they could listen. He began with the sinkholes, barely getting through Molly's death. He told them of the visitations, pulling up his shirt and showing them the hand-shaped brand on his chest. His leg throbbed as he swiveled to give Greg a good look. He told them of his trek to Florida, his discovery of the Chance-Gamble connection. He ended with his search for the canal. When he finished, he fell silent. He felt like a man on trial, waiting for the jury's verdict.

"I believe you," said Andie finally. "I believe every word. Greg?" Her husband thought about it. Garrett could see that he was struggling.

"Yeah, I guess I do too," he said at last. "I don't want to, but…I can feel something here, and I know two things about it. It's following us, and it's evil."

"So what gives you the right to do this to us?" hissed Andie. Garrett shook his head.

"Nothing," he muttered. "What I've done is…"

"Inexcusable," supplied Andie. Garrett nodded.

"We can worry about that later," said Greg. "First we get out of here." To Garrett's relief, Andie did not reply. Instead she gripped her paddle and set to it with a will. They moved along at a rapid clip. Garret estimated that they made a good mile, although he could still feel the entity nipping at their heels. With his awakened senses, he could see it sending out shoots of dark power through the water beneath them. The barrier that had prevented their escape shadowed them, growing steadily thicker. The way ahead was still clear, but Garrett knew that their time was running out.

Erica let out a yelp, and an instant later both canoes slid to a halt.

"What the…" Sean began, but Greg was a step ahead.

"We hit something," he snapped. "Back up, back up." They went to work, but despite their efforts, they could not budge the stuck craft. Garrett watched them, feeling both helpless and afraid.

He's got us, he thought. *We weren't fast enough.* He closed his eyes and saw the darkness rushing toward them.

Chapter 13

Light in a Dark Place

*G*reg and Andie back-paddled frantically, but the canoe did not budge. Gripping the side with both hands, Garrett peeked over the edge. He half-expected to see the rotting corpse of John Gamble rising from the depths, arms outstretched, ready to drag him down to everlasting torment. Instead, there was only the bottom of the canal a few feet below. He could see gently waving fronds, moss covered stones and sand. His eyes darted toward the bow of the canoe. This time, no real-yet-unreal barrier was stopping them. They were hung up on a very solid, very perceptible sand bar. He remembered from his research that Gamble's barges were constantly getting stuck in the same manner.

"Sean, you jerk! Stop it!" Garrett looked over at the siblings and saw that Erica was now drenched. At first, he thought that Sean was deliberately soaking his sister. Then he saw the young man's face and realized that he was one step away from full-fledged panic. He beat at the water with his paddle, sending thick flumes straight at his sister.

"SEAN!" Greg's commanding voice rang out, cutting across the canal. Sean jerked as if he had been slapped. He froze, holding his paddle half in and half out of the water. He stared at his parents. "Ease off the juice, son," said Greg, lowering his voice. "We're going to get out of here, but we need your help to do it. Now calm down and use your head." Greg's voice held about three parts encouragement and two parts rebuke. Sean's dark cheeks flared deep crimson. His shoulders slumped, and his head bowed.

"Sorry," he muttered. Garrett's heart went out to him. He knew humiliation when he saw it. Greg could see it as well.

"Just relax," he said. "There's no shame in being scared. You've just got to control it. Okay?" His words had a remarkable effect on Sean. The young's man's shoulders straightened again. He raised his head slowly and met his father's eyes.

"Okay," he replied.

Despite the growing darkness, Garrett could not help but be impressed by both the way Greg dealt with his son and the way Sean received his father's instruction. He had been on the receiving end of his own father's biting tongue more times than he could count. Harold Webb could stand to learn a few things from the reverend.

The canoe rocked suddenly, jolting him out of his thoughts. Greg had jammed his paddle into the bottom of the canal and was pushing hard. Andie did the same, but neither was able to budge the craft. The bow had wedged itself deep into the soft earth.

"We're too stuck and too heavy," grunted Greg.

"No," whispered Andie. "We can't."

"No choice," said Greg. Then, before Garrett could object, he swung his legs over the canoe's edge and slid into the water.

"Greg, don't."

"Andie, relax! Look." He was standing next to the canoe, feet planted firmly on the bottom. The water barely came up to his knees. "Now just hang on. Sean, you know what to do." There was a shout and a loud splash. Showing considerably less grace than his father, Sean tried to get into the water. His foot caught on the edge of the canoe, and he went in head first. Erica yelped as the canoe rocked back and forth. Sean got his feet under him and stood, wiping the water from his eyes.

"Hurry," said Andie in a low voice. "It's getting closer. Erica, stay in the boat. I…I think it wants you more than any of us." She met her husband's eyes. "Hurry," she whispered again. Greg splashed past Andie to the back of the canoe. Sean followed his father's example.

"This would be a lot easier if you two would get out," said Greg. "No," said Andie, speaking for Garrett as well. He shook his head. Exasperated, Greg grabbed the canoe.

"All right, then," he said and shoved hard. The canoe lurched forward a few inches. Sean managed maybe a foot. Greg took a deep breath, wiped the sweat from his forehead and made ready to push again.

"Greg!" Andie's voice was low and urgent.

"I know, I know." Greg heaved again, but this time the canoe did not budge. Garrett closed his eyes and groaned. The dark fog was closing in. He could almost see it with his natural eyes. It billowed around them, growing thicker by the second. The way ahead was nearly blocked.

"We've got to go now," he grunted. Greg heaved again, but again the canoe did not move.

"This isn't working," he said after a third try. "We're going to have to carry the boats. There's no way that we can push them across this thing."

"We can't," whimpered Andie. Garrett felt the outer wisps of the fog grow closer. It was the last thing he wanted to do, but he knew that Greg was right.

"No choice," he said. He swung his good leg over the edge and levered himself into the water. Given the Florida heat, it was surprisingly cold. A sudden splash diverted his attention. Erica had jumped into the water.

"Erica! Don't!"

"I'm sorry, Mom," said Erica, nearly in tears, "but I can't stand this anymore. This is the only way." She moved to the front and, in perfect unison with her brother, hoisted the canoe. They started over the sand bar.

"Come on, Andie," said Greg. "The sooner we do this, the sooner we're out of here."

"No."

"Andie."

"No, Greg. I can't." Keeping his weight on his good leg, Garrett leaned over until his face was even with Andie's.

"I can't help you," he said softly. "Not with this bad leg. Please, Andie. We're running out of time." He barely managed to register a blur of movement. Then Andie's open palm collided with his right cheek. He staggered and nearly fell. Andie's slap had caught him completely off guard.

"Screw you," she hissed. The venom dripping from her voice stung him almost as much as the slap. "This is your fault. We're being hunted by that…that thing, and it's your fault."

"That's enough." Greg's voice whipped out through the air, stern and commanding. Andie turned and met her husband's glare with one of her own.

"Not nearly," she snapped. "And don't you dare speak to me that way. I'm your wife, not your child."

"Then stop acting like a child," said Greg. "How many times have you heard me preach about evil? Well, there's evil here, all right. It's all around us, so get your ass out of the boat and let's get moving." Andie jerked backward, as if she was the one who had just been slapped. Then, glaring at Garret, she threw her legs over the side of the canoe and splashed into the water. Garrett felt the darkness surge toward them. He backed away and bumped into Andie.

"Get away from me," she snapped. Garrett bit back a reply and moved aside. He glanced over at Sean and Erica and was gratified to see that they had already cleared the sand bar. Andie and Greg grabbed their canoe and lifted it. Then they marched past Garrett and over the bar. Garrett fell in behind them. The dark fog rolled in, growing more impenetrable by the second.

"Come on, Garrett," said Greg over his shoulder. Glad to obey, Garrett crossed the sand bar. At its zenith, the water barely covered his ankles, but his bad knee argued against every step. Once on the other side, he slid back into the canoe as Greg held it steady. Andie was already inside. Garret settled down into his seat, grateful beyond words to be out of the water.

"All set?" asked Greg. Garrett looked over his shoulder, raising a hand to give a 'thumbs up' signal, but suddenly his chest flared with black heat. He gasped and doubled over.

"Garrett?" Greg's voice sounded very far away. "What is it?" Garrett opened his mouth but could not make a sound. He clutched at his chest, clawing at the dark fire burning him.

"Go," snapped Andie. "Now!" The canoe rocked as Greg jumped in. Andie was already paddling. The canoe edged forward, gaining momentum, but Garrett's new senses were running white hot. The delay had cost them. The dark fog surrounded them, cutting them off in both directions.

"Stop," he managed to gasp, but no one was listening. He tried again, but the pain in his chest doubled. The two canoes barreled headlong toward the writhing darkness. His hands flew up in front of him, a useless reflex. They reached the edge of the darkness, and he knew that once they entered, they would not be coming out. He braced himself for the violent assault on his mind and spirit.

Then, against all reason, the fog parted. It split in two and moved back toward both banks, forming a narrow pathway down the center of the canal. He glanced to his right, and his senses reeled. His natural eyes saw the bank, lined with trees and thick brush, but his new sight saw an opaque wall of concentrated dark power...the same kind of power that was infecting his soul. The nausea he had experienced earlier made a curtain call, and he struggled to control himself.

Then they plunged into the narrow valley that was both there and not there. The dark barrier rose up on either side of them, and Garrett was certain that it would come crashing down and bury them alive. He closed his eyes and covered his head with his hands. Long seconds ticked by. The only sound was the rapid 'slurp gurgle slurp' of four paddles attacking the water. When nothing happened, he opened his eyes again.

The barrier was still there, but it was motionless. The way ahead was open, just wide enough to get through. Garrett watched as Greg and Andie, following Sean and Erica, threaded their way straight down the middle of the narrow valley.

"Can you see it?" he asked.

"I know it's there," snapped Andie. Garrett glanced back at Greg, who nodded grimly.

"Yeah, I can feel it too," he said. "It's like it's waiting for something." He looked hard at Garrett. "Any idea what?"

"Yeah," said Garrett, looking away. He could not meet the preacher's glare. "I think it wants your wife and daughter." Greg's dark eyes flashed. He pressed his lips together in a thin line.

"Over my dead body," he snarled.

Fool.

Dark tentacles shot out from both sides of the barrier. There were hundreds of them. Garrett screamed. The pain surged in his chest, and he doubled over again. He held up his hands, trying to ward off the tentacles, but they ignored him and made straight for Andie and Erica. Horrified, Garrett watched as they wrapped themselves around the women, cocooning them. Some of them, Garrett saw, actually entered them, burrowing deep. Andie slumped over. She dropped her paddle into the water. It floated away as if under its own power. Erica was also frozen. Her body was limp, and her hands were dangling at her side, but her face...

Garrett barely managed not to scream again. Erica's eyes were alert and aware. They darted back and forth, searching for something…anything…that would allow her to escape. *She knows*, thought Garrett. *She knows exactly what's happening to her.*

"Andie!" Greg's shout jolted Garrett out of his stupor. "Erica! Look at me!" Neither woman obeyed. They were unable to obey, but Greg's voice had cut through the terror in Garrett's mind. The pain in his chest eased off, and he managed to sit up.

"It's got them," he managed to gasp.

"The hell it does," growled Greg. He kept paddling, but now both sides of the barrier were moving toward them. It was as if the tentacles had anchored themselves into Andie and Erica and were reeling it in. "Sean! Are you all right?"

"I…Dad, something's wrong with Mom…Erica too."

"I know. What about you?" Garrett could easily see the answer to that question. Sean was losing it. Greg could see it as well. "Answer me, son. Are you all right?"

"No. I don't…I don't think I can…"

"That's enough," snapped Greg. "Your mother and sister need you. *I* need you. Now get a hold of yourself."

"Ye…yes, sir."

"Keep paddling," ordered Greg. "This thing hasn't got us yet. We can still make it."

"Okay." Sean's face managed an amazing range of expressions, from pure terror to utter hopelessness, but then settled down into grim determination. He bent to his work with a will, paddling hard.

The kid's got guts, thought Garrett. *For all the good it will do.* He watched hopelessly as the tentacles wound even tighter around Andie and Erica. The dark barrier drew closer. He could see that the tentacles did not stretch as the canoes continued forward. Rather, they moved with them, as if they were rooted in dark liquid and could move at will.

"Andie? Come on, sweetheart. Talk to me." Andie did not answer. Garrett had a feeling that she might be able to hear her husband, and that made it all the worse.

"We're not going to make it," whispered Garrett.

"Shut...up," gasped Greg. His breathing was ragged and uneven. He was near the end of his endurance, but still he kept paddling. He even managed to pick up the pace a little. Sean, with the strength and endurance of youth, began to pull away. Garrett peered ahead, but there was no sign of the canal's end.

"How far?" he asked. Greg did not answer.

The barrier slammed shut. There was no warning. Garrett blinked, and in that single instant that his eyes were closed, existence as he knew it disappeared. This time, there was no double vision. This time the darkness was both real and impenetrable. He tried to scream, but the sound was choked off before it left his throat. He could not move, could not even feel the canoe under him. Greg, Andie, Erica and Sean...all were forgotten. They were no longer a part of his world. He sat alone in what could only be described as non-existence.

This is hell, he thought, or thought he thought. His mind was fading. *No light, no sound, not even memory. This has to be hell. It can't be anything else.* Then even that thought was gone. His name, his life, even the fact that he existed, all of it was forgotten. He sat in the darkness, nothing more than a non-entity.

Time passed.

And Time did not pass.

Then...

A flicker of light caught his attention. He stirred, and for just a moment his mind flared. *What was that?* He waited, but there was nothing else. His mind dimmed again, and he sank back into the oblivion that cocooned him.

Another flicker, and this time it was brighter. Again he was roused out of the muck that used to be his mind.

Light. The single thought flashed through his mind. *Light.* He waited, and this time he did not wait in vain. The light returned, only now it stayed. It was weak and dim, but it was there. It penetrated the darkness, and Garrett...*that's my name,* he remembered with a fierce joy...was certain he heard a faint howl of rage and pain. He focused every scrap of his battered mind on the light. It was coming from behind him. He commanded the muscles in his neck and shoulders to move, and after arguing about it for a few seconds, they obeyed. He turned, and gasped. Greg was the source of the light. As he watched, it grew, and against all hope the darkness retreated...not all the way, but it gave ground.

You don't like this, he thought. *Whatever this is, it can hurt you.* Greg opened his eyes, and again Garrett gasped. They were glowing an intense green, and as the light surrounding him grew, so did the glow. Garret thought of the light Andie had brought to bear in her futile attempt to escape the canal. *This is different. Andie's felt more...earthy. Greg has tapped into something different; something...not of this world...something alien.* He shuddered. Even though it seemed to be helping them, in its own way the light was just as frightening as the darkness.

Without warning, the darkness within him burned. He gasped in pain and was forced to look away. The light flared brighter. No longer a dim glow, now it was a miniature emerald sun. It battered the darkness, driving it back toward the land. Again Garrett heard the entity's voice, only now it shrieked in agony. At the same time, the dark power within Garrett screamed. He felt it writhing inside of his soul, trying to escape the piercing light.

"Greg." He could barely whisper, but Greg heard. His glowing eyes locked onto him.

"The power that seeks to imprison you...you carry it within you," he said.

"I...I...yes." Greg pointed a glowing finger at him.

"My power here is limited, but I can free you of it. Are you willing?"

"Yes," sobbed Garrett. "Oh, please yes!" Greg's light flared even brighter. Then a beam, pure and intense, streaked out from his forehead, striking Garrett squarely in the chest. The darkness within Garrett rebelled. It lashed out at the beam and drove it back.

"You're...fighting me," said Greg in a low voice. "You have to let it in, Garrett. It's the only way."

"I don't know how," sobbed Garrett.

"Just...let...it...in," said Greg. Garrett stared at the preacher. He felt the two forces battling for his soul. He closed his eyes.

The dark power boiled inside of him. The entity...maybe its name was John Gamble, maybe not...had planted it there like a malignant seed. Garrett had watched helplessly as it put down roots, knowing that it was only a matter of time before it overwhelmed him.

Now, for the first time, he had a way of escape. Greg, or whatever he had become, was providing the power, and at that moment it was a match for the darkness within him. All he had to do was provide the will.

Fool. You're mine. Your wife is mine. These women are mine!

"Screw you," growled Garrett, echoing Andie. "No. Damn you. Damn you to hell." He did not give the entity time to answer. Moving on instinct alone, he reached out for the beam. The darkness rebelled, but for an instant Garrett was stronger. He fought it, and won. With every ounce of his being, he reached out…

…and touched the green light.

He screamed…maybe. It was hard to tell. The beam rushed forward, shattering the darkness. It plunged into him like a heat seeking missile, driving deep. Wherever it found the darkness, it obliterated it. Garrett's mind blazed with a power and light he had never known. He looked down at his hands and was not surprised to see that they were glowing.

And then the darkness that had infested him for so long and had cost him so much was gone. He screamed again, this time in defiant victory. He half-expected to hear that far off voice call him a fool again, but there was only silence. With a thrill of joy, he realized that he would never hear that voice in his mind again. It had used the darkness within him as a conduit, and now that darkness was gone.

"One more thing," whispered Greg. Garrett could not tell if he heard the preacher's voice with his ears or his mind. It did not matter because now the light infused him. He felt his body glow, and then suddenly his bad knee flared with white hot heat. He cried out in both shock and pain, but it was over in an instant. The heat dimmed, and Garrett knew without even checking that his knee was whole again. "I can't give you back the years that were taken from you," said Greg, and now his voice was much fainter, "but I can heal you. I can do that much." Garrett looked at Greg. He was still glowing, but now his glow was much fainter.

"Who are you?" he gasped. "*What* are you?"

"A friend," said Greg.

"You're not Greg," Garret whispered in awe.

"He's here, and he's safe," said Greg's voice.

"Mo…Molly? Is that you?" Greg's head shook.

"She is not here. This is not her place." The writhing darkness that surrounded them was forgotten. Garrett stared at the being inhabiting Greg's body. A million questions piled into his mind, but he asked the only one that mattered.

"Melody," he whispered.

"She's here, and she is alive, but I cannot save her. I have…limitations. This is your realm. The two of you are connected by a bond that cannot be broken. It is that bond that will be her salvation, but I warn you now, Garrett Webb, the price will be high."

"How can I find her?" asked Garrett.

"Follow the lost," was the enigmatic reply. "They will lead you."

"I don't understand."

"You will, but first you must get this innocent family to safety. They are your responsibility."

"But…"

"They are trapped because of you. You must get them out, or their blood, and their souls, will be on your hands."

"You've got to help me," said Garrett. "I can't fight this by myself."

"Yes, you can," said Greg's voice. "You are stronger than you know. Don't give up. I will protect you as much as I am able. Now please, go. I have power, but this darkness is stronger." With a thrill of fear, Garrett saw that Greg's light was fading. He reached out with his new senses. The pain he had sensed a moment ago was still there. Greg had hurt the entity, but it was recovering. It still held Andie and Erica in its grasp, and it was growing stronger by the second.

Something bumped against the canoe. He looked down and saw Andie's paddle floating in the water beside him. He scooped it out of the water.

"Did you do this?" he asked, holding up the paddle.

"Yes," said Greg's mouth. "Hurry." The light dimmed, and the glow in Greg's eyes disappeared. The darkness moved closer. Garrett did not have to be told twice. He started paddling.

Chapter 14

The Valley of the Shadow

*G*arrett pulled hard, his clumsy strokes battering rather than cutting through the water. All around them, the darkness fluttered. It began to close in on them again, only now it seemed hesitant.

He hurt it, thought Garrett. He knew that he was right, but he also knew that they were still in deep trouble. The tentacles remained wrapped around Andie and Erica, holding them fast, and while the darkness was moving much slower, it was still coming at them. A sudden thought struck him.

"Why can I still see you?" he muttered. He had been able to discern the dark power because Gamble had planted the same power in his soul…or so he thought. Now, that seed had been obliterated, so why could he still sense the darkness?

"You've been touched by that power, just like me." Greg's voice was weak, but it was his own. "It's changed us, and I don't think that we can ever go back." There was an almost silent splash. Garrett glanced over his shoulder. The preacher had regained the use of his body and was actually paddling. His eyes were wide with both terror and wonder.

"You can see it," Garrett said.

"Yeah, I can see it," said Greg. He shook his head. "But now's not the time. Paddle Garrett. Paddle for our souls." Garrett was only too happy to obey. He looked to his left and saw that Sean had started paddling again as well and wondered if the young man had even been aware of what had happened.

"If you can see the darkness," said Garrett, "Then you can see…"

"That it has my wife and daughter," finished Greg. "Yeah." He raised his voice. "But I swear that you won't keep them," he said to the darkness. Garrett tensed, expecting to hear John Gamble's dead laughter echo through his mind, but there was nothing.

His hold on me has been broken, he thought, and suddenly tears began to run down his cheeks. He touched his chest and knew without looking that Gamble's mark was gone. *He'll never use me again, and if that can happen to me…*he looked at Andie, who was still slumped over…*then they can escape as well…and not just them. I can save Melody too.* He braced his legs against the bottom of the canoe, reveling in the absence of pain from his now strong knee, and pulled harder. They drew even with Sean and then pulled ahead.

"Sean," called Greg. "You still with us, son?"

"Yeah," grunted Sean. He was breathing hard, but he kept paddling.

Garrett kept his eyes on the dark walls that bracketed them. They seem to stretch ahead to infinity. Above, the sky was a dull gray rather than the vibrant blue it had been when they entered the canal. The light was fading with each passing second.

That can't be right, thought Garrett. It was too dim to make out the numbers on his watch, but by his reckoning it should be mid-afternoon. *Just how long were we trapped,* he wondered...*an hour...a day...a week?* It was a disturbing question, but one that would have to be answered later.

The tentacles flowed with them. Gamble, it seemed, was not about to let his two prizes escape, at least not without a fight. *And whoever or whatever saved us isn't here anymore,* thought Garrett. He peered ahead, searching for a sign that they were coming to the end of the canal, but he could see only the darkness.

"Does this thing ever end?" he grunted.

"Just...keep...going," gasped Greg. The preacher's fatigue mirrored his own. He was running out of steam.

"I...don't think that...we're going to make it," he said.

"Don't you dare quit on me," snapped Greg. There was real anger in his voice.

"We...need help," said Garrett. His arms were on fire now, and his fingers were growing numb. Every stroke was agony. He kept switching sides, trying to use different muscle groups, but it did not help. He was nearly spent.

"We're all we've got," snapped Greg. "Now pull!" Garrett closed his mouth and paddled. The darkness continued to close in from both sides. It was moving faster now, as if it could sense that they could no longer resist it.

Why? he thought. *Why save us if we didn't stand a chance?* Sweat was pouring off his face. His arms were on fire. The pain made it nearly impossible to think, but he had no choice. They were not going to escape by brute force. *What am I missing? That creature...angel?...Gregangel?...freed us. It said that I had the power to save Mel. It said...*

"It said that I was stronger than I knew," he said aloud.

"Garrett," hissed Greg. "For the love of God, shut up and paddle." Garrett shook his head.

"We need time," he said. "And we need to free Andie and Erica." He pulled his paddle out of the water and laid it across his lap.

"Are you insane?" screamed Greg. "Pick up that paddle, Garrett. Pick it up, or I swear I'll..."

"Greg," hissed Garrett. "Do you remember that creature being inside of you?"

"I remember everything," said Greg, "but now's not the time."

"Yes, it is," said Garrett. "We can't get out this way. We've got to free Andie and Erica."

"We'll free them once we're out," snapped Greg. He jammed his paddle into the water. It made a sickly gurgle, as if the water had suddenly turned to oil. "It can't keep them once we're out. It can't." He sounded desperate.

"Are you sure?" demanded Garrett. "Gamble's planted himself deep into this place, and he's been spreading out for over a hundred and seventy years.

"Garrett..."

"He reached all the way to Kentucky and took my wife," he said. "And I think our buddy Kyle is under his spell as well."

"It's getting closer," said Greg. "And if it closes on us this time, I don't think we're getting out."

"Oh, we're getting out," said Garrett. Suddenly, he was absolutely certain of that. "I don't know what's going to happen afterward, but we're getting your family out of here."

"Then…start…paddling," said Greg. His voice was low and weak. He was spent. Garrett did not bother to reply. He closed his eyes and bowed his head, as if in prayer. But this was not a desperate attempt to reach out to a God he did not believe in. Since the moment his knee had been healed, something had been stirring inside of him. He could not discern it at first, but as they forced their way through the canal, it began to manifest itself. Now, Garrett took a few precious seconds to study it, and as he peered into his mind and soul, he realized a simple, shattering fact. The entity had done far more than mend his knee. It had left something behind.

It had given him *light*.

"Oh…my…God," he breathed. It was there, deep inside of him…and it was *good*. Garrett stared at it with eyes that saw beyond the physical realm. *Can I use this?* The light blazed within him. It was a raging furnace, filling him with a kind of strength he had never known.

Now that he could see it, he could not un-see it. It infused every part of his being, and he was certain that when he opened his eyes, he would see it leaking out of every pore. *Do I dare use it?* It was a staggering question. If he tried, would he be burned to a crisp?

It was the power of life itself. It was not the same power the Gregangel had used to keep the darkness at bay, nor was it the same power that had healed his knee. He had perceived that as green. This was a pure, blazing white. He had no idea what it was, but it was there, and it was demanding to be released.

It's going to burn me, thought Garrett as he stared into the heart of the white power permeating his soul. Then he discovered a wonderful fact. He did not care. He could no more be afraid of this incredible power than he could be afraid of breathing. The power of the Gregangel had been strange...alien. Somehow, this was a part of him. It *belonged* to him.

"Garrett," said Greg, his voice barely audible. "If you're going to do something, now's the time." Garrett's eyes snapped open. He saw that the dark walls were much closer now. He swiveled to look at Greg. When the preacher saw him, he gasped.

"What?" he demanded. Greg scrunched his eyes shut and turned his head away.

"Your eyes," he whispered. "Your...they're...they're glowing. What...what are you?"

"I'm still me," said Garrett. The power within him was expanding now, straining to get free. It was as if it was eager to take on the darkness. Garrett was happy to oblige it. He turned to face the oncoming walls. For a brief instant, his fear made a curtain call. Once he released it, would he be consumed? Would the light burn him to dust, destroying not only his body, but his soul as well? Would he simply wink out of existence? The he looked at the light again, and his fear vanished into a puff of nothingness. He knew what he had to do, and for the first time since his ordeal had begun, he knew how to do it.

First things first, he thought. He turned his attention to Andie. Now, thanks to the light, he could see beyond the dark tentacles binding her. He could see the vile power oozing into her, penetrating through her physical being and seeping into her soul. He could see that it was imprisoning everything that made up the unique being that was Andie Powell. Anger flared inside of him, and this time it wasn't dark. This time, it was white hot. He reveled in it, knowing that it was justified.

How dare you, he thought, not knowing or caring if Gamble could hear him. *These women are innocent. How dare you do this to them?!* Doubt bubbled up again. Could he free them? Could he command the power that raged within him? Then, in a flash of insight, he saw the truth. He commanded nothing. He was the conduit. He provided the will. This power did the rest. *Fine by me,* he thought.

He released the light. It was a simple thing, like opening a kitchen faucet. He focused his attention on the dark power binding Andie and turned the handle.

Power, pure and wonderful, burst out of him. It formed itself into a thin lance, tapering down to an impossibly fine point. Garrett let it loose and watched in awe as it knifed into Andie.

The effect was immediate. For the first time since she had been bound, Andie screamed. From somewhere far away, Garrett might have heard another scream…a scream of pain. *That's for Mel, you son of a bitch,* he thought. The light flooded into Andie, and as it did, the tentacles started to shrivel. Garrett stared in amazement as the white power collided with the dark, obliterating it. It plunged deep into Andie's soul, and everywhere it went, the darkness fled.

In an instant, Andie was free. She doubled over, gasping for breath. Garrett immediately turned his attention to Erica. The dark walls were almost upon them. Dismayed, he saw that his power was already fading. While potent, whatever the Gregangel had poured into him was finite, and he was using it up at an alarming rate.

"Andie?" Greg's voice barely registered in Garrett's mind. "Are you there?"

"B…barely," gasped Andie. "That…that thing…oh my God, Greg, it *raped* me!" She began to sob. "It's raping Erica. Please, make it stop."

"Andie? Please listen to me." The desperation in Greg's voice penetrated Andie's agony. Her shoulders straightened, and she half-turned to face him. "We're going to make it stop, but you've got to help," he said. "Turn around and take Garrett's paddle. We've got to keep moving." Garrett saw Andie shudder. Then, incredibly, she reached out grabbed the paddle out of Garrett's limp grasp. As she did, she looked into his eyes.

"What…"

"Let him be," said Greg. "It's almost here." Andie tore her eyes off Garrett and looked toward the bank. Garrett could tell by her reaction that she could see the approaching darkness, but there was nothing else he could do for her. Once again he let the light within him well up, and when it was ready, he released it.

Again it formed itself into a shining lance. The lance penetrated Erica, but as it sank deeper into her soul, its progress slowed. Then, before it could destroy the dark power, it stopped.

It's fighting me, thought Garrett. *I took it by surprise with Andie, but now it's ready.* A single terrifying fact presented itself. The darkness infesting Erica did not have to defeat the light. It only had to delay it long enough for the walls to slam shut and imprison them. He felt the light strain within him, and he opened his internal faucet wider. The darkness resisted.

You're not going to keep her, thought Garrett. He was straining now. The light was flowing out of him, and he could feel the darkness inside Erica weakening, but his time was running out. That miniature sun was dimming, and once it went out, he would be finished.

He reached deep inside himself, grabbed that internal valve that controlled the flow, and twisted it as far as it would go. For an instant, the two powers raged against each other. The light won. The darkness shattered and the light infused Erica. In seconds, she was free.

Like her mother, Erica screamed, only this time it was different. Andie's scream had been one of despair and loathing. Erica's scream was pure, animalistic triumph. Garrett suddenly understood. She had been fighting it the whole time. It was probably why the darkness had tightened its hold on her. She refused to give up, and because of that, the darkness had never truly held her. She sat up straight and looked over at Garrett.

"Thank you," she said. Her voice was strong and even. Garrett nodded a silent response. Erica glanced at the closing darkness, regarding it the way a mongoose might regard a cobra. Garrett could see that she was spoiling for a rematch. Then she grabbed her paddle and got to work. *I wonder if either Greg or Andie realize just how special these children are*, he thought.

"You did it," whispered Greg.

"Yeah," said Garrett. "You got anything left?" He looked at Greg and saw that the preacher was paddling hard, his jaw set.

"Just watch me," he snarled. Garrett turned back and saw that Andie was paddling as well, although her entire body was trembling. Garrett realized that she was sobbing.

"Andie?"

"Shut up, Garrett," she said. "I know what you did, and I'm grateful. Believe me, I'm grateful, but I haven't forgotten why we're here. Now just be quiet and let me do my part." Garrett shut up.

Whatever the tentacles had done to them, it didn't seem to affect the two women physically. Both Andie and Erica dug into the water with a strength that surprised Garrett. Now, with two fresh sets of arms working in tandem, the canoes picked up speed.

Again Garrett tried to see the end of the canal, but there was only darkness. *We can't be too late*, he thought, *not after all this*. But there was no sign of light anywhere, and the dark walls were almost upon them. Even the light from the sky was nearly gone. Andie was only a few feet in front of him, and he could barely see her. He closed his eyes and tried to grab hold of that incredible light that had infused him, but where once had been a raging sun now was only a few barely glowing embers. He had used up nearly everything the Gregangel had given him. Now it was up to the brute strength of Greg, Andie, Sean and Erica.

Then he felt it…a cool breeze on his face. His head jerked up, and his eyes snapped open. He took a deep breath, reveling in its moist freshness. It was like walking into an air conditioned room on an unbearably hot day. It felt open and alive, but most of all, it felt free. He looked back at Greg.

"Did you…"

"Yeah, I did," said Greg. He was gasping for breath. "I think…we're almost there."

Sean and Erica were now a full boat length ahead. Garrett silently cheered them on. As they pulled ahead, they began to disappear into the darkness. Again Garrett looked up, and as he did, the last remaining light faded.

He could feel the dark walls on either side of them growing closer and closer. Soon, they would slam shut.

"It's coming," cried Andie. Garrett could feel it as well. The dark walls were within arm's reach. The Gregangel had weakened them, but they were regaining their strength.

In desperation, he reached inside and tried to scrape together the fading embers of the incredible power. If he could manage just one more blast, it might give them enough time to get clear. But even as he tried to latch on to them, they flickered and died. A terrible sense of loss welled up inside of him, and he realized that, for the first time in his life, he had felt complete. The power had filled a void that he did not even realize existed. Now it was gone, and in its place was a gaping hole that bore all the way to the center of his soul. *It's gone*, he moaned silently. *It's all gone*. Overhead, the last light from the sky fled, and they were left in absolute darkness. He could not even make out Andie's silhouette. He felt the dark walls flutter again

"YES!" Suddenly, Sean's shout echoed out from somewhere close by.

"SEAN!" shouted Greg.

"We're here," Sean shouted back.

"I can't see you," cried Andie.

"Just keep coming, Mom," called Erica. "I can see you now. You're almost there." Greg snarled and, despite his exhaustion, paddled harder.

"Get out of here," he shouted. "Both of you; GET OUT!"

"We're already out," shouted Sean. "We're free, Dad. Just keep coming!"

"Thank God," whispered Greg. "Oh, thank you, God." Andie said nothing. She just kept paddling. The walls were on them now. They could no longer see them, but that made no difference. They could feel them. If they veered off even slightly in either direction, they would be trapped.

"HURRY," screamed Erica. "It's..." Andie screamed. An instant later, so did Greg. The walls slammed shut. Garrett cried out and covered his head. Then he sat up straight. The walls had closed behind them. Another breeze wafted across his face, and he actually shivered. He looked up and again saw only darkness, only this time it was the simple, elegant darkness of night. A full moon hung just over the horizon, and countless stars blazed in the black velvet sky. He took a deep breath and tasted freedom.

How much time did we spend trapped in the darkness before the Gregangel got us out? he wondered again:

"We made it," gasped Greg. He and Andie had both pulled in their paddles and were slumped in their seats. They gasped at the air, gulping it in. Then Andie sat up straight.

"Sean! Erica!" She could barely speak, but it did not matter.

"We're here," said Sean's exhausted voice. A long, low shadow appeared out of the night. Sean and Erica's canoe bumped against theirs as they drew alongside. Andie couldn't have cared less if she tipped the canoe. She leaned over and grabbed Erica in a fierce hug. Both canoes rocked back and forth as Greg grabbed onto Sean. Garrett hung on, waiting.

"Let's get out of here," said Greg, releasing his hold on Sean. Andie held on to Erica for a few more seconds before reluctantly letting her go. Feeling awkward and out of place, Garrett looked around, trying to get a feel for their surroundings.

"Where are we?" he muttered. The moon rippled on the water, and he could feel that there was now a current. Both canoes were moving on their own accord. That suited him just fine. He wanted to put as much distance between them and the canal as possible, although he knew that he was going to have to go back. *Follow the lost,* the Gregangel had told him. He had no idea what that meant, but he was certain that sooner or later it would lead him back to Gamble's Run.

"The Wacissia," said Greg, answering his question. "I know this place. Just around that bend is Nutall Rise." Garrett nodded, looking ahead to where the river veered off to the right. If Kyle did what he said he would do, both of their vehicles would be waiting. He would see his charges safely on their way and then figure out what to do next. His stomach suddenly growled, and he realized that he had not eaten since his breakfast at the motel.

"Let's get going," said Andie as she released her hold on her daughter.

"Amen to that," said Greg. They pushed off and oriented their canoes. In moments, they were paddling toward Nutall Rise.

"I see light ahead," said Andie. Garrett squinted ahead and saw that Andie was right. There was a dull but harsh glow filtering through the tree line directly ahead.

"Is there a store or something at Nutall Rise?" asked Garrett.

"Nothing," said Greg. "It's just a clearing pretending to be a hill." Garrett could hear the frown in his voice. "Maybe Kyle's there, waiting for us. We're late. In fact…we're way too late. He should have…" He faded off.

"He should have sent out a search party after us," finished Andie. "This entire section of the river should be swarming with people." The alarm in their voices triggered a memory in Garrett. He thought about how Kyle had grown cold and distant when he had asked him about Gamble's Run.

"Something's not right," he said.

"I…think you might be right," said Greg.

"So what now?" demanded Andie, choking back a sob. She was working well beyond her emotional limit. Garrett suddenly understood that she would be healing for a long time, if she ever healed at all. "We need to go *home*, Greg."

"Just take it easy," said Greg, although his voice was nearly as ragged as Andie's. "Let's ease over to the far bank. I doubt that anyone can see us there. If our cars are there, we take them and go…and never come back. If not, the main road is not far past the rise. We'll get on it, flag down some help and get out of here. Okay?" Andie nodded. "You two got it?" asked Greg.

"Got it," said Sean and Erica in unison.

"Then take it slow," said Greg. "Let's see what we can see." They started paddling again, easing along the bank opposite Nutall Rise. The light grew brighter as they drew closer. Then they rounded the bend, and Nutall Rise came into full view.

"Oh no," said Greg.

Five vehicles were parked side by side. Four of them were pickup trucks, the other an SUV. Neither Greg nor Garrett's cars were in sight. The headlights were all on, pointing straight at the river. A least a dozen men stood around the trucks. All of them were armed, and all of them were staring straight at the five refugees from Gamble's Run. One of them waved.

"Hey, Mr. Webb," he called cheerfully, and Garrett recognized Kyle's voice. "I was wondering if I would ever see my canoes again. Now if you'd just bring them over here, I'll take those niggers off your hands. The master wants to see them, and he gets real ornery when he's kept waiting!" There was the harsh sound of metal striking metal as twelve deadly weapons were cocked and aimed straight at them.

Chapter 15

Downriver

"**D**addy?" Erica's voice trembled.

"Hush," commanded Greg.

"Come on, Greg," shouted Kyle. "Get that bitch and those brats of yours over here. Don't make me tell my boys to open up."

"You won't," shouted Greg. "Your master wants us alive. You said so yourself."

"He's not my master, nigger," sneered Kyle. The friendly, easygoing store owner was long gone. "He's yours, and if I have to give him your bloody corpse, I'll do it. It might be bad for me, but it will be worse for you, and a lot worse for that worthless brood of yours. They may bleed, but I'll deliver them alive. Now move, *boy*. I don't have all night."

Garrett closed his eyes. He reached out with his other sight, the sight that could see powers of both light and dark. Sure enough, it was there. Even from across the river, he could easily sense Gamble's dark power infesting Kyle and his men. *You're wrong*, he thought, opening his eyes again and looking straight at Kyle. *He's your master too. You're just too much of a fool to realize it.*

"Greg, we can't," said Andie, her voice low and urgent. "He'll kill us…or worse."

"I think it's 'or worse'," said Greg, his voice betrayed his exhaustion.

It's not fair, thought Garrett. *This should have been over for him.* The canoe lurched, and he grabbed on to the sides to steady himself.

"Dad! NO!" This was from Sean. Greg had pointed his canoe toward Kyle and was now paddling steadily.

"Hush," snapped Greg, his voice barely loud enough for his son to hear. "When I give the word, go over the side. Dive as deep as you can and swim with the current." He eyed the lynch mob standing on the bank. "Nutall Rise is surrounded by overgrowth. They might be able to force their way along the bank on foot, but I think we can move faster in the water. If they want to catch us, they'll have to backtrack to the road, and that means they'll have to find us again. We won't let that happen." He paddled slowly, letting the current carry them off toward the left. "Garrett, can you swim?"

"Yeah," said Garrett without nodding his head.

"Good," said Greg. "We all go at once. Once we get past them…and we *will* get past them…we meet up at the 98 bridge. From what I remember, that's less than a mile from here."

"A mile's a long swim," said Garrett.

"We'll have the current," said Greg. "And from my seat, we really don't have a choice." They were now in the middle of the river.

"Move it, Greg," shouted Kyle. "Or I'll put a bullet in your son's head and to hell with the consequences. It's your women he wants. I think he's going to enjoy Andie, but maybe he'll let me and my boys have a go at that sweet little blackbird of yours." Erica groaned, but Greg was not about to surrender his family.

"NOW," he shouted. The canoe rocked hard as he, Andie and Garrett went over the side. Garrett had just enough time to see Sean and Erica dive into the dark water before he went under.

The water roared in his ears as he dove toward the bottom. It was cool, but not cold. It was also dark, and in seconds he could see nothing. He kicked hard, sinking into the water, wondering when the mob would start firing.

He did not have to wait long. As he dove, he heard the muted 'thwup thwup thwup' of bullets plunging into the water. Adrenalin surged through his system, and he kicked again, going even deeper. Something brushed past the side of his face, and he prayed that it was some species of fish and not one of the poisonous snakes that infested the Florida waters. He swam as hard as he could, trying to put as much distance between him and the mob before he was forced to come up for air.

Fire blossomed in the middle of his back. *OhmygodI'vebeenshot.* He screamed, the air bursting from his lungs. His body tried to take a breath to replace the lost oxygen, and he had to clamp his mouth shut. Vivid colors...red, orange, violet...exploded in his vision. He had no choice. If he did not surface, he would drown.

The impenetrable darkness disoriented him. He kicked and flailed, but he did not know if he was going up or down. Then his head broke the surface. He gulped in the air and made ready go under again. Miraculously, despite the searing pain in his back, both his arms and legs seemed to be working, and that was the only thing that was right with the world. He had to resist the urge to feel the wound. From somewhere behind him, he heard shouts.

"There! Get a light on him!" There was a dim flash as someone pointed what was probably a hand held searchlight in his direction. Garrett took another gulp of air and dove. Amazingly, the pain in his back did not get worse.

I'm in shock, he thought as he swam. *And when that wears off, I'm going to be in real trouble.* In seconds, his lungs were burning again. He twisted his body around, trying to change directions, although he had no idea where he was in relation to Nutall Rise. A moment later, he again broke the surface, gasping in the air and choking out the fetid water.

He blinked his eyes, trying to clear them. There was no immediate hail of bullets, and he risked a quick look. He saw Nutall Rise almost immediately. He had managed to put a good twenty yards between it and him. The headlights from the parked vehicles danced back and forth. For a moment, he thought that his vision was blurring, perhaps from losing too much blood. Then he realized that the vehicles themselves were moving. The mob was leaving.

Probably heading for the bridge that Greg said to make for, he thought. He took another look around, trying to spot Greg, Andie or the kids. There was a shape in the water several yards away that could have been a head bobbing, but it was too dark to tell. His back was burning, but now the pain seemed to be lessening.

He wasted a moment, reaching around to feel under his shirt.

"Gaggh! Crapcrapcrap." Water spilled into his mouth as he spoke, making it come out "crrrrrapcrrrrrapcrrrrrap." He coughed and spat out the water, trying not to gag. It tasted of sulfur and algae.

Touching the wound delivered a dose of instant agony. He jerked his hand away but then gritted his teeth and tried again. He needed to know how bad he was hurt. Again the pain hit, but this time he was ready. He felt where the bullet had struck him and was both amazed and relieved to find the skin unbroken. It seemed that he had been deep enough so that the water blunted most of the bullet's velocity. The skin was tender, and he had no doubt that by tomorrow he would be sporting a dark, ugly bruise, but other than that he seemed to be fine.

"That's gonna leave a mark," he muttered aloud, and then actually managed a rough laugh.

Another glance toward Nutall Rise told him that the mob was gone. No one seemed to be lingering around, waiting to see if anyone tried to get out that way. *We should have waited*, he thought. *We could have…* He realized that he was wasting time and started swimming.

Despite the pain in his back, he managed a strong, even stroke. His newly healed knee worked just fine, and in seconds he was moving at a good pace. The current was weak, but it was there. Thankfully, there was no undertow. He picked up his stroke, trying to spot the bridge. He tried to visualize the maps he had studied, but he could not translate the abstract images into reality.

In the end, he nearly smashed into one of the pillars that supported the bridge. He was so engrossed in both the mechanics of swimming as well as trying to figure out the distance on the map that he did not see it until he was right up on it.

Suddenly, something dark reared up before him. He cried out and pulled up. For an instant, he actually thought that John Gamble had risen out of the river, arms outstretched, ready to carry him back to the canal. Then his eyes cleared and the image resolved. He had reached the bridge. He treaded water, clearing his eyes. There was no sign of traffic. Garrett suddenly remembered that he had no idea of the time, although the lack of traffic probably meant that it was very late. Again he wondered just how much time had been lost in the canal.

"Hsssst! Garrett! Over here!" He jerked in surprise. Greg's voice seemed to come from everywhere.

"Where?" he called out.

"Over here, under the bridge," said Greg. Blinking the water out of his eyes, he looked to his right. Two sets of streetlights, placed at either end of the bridge, gave off a harsh white glare. The bridge itself was nothing special. There were no steel girders or suspension cables, just an even stretch of concrete. Only two lanes wide, it was built twenty feet above the river and ran for about thirty yards. Three sets of concrete pylons supported it.

Beneath the bridge, the land sloped upward, creating a small cove that was invisible from the road. There, a few feet away from the water, were three kneeling figures huddled together. Garrett could see another form up near the road, and he recognized Sean, keeping watch. Greg stood and waved him over.

Thank God, thought Garrett as he swam toward them. The river bed came up under his feet, and he managed to stand, wincing at the pain in his back. Greg extended a hand and helped him out of the water. Garrett collapsed next to the preacher, breathing hard. He had to stifle a yelp when he sat down. The pain in his back flared but then subsided.

"Took you long enough," said Andie. Her tone told him in no uncertain terms that she was not close to forgiving him.

"Sorry," he muttered.

"We're just glad you made it," said Greg. Andie snorted at that. "What kept you?"

"Oh, you know," said Garrett deadpan, "chased by a bunch of maniacs, shot in the back…the usual."

"Are you serious?" said Greg. "Let me see."

"It's all right," said Garrett. "The water stopped the worst of it. The skin's not even broken."

"Then I'd say that you're extremely lucky," said Greg. "But I need to take a look anyway. Lean forward, Garrett." Garrett hesitated and then complied. "Move over a little, into the light," said Greg. Garrett obeyed, wincing as Greg lifted his shirt and felt around the wound.

"The skin *is* broken," he said at last. "It's just a scratch, but we need to get some antiseptic on it as soon as possible. There's a lot of bacteria in the water, and that could get infected real easy." He lowered Garrett's shirt and clapped him gently on the shoulder.

"Are you guys all right?" Garrett said as they scooted back under the bridge.

"That's a stupid question," snapped Andie.

"Stop it, Andie," warned Greg.

"No Greg, I won't," said Andie. "It's his fault that we're here." Venom dripped from her voice. "That…that thing back there *violated* me. It violated

Erica too." Erica shuddered but said nothing. "Cut him loose, Greg. Make him go away." Garrett closed his eyes. He could not bear the agony saturating her voice, nor could he fault Andie for her hatred of him.

Just hours ago Andie Powell had been a happy wife and mother, out for a pleasant day trip with her family. That woman was gone now, destroyed by the thing in the canal. One day she might find healing. Some version of her former self might be resurrected, but no matter how much she recovered, she would never be the same. She needed someone to blame, and he was the only real choice.

"Just make him go away," she whispered again.

"No," said Greg. He reached out and took her hand. She started to pull away, but he held on tight.

"It's his fault," said Andie.

"Maybe it is," said Greg. "Although after the way Kyle spoke to us at the Rise, I'm not so sure. Either way, Garrett saved our lives. Even if he wasn't here, I don't think we were ever meant to get out of the canal." Andie started to argue the point but thought the better of it. She looked away.

"Dad?" Erica looked up at her father. "We've been through the canal half a dozen times. Why should today be any different?"

"I don't know," said Greg. "But something *is* different. I'm sure of it." The sinkhole pattern Garrett had discovered on the map flashed into his mind, but he kept his mouth shut. Greg looked at his wife.

"Let it go, babe," he said softly. "I can't begin to understand what that thing did to the two of you, but right now our only priority is to get out of here, so until we can get home, please let it go." Andie looked away, shooting Garrett another hate-filled glare.

"Car's coming," called Sean from his post above them. Alarmed, Greg asked,

"How many?"

"Just one …I can't tell what kind." He came sliding down the grassy slope and ducked in under the bridge. There was a flash of headlights and a loud 'thump-thump, thump-thump, thump-thump.' The car sped across the bridge and continued on its way. Greg breathed a sigh of relief.

"We've got to move now," he said. "This is the only logical place for us to get out of the river, which means that Kyle and his friends are on their way here."

"So where do we go?" asked Garrett. "They're sure to catch us if we take to the road. Can we cut across country?"

"No," said Greg. "We can't go stumbling around in the dark. Our only real choice is to go further downriver, but to try that without a boat is insane."

"The Wacissia leads to the Warriors," said Garrett. "You said that you almost got lost in there." Greg managed a dry chuckle.

"I'd rather be lost than meet up with Kyle and company again," he said. "They won't find us there. I'm sure of that. We can make it as long as we keep heading south. Once we're through, we can find the nearest town and contact the police."

"No," said Andie. "For all we know, everybody within fifty miles is in on this. We rent a car and don't stop until we're home. We can tell our own police. Let them deal with Kyle and his boys." Greg nodded in agreement.

"Terrific," said Sean. "Only, just how are we supposed to get through the Warriors without a boat?"

"We use that," said Greg, pointing upriver. Garrett followed his arm and saw one of the canoes slowly floating toward them. "We managed not to tip it over," said Greg. "I gave it a good push before I went under. Thank God it managed to get here." He nudged Sean. "Go get it, will you, son."

"On it," said Sean and splashed into the river.

"How long before they get here?" asked Garrett.

"They'll have to take the back roads," said Greg. "I don't know where they'll come out on 98, but it can't be far. They could be here anytime." They watched anxiously as Sean reached the canoe and began to push it toward them. Another car whizzed past without slowing down. When Sean drew close, Greg and Garrett helped haul the canoe onto the bank.

"Yes," exclaimed Greg. "They're still here." He reached down and pulled out a paddle, along with one of the packs. He opened the pack and passed out foil packs of dried food. "We need to eat, but we'll have to do it on the way," he said.

"There's five of us," said Andie, throwing Garrett another glare. "This thing won't hold five."

"It will if we're careful," said Greg. "Garrett, I want you in front." He laid a hand on Garrett's shoulder. "I know that you can see things," he said. "You know the kind of things I mean."

"Yeah," said Garrett.

"Erica, you go in next," said Greg. "Andie, you're behind her. Sean, help me get this thing back into the water." Garrett, Erica and Andie got in and sat down. As soon as they were settled, Sean and Greg slid the canoe back into the river and climbed in. The canoe sank low in the water, its edge bare inches above the water line, but it floated and that was enough. Greg pushed off the bank with the one remaining paddle. He strained hard, and after a few moments the unwieldy craft began to pick up speed. The bridge slid by above them.

The glow from the streetlights faded, but it was a cloudless night and the moon was full. It was not hard for Greg to steer the canoe down the center of the now rapidly narrowing river. He pulled hard, and soon they were making good speed.

Garrett tore open his packet and wolfed down a mixture of dried apricots, apples and bananas. He washed it down with the bottled water Greg had also pulled from the pack. Feeling stronger, he focused his senses ahead.

The river continued to narrow until it was barely twenty feet wide. Just ahead, two rows of oak trees, dripping with Spanish moss, came into view. They lined both banks like silent sentries. Overhead, their branches intertwined. To Garrett, it almost looked like some kind of natural gate. As it turned out, he was not far from wrong. Greg guided the canoe down the center of the river, through the tree gate. The branches were so thick that the moonlight disappeared completely.

A moment later, they were through. They cleared the gate, and suddenly the land on either side disappeared. They edged out into what could only be described as a smallish lake, maybe fifty yards in diameter. The current disappeared, and the dark water stilled. Garrett suppressed a shudder. *Just how deep does it go? And what does it connect to down there?*

They were barely into the lake when they heard the sound of screeching tires. All five of them looked back. They could still see the bridge through the tree gate. A half dozen cars and trucks, no doubt the same vehicles that had been parked at Nutall Rise, now lined the bridge. Greg hissed and paddled furiously, forcing the canoe to the right. They floated past the tree gate and slid up against the bank. Peeking through the undergrowth, they could just make out the bridge. Because of the distance and the darkness, Garrett doubted that the bridges current occupants would be able to see them.

Several dark figures, silhouetted by the glaring headlights, ran back and forth. Almost all of the figures were waving flashlights. A few disappeared under the bridge, only to reappear moments later. The figures grouped together for a moment. Then they scattered, returning to their vehicles. They screeched away, half in one direction, half in the other.

"Good," muttered Greg. "As far as they're concerned, 98 is our only option."

"Think they left anyone behind?" asked Sean.

"I would," said Greg. They kept watching. Moments later, two shadowy figures walked across the bridge.

"Let's get away from here," said Andie.

"Yeah," agreed Greg. He pushed off against the bank and, keeping close to the land, began to skirt the lake. They floated in silence for several minutes. Garrett kept watch for powers both natural and supernatural, but there was no sign of either. Something rattled under his feet. He looked down and saw his cane. He picked it up and looked at it for a moment. Then he dropped it into the water and watched as it floated away.

"Garrett," said Greg, breaking the heavy silence. "I've been thinking about what happened in the canal."

"Don't," pleaded Andie in a very low voice. "Please don't."

"I have to, babe," said Greg gently. "This is important."

"I'm listening," said Garrett.

"I remember everything that happened when that being was controlling me," said Greg. Andie whipped around, rocking the canoe in the process.

"What are you talking about?"

"Not now," said Greg, but Andie would not be put off.

"Yes, now," she snapped. "We have the time. I know what forced its way into me." Her voice broke, and it took her a moment to get herself under control. "What happened to you, Greg?" Greg took a deep breath and then quickly told Andie everything. He stressed how Garrett had used the power channeled into him by that same being to save both her and Erica.

"It let me hear some of its thoughts while we were joined," he said. There was both terror and wonder in his voice. "They were…different. Yeah, that's the word…different."

"What can you tell us?" asked Garrett.

"More than a little," said Greg. "First off, and most important, that being, whatever it is, is not our enemy."

"You can't know that," snapped Andie. "That thing took your body and used it for its own purpose."

"Because I let it in," said Greg. "I allowed it to use me."

"You *what*?"

"It came to me in a vision," said Greg. "It seemed to last a long time, but I guess it was only a few seconds. It showed me what was happening to us…at least in part. It was hard for us to communicate, even when we were joined. It told me that it could help, but only if I allowed it to use me." Garrett stiffened, wincing at the pain in his back. Even from the rear of the canoe, Greg noticed.

"You had that dark power inside of you," he said gently. "It couldn't use you until it was…exorcised? That's about the only word that fits."

"Yeah," said Garrett.

"Greg," said Andie, her voice breaking again, "how can you know all this?"

"Because we got out," said Greg simply. Andie had no answer to that.

"It was a higher being, a being not of flesh or blood," continued Greg. Awe tinged his voice.

"A Gregangel," muttered Garrett. He did not intend for Greg to hear, but his voice carried over the water. Greg managed a weak laugh.

"Funny," he said.

"Was it an angel, Daddy?" asked Erica. Her voice was hushed, almost reverent. Greg shrugged.

"Maybe," he said. "Maybe not. I honestly don't know, sweetheart."

"But whatever it is, it's on our side," said Sean. "And it's powerful. That's a good thing, right?"

"It's good," said Greg, "but with all its power, it was limited in the canal."

"Why?" asked Garrett.

"I don't know," said Greg. "All I do know is that it is not of this Earth." He trailed off.

"There's something else," said Garrett.

"Yeah, I saw through its eyes," said Greg, and his voice trembled. "I saw the darkness the way it saw it. I don't know what it is, but I know what it's not." Garrett swiveled in his seat, leaning over to look at Greg. The canoe tipped dangerously low to the water, and he quickly faced front again.

"What are you saying?" he asked.

"I saying that whatever was controlling that darkness, it wasn't human...and it never was." It took Garrett a few seconds to understand exactly what the preacher was saying.

"That can't be," he said. "John Gamble..."

"May indeed be haunting the canal," said Greg, interrupting, "or some form of him, at least, but there's something else in there with him." He stopped paddling. "And whatever it is," he continued, "it's very evil, very powerful, and very, very hungry."

Chapter 16

The Warriors

"That doesn't make sense," said Garrett. Greg barked a harsh laugh.

"Repeat that sentence with a straight face," he said. Garrett opened his mouth and then closed it again. He shook his head.

"Point taken," he said. "But what are you saying…that John Gamble is some kind of demon possessed ghost? That doesn't…"

"Garrett," warned Greg, and Garrett waved a hand in surrender.

"Fine," said Garrett. "I'm listening."

"The dark power came up from below," said Greg. "Far below, I think. I know that the canal is only a few feet deep, but it's...it's…oh crap." He bit out the last two words. Garrett understood. How did one go about explaining the unexplainable?

"The waters run deep," he said softly. He could feel Greg nod.

"Yeah, they do," he agreed, "and I think that the canal is a lot deeper than we've been allowed to see."

"Not something I want to think about. This lake might just connect to it," said Garrett.

"Yeah, we need to not be here," said Greg. "But Garrett, I need to ask you something. Why are you so sure that it's John Gamble's ghost down there?"

"Because of Melody," said Garrett, "and her mother. Both of them told me about Gamble."

"But are you sure?" asked Greg.

"I'm not sure of anything," said Garrett. His voice was heavy. "I only know that whatever it is, it has my wife. It's had a hold on her family for generations, dating all the way back to the digging of the canal." Maybe it was something left over from his experience with the Gregangel, or perhaps his natural intuition was simply running hot. Whatever it was, he felt something in Greg stir. He glanced back at the shadowy form of the preacher.

"What?" Greg shook his head.

"What I'm thinking…it doesn't…"

"If you end that sentence with 'make sense', I'm going to tip this canoe over," warned Garrett. He felt rather than saw Greg's weak smile.

"Point taken," he said. "It's just that…Garrett, I don't think that the canal is just deeper, I think that it's a lot *older* than we've been allowed to see."

"It was dug in the mid-1800s," said Garrett. "That's a fact."

"Its current version," said Greg. "But I think that maybe it's been around a lot longer than that." He shook his head. "No, I don't think it. I *feel* it." Garrett swiveled back to face front. He kept scanning the lake but could detect no sign of the dark power.

"I read some of the history of the place," he said after a moment. "Geologists have found artifacts from thousands of years ago."

"The Paleo tribes," said Greg. "But that's just a name some archeologist gave them. No one really knows who or what they were."

"Are you saying that…"

"I'm not saying anything," snapped Greg. His frustration, fear and exhaustion were getting the better of him. "I just think that the canal, in some form or another, has been around a lot longer than John Gamble's time."

"Are you sure that your wife is still alive?" Garrett jumped a little at the voice behind him. Andie was the last person he expected to join the conversation. Her voice was flat, but she had asked a valid question. He thought about Melody's apparition in his apartment and the otherworldly visit from his daughter. Then he remembered the words of the Gregangel.

"Yeah, I do," he said. "But she's running out of time."

"But where is she, Garrett?" said Greg. "How the *hell* are you going to find her?"

"Follow the lost," muttered Greg.

"What's that supposed to mean?" demanded Andie. Garrett shook his head.

"I wish I knew," he said.

'There's the Gregangel," said Erica, chiming in. "It helped us get away. Maybe it'll help you find your wife." Garrett nodded, but he could almost hear Greg's thoughts. *Don't count on it.*

They were now well over halfway across the lake. Garrett took a quick look behind them and saw that the bridge was out of sight. Only the faint glow of the streetlights shining through the tree gate marked its location. That was something, at least. He did not think that Kyle and his merry band would be able to find them now.

They moved along at a good pace, although judging from Greg's heavy, labored breathing, the preacher was at the end of his strength.

The conversation died. The water gurgled as Greg continued to paddle. It was an oily, sickly sound, like mucus sliding down a sick man's throat. There was nothing else…no crickets chirruping, no rustling as some nocturnal animal made its way through the night…nothing. Garrett was a child of the suburbs, so he missed the significance. Sean did not.

"It's way too quiet," he said.

"I know," said Greg. "Here in the backcountry, especially on the water, the noise should be deafening. I don't hear anything…no frogs, crickets…nothing." He angled the canoe away from the shoreline. "Garrett, do you see anything?" Garrett shook his head.

"No," he said. "And believe me, I'm looking."

"Don't let up," warned Greg. "This silence isn't natural, and I've had my fill of things not natural."

"Yeah," muttered Garrett. In the pale moonlight, he could see that they were coming to the end of the lake. The land was gradually closing in on them, funneling them into a narrow passage.

"This is the beginning of the Warriors," said Greg. "Hang on, gang. We'll get through this yet."

"We've got a long way to go," said Andie softly, and Garrett understood that she was not just speaking about physical distance.

"I know," said Greg. "But I think that Kyle and his mob are far away. They're not going to take us, Andie."

"It's not just Kyle that I'm worried about," whispered Andie.

"Me neither," said Greg, "but we got away once. We'll do it again." As he spoke, the lake disappeared and they passed into the Warriors. The passage narrowed until they could almost touch the land on either side. There were few trees, but the Florida plant life was alive and well. The brush rose well above their heads, concealing them effectively. Long stemmed fronds reached out and brushed against Garrett's face. He batted them away.

"How far?" he asked.

"I don't know," said Greg. "Like I said, we came here a few years ago, just to see what it was like, but we didn't go in very far." There was a thump. Garrett looked back to see that Greg had pulled in the paddle. "Sorry guys, but I need a break."

"Let me," said Sean. He reached out to take the paddle, but Greg shook his head.

"You would need to sit here," he said. "It's the only way you can steer. I just need a…" He never finished the sentence. Sean rolled over the side and splashed into the water. The canoe rocked hard. Water sloshed over the edge, and for a moment, Garret was sure that they were going to capsize.

"Sean! What the hell…" Again Greg was interrupted.

"Tell you what, Dad," said Sean. "You lay off the swearing like a good preacher, and I'll paddle for a while." He was standing chest high in the water now and making his way toward his father. Unlike the lake, it seemed that the Warriors were quite shallow. Garrett looked back to see Greg staring at his son.

"Sean," he said in a low, dangerous voice.

"You've had it," said Sean. "I haven't. Come on, Dad. Let me take it for a while."

"Do it, Greg," said Andie without looking back. "You need to rest, and we need to keep going." Greg seemed ready to argue the point. Garrett could see that the preacher's pride was putting up a fight. He needed to personally save his family, but after several seconds his good sense won out. Silently, he handed Sean the paddle and scooted forward to make room for him.

"Okay," said Greg. "Just keep us heading south."

"Got it," said Sean, settling into Greg's seat. He paused. Then, "Um, the big flat end goes in the water, right?" Garrett was thrilled to hear Erica laugh, although Andie remained silent.

"Just paddle," said Greg, although Garrett could hear the laughter in his voice as well.

They're strong, he thought. *They might just get through this.*

With Sean's slow, steady stroke, they moved deeper into the Warriors. The canal narrowed until there was barely room enough to maneuver the canoe. It twisted and turned, and every now and then it forked. Twice they had to backtrack when it veered north. Finally, it disappeared altogether. They rounded a turn, and the land closed in on three sides. Sean pulled up, and the canoe scraped into the mud in front of them.

"I think I'm going to need help to turn around," he said. Greg shook his head.

"Don't bother," he said. "We need to keep going south. We'll carry the canoe until we come to the water again."

"What if we don't?" asked Erica.

"We will," said Greg. "We're not even close to being out." He levered himself out of the canoe and waded onto the muddy land. His boots sank deep into the mud, and when he pulled them out, they made a slurping sound that Garrett found vaguely disturbing. He reached into the canoe and pulled out the pack. "Sean and I will carry the canoe," he said. "Erica, take the pack. Andie, you've got the paddle." He held out his hand to his wife to help her up.

"I'm not an invalid," she snapped. There was real anger in her voice, but even Garrett could tell that it was not directed at her husband.

"I know," said Greg quietly, "but I'm still a gentleman. Please?" Andie relented and took his hand. Once they were out, Greg and Sean pulled the canoe out of the water, flipped it upside down and lifted it above their heads.

"Garrett," said Greg, "you lead the way."

"Are you serious?" objected Garrett. "I don't have a clue where we're going." Greg laughed at that.

"Like any of us do," he said. He nodded toward the horizon. "See that bright star up there?" Garrett looked up and saw a single bright point of light hanging high in the sky.

"Yeah," he said.

"That's Venus," said Greg, "And it's always hangs low in the west this time of the year. Keep her to the right, and you'll get us there. Trust me; sooner or later the water will come back." He lowered his voice. "And remember to keep *both* sets of eyes open." They started out in single file with Garrett in the lead. Erica fell in behind him with Andie behind her. Greg and Sean brought up the rear.

Whatever was wrong with the nocturnal population was not affecting the mosquito life. Swarms of the beasts were suddenly buzzing around them, biting at will. Greg and Sean had it the worse. Unable to use their hands, they had no choice but to be a banquet for the ravenous blood suckers. Garrett, Erica and Andie were not much better off, although they at least could wipe the sweat out of their eyes.

Garrett kept moving forward, even though he could barely see. Bushes with thick trunks constantly barred his way, along with a host of other tall plants whose names he had never bothered to learn. Many of them ended in sharp spikes, and soon his arms were covered with scratches.

He tried not to think of what critters might be lurking about. He struggled to clear a path, but like Greg, he was running out of steam. Every few minutes, he would glance upward at the glowing Venus. If it had not been for that single fixed point, he would have become hopelessly lost. After several minutes, he put a foot down and felt it sink into the water. He emerged from the brush to find a narrow canal angling off toward the southwest.

"Water's back," he called over his shoulder.

"Excellent," panted Greg. "Move over, guys." He and Sean shouldered past the rest of the group. Breathing hard, they flipped the canoe and slid it into the water. Greg put his hands on his knees, gasping for breath. Garrett was sure that he was going to throw up, but he managed to get himself under control. He stood up straight. "All in," he said. "Sean, you got enough left to paddle?"

"Just watch me," said Sean, getting into the back of the canoe. The rest of them piled in, and seconds later they were off again. For a while, they made good time. The canal continued southward, and for the first time since the bridge, Garrett began to hope that they would make it out.

"Sean, hold up." Garrett swiveled in his seat. Greg's voice was suddenly tense. Sean pulled the paddle out of the water.

"What?" asked Garrett.

"Shush," snapped Greg. "Listen." The unnatural silence settled over them again as the canoe slid to a halt. It drifted to the right and bumped against the land. Garrett cocked his head, and after a few seconds he heard it. The low thrum made him think of a small prop plane, flying close to the ground. The idea seemed ridiculous. Who would be buzzing the Warriors at this hour?

"Greg," he called. "What…"

"Damn," snapped Greg. "I should have seen this. It's Kyle's airboat, and it can navigate the Warriors a heck of a lot faster than we can." Garrett remembered the speedy craft he had seen tied to the small dock. It sounded as if it was heading straight toward them.

"Get into that brush and get down," snapped Greg. "Sean, help me get this thing out of the water." They spilled out, splashing noisily. This time there was no muddy bank. The brush started at the water's edge, and they struggled to push through it. Far too close for comfort, the airboat's engine sputtered and stopped.

"Keep going," whispered Greg. With Garrett in the lead, they forced their way deeper into the brush. They made a sizable racket as they pushed forward.

"That's far enough," said Greg. "Get down. Don't make a sound." They crouched low, waiting. For long minutes, there was nothing. Then they heard the airboat's engine sputter and start. Seconds later, it was moving again. Garrett closed his eyes and stifled a groan. Once again, it sounded as if it was coming straight at them. He tried to peer through the brush, but it was too thick. The resilient growth had even sprung back where they had forced their way through, covering their tracks.

"We can't stay here," hissed Andie.

"Quiet," snapped Greg. "They're guessing. There's no way they can track us in here." The airboat's engine shut off again, but not before it had drawn much closer. Garrett strained his ears, but the only thing he could hear was the heavy breathing of his four fellow fugitives. He hunkered down, gripping the side of the canoe for support. His legs burned, but he refused to move. The silence dragged on.

What are they doing? They can't just be sitting out there, waiting for us to make a run for it. From somewhere nearby, a light came on. It flashed above them like the blade of a giant fan and disappeared. A few seconds later, it flashed again, this time traveling in the opposite direction.

"Searchlight," whispered Sean. Greg gripped him hard on the shoulder. The gesture said in no uncertain terms, 'shut up'. The light went out, and a moment later the airboat's engine coughed and came to life. To everyone's relief, it started to move away from them. Seconds later, it faded completely.

"Okay," muttered Greg. He grunted and swiveled to face his family. In the darkness, he was nothing more than a crouching silhouette. "We'll give it a few more minutes. Then we're out of here."

"Daddy?" The terror in Erica's voice was palpable. She had bravely resisted the dark power in the canal, but she was terrified of the slaves of that power.

Greg did not bother with a reply. He scooted over and threw his arms around his daughter. She collapsed against him, sobbing. After a moment, Andie embraced her as well, cocooning their daughter between them. Sean joined them. They huddled there, hunted and on the run, but still a family, and still strong. Garrett looked away, thinking of Melody and Molly. Long minutes later, Erica's sobs slowed and finally disappeared.

"All right," said Greg, his voice low, "judging from the moon, we've got maybe an hour until daybreak. Let's see if we can find our way out of here before then." He kissed the top of Erica's head. "You ready?"

"Yeah," sniffed Erica. She pulled away from her father and stood up.

"Then let's get the…let's get out of here," said Greg. He glanced at Sean. "Better?"

"A little," said Sean. "But unless I can get my driver's permit on my birthday, I'm telling the whole church that you cussed."

"Hey, that's extortion," said Greg. Sean shrugged.

"Is it working?" he asked innocently.

"Yeah, it is," said Greg with a sigh. "All right, let's get going." They shoved the canoe into the water and got underway. Garrett had to resist the urge to scratch himself raw. While they were hunkered down, the mosquitoes had enjoyed an early breakfast. His neck and arms were covered with welts.

The canal continued south. Sean worked hard, and for thirty minutes or so they made good time. Garrett tried to stay alert, but his body was demanding rest. After a while, his eyelids began to sag. He shook his head and sat up straighter. Then he splashed some fetid water into his face. Blinking his eyes clear, he suddenly realized that he could see the surrounding foliage in greater detail. He glanced up at the sky and saw that a small part of it was now a very dull gray.

"Daylight's comin'," he said.

"And I wan' go home," sang Greg. Sean groaned at his father's off key tones. The light grew with each passing minute, and with it, Garrett's spirits. Once Greg and his family were safe, he would find his wife. He would get her away from Gamble, or whatever it was that was imprisoning her.

A dull rumble came from overhead as a passenger plane made its way across the faintly glowing sky. It reminded him that there was a world far away from the darkness of the canal. It was a world of light, and it was waiting for him and Melody.

Something moved, or seemed to move, off to his right. He glanced over, peering into the brush, but could see nothing.

"Garrett?" Greg's voice was suddenly tense.

"You saw that?" he asked, keeping his eyes on the brush.

"I thought…" began Greg, but he trailed off. Garrett shook his head.

"Yeah, me too," he said. He stared at the brush a moment longer. Nothing presented itself, but after everything that had happened, he was not about to get careless. He gripped the sides of the canoe, scanning with both sets of eyes. There was no hint of the dark power, but he was getting worried.

"Something's not right," said Greg. Sean stopped paddling, and the canoe eased to a stop. Overhead, the sky now sported a faint glow of pink in the east. Venus was near the horizon and would disappear soon.

"Garrett? Do you…"

"Nothing," said Garrett. They floated silently for long seconds.

"Get us moving, Sean," said Greg finally. "Garrett, for the love of God, don't miss anything." Garrett did not bother to reply. He sat ramrod straight as they eased down the canal. Sunrise was now minutes away. *Darkness can't exist in the light*, he kept telling himself. *We'll be safe when the sun comes up. If we can just...*

Again something moved. Garrett started to turn but forced himself to keep looking ahead. He tried to pinpoint the movement with his peripheral vision but could not. Then he groaned. He was not seeing the movement with his natural eyes. Something was tickling the corner of his other vision. He closed his eyes, concentrating, but whatever it was remained hidden. *Come on come on come on.* He tried to focus that unique sight he had been gifted with since the canal, but he still had no idea how to control it. Frustrated, he opened his eyes again.

"Greg, there's something there," he said. "I can...feel it, but I can't see it."

"You know," said the preacher, his voice deceptively casual, "people who don't understand Christianity think it's just a list of rules...dos and don'ts that we're supposed to follow to the letter. If we don't, God is waiting to strike us down with a lightning bolt." Garrett's eyes widened, and his mouth hung open.

"This is not the time for a sermon," he managed to say.

"Nonsense! There's always time for a sermon," said Greg calmly, "especially if you're me." Garrett started to speak, but Greg held up a hand. "Hear me out. True Christianity isn't just a bunch of rules. Really, it's nothing more than an acknowledgement that we all need a little help. We trust God to help us through the rough patches in our lives, and he gives us the strength to conquer whatever challenges we face." His eyes locked in on Garrett's and held them.

"Listen to me, Garrett. We don't force the power God gives us. We don't use it. We let it use us." Greg's voice was low and quiet, but in a way Garrett could not begin to describe, it thundered through the short distance between them. He stared at the preacher and realized one single, powerful fact. For the first time in his life, he had come face to face with a true man of faith. Even after everything that had happened to them, Greg Powell's belief was alive and well. It surrounded him like an impregnable armor that no darkness could penetrate.

"But I don't believe like you do," he said at last. "I don't really believe in anything, let alone any kind of god." Compared to Greg's, his own voice seemed thin and puny.

"You can call it whatever you want," said Greg. "God, light, a higher power, but whatever you choose to call it, you're still a servant of that Light," said Greg. "You proved that in the canal. You made a choice and took a side. That strength is still inside of you, but you don't use it. Let it use you, Garrett."

"Greg…"

"No more excuses," snapped Greg. Now his voice reeked of tension. "There's something close by, and we need to know what it is. Now do what you need to do to save my family!" Garrett saw the uncompromising look on his face and knew that any further argument would be useless. He turned around and closed his eyes again. This time, he did not try to focus his special sight.

Maybe Greg's right, he thought. As Sean continued to paddle, he tried to clear his mind.

He could not do it. Stray thoughts kept creeping in. The night of Molly's death, the divorce hearing, the visitations, the vision of his daughter, full grown and beautiful; his mind flashed back and forth, unwilling and unable to settle down.

Dammit! Again he felt something move. *Help me*, he thought, unsure of whom he was calling out to. He refused to believe in Greg's god, or any god who allowed his daughter to die.

You are a servant of the Light.

Am I? Did I really make that choice? He thought back to the canal and suddenly realized that yes, he had chosen to be free of the darkness and he had chosen to let the Gregangel empower him with the light. *But it's gone*, he thought, despairing. *I used it all up getting us free.* The terrible sense of loss he had felt in the canal returned, but at the same instant, from somewhere very far away, or perhaps from somewhere from deep in his soul, he heard a single, simple question.

Did you? Those two words brought him up short.

Did I? He thought about it. He remembered trying to gather the last glowing embers of the light the Gregangel had given him, only to have them wink out. *Did I?* He had not really thought about it since they escaped the canal. Now he did. He turned his attention inward, searching. He remembered the blazing furnace of light that had once indwelled him. It was gone, used up in the desperate battle to free Andie and Erica. All that was left was emptiness.

He almost gave up. And then he saw it. There, in the center of the emptiness was a tiny spark. It was dim, and for long moments, he was sure that it was merely a product of his desperate imagination.

"Garrett?" Greg's voice, low and urgent, seemed to come from a great distance. He ignored it and concentrated in that single tiny spark. He wanted to reach out to it, but was afraid that if he did, he might extinguish it forever. Instead, he simply watched it until he realized a simple, wonderful fact. *It was growing.*

It was never really gone, he thought in awe. *It's a living thing, and it's a part of me.* He focused every ounce of his attention on it, willing it to grow.

Garrett? Garrett, is that you? This was not Greg's voice. It echoed not in his ears but through his mind. He wanted to scream with joy.

Melody! I'm here babe! For a moment, there was nothing. Then…

Hurry!

MELODY! She was gone, but now Garrett understood. *The two of you are connected by a bond that cannot be broken.*

Somehow we are bound by the light, he thought. He stared at the tiny-but-growing speck of light, and suddenly he realized that he could see again. Even this tiny spark was empowering him. Keeping his eyes closed, he looked outward.

And every hope he had managed to resurrect shattered into dust.

The dark power was everywhere. He had been unable to see it because his sight was limited. In the canal, it had been so powerful that it had nearly overrode his senses. It was impossible *not* to see it.

Now it was subtle, barely discernible, but it was there. Thousands…millions…of tiny threads, each no thicker than the strands of a spider's web, infested the water. They were not powerful enough to harm them, but Garrett understood that their purpose was far more sinister.

Eyes, he thought, remembering how Kyle's airboat had seemed to make a straight line toward them until veering off. *He knows where we are*, he thought. *He's known all along. He's been driving us forward.*

His eyes snapped open. Brightness flooded in. The sun was rising. The eastern sky was a blazing orange. Blinking, he turned to warn Greg, but at that instant, an airboat's engine roared to life.

Chapter 17

A Crack in Nothing

"**N**o," cried Erica.

"Greg?" Andie's terror mirrored her daughters. Garrett looked back at the preacher. When he saw the raw panic on Greg's face, his heart sank. He had been their rock and their strength, but now his eyes were impossibly wide and his mouth was hanging open.

"I don't…" he managed, shaking his head, but that was it. He was finished. He had given everything he had to give. They had no place to run. Even if they tried to hide in the tall brush, Kyle would hunt them down.

The canoe rocked violently. Garrett grabbed the sides, to no avail. Panicked, Erica jumped into the water. The force of her leap capsized the overloaded craft. Garrett went under and came up sputtering. He managed to gulp down a mouthful of the slimy water and instantly felt sick. Far worse, the threadlike strands of dark power slid over him, caressing him from head to toe. It was as if he had just fallen into a thousand clinging spider webs. He wiped his eyes and saw Erica struggling out of the water and into the brush.

"Erica!" cried Greg.

"They won't take me," screamed Erica. "They won't."

"Just…wait!" Greg made it to land, but Erica had already disappeared.

"No," she shouted, her voice muffled. With a growl, Greg followed his daughter into the heavy brush. Andie and Sean were right behind him. Garrett shoved the overturned canoe aside and struggled forward. His feet sank into thick muck, dragging him down. The dark power kept trying to wrap itself around him, but he kept going. His imagination kept showing him all too vivid images of Erica and Andie with Kyle and his friends.

He made the bank and heaved himself onto the land, the dark power still clinging to him. He swiped at it with his hands, as if it was a real web. He could feel it probing, searching for a way in, and for an eternal second he was terrified that it might succeed. Then that tiny spark of light deep within him flared. It was not a big flare, but it was enough. The dark power recoiled and fell away. He nearly cried out in relief. He used a precious second to scan Greg, Andie and Sean and saw that they were clean.

The roar of the airboat's engine suddenly grew louder. He could not see it, but it sounded as if it was only yards away. He plunged ahead, trying to keep Sean's bright red shirt in sight. The brush was so thick that he could barely see it.

Suddenly, the airboat's engine died. The plants and bushes cracked and crunched as they forced their way through. The racket was deafening. If Kyle was really that close, he had to hear it. Sure enough…

"I've had enough of this, Greg." Kyle's angry voice sounded out through the brush. Garrett cast an involuntary glance over his shoulder and ended up crashing into Sean. The two of them staggered and fell. Thorns of all sizes and shapes slashed at their arms and necks. Then Greg's strong hands reached down and yanked both of them to their feet. Blinking, Garrett saw that the brush had thinned out a little. It was not a clearing by any stretch of the imagination, but at least they had a little more freedom of movement.

"I can hear you," said Kyle, his voice mocking. "Believe it or not, I can track you in here. Make it easy on all of us and stop running. If you do, I'll do everything in my power to see that you're family lives through this. They'll suffer, but they might survive, at least some of them. That's all I can do, and I promise you that if you keep running, it'll be a lot worse. Now stop wasting my time." Garrett glanced over at Greg and gasped. The hopelessness he had seen on the preacher's face was gone. In its place was pure, feral rage. He could almost feel the heat of it blazing through Greg's eyes.

"I'LL KILL YOU," Greg screamed, loud enough to make Garrett's ears ring. "I swear to God, if you lay one hand on my daughter…"

"SHUT UP, NIGGER." Kyle's rage easily matched Greg's.

A pause.

Then…

"Go ahead then, Greg," he called. The mocking tone was back. "Run all you want. When I get to you, I'm going to put a bullet in your gut and one in your son's as well. Then me and Reggie here are going to have some fun with Erica and Andie, and you're going to watch. If they're lucky, we'll be through before the rest of my boys get here. If *you're* lucky, you'll die quick, but you never know with gut wounds. They're a real bitch." The airboat's engine roared to life.

"You bastard," sobbed Greg. "You god-damned bastard." He staggered as Andie grabbed his arm.

"Which way?" she demanded. "Greg, for the love of God, which way?" Greg stared at his wife. The look on his face said plainly, 'I don't know'.

Garrett wanted to scream. Kyle had no right to torture them like this, and Gamble had no right to brutalize Melody. *We can hide*, he thought wildly. *We can let Kyle find Erica or Andie, and the rest of us can hide. That airboat only holds two. The three of us can take them.* It was a lousy idea, and he knew it. Two men with guns would almost always beat three men without guns. The airboat drew closer. Garrett heard its engine rev and then shut off. Metal scraped against metal.

"Found your canoe," called Kyle. He was only yards away now. "Come on, now. There's nowhere for you to go. You can't walk out of the Warriors, and you know it." Greg snarled but had the good sense not to answer. "I can sense you," called Kyle. "I've got an edge, you see. There's a power at work here that you can't begin to understand, and it's led me straight to you. Now quit this crap and get out here." There was a loud CRAAAK. Something tore through the brush a few feet away. It took Garrett a moment to realize that Kyle had just fired off a shot.

"That was a few feet to your right," said Kyle. "Last chance. Get out here, or we're coming in."

Something tickled the back of Garrett's head. He swatted at the supposed insect without thinking.

"Sean," hissed Greg. Miraculously, he was back in control, at least for the moment. "Get in there and hide." He pointed at the thick brush to his left. "When they come, we'll jump them." He shoved Sean toward the brush and made to follow. Garrett grabbed him by the arm.

"It won't work," he whispered, but Greg threw off his hand.

"You're with us," he snarled. "We'll rush them together. They can't kill all of us, and when I get my hands on Kyle…" Behind them came the loud sounds of two men forcing their way through the brush. Kyle and Reggie were on their way.

The tickle returned to the back of Garrett's head, only now it was much stronger. It grew quickly until it felt as if an impossibly long, thin needle was being slowly pushed into his skull. He cried out and grabbed his head with both hands. From somewhere both very close and impossibly far away, he heard the voice of the Gregangel.

It's all I can do for you. The rest is yours. The voice faded, but the tickle suddenly transmuted itself into stabbing pain. Then there was one last message. *Follow the lost.*

How? demanded Garrett, but the voice was gone. Whoever was pushing the ice pick into his head gave it one last hard shove. His vision blurred, and he fell to his knees, knowing that it was over. He could hear Kyle and Reggie coming straight at them. They were just yards away.

Then, as suddenly as it came, the pain disappeared. Garrett's vision cleared. He blinked, trying to get the tears out of his eyes, and immediately saw it. He acted without thinking.

"Come on," he shouted, knowing that Kyle could hear him. "This way!" He grabbed Greg again and this time would not allow the preacher to shake him off. He gripped his arm and brought his face to within inches of Greg's. "If you want to save them, follow me." Greg stared at him. His eyes widened, and the hatred that had so disfigured his face disappeared, replaced by what could only be described as desperate hope. His mouth worked, trying to speak. Then, finally, he managed a single word.

"Go." That was enough for Garrett. He swung around, started off, heading away from Kyle.

"Come on," he shouted. It no longer mattered if Kyle could hear them. He lunged into the brush, keeping his eyes on a path that only he could see. He both heard and felt Greg and his family fall in behind him. Kyle heard it as well.

"That does it," he snarled. "You're going down hard, Greg!" Garrett risked a quick glance over his shoulder and saw the brush behind them wave madly. Then Kyle burst into view, followed immediately by a tall, gaunt middle aged man. His face was covered with a thick beard. He wore a dirty white T-shirt and tattered green cap. Kyle was gripping a rifle while the man...Reggie no doubt...was lugging a shotgun. Kyle saw them and without hesitation raised his rifle.

"Gotcha," he shouted and fired. Garrett felt the bullet scream past them, and the branch of a thorny bush to his right exploded. Bits of damp wood flew out, slapping him hard in the face. He staggered but kept going. His quick look back had cost him. He had nearly lost the path.

"What the hell?"

"You missed," shouted Reggie in a high pitched voice. The man had a noticeable lisp, and it came out, "You mithed!"

"At this range? No way," snarled Kyle. He fired again. This time his shot went wide left. Garrett kept his attention focused ahead.

"Idiot," he heard Reggie say. A second later, the shotgun popped, sounding like a firecracker on steroids. The scattershot flew through the brush, straight at the fleeing family. Plants shattered all around them, but again, no one was hit. "That's impothable," cried Reggie.

"Shut up," shouted Kyle. "Get after them."

"Thith ain't right," whined Reggie. "Thith ain't right at all."

"MOVE," screamed Kyle.

"Garrett, are you sure?" Greg was panting hard. Garrett did not bother to answer. He had to stay focused on the path. It was nearly invisible, and he was fairly certain that if he lost his concentration, it would disappear altogether.

It stretched out before him, weaving in and out of the brush. In his mind, he saw a dimly glowing string, like the kind a child might use to fly a kite. It was thicker than the web-like manifestation of the dark power, but it was also somehow more ephemeral.

It's like it's not really here, he thought as he followed it through the brush. *It's somewhere else.* He could see that it was already fading away. Soon it would disappear entirely.

BOOM! Another blast from the shotgun scattered through the plants around them. Reggie had given it another try, only to produce the same results.

"Kyle," Garrett heard him say, "Let 'em go. I don't like thith. I don't like thith at all."

"You'll like it a lot less if we let them get away," said Kyle. "You want to explain it to *him*?" Reggie did not answer, and Garrett felt rather than saw the two men close in on them.

"Something's happening," grunted Sean. He was right behind Garrett.

"Keep going," gasped Greg. "Whatever it is, it's working for us." Garrett did not dare to speak for fear of losing the string, but he could feel it too. It was mainly the sounds. The crash and crackle of the brush as they forced their way through was no longer deafening. Now it sounded thin, empty…*transparent*. The ground felt solid under his feet, and the resilient plants still slapped him in the face, but it felt as if the world was somehow fading.

"Dad! Look!" Sean's voice sounded thin as well.

"Don't look back," Garrett shouted, already knowing that it was too late.

"Sean," shouted Greg, "turn around!" A vivid image presented itself in Garrett's mind; Sean, stopped in his tracks, standing with his back to his family. He was staring at Kyle and Reggie as the two men bore down on him. Then Greg's hand reached out and grabbed the back of his shirt. Sean was yanked backward. He staggered and turned around. He took a step forward but then stopped.

"Dad? Where are…I can see you but…" His voice was distorted, as if someone had found a treble knob on his vocal cords and cranked it to maximum. Again Greg's hand reached out. This time it grabbed Sean by the throat.

"Andie," shouted Greg. "Take my hand, and for God's sake, don't look back." Andie grabbed hold of her husband. Greg turned around. Garrett felt him waver. Despair slammed into his gut like a club. *I'm going to lose them both.*

As it turned out, he was wrong. Greg still had some strength left, and he was not about to lose his son. He grabbed on to Sean with one hand and, with a will that could only be described as heroic, pulled him forward. Then, gripping Andie's hand, he turned around.

"Are you with us now?" he asked. He was panting so hard that he barely managed to wheeze the words out.

"Y…yeah," gasped Sean. His voice was normal again. Through the sheer force of his love, Greg had saved his son. *That was way too close*, Garrett thought as he started forward again.

"Don't look back," he shouted again. "Something's happening. If you look back, you're lost."

"What…what's happening to us?" gasped Andie. "Where are you taking us?"

"Don't know," said Garrett. "But anywhere's better than back there." He desperately hoped that he was right.

They kept going, and Garrett suddenly felt walls. They reared high up on either side of him. For a moment, he was back in the canal, the walls of dark power closing in on him. Then he focused his new senses.

They're different, he thought. The dark walls of Gamble's Run had been vile and unnatural…a made thing. The walls now hemming them in felt slightly different. They were still artificial, but they also felt as if they were a part of the land itself. And they also felt old…ancient.

The glowing string faded.

No, he cried silently. *Not yet!* He tried to will it back to its former brightness, but with a wink it went out. The walls remained, only now they felt closer. Garrett stopped abruptly, trying to recover the lost path. Close behind, Kyle was coming on fast.

"Garrett! What are you doing?" Greg shoved past Andie and Erica and grabbed him by the shoulder. Garrett opened his mouth to say 'It's gone!', but at that instant, Kyle and Reggie arrived. Despite his own warning, Garrett swung around. Their two pursuers staggered up, with Kyle in the lead. Greg, still gripping him, tensed. He was ready to charge, but Garrett grabbed his hand and squeezed.

"Wait," he said in a low voice. Greg seemed ready to argue the point, but suddenly Kyle shoved past Sean. Eyes forward, he reached Greg and Garrett. He kept going for a few more paces and then stopped. Then he turned, facing them. His pale face was bright red, and he was breathing hard. A moment later, Reggie joined him. They gripped their weapons and stared in Greg's direction, but Garrett could see that their eyes could not focus on them. Not only that, but both men seemed pale. Reggie's formerly bright green hat now held only a hint of color. Their faces had a grayish tint. Garrett felt as if he was looking at them through some kind of dark filter.

"Garrett," whispered Greg.

"We've moved," said Garrett. "We're not here." He could not have explained those two short sentences if his life depended on it, but it did not matter. They were true. Kyle's eyes moved back and forth. He would focus in on them and start to move, but then he would look away.

"They can't see us," said Greg. His voice held equal amounts of wonder and terror.

"I don't think it's that simple," said Garrett. "I…I don't think that they can *acknowledge* us."

"Can we touch them?" asked Greg. Garrett shook his head.

"I have no idea," he said.

"Let's find out," said Greg. Shaking off Garrett's hand, he took a step forward, curled his right hand into a tight fist and let fly. His roundhouse punch was both clumsy and powerful. In a real fight, it would not have landed, but Kyle never saw it coming. Greg's fist met Kyle's jaw with a loud SMACK. Kyle let out a sharp yelp that was cut short by a second punch to his nose. He hit the ground hard, hands over his face. Blood spurted through his fingers. Then his eyes glazed over and he stopped moving. Greg's combination had put him down for the count. Wherever the glowing string had led them, it seemed that Kyle and Reggie had followed them close enough so that they could interact, at least on a physical level.

Greg did not hesitate. He rounded on Reggie, who was waving his shotgun wildly. This time, Greg took his time and aimed. His blow connected squarely with Reggie's left temple. The tall man started to crumble with a whimper, and Greg followed up with a hard left to his other cheek. As Reggie hit the ground, Greg grabbed the shotgun. He took a step forward until he was standing directly above them, and pointed the barrel straight at Kyle's head. He looked back at his wife, his intentions clear. Andie shook her head.

"I won't stop you," she said, her voice flat. "Not after what they were going to do to my baby." Greg nodded and turned his attention back to the two men on the ground. Kyle was barely conscious. His hands had fallen away from his face, and Garrett could see that the blood was flowing freely from his nose. Reggie was dazed, but he was coming out of it. He rolled over, trying to stand. With a snarl, Greg raised the butt of that shotgun and brought it down hard on the back of Reggie's neck. This time, Reggie did not make a sound. He fell face first into the ground. Greg brought the barrel of the shotgun to bear on Kyle's chest. Then he looked back at Garrett.

"Give me a single reason," he snarled. Instantly, Garrett understood one thing. For all his anger, all his hatred, Greg did not want to pull the trigger. If he did, Kyle and Reggie would already be dead, their faces shattered into tiny bits of blood, bone and brain. Garrett stared at the preacher, but he was thinking of his vision in Kyle's truck. He remembered how the dark power that Gamble had planted inside of him wanted nothing more than to beat Kyle into a broken, bloody mass.

Their narrow escape from the canal flashed into his mind. He saw the power of the Gregangel as it burned the darkness out of his soul.

"You're a servant of the Light," he said softly. Greg jerked as if Garrett has slapped him. He closed his eyes and tears rolled down his cheeks. Garrett nodded at the fallen men. "They don't matter anymore," he said. "This is about you." He kept his eyes on Greg, hoping that the preacher would make the right decision. Greg opened his eyes again and stared hard at Garrett.

"You're a real pain in the ass," he said, his voice breaking. He looked at the shotgun with the kind of loathing usually reserved for a cockroach infestation. Then he grabbed it by the barrel, reared back and threw it into the brush. "Never again," said Greg, wiping his hands as if they were soiled. "I will never touch a gun again." He looked at his wife. "I'm sorry, Andie. I couldn't do it." Andie glanced at Kyle and Reggie.

"Garrett's right," she said, fighting back the tears. "They don't matter anymore." She moved into Greg's embrace. Sean put a hand on his mother's shoulder, but Erica had something else in mind. She shoved past her parents and moved to stand next to Kyle. Then she planted a kick deep into Kyle's stomach. Kyle whuffed as air exploded from his lungs, but he did not regain consciousness.

"I'm not a saint like my dad," she said in a low voice, "but I'm still a nice person." She kicked him again, this time in the groin. "Well, maybe not so nice," she said. She turned to face her parents. "You two have a problem?" she demanded.

"No," said Greg. "Feel better?"

"As a matter of fact, I do," said Erica. She turned to Garrett. "What's happening to us?"

"I honestly don't know," said Garrett.

"Can you get us out of here?" asked Andie. Her tone had softened a little. Garrett hoped that maybe she was beginning to forgive him.

"All we can do is to keep going," said Garrett. "We don't want to go back the way we came. Kyle's friends can't be too far behind, and those two are going to wake up sooner or later."

"Then lead on," said Greg. "You've got us this far." Garrett looked the question at Andie, who shrugged.

"What he said," she said. Garrett did not bother to answer. He opened his senses and reached out. Now that they were not on the run, he was able to get a better feel for the walls. *Except that they're not walls*, he thought. They felt rough and jagged. *It's a crack*, he thought. *But a crack in what?* It really did not matter. There was only one way for them to go.

"All right," he said, pointing ahead, "that way."

"What about those two?" asked Sean, toeing Reggie's leg.

"Leave 'em," said Greg. "Let the mosquitoes and whatever other critters there are here have their fun." He motioned for Garrett to lead the way.

"What are you seeing?" he asked as they started off. "I can feel something, but I can't tell what."

"It's like being in a tight canyon," said Garrett. "There are high walls in either side. The path ahead is straight, but narrow." Greg actually laughed at that. Garrett looked at him.

"What's so funny?" he asked.

"The straight and narrow path," said Greg. Garrett got it and managed a smile.

"I've afraid I've never been one to follow it," he said.

"Until now," said Greg. Garrett nodded.

"Literally," he said. They kept moving forward, threading their way through the foliage they could all see and a crack that only one of them could see. They were moving much slower now. The long day, the endless night, and the mad dash to escape Kyle and Reggie had taken their toll. Garrett knew that they would have to find food and water soon. Their snack in the canoe was not nearly enough to keep them going.

"There's water ahead," said Greg. Sure enough, another canal, this one much wider than the others, appeared before them. The brush fell away, and they stepped out onto a bank that was maybe ten feet wide and very muddy. To their left, the canal ran straight for as far as they could see. To their right, it curved out of sight after about fifty yards. They stood there, blinking in the bright, hot sun.

"I'd give a lot to be clean and cool right now," muttered Erica.

"Which way?" asked Greg. Garrett shook his head.

"The crack is gone," he said.

"Meaning that we're through," said Greg. "To where? Another time? Place?" Garrett glanced up at the cloudless blue sky.

"Not another time," he said, pointing up. Greg followed his finger and saw two distinct white contrails etched in the blue, the kind ordinary passenger jets made flying at high altitude.

"And since we're still obviously in the Warriors," said Greg, "we're not in another place. So…what now?" Garrett shook his head again.

"Do you hear that?" asked Sean, moving to stand next to his father. Garrett strained his ears, listening. He half-expected to hear Kyle's airboat again. Instead, he detected a strange mechanical sound….wheeze-whoosh…wheeze-whoosh…wheeze-whoosh.

"What the…" Greg never finished his sentence. Garrett followed his gaze to where the canal curved away. He could detect movement behind the trees and brush. Something was coming up the canal. A few seconds later, that something hove into view. Greg and Garrett looked at each other, and then back at the something. Andie, Sean and Erica merely stared.

Coming around the bend, its twin smoke stacks belching black steam and its stern paddle wheel slowly churning the water, was an old-fashioned river boat.

Chapter 18

The Shamrock

*T*he riverboat cleared the bend and slowly turned towards them, its stern wheel churning the water at a leisurely pace. It was maybe fifty feet long and half as wide. There were no cabins. The two decks were open with only a wooden guard rail surrounding them. It's faded and peeling white paint was accented by equally faded dark green trim. There was a name painted on its side.

"Shamrock," Garrett said aloud. It was printed in large, black lettering, bordered with the same shade of green as the trim. In the center, between the 'M' and the 'R', was a stylized dark green four leaf clover.

"We need to get out of here," whispered Andie.

"Yeah," said Greg. "I think you're right." He laid a hand on Garrett's shoulder. "You need to lead us back," he said. Garrett nodded, but when he reached out, searching for the crack, he could not find it. It had not disappeared…at least, he did not think so…but he could no longer sense it. The there-not-there walls seemed to have merged into a single, solid mass. They were effectively trapped.

"I can't…I…" He shook his head and tried again. "I can't see the way back," he cried. The riverboat was now coming straight at them.

"Like hell," said Andie. With a snarl, she pushed past him.

"No!" cried Garrett, but Andie had had enough. She grabbed Erica's arm and pulled her along, but when she drew near to the edge of the wall, even though she could not sense it, she stopped. She stared straight ahead for a few seconds and then took another hesitant step forward. She penetrated the wall, but the instant she did, her body went rigid, as if she had just brushed against a strong electrical current. She looked to her left and right, swinging her head back and forth wildly. Then she stumbled back a step and whirled on Garrett.

"What have you done?" she demanded. Greg reached out to steady her, but she shoved his hand away.

"Mom?" This was from Sean.

"It's blocked," said Andie, keeping her eyes on Garrett. "Like when we tried to get out of the canal. You did this, didn't you?" Garrett shook his head, stunned at the accusation.

"You can't think…" he began, but Andie wasn't having any.

"Get us out of here," she said. "Now."

"I can't find the way out," cried Garrett. Behind him, the sound of the riverboat's chugging engine grew closer. Andie stepped toward him, her eyes wide with terror.

"If that thing gets to us, we're dead." Her voice was shrill, just one note short of a full scream. "You know that. Now find the way back."

"We can't go back," said Greg. "Not with Kyle…"

"Would you rather deal with that?" cried Andie, pointing at the Shamrock. Almost against his will, Garrett looked at the riverboat. It was much closer now. He raised his eyes to the pilot house, perched on the front of the top deck. He could just make out a shadowy figure through the dirty glass.

"We can get past Kyle," said Andie. "Garrett proved that." She reached out and grabbed Garrett by the arm. Her fingernails bit deep into the exposed skin. He grimaced but did not pull away. "I know that this isn't your fault," she said in a low voice. Garrett understood that she really did not believe that. "But you've got to get us out of here."

At that moment, the Riverboat's steam whistle sounded out. It echoed across the water, a high-pitched banshee wail. If any of them had harbored any doubts that the Shamrock might not be dangerous, that whistle erased them. One word popped into Garrett's mind…damned. The whistle reeked of damnation, and the instrument of that damnation was pointed straight at them. Erica put her hands over her ears and squeezed her eyes shut. Both Sean and Greg hunched down, as if a heavy weight had just been dropped onto their shoulders. Andie shuddered and gripped Garrett's arm even tighter.

"Please, Garrett," whispered Andie. She was begging now. "Please lead us out of here."

"I'll try," said Garrett, throwing another glance at the Shamrock. It was now less than thirty yards away. There was no sign of any passengers, just the dark silhouette in the pilot house. *But that's a lie*, thought Garrett, tearing his eyes away and turning his attention to the thick brush behind them. *There are people aboard, all right, and whoever they are, they aren't nice.* He approached the brush, desperately trying to sense the crack, but it remained hidden. The wall that blocked their way was not made of stone or steel, but it was just as impenetrable. Garrett cringed as he drew close to it. It seemed to rise above him, stretching into infinity. He suddenly felt dizzy. *Come on, come on.*

He started to raise his hands to feel his way but caught himself at the last moment. He could feel eyes boring into his back…not just those of the Powell family, but those belonging to the hidden passengers on the Shamrock. He closed his eyes, trying to locate the crack. In front of him the brush, stirred by a slight breeze, rustled gently. Physically, he could have reached out and touched the nearest tree, but it did not matter. The way back was blocked.

The Shamrock's whistle sounded out again. It was all Garrett could do not to scream. He could hear a million damned souls in that whistle and understood a terrible truth. There was room for five more.

Then he felt it. The crack appeared, and it was just a few feet away.

"Here," he cried. "This way." He turned to wave Greg and his family toward him, but at that moment, the Shamrock swerved toward the bank. The engine shut off, and the bow bumped gently against the land. The twin stacks wobbled for a moment and then stilled. Greg grabbed Andie's hand and pulled her toward Garrett. Sean and Erica were moving, already two steps ahead of their parents. Garrett opened his mouth to urge them on, but suddenly a narrow gangplank was released. It hit the ground with a heavy thud, sinking several inches into the mud.

Garrett's eyes blurred, and his head spun. He blinked rapidly, trying to clear both his head and his vision. He refocused and immediately saw that their time had run out. At least a dozen men were running down the gangplank, heading straight toward them. Garrett had not seen them on the boat because he had not been allowed to see them. Now they had dropped their cloak of secrecy. All of them were carrying guns, both rifles and pistols. They were clad in everyday wear. Most of them were wearing jeans, pullover shirts and heavy boots. Garrett tried to make out their faces, but his eyes refused to focus on them.

The Shamrock had landed barely ten yards upriver, and the men moved unnaturally fast. They caught Greg and Andie when they were only a few feet from the crack. Two of the men tackled them. They went face first into the mud, crying out as they fell. Sean turned to try to help, but he was caught seconds later.

Erica reached out for Garrett. In the canal, she had been violated, but she had resisted the dark power. Her formidable courage had saved her. Now that courage was gone. Her face was contorted with terror, and Garrett could see that she was running on blind panic. She knew exactly what would happen when the men from the Shamrock caught her.

Garrett tried to grab her hand and pull her into the crack. If he could save her, then maybe he could somehow come back for her family. The idea flashed into his mind, taking full root in an instant. Then, just as quickly, it withered and died. She was grabbed from behind and thrown to the ground. She landed hard on her left arm and cried out in pain. There was no sickening snap, so Garrett was reasonably sure that it did not break, but her shoulder was probably dislocated.

Greg, Andie and Sean struggled, but they were spent. The man holding Sean down jammed his knee against his neck, pushing hard. Sean gagged, choking on the mud that was forced into his mouth. Greg and Andie were hauled to their feet. There was a heavy clanking and Garrett looked back at the Shamrock. Two more men were trotting down the gangplank. Both of them were carrying chains that ended in what looked like…

Shackles, thought Garrett. He was numb now. The men with the chains went to work, binding Greg and Andie's hands and feet with ruthless efficiency. Then they dragged Sean upright and shackled him as well. The men were silent, going about their task without speaking a word. One of the men reached down and grabbed Erica by the hair. He yanked hard, pulling out a large wad. Erica screamed, and Greg lunged forward.

"Bastards!" he screamed. Instantly, he was thrown to the ground. The men nearest him began to kick him hard. Greg tried to curl up and protect himself, but one of the booted feet caught him squarely on the temple. Greg let out a 'whoof' and then lay still. The man who had grabbed Erica grabbed her again, this time by her undamaged arm. He yanked her to her feet, and Garrett could see that her shoulder was indeed dislocated. She screamed again, but the men paid her no mind. Moments later, she, Sean and Andie were herded toward the Shamrock. Two other men grabbed Greg by the ankles and began to drag him toward the riverboat as well.

Garrett watched the scene play out in front of him. It happened so fast that his exhausted mind was barely able to comprehend it. He could only stare as the family he thought he had saved was bound and dragged away.

Andie, Sean and Erica were forced up the gangplank and shoved against the far rail. Greg was dragged onto the Shamrock by his feet. His head bumped against the hard wood, whipping back and forth until Garrett was sure that his neck must be broken. Once the preacher was on board, he was left lying on the deck. His family tried to rush to him, but they were shoved back against the rail and forced to sit down.

This is not happening. This is NOT happening. The single thought chased its tail in Garrett's mind. He desperately tried to deny the evidence of his eyes, but it was useless. What he was seeing was all too real.

One of the men had his back to him, watching as the Powell family was taken away. As soon as they were all on board, he turned toward Garrett. Garrett stared at him, and when the man started toward him, he cried out and backed away. He was not all that tall…just a little over five feet…and his build was slight. With his mended knee, Garrett might have even taken him in a fight. He carried a single barrel pump action shotgun and wore what looked like a .45 pistol in a holster around his waist.

But it was not his average physique that made Garrett cower in terror or the impressive hardware. At Nutall Rise, he had scanned Kyle and his gang. The men had reeked of the same dark power that Gamble had used on him. They were controlled by it, but the man coming toward him was not just under its command. He *embodied* it. He was the dark power made manifest. Maybe he had once been human, but Garrett could sense that any shred of that humanity had long since been crushed out of existence. He was no longer a man.

He could sense something else as well.

The man…un-man…was very, very old.

Garrett could not take his eyes off his face. It was a pale, empty mask. All of the features were there; narrow eyes, large, bulbous nose and wide mouth. Taken separately, they were bland and ordinary, but when Garrett's mind tried to form them into a face, the entire effect fell apart. It was as if the dark power had taken the original face, pulled it apart like a damp jigsaw puzzle and then tried to put it back together. The pieces no longer fit. Garrett got the distinct impression that he was seeing what the un-man wanted him to see. His true face was hidden.

The un-man walked slowly, deliberately. Eyes that once might have been brown but were now a dark, murky black stared at him. Garrett held up his hands, trying to ward off the dark power coming toward him. It radiated off the un-man like a blazing heat.

The tiny spark of light that had already saved him twice flickered, and for a moment, he was terrified that it would die. It continued to burn, but it was weakening. The un-man came to a stop a few feet away, staring at him with his black eyes. After a moment, he spoke, not to Garrett, but to four other men who were waiting behind him.

"Go get those fools," said the mouth. The voice, like the face, was ordinary and bland, with just a hint of a southern drawl. The men obeyed instantly. They moved single file straight toward the crack. When they reached it, they did not hesitate. They went in and disappeared into the brush. The un-man turned his attention back to Garrett.

"You need to listen to me," he said. "You're never leaving this place. Get that in your head. This is where you make your choice. You can join us, right here, right now. Renounce what you call the Light, and you live.

You can be reunited with your wife, and the two of you can live out your lives here. Reject us, and you die, but she doesn't. Let me repeat that. *She doesn't die.* It's that simple. Choose…now." Garrett stared at the un-man. His only thought was to somehow stall, although he had no idea what he might be stalling for. He shook his head.

"I don't under…" The un-man moved fast. Garrett did not even realize what was happening until the butt of the shotgun slammed into his midsection. He doubled over, the air exploding from his lungs. He fell to his knees, hands on the ground, retching.

"Last chance," said the un-man again. The dark power flared even hotter. Garrett felt it trying to enter him. His own light was holding it at bay, but it was slowly dying.

I'm sorry, Mel, he cried silently. Not long ago, he believed that he would have done anything to save his wife, but now he understood that there were some lines he could never cross. His insight, perhaps guided by that spark of light within him, was working overtime, and it was showing him a very simple, undeniable truth.

The un-man was lying. Maybe he would indeed be reunited with Melody, but if he chose to join the men of the Shamrock, he would cease to be Garrett Webb. He would, in fact, become just like the abomination standing over him.

The Gregangel had given him a choice in the canal, and that choice was still his. He would *not* join the darkness…not even to save Melody. If he did, it would destroy them both. He looked up at the un-man, gasping for breath. Then he mouthed a single, defiant word.

"No." The un-man's arms blurred as again he moved with unnatural speed. The barrel of the shotgun swung down, stopping barely an inch away from his forehead. Garret understood that there would be no second chance. He had made his choice, and now he would die. He closed his eyes and thought of Melody. Her beautiful face, young and prefect, appeared in his mind. Gamble might have stolen his secret place, but it did not matter. At that moment, she was with him.

Nothing happened. There was no loud 'BANG', and his face did not disintegrate. After a few seconds, he opened his eyes again. The shotgun was still there, and it was still pointed straight at his forehead, but the un-man's head was cocked at a strange angle. He was looking back toward the Shamrock, as if he was listening to something that only he could hear. After a moment, he turned his attention back to Garrett.

"On your feet," he said.

"Wh…what?" gasped Garrett.

"Don't make me ask twice," warned the un-man, pressing the barrel of the shotgun against his forehead. Garrett struggled to his feet, wondering what new cruelty his captor was planning. The idea of mercy did not enter his head. The creature holding the shotgun knew nothing of the concept.

Something thrashed behind him. He looked to see the two men who had went into the crack returning. Each of them now had a companion. It took Garrett a moment to recognize that the two new arrivals were Kyle and Reggie. Both men looked the worse for wear. Dried blood was caked under Kyle's nose, and Reggie sported wicked bruises on both sides of his face. At first, Garrett thought that the un-man was merely gathering his troops, but the looks on the faces of both Reggie and Kyle contradicted that idea. The two men were terrified. They were herded over to stand next to him.

"This should have been finished hours ago," said the un-man. Reggie whimpered and sank to his knees. Kyle managed to stay on his feet, but he was trembling from head to foot. He glanced at Garrett, his face a strange mixture of terror and hatred.

"We had them," he said in a trembling voice. "They just got lucky." The shotgun swung away from Garrett and centered on Reggie. Reggie started to say something…what it was no one would ever know…but the un-man pulled the trigger. There was a blinding white flash and a loud 'BANG'. Reggie's face flew apart. His forehead shattered and the top of his head from the nose up disappeared. Blood flew in every direction, accompanied with bits of bone and brain.

Garrett screamed and tried to turn away, but it happened too fast. Reggie's blood sprayed him from face to belly, soaking his shirt. Tiny bits of Reggie's skull dug into his exposed skin. Kyle screamed as well, and as it turned out, that scream was the last thing he would ever utter. The instant Garrett turned away the un-man fired again. Kyle was cut off in mid scream and again, Garrett was doused in blood. His stomach lurched and tried to climb up his throat. He sank to his knees again, retching, but almost instantly strong arms grabbed him on either side and hauled him to his feet. He saw the un-man regarding his handiwork.

"Get him on board," he said without even bothering to glance in his direction. "The Master isn't through with him, it seems." Garrett was hauled across the muddy bank, up the gangplank and dumped onto the deck of the Shamrock. He landed inches away from Greg. The preacher was laying very still, his eyes closed, and for a moment Garrett feared the worse. Expecting to be beaten at any second, he reached out and laid his hand on Greg's cheek. It was warm to the touch. His hand slid down to Greg's left arm and came to rest on his wrist. The pulse was weak, but it was there.

"Garrett?" He looked over at Andie, huddled on the deck with her children.

"He's alive," croaked Garrett. His mouth was so dry that he barely managed to get the words out.

"Oh thank God," cried Andie. She tightened her grip on her children. Erica cried out in pain, cradling her dislocated shoulder, but Andie did not seem to hear. Garrett managed to get his hands and knees under him and crawl over to her. None of the men stopped him and, in fact, seemed to ignore him. He slid next to Erica and took hold of her hand.

"We've got to get that fixed," he said and then coughed. He was badly dehydrated. He reached over and put a gentle hand on her dislocated shoulder. Erica cringed away. "If we're going to have any kind of chance, we've got to be ready," he said in a low voice.

"Let him, baby," said Andie. She looked hard at Garrett. "You know what you're doing?" Garrett nodded.

"It won't be my first," he said. He slid his other arm around Erica's shoulders and braced himself. "This is going to hurt," he warned. From behind him, footsteps clattered across the wooden deck. They were heading in his direction.

"Hurry," whispered Andie. Garrett knew that he could not afford to be gentle. He gripped Erica tight, put the heel of his hand over the protruding shoulder, and shoved hard. Erica screamed and at the same time, her shoulder popped back into its socket. Barely a second later, Garrett was grabbed by his collar and yanked backward. He went sprawling onto the deck, landing next to Greg again.

"Y'all wanna stay away from that bitch now," said one of the men. Garrett risked a glance at him. Like the un-man, he was physically unremarkable. His pale face had a good dose of sunburn. His head was bare, and he wore his black hair long. It had a greasy look to it, as if it had not been washed in days. His faded jeans and dark green T-shirt were filthy.

Unlike the un-man, he was still human. Garrett felt the dark power writhing inside of him, but it was only infesting him. The man saw Garrett looking at him. He sneered and spat on the deck.

"What the hell are you looking at?" he demanded. His thick southern accent made 'hell' sound like 'heeell'. White hot rage flared inside of Garrett. He propped himself up on one elbow and spoke without thinking.

"One sorry son of a bitch," he rasped. It was a mistake. The man spat again, this time in his face. Then he leaned down, balled his fist and slammed it into Garrett's right cheek. Garrett's vision blinked and he fell backward, hitting his head on the deck. Miraculously, he did not lose consciousness.

"Y'all wanna mind your manners now," said the man.

"That's enough, Roy," said one of the other men.

"Tain't nearly," grumbled Roy. He was still leaning over Garrett, readying another blow. His friend caught him by the shoulder.

"Leave him be," he said. "You'll get your turn with that pretty little blackbird soon enough." Roy thought about it. Then he spat into Garrett's face again and stood up straight.

"Lucky for you, boy," he said. Then he walked away. After a moment, so did his friend. Garrett kept his eyes closed, listening to them leave. His face was burning from Roy's blow, and his head throbbed in time with his heart.

Are you there? he cried out in his mind. The Gregangel did not answer. *Melody! Can you hear me?* There was only silence. He reached up and wiped Roy's spittle from his face, gagging at its foul stench. Roy was a tobacco chewer. Then he opened his eyes and saw that he was alone. He wondered where the un-man might be and then decided that, at least for the moment, he did not want to know. He glanced at Greg and saw that the preacher was still out. Then he rolled over and checked on Andie. She was still there, cradling Erica in her arms. Sean had pulled away and was sitting against the rail. Garrett could see the seething hatred and rage burning his face. His arms were folded, and his fists were clenched. Garrett needed no special insight to see what the kid was planning.

"No," he whispered. Sean did not seem to hear him. "Sean," he said, this time a little louder. Sean looked at him, and Garrett shook his head. "It's…not the time," he said and then started coughing. Sean looked away, and Garrett struggled to get his body under control. "Please," he managed at last. "Wait. You'll…you'll get your chance." Sean glanced at him again and after a moment gave him a barely perceptible nod.

At that instant, two things happened. The Shamrock's whistle sounded out again. This time, it was far worse. The countless voices trapped within that whistle all seemed to be shouting at Garrett. *Here you will stay*, they cried. *Here you are damned.* At the same time, another voice echoed inside his mind. Garrett nearly cried out in relief. The Gregangel was back.

It's time for you to learn, it said. Garrett could only think of one response.

About damn time.

Chapter 19

History Lesson

*Y*ou *need to come with me*, whispered the Gregangel.

Not without them, Garrett replied, pointing a mental finger at Greg and his family, *and not without my wife. You save us all or get the hell out of my head.*

Your loyalty is a good thing, said the Gregangel. *Indeed, it is a great thing. And it is one of the reasons that you might succeed where I have failed.*

What do you mean?

I need to show you, said the Gregangel. *Words are useless, even at this level of communication.*

I'm not..., began Garrett.

...leaving them, finished the Gregangel. *You won't. I am not bound by time, and for a short period, I can free you from its bonds as well. In addition, only your spirit will travel with me. Your body will stay here. No one will know that you are gone.*

Why me? asked Garrett. *Greg would be a better...* Again the Gregangel interrupted.

He is the key, but you are the chance.

Speak plainly.

HE did not expect you. You were never supposed to get this far, and because of that, you may still prevail.

He, said Garrett. *You mean John Gamble.*

What lives in that rotting shell is no longer the man called Gamble. He was consumed long ago.

So what consumed him? demanded Garrett.

Like me, something that does not belong here. You call me the Gregangel. For want of a better name, you may call him the Gamblemonster. Garrett felt the Gregangel reach out a hand that did not exist in his world. *Now, will you come with me? Your time is running out.*

You want to take me out of my body, he said. He felt the Gregangel agree.

Something usually reserved for death, he replied. *It is not without its risks, but you must learn. Please, for all of those you hold dear, come with me.* Garrett thought about it and realized that he was out of options.

Do it, he said. The Gregangel drew close. Garrett could feel its presence hovering as near to him as his own skin. Then he moved even closer. He entered Garrett. Garrett's mind exploded. He felt as if the Gregangel had shoved a thick garden hose deep into his head and had started pumping gas. He felt his body convulsing.

They'll see, he cried out.

Do not struggle, commanded the Gregangel. Its voice was no longer quiet and gentle. It ripped through Garrett's mind, and again he cried out. *Garrett, I won't hurt you, but you must stop fighting me. Remember the canal. Remember how you asked me to free you of the darkness. This is no different.*

You're...killing...me.

No, said the Gregangel. *Please...trust me.* Garrett struggled some more, but gradually he calmed down. As he did, an amazing thing happened. He felt the Gregangel reach out and wrap him in arms both powerful and invisible. For the first time in a very long time, he felt safe and protected. He stopped struggling.

The Gregangel moved swiftly, a skilled surgeon wielding a spiritual scalpel. Garrett felt himself coming loose. The ties that bound him to his physical presence were being severed. He felt another surge of panic.

Stop, he cried. To his amazement, the Gregangel obeyed. *Is this death?*

On a certain level...yes, said the Gregangel. *But what I take, I can put back, for a time. Will you trust me?*

Will this take me to Melody?

No, but it will show you how to find her. Please, Garrett. I know that this is hard for you, but it is also very difficult for me. Garrett took a deep mental breath.

Go, he thought.

The surgery was terrifying. Garrett had always taken his physical presence for granted, but now that presence was being methodically sliced away. The links that bound him to his body were severed and cauterized. His vision winked out, followed by his hearing, sense of touch smell and taste.

Through it all, the Gregangel worked silently and efficiently, and as he did, Garrett slipped deeper and deeper into a bottomless pit. He was suddenly surrounded by a kind of darkness that was beyond his experience. It had nothing to do with the dark power of the Gamblemonster, nor was it the simple absence of light. It was the darkness of oblivion. But for that tiny spark of light that still glowed within his spirit, he might have been consumed by it.

Almost there, whispered the Gregangel. The last bond was cut. The Gregangel's arms tightened their grip, and Garrett was lifted. The well of oblivion shattered, and light, pure and living, bathed Garrett in a warm glow. He gasped, or would have gasped if he still possessed lungs. The remnants of his physical senses fell away, left behind in his now unconscious body. New sensations rushed in to take their place.

Easy, cautioned the Gregangel. *I have you.* Garrett struggled against the Gregangel's grip, his mind desperately trying to ride the wave of raw power that assaulted him.

What's happening to me?

Birth, said the Gregangel, *or to be more precise; rebirth.* Garrett's mind exploded. In an instant, he understood that he would never fear death again. It was not the end. It was not even close to the end. He could feel the universe spread out at his feet. He could even sense where that universe ended and others, far more wondrous, began. He took a deep non-breath and screamed, and it was a scream of wild joy.

There was life everywhere. It smelled of moist earth and pure water. He could taste the struggle of billions beyond billions of lives, and it was both bitter and sweet. He could hear the heartbeats of each and every being that inhabited his own level of existence, and the sound was a symphony that rang out across the cosmos.

This is your great gift, whispered the Gregangel, and for the first time, Garrett heard the envy in his voice. *You have the magnificent ability to leave your physical shell and journey beyond the reaches of creation itself. I find it a great tragedy that your people fear the one thing that frees them.*

Death, said Garrett. The wave of new sensations was still strong, but he was rapidly learning to cope. Acting on sheer instinct, he drew his senses in tight, allowing the cacophony of creation to fade.

Yes, replied the Gregangel. *Death is a transition, nothing more. It makes it possible for you to journey to places that my own people can never imagine. We are trapped here by our own hands.* That last statement was infused with such a great sorrow that Garrett managed to turn his attention away from the wondrous vista spread out before him. He focused his mind on his companion and saw the truth.

You're not from around here, he said. The Gregangel shimmered and took shape. Garrett perceived an old man, hairless and stooped with age. His skin was wrinkled with countless years, and his dark eyes were tired and sad. He appeared to be clothed in a sagging white robe.

I am not, agreed the Gregangel. *But I have been here for a very long time. I was here when your progenitors were nearly destroyed, and I stayed as they recovered and rebuilt their world.*

I don't..., began Garrett, but the Gregangel ignored him.

I watched as humanity spread out from its second cradle so far away and eventually came here. Again Garrett felt deep sorrow emanate from the Gregangel. *What we have done to you is inexcusable, but I hope that someday you might forgive us.*

What do you mean?

I will show you, said the Gregangel. *Come*. The old man held out a withered hand, and after a moment, Garrett took it. *Focus your thoughts into your own world*, said the Gregangel.

I don't know how... began Garrett.

Yes, you do, said the Gregangel. And, as it turned out, he was right. Garrett turned his thoughts back to the riverboat, and suddenly there it was, right below him. He was floating above it, a few feet higher than the pilot house. He could see his own body, lying next to Greg. Near the rail, Andie still clung to her children. He saw something else as well, and despite the absence of his body, he suddenly felt sick to his non-existent stomach.

That...that thing...

A relic of the past, said the Gregangel. *Something that was once used for great evil, and unfortunately, great evil abides.* The Shamrock chugged along below them, making its way through the steadily narrowing canal. With his expanded senses, Garrett could easily see the physical aspect of the boat. The wood and metal were real. The rivets that held it together were made by man. The riverboat was a physical object with height, depth and width, but it was much more than that. The dark power infested every nut and bolt. Garrett's eyes were drawn to the pilot house, and he cried out.

Easy, said the Gregangel.

I was on that thing, cried Garrett. *My friends are STILL on that thing.* The pilot house was empty, at least of any human form. Within its confines, the dark power thrashed like a caged beast, as if straining to get out. From there it seeped into every part of the Shamrock.

That power cannot harm your friends, said the Gregangel. *Look.* He pointed a wizened finger. Garrett looked to where Greg lay, still unconscious.

Wha... The preacher was surrounded by the dark power, but it formed a circle around him. It was as if he was lying in a pool of light cast by a powerful spotlight. Garrett looked to where Andie sat against the rail and saw the same thing. The dark power surrounded them, but something seemed to be holding it at bay.

This is what you have done for the woman and her children, said the Gregangel. *And what I did for the man. When you freed them, you left a part of that light I channeled into you inside them.*

What about Sean?

The boy is protected by his mother, said the Gregangel. *They are in grave danger, but they can no longer be corrupted by the power surrounding them.*

It's a part of the Gamblemonster... the Shamrock, I mean.

He controls it, said the Gregangel. *He uses it to keep watch on this place. The men aboard gave themselves to him long ago.*

How long? asked Garrett. The Gregangel shook his head.

A very long time, he replied. *Now come. We are no longer bound by time, but our time is short nonetheless.*

That makes no sense, said Garrett.

It is nevertheless true, said the Gregangel. Garrett felt the Gregangel tug at him. As he turned away, he gasped, this time in amazement.

That's what we passed through, he said and felt the Gregangel nod.

For want of a better word, call it the Barrier. Garrett had originally sensed a great wall, infinitely high and infinitely old. Now he saw it for what it was; not a wall, but a sphere. He could sense that it existed in the world he now inhabited, but he could also see that it protruded into the physical world as well. It arced across the sky and dove deep into the earth, covering the Warriors and reaching all the way back to the canal. Garrett suddenly understood its purpose.

It's a prison, he said. *It's the Gamblemonster's prison.*

Yes, agreed the Gregangel. *Now look closer.* Garrett looked. If he had been in his physical body, he would have shuddered.

It's cracked, he said, dismayed. *That's why we got through.*

It is deteriorating, said the Gregangel.

We got out, said Garrett. *We made it, but…*

But that boat patrols the parameter, said the Gregangel. *The Gamblemonster knew which route you would take.*

You sent us, cried Garrett. *I followed your path.*

It was the only way, said the Gregangel. *I had hoped that you might escape, but I was wrong. Now please, follow me.* Garrett felt inclined to argue but thought the better of it. Whatever else might be happening, he believed that his companion was telling the truth. He had tried to aid in their escape. The fact that he failed simply meant that he was not all powerful. Together they moved toward the dome.

We're going back, said Garrett.

Yes, said the Gregangel. Garrett saw the crack they had traversed just moments ago. They sped toward it and without hesitation entered it. Garrett did his best to ignore the bodies lying at the crack's entrance. The Gregangel threaded his way through the crack with both precision and ease. In moments, they were through.

You've come this way before, said Garrett.

Many times, said the Gregangel. *Look.* Garrett obeyed and saw Kyle's airboat.

What? The airboat was lying on its side, half in, half out of the water. Next to it was the canoe, also half-submerged. Both craft were covered with moss and slime. The wooden propeller of the airboat had rotted into uselessness, and the engine had come loose from its mounts and fallen into the water. It looked as if they had been there for years. Garrett turned to the Gregangel. *How?*

I told you, said his guide. *We are outside of time. What you perceive as the past, present and future are meaningless now.*

The Gamblemonster, said Garrett. *Is he also outside of time?* He sensed the Gregangel's surprise.

Your insight is strong, he said. *You see much that should be hidden. The answer is no. He was, but when he merged with John Gamble, he became as much a prisoner to time as you. Look...there.* Garrett followed the wizened hand. They were now flying over the Aucilla, and there, making its way down the center of the river, was the Shamrock. Garrett cringed but looked closer. He saw the difference immediately.

The dark power that had infested the riverboat was gone. Garrett realized that they were seeing the Shamrock as it once was, a simple riverboat from the mid-1800s. As they drew close, he saw that the lower deck was dangerously overcrowded. Men, women and more than a few children...all of them dark-skinned...were crammed in tight. Looking closer, Garrett could see that they were chained together, ankle to ankle. He could feel neither heat nor cold, but judging from the way the passengers were sweating, the day was stifling hot. On the upper deck, a dozen white men loitered casually. All of them carried flintlocks as well as pistols and machetes. A pack of six large hounds lay near the stern, dozing in the heat. Again his insight flared.

These are Gamble's slaves, he said.

Yes. They dug what Gamble, in his pride, would call Gamble's Run.

And the men above…

Overseers, said the Gregangel. *Now watch closely.* The Shamrock suddenly swerved toward the bank, and even though he was peering over one hundred and sixty years into the past, Garrett had no trouble recognizing the entrance to the canal. It was blocked by a crude earthen dam, obviously designed to keep the water out so that the slaves could dig. The paddlewheel stopped turning and the riverboat bumped gently against the land. Garrett felt his non-existent stomach clench as the gangplank was lowered.

The men on the upper deck began shouting, although Garrett could hear nothing. The slaves began shuffling down the gangplank, hampered by the chains. When they were all off, eight of the overseers, two of them accompanied by the now alert hounds, joined the slaves and began to unchain them. The other four remained on the upper deck, guns at the ready. Once they were freed, they were marched single file into the canal. Garrett and the Gregangel followed them.

The canal was not even half-completed. The land had been cleared for maybe a mile, and the digging barely begun. The slaves were divided into several smaller groups. Some were set to clearing the land, others moving the heavy rocks, while still others began to dig. It was backbreaking work, and Garrett wept non-existent tears for their agony.

That would have been Melody if she had lived in this time, said the Gregangel softly, *and her brothers and mother.* He paused. *Your daughter would have also suffered here.* Garrett tried to close his eyes, but since he lacked both eyes and eyelids, he failed.

Look there, said the Gregangel. Garrett saw that one of the male slaves had fallen to the ground. He looked sixty, but Garrett could tell that he was barely forty. A younger woman, perhaps his daughter, was shaking him. He was lying face down. Two of the overseers came over and knelt down next to him, forcing the young woman away. One of them placed a finger against his neck, checking for a pulse. A moment later, he shook his head.

The woman cried out. She lunged toward the fallen slave but was again pushed away by one of the overseers. The other overseer called two male slaves over. They spoke to them, motioning toward the edge of the unfinished canal. The two slaves grabbed the unfortunate man by both arms and dragged him to the edge. There, they left him, half-covered by the foliage.

Garrett was sickened by the sheer heartlessness of the overseers. They were not overly cruel. They were not beating the slaves or abusing them in any other way as far as he could see. What they were doing was much worse. A human can be cruel to another human, or an animal, but not a thing. The overseers did not see the slaves as anything other than property…cogs in a living bulldozer. One of the pieces had failed, so they merely discarded it and replaced it with another.

This is where it began, said Garrett, watching the slaves dig.

This is a beginning, said the Gregangel. *But it is not the beginning. Come.* Garrett followed the Gregangel up river until they came to a landing. From there, they followed a narrow dirt road until it ended at a stately colonial mansion. The mansion was two stories high and painted white. In the front, a wide porch ran the length of the structure and boasted half a dozen rocking chairs. Two older white women were sitting there, rocking slowly back and forth. They did not speak to each other, and their worried looks said that all was not right with their world. A balcony, devoid of either people or chairs, protruded from the second floor. It was supported by four equally spaced white columns. The mansion spoke clearly of aristocratic southern wealth, built the backs of men, women and children who were considered nothing more than property.

Look closer, said the Gregangel, as if reading Garrett's thoughts. Garrett did and saw that all was not as it appeared. The signs of decay were nearly hidden, but they were there. The paint was fading and peeling, and in many places the wood was rotting. The roof sagged in at least two places, and one of the porch steps was held in place by a large rock.

Just behind the mansion to the left was a long low building that held several stables, and next to that was a large, two story barn. Like the mansion, they were showing signs of neglect. Several dozen slaves milled about. Some were working with the livestock, but most seemed to be looking for something to do. All of them cast worried glances toward the mansion.

With his enhanced sight, Garrett could easily see past both barn and stables to the cotton fields beyond. The fields were deserted, and although he had no real knowledge of farming, he could easily see that the cotton was neglected. Weeds grew everywhere, choking the life out of the plants.

These were the last days of Gamble's plantation, said the Gregangel.

We moved in time again, said Garrett. *From the canal, I mean.*

It now stands empty, said the Gregangel. *A monument to both Gamble's ego and foolishness. Come.* He led Garrett up to the second floor. They passed through an open window into a large, ornate bedroom. A wide four poster brass bed sat in the center of the room. On it was a dying man. A second man, obviously a doctor, hovered above him. The dying man motioned feebly, ordering the doctor away. The doctor started to argue, but another gesture cut him off. Garrett could see that there was no love lost between the two men. The doctor grabbed his black bag off the floor and left, closing the door behind him. The dying man…Garrett knew without asking that it was John Gamble…tried to sit up but failed. He lay on his expensive bed, gasping for breath.

Garrett stared at the source of so much tragedy. He looked nothing like the picture Garrett had found online. There he had been a man in his prime, a wealthy and powerful conqueror. Here, he was a withered skeleton of a man. His eyes were dull and watery, his skin pale and pasty. A thin film of sweat covered his face, giving it an unnatural sheen.

But it was not the hollowed out shell of the man that filled Garrett's spirit with such loathing. The instant they entered the bedroom, he felt the dark power. It raged inside Gamble's body, and Garrett could see that it was both sustaining him and eating him alive. It was as if the dark power was some kind of spiritual scalpel, cutting away at his soul, hollowing him out. Garrett recoiled, but the Gregangel steadied him.

You must see, he said. *You must understand.* Garrett had a wild urge to tear himself free and flee back to his body. He knew that the Gregangel would not stop him, and that alone gave him the strength to stay. *Watch,* whispered the Gregangel. Gamble took a shallow, rasping breath, followed several seconds later by another. *This is where everything changed,* said the Gregangel. *This is where we ...I...failed.* Gamble's breathing was slowing, and Garrett understood that the end was close.

He died alone, he said.

Alone and un-mourned, said the Gregangel. Gamble took another breath. His chest shook, and even though there was no sound, Garrett fancied that he could hear the deep, wet rattle. Another breath…and another…and then nothing. Gamble's chest stopped moving. There was nothing else. His head did not fall to one side nor did his hands slide off the bed. He simply stopped living.

Watch, said the Gregangel again. *And remember, I have you. Nothing here can harm you.*

I don't like the sound of that, said Garrett.

Nevertheless, you must see this. Something seeped out of Gamble's body, something both real and ethereal. It rose a few inches into the air and hovered, a shapeless mist.

His soul, said the Gregangel. *Here is everything John Gamble was…his memories, his thoughts, his feelings, his very consciousness.* The mist moved back and forth, as if trying to find its way. Then it began to rise, and as it rose, it faded.

Suddenly the dark power still seething in Gamble's body reacted. Tendrils shot out. Garrett could not help but remember how it had cocooned Andie and Erica in the canal. The tendrils grabbed Gamble's soul, immobilizing it.

Aiieeeee! The scream tore out of Gamble's soul. Garrett was not able to hear the sounds of Gamble's physical world, but this he heard all too well. It grew and grew until he felt as if his own spirit would shatter into billions of microscopic shards that would be scattered throughout eternity.

Watch, commanded the Gregangel. Garrett struggled, once again fighting the nearly overwhelming urge to flee. Then, mercifully, the scream faded. The tendrils of dark power wrapped themselves around Gamble's soul and dragged it back into his body. Garrett could only watch in horror as Gamble's body jerked. The thin arms flailed, and the bony legs kicked off the expensive silk sheet.

He gave himself to the dark power long ago, said the Gregangel. *Now he has to pay the price for his idiocy.* Images flashed through Garrett's mind; a boy of sixteen standing tall and proud in the cotton fields. He was the lord of his domain, and the world lay at this feet. The image shifted to a young man of twenty-five, assuming the ownership of his father's plantation. He would marry and have children, not only with his wife but with several of his female slaves, many of whom would barely be old enough to menstruate. The young man disappeared and was replaced by the same man in his thirties. This version conferred with his business partners, making plans to expand their empire. Garrett could see the first seeds of darkness worming their way into Gamble's soul.

Did he know? asked Garrett. *Did he understand?*

Not at first, said the Gregangel. *He was a natural leader, with the ability to both persuade and dominate.*

The dark power enhanced these abilities and made him one of the most powerful men in the region. When he finally understood, he welcomed that power. It became a part of him.

How? asked Garrett.

The Gamblemonster revealed itself to him in a vision. It offered Gamble more of everything he had, and the fool accepted.

A deal with the devil, muttered Garrett.

I understand the reference, said the Gregangel. *It is something that has nearly destroyed your race, and it is my fault…mine as well as the others.*

Others?

In a moment, said the Gregangel. *Watch.* Garrett saw that Gamble…now the Gamblemonster…had left the bedroom and was making its way down the spiral staircase to the foyer below. He did not lurch or shamble like the zombies Garrett has seen in dozens of horror movies. The dark power knew Gamble's body intimately, and the unseen puppeteer pulled the strings effortlessly.

The Gamblemonster reached the main floor, pushed open the double front doors and stepped through them. Startled, the two old women jumped to their feet. They stared at the man they thought they knew. One of the women put her hands to her mouth, while the other took a step backward. They did not know what was coming toward them, but both of them instinctively knew that it was not John Gamble.

The Gamblemonster's right fist flew out, connecting with the first woman's throat, instantly crushing it. She went down in a heap. The second woman started to scream, but the Gamblemonster was on her in an instant. His hands went around her neck. Seconds later, they went through her neck. Blood spurted from her mouth as well as her shattered throat. She gagged once and then went limp. The Gamblemonster threw her aside, turned and studied the first woman. She was still alive, although her face had turned blue from lack of air. The Gamblemonster aimed a vicious kick into her stomach, and even though there was no sound, Garrett fancied he could hear her brittle spine shatter.

The Gamblemonster stepped over her. Some of the slaves were just now focusing their attention on the porch. Garrett could see their faces register surprise, shock and horror in rapid succession as they realized what was happening. Some of the men started toward the Gamblemonster as it moved off the porch and into the front yard, but when they saw the old man's face, they stopped short. A few turned to run, but it was too late.

Tentacles of the dark power, invisible in the physical world but all too visible to Garrett, shot out from the belly of the Gamblemonster. Each one found and entered a slave. Those who tried to run stopped short. The Gamblemonster did not even spare them a second look. He started down the long path to the river, and as one, the slaves fell in behind him.

Come, whispered the Gregangel.

Why? demanded Garrett. *I get it. Gamble was consumed by the dark power. He dragged these slaves back to the canal. He's there now.*

Yes, said the Gregangel.

Then why...

Because you need to understand exactly what the dark power is. You need to know how to fight it, said the Gregangel. Again Garrett felt the Gregangel's shame.

What else? he demanded.

You need to witness our great crime, said the Gregangel. *You need to understand how we destroyed the world that should have been yours.*

Chapter 20

History Lesson, Part 2

here are we going? asked Garrett.

To another beginning. It will be difficult for you. It will, in fact, be difficult for me. It is always painful to relive past sins. Will you come with me?

Yes, said Garrett, feeling a little like Scrooge in the presence of the Ghost Of Christmas Past. Suddenly he was catapulted upward. The mansion fell away, followed by Florida, and seconds later, the Earth itself. At first, Garrett thought that they were going to hover above the planet, the way he had with Molly. Instead, they kept going.

The stars exploded in a blaze of light, burning with a multitude of colors...blue, white, red, purple and yellow. Entire solar systems hurtled toward him, only to disappear behind them. He drew in his senses, wrapping them tight around his spirit. Seen firsthand, the sheer size of the cosmos was beyond overwhelming. Faster and faster they flew, until suddenly the stars disappeared.

Cast your senses behind, said the Gregangel. Garrett did and saw the pinwheel shape of what he could only assume was his own galaxy growing smaller and smaller. In a heartbeat, it was nothing more than a dull point of light. It was joined a moment later by another and another and still another, until there were thousands…millions…*billions* of them.

Those aren't stars, said Garrett. *They're galaxies.*

Every one of them, said the Gregangel. *Look ahead. We are nearly at the end of our journey.* Garrett cast his gaze forward.

This new galaxy filled the black void of space, rising impossibly high above him. His vision blurred and everything seemed to wobble as he experienced an almost physical sensation of vertigo. Like his own, it was pinwheel shaped, with at least six arms spiraling out from a central hub, but that was where the similarities ended. His galaxy had been filled living stars. This galaxy boasted a few glowing points of light but spread across each arm were great splotches of red and black. It seemed as if a great, malignant cancer was devouring it from the inside out.

It's…diseased, he asked.

It's dying, replied the Gregangel. *It has been dying for countless eons.*

This is where you come from, said Garrett.

No, said the Gregangel. The decaying husk of the galaxy rushed toward them, and suddenly they were surrounded by dead and dying stars. With the help of his companion, Garrett was able to sense the galaxy in its entirety. It was as if he had become a giant capable of walking among the stars, regarding them the way a child might regard Christmas lights hanging from a ceiling. Another time and place, it would have been an exhilarating experience. Now all he wanted was to be small again. There was something very wrong here, and that wrongness pulsed at him from every direction.

What happened here? This isn't...natural.

War, answered the Gregangel. *It was a terrible, unimaginable, devastating war.* Garrett squeezed his senses even tighter. Even wrapped in the Gregangel's unbreakable hold, he felt exposed and vulnerable. Whatever destroyed this galaxy still existed, and it was still powerful. *All this happened long ago,* said the Gregangel

It's still here though, said Garrett, meaning the menacing force.

Yes, said the Gregangel. *And it is still dangerous, even for me. We must be very careful.*

Is this now? asked Garrett. *Is this what it looks like in my time?*

Yes, said the Gregangel. *Now prepare yourself.* Garrett laughed at the absurd command.

How am I supposed to prepare myself for any of this?

As best you can, said the Gregangel. *Watch.* The dead stars shimmered. Garrett gasped as they burst to life, first one at a time, then thousands and then millions. They spun around him in patterns so complex that he could not begin to decipher them. The black and red cancer receded until it disappeared completely. It took Garrett long moments, but he finally understood what was happening.

How far back are we going?

Billions upon billions of your years, said the Gregangel. *Even in your expanded state, you cannot*

comprehend the depth of time and space that we are traversing. Garrett was not inclined to argue. The stars swarmed about them moving faster and faster. Then they began to slow until finally they stopped. Garrett felt the Gregangel's hold on him loosen. *Open your mind,* he said. Hesitant at first, Garrett nevertheless did as he was told. He reached out and stared in wonder at the now vibrant galaxy.

It's...alive, he whispered. *It's all alive.*

Yes, said the Gregangel. *Millions of worlds holding uncounted billions of lives, each a unique and irreplaceable spark.*

I can feel them, but...there's more. Garrett felt the Gregangel's approval.

Go on, he said. He released his hold on Garrett, letting him fly free. Garrett soared in the emptiness of space, expanding his senses out in an ever widening pattern. The fertile smell, the feel, the *texture* of life nearly intoxicated him. He reached further and further, until...

I can feel....I... Suddenly, he hesitated. He floundered, recovered, reached out again, and screamed. In an instant he drew his senses back into himself, wrapping them around his spirit like a heavy cloak. It wasn't until he felt the comforting arms of the Gregangel return that he managed to collect himself.

What did you sense? asked the Gregangel. Garrett shook a nonexistent head.

I don't...know, he whispered. *It was...too big.* He opened his senses just wide enough so that he could see the Gregangel. The old man was regarding him with an expression that held both envy and pity. His insight flared. *You don't know either,* he said. The Gregangel nodded.

As you say, it's too big…even for us.

It's alive, said Garrett. *It's like…the entire galaxy is a living being.*

Garrett, said the Gregangel, and now there was infinite sadness in his voice, *it's all alive. Your physical body is an entire universe unto itself, with galaxies of particles too small to be measured even by my people, let alone your own primitive science. The further in you go, the bigger you become. Likewise, the further out you go, the more there is to discover. Space is infinite in both directions.*

I touched a mind, said Garrett. *It…it…*

Don't try it again, warned the Gregangel. *It would destroy you. As I said, it's too big. For the sake of a label, call it the Galactic Mind.*

Is my own galaxy…?

Yes, said the Gregangel. *It is as alive as this one.*

Why have you brought me here?

To see this, said the Gregangel. The old man pointed, and Garrett followed the withered finger. He stared into the living light of the stars.

Space split open. A jagged rip tore across the blackness, racing across the galaxy with the speed of thought. From within the rip came a blazing, diseased green light that Garrett remembered all too well. He had seen it in his wife's eyes the night his daughter died. He had seen it in the bowels of the earth when that same daughter had penetrated the veil between life and death. His spirit quailed.

Open your senses, said the Gregangel.

No, said Garrett. *I can't.*

You must, said the Gregangel, *or this is all in vain.* It was the urgency in his guide's voice that made Garrett obey, not the command itself. He expanded his sight, watching as the rip tore across the very fabric of reality. Thousands of stars were in its path. They were destroyed in an instant. Billions of lives winked out, their worlds incinerated, but that was not the worst. Garrett's mind rang with another scream, one that threatened to blast him into oblivion. It was a scream of mortally wounded being. He knew at once who…what…it was.

The Galactic Mind, he gasped and felt the Gregangel's agreement.

Here, in this time and place, is where this galaxy died, he said. *It took billions of years for it to end completely, but this is where the real death happened. From this moment on, nothing could save it.* Garrett could only watch as something that happened so long ago that he could not comprehend it continued to play itself out. From the jagged rip, the green power continued to pour out. Unhindered by either time or space, it blasted a million worlds, and again countless billions died.

And there was war in heaven, said the Gregangel.

What? gasped Garrett, staring at the obscene destruction spreading out before him.

Something from one of your holy books, said the Gregangel. *It speaks of a great war between good and evil. I believe that that passage is an echo of a memory…a memory of this terrible tragedy. You would be amazed at how many other worlds have records that speak of the same thing.*

Is that what this was? asked Garrett. *A war in heaven…a war between good and evil?* The Gregangel did not reply. The tear widened, and the green light continued to pour out, destroying everything in its path. Garrett forced his senses away from the terrible spectacle and focused his attention onto the Gregangel.

When he saw the anguish etched into the ancient face, he faltered. His senses wavered for a moment. Then he managed to steady himself.

We thought so, said the Gregangel at last. Garrett flinched as the grief in his voice. *We waged our war in our own reality, so certain that we were on the side of good. Those we fought wanted to destroy us. They hated us with every fiber of their being. After a while though, the war seemed to take on a life of its own. It was as if we were both goaded by something else. In the end...*

You destroyed each other, said Garrett. He was surprised when the Gregangel shook his head.

No, he said. *We won. We defeated our enemies, but our own reality was nearly destroyed, and the power we used blasted a hole into your universe. This is the result.* Garrett turned his senses back to the tear. It was still expanding, but at a slower rate. As he watched, it stopped, an unimaginably long, glowing jagged wound hanging in space. A question formed in his mind.

In your world...your reality...were you like us?

You mean did we once exist in what you think of as the physical realm? said the Gregangel. *I honestly don't know. If we did, that knowledge is lost to us, and our memory reaches back billions of years even before this tragedy.*

Garrett could not think of a reply to this. Cautiously, he opened his senses again. He flinched at the vile, searing heat coming from the tear, but the Gregangel shielded him. All along the tear he could see enormous dust clouds glowing in its light. The green refracted into a rainbow of deep blues, purples, yellows and pinks. Garrett found it obscene that a holocaust of such magnitude should be marked by such stunning beauty.

He expanded his sight and saw the other worlds, the worlds that had been in the path of the green light. Some of them were already dead, and others were dying. He could almost hear their screams of agony, and he realized that those who had been blasted into dust were perhaps the lucky ones.

I want to go home, he whispered. Suddenly he was overwhelmed by grief, not only for the unimaginable loss of life, but for his own loss as well.

Soon, said the Gregangel, *but there is more to see*.

I can't, moaned Garrett. *It's just too big. Nobody should have to endure this. Please, take me back.*

I will Garrett, but you must understand why I brought you here. It is the only way you can defeat the Gamblemonster. And understand this...you must defeat him. Garrett suddenly understood.

He's one of yours, he said, whirling on the Gregangel. *It's wasn't just some kind of impersonal dark power that consumed Gamble. It was one of your enemies. How? How is that possible?* The old man gestured toward the tear.

Watch, he said. The green power was still pouring out, only now there was something else coming through. Garrett frowned mentally and looked closer. *This is what you need to see...what you need to understand*, said the Gregangel.

Your enemies, said Garrett. *They escaped through the tear.*

Some of them, said the Gregangel.

How many?

By your count, hundreds of billions, said the Gregangel. *They came into this reality and scattered.*

And you followed, said Garrett.

Yes, said the Gregangel. *Along with many of my own forces. We pursued them here, tracked them down and fought them. Watch.* The stars began to move again, and Garrett understood that they were moving in time, only now they were going forward. *The conflict in this galaxy alone lasted another billion years. By then, there was not much left. We tried to protect it, but in the end, everything died.* They stopped again.

All around him, Garrett could see the war raging. Energies capable of setting a universe on fire were hurled across unimaginable distances. With every attack, a few of those who had escaped through the rip in space were destroyed, but at the same time entire worlds died. He could not see the combatants, but watching the devastating effects of their war was more than enough. He looked away.

This is what you call 'greatly weakened', he whispered.

I could not show you the war in my own realm, replied the Gregangel. *Even I could not protect you. It would obliterate your soul.* He gestured to the ongoing battle. *You understand now*, he said.

All too well, said Garrett. *One of your enemies found my world.*

More than one, said the Gregangel. *We fought them across your universe, through galaxy after galaxy, and slowly we gained the advantage.* The Gregangel moaned softly. *But the cost*, he whispered, *the terrible cost. Thousands of worlds got caught in the crossfire. Most of them were utterly destroyed, but in the end, we beat them. They scattered and fled, hiding on a million worlds.* He paused, watching the destruction play itself out. Garrett thought that he was done, but after a moment he spoke again.

When the fighting finally ended, we took stock, he said. *The tear sealed itself, but of course the damage was done. The war had spread to thousands of other galaxies, including yours. The damage to them was horrific, but at least it was not catastrophic. They still lived.*

Tell that to the people caught in the middle, snapped Garrett. The Gregangel whirled suddenly on Garrett, his eyes blazing. Garrett flinched away from his anger.

I do not need you to damn me, he said, his voice cold steel. *I am already damned by my own hand.* Garrett opened his mouth to say 'I'm sorry', but abruptly realized that he was just as angry as the Gregangel. He met that blazing gaze with one of his own.

What gave you the right to bring your war here? he demanded. *What gave you the right to end those lives, and what the HELL gives you the right to bring your mess to my world?* The two of them stared at each other for long seconds, but it was the Gregangel who looked away.

It was never meant to happen, he said. *We never wanted this.* Garrett held on to his anger a moment longer and then let it go. He could not afford it. Somewhere impossibly far away in both time and space, his wife, along with an innocent family, desperately needed his help. It was the single thing that anchored him in the madness he was witnessing. He could understand the fact at billions had died in the Gregangel's war, but he could not feel it. Like the Galactic Mind, it was too big. What he could understand was that his wife and friends needed him.

So what now? The Gregangel looked back at him.

You've seen the tapestry in its whole, he said. *Now you need to see one tiny part of it. Will you follow me for just a little longer?*

Can I get home by myself? asked Garrett sarcastically. The Gregangel shook his head.

No, he said simply.

Then lead on, spirit, lead on, said Garrett, once again mimicking Scrooge. The Gregangel reached out and for the last time wrapped Garrett in his strong arms. They began to move. The dead galaxy fell away, much to his relief, and once again they were hurtling through the vast gulf that lay beyond. The field of galaxies before them began to drift apart, and a moment later, one of them began to grow larger. Garrett recognized it as his home galaxy. Somewhere, circling one of those tiny glowing points of light was a beautiful blue and green world. There, a riverboat that had no right to exist was making its way toward a creature that had lived for far too long.

The pinwheel of stars rushed toward them until it swallowed them whole. Countless planets zoomed past them until at last they hovered above one single world. Garrett looked down, thinking that they had returned to Earth, but when he saw a single, unfamiliar continent, he felt a surge of disappointment.

That's not my world, he said.

Yes, it is, said the Gregangel. *I have brought you home.* Garrett stared at the planet below. Only a single large round landmass, completely surrounded by water, was visible. Garrett's insight flashed.

This is still the past, he said.

Yes, said the Gregangel. *But it is the much more recent past, as far as your world is concerned. We are less than ten thousand years away from your present.*

Only ten thousand years, whispered Garrett.

Open your senses, said the Gregangel. *Understand the final act of this tragedy.* Garrett looked down at the spinning globe, marveling at its beauty. The single ocean was a deep, pure blue, and he knew without knowing how he knew that it was filled with fresh, not salt water. There was no brown on the land, only lush shades of green. The sky was clear. No cloud patterns dotted the globe. Taking a deep mental breath, Garrett did as the Gregangel asked. He opened his senses.

Oh my God, he whispered. He reached out non-existent arms, wanting nothing more than to wrap the entire planet in a hug.

This is what should have been yours, said the Gregangel. Energy, pure and powerful, exploded out from the surface. It was the energy of life itself. Garrett wanted to bathe in it. He drank it in, marveling at its taste and texture. It felt warm and comforting, cool and exhilarating, hot and erotic, all at the same time.

It felt like home.

This is your birthright, said the Gregangel.

The power I'm feeling... began Garrett.

Is the power of life, said The Gregangel. *I told you before, that everything is alive, including your world. What you are feeling is its own life force...its soul.*

This power, said Garrett, *is it everywhere...on other worlds, I mean?*

Not like this, said the Gregangel. *It is, in fact, incredibly unique. It is as if its very soul sustains and unites your people.*

Earth...soul, said Garrett. It felt right.

A good name, agreed the Gregangel. *There is more. Come and see.* Together they sank through the atmosphere. As the continent grew larger, he began to see it in greater detail.

That's…that's not possible, he said.

On the contrary, it is not only possible, it is the truth, said the Gregangel. Despite the power he felt…the earthsoul…Garrett had expected to find humanity dwelling in caves, hunting in packs, perhaps forming the beginnings of a rudimentary society.

The approaching city blew that assumption into so many pieces that he would never be able to put it back together. It gleamed like crystal under an intense blue sky; its buildings stretching upward to reach heights no architect could dare dream. Many ended in long spires that tapered to impossibly sharp points.

Every building looked as if it had been carved out of a single diamond. Wide streets were paved with a milky white stone that was streaked with blues, reds and yellows. The buildings themselves, if they could even be called buildings, were of every shape and size. Each one stood alone as a magnificent work of art, and yet each one was a part of an intricate pattern.

Looking at the city as a whole, Garrett could see circles, triangles, squares, tetrahedrons, and a thousand other shapes, each one a vital part of that pattern. The blazing sunlight struck the buildings, refracting into every possible color. Even in his disembodied state, he felt the need to squint at the intensity of the light.

The city itself did not occupy a great deal of land. Its advantage in space lay in its height, not its breadth. It was surrounded by a thick green forest that was divided by wide roads leading away in every direction. Garrett could not help but notice that the city had not merely ploughed the forest under to make room. There was green everywhere, from the impossibly tall trees that seemed to grow right out of the milky pavement to the vines that wrapped around many of the buildings. Somehow the city planners had managed to design and maintain a true balance with nature. The city and the forest existed in perfect harmony.

Let's take a closer look, said the Gregangel, and Garrett eagerly agreed. They descended between two buildings, giving Garrett the opportunity to study them in greater detail. He could not see through the walls...not entirely at least. He could detect shapes moving within, but they were blurred. There were no windows, and he wasted a moment wondering how the people inside managed to get fresh air. Then he wrote the question off as foolish. A people brilliant enough to fashion this city would certainly be able to figure out the air conditioning.

They reached the street, touching down on the glassy pavement. All about them the city's inhabitants moved to and fro. Garrett stared at them for long seconds and then looked at the Gregangel.

Are they... He could not bring himself to finish the question. The Gregangel could.

Human, he said. *These are your far distant ancestors.* Garrett stared some more. The adults were all tall...most of them well over six feet. They were all lean and graceful. Each step they took would have made the greatest dancers of his time weep with envy. Their complexions were clear. No blemishes marred their perfect beauty. Hair was, for the most part, kept short on both men and women, with shades running from blonde to jet black. Their skin was more uniform, ranging medium to dark brown, but Garrett could see that the color of the skin had nothing to do with race. There was in fact no race. Rather there was only a single race.

Staring at the faces of the city's citizens, Garrett could see traces of each and every ethnic group that populated his own time.

There was something else that Garrett found oddly disturbing. Something about these people was not quite right…or rather was not quite like the human race he knew so well. For long seconds, he could not put his finger on what bothered him. Then it hit him. Everyone looked young. Each and every adult seemed to be in the prime of both life and health. There was no gray hair or wrinkles or any other sign of aging.

Where are the old folks? he asked.

You're looking at them, said the Gregangel. *At this point in their development, the lifespan of these first humans was over a thousand years, and even at the end of their lives, they did not show their age…at least not in the way you would recognize it.* Garrett stared some more. He could see now that no one wore a look of stress or anger or worry or any other negative emotion. They certainly seemed to be focused, going to and fro with an air of purpose, but they also appeared to be quite contented.

There is more to see, said the Gregangel. *Come.* They flew out of the city into the forest. A moment later they came upon tilled fields, laid out in neat, orderly squares. *There was no need here for any type of artificial watering,* said the Gregangel. *The entire continent floated on a thick layer of highly pressurized water. Whatever was planted grew in abundance.* Realization hit Garrett like a runaway train.

This is Eden, he whispered.

Yes, said the Gregangel. *No war, no famine…just people living in perfect harmony. By this time, humanity had been thriving on this world over a million years.*

You see them here at the pinnacle of their success. Soon, if they had been left alone, they would have begun to reach out to the stars. Suddenly Garrett's non-existent gut clenched. If this was Eden, then...

The serpent, he said, turning his full attention onto the Gregangel.

Serpents, he corrected. *Many of them fled to your world. See for yourself.* Garrett turned his attention back to the magnificent world, just in time to see fire rain from the heavens. He cried out in agony as millions of acres of the lush fields were destroyed in an instant. *By this time, both we and our enemies were so weakened that we could barely fight,* said the Gregangel. *That is why your world was not destroyed outright.* Garrett could only watch as the final stages of the war ravaged his world. Fields and forests burned. The cities melted with heat that rivaled the sun.

Come, said the Gregangel. Stunned, Garrett obeyed. They shot upward until, as before, they were hovering above the planet. Now, continent sized clouds of smoke obscured his view. The land burned, and the seas boiled. He groaned. How could anyone survive? *Here is the end,* said the Gregangel.

There was a flash of deep green light. It formed into a thin, jagged line that streaked across the vertical axis of the continent. The entire planet seemed to shudder. Then, the continent split into five pieces and broke apart.

That's not possible, he said.

I told you that the land rested on a layer of pressurized water, said the Gregangel. *Think of throwing a rock across an ice covered pond.* The five pieces flew away, sliding on that layer of water. The ocean boiled as geysers, hundreds of miles wide, erupted. Again the planet shuddered, only now it began to tilt. The water that was shot high into the atmosphere began to pour down.

Then, as suddenly as they started, the pieces slammed to a halt. The land buckled and wrinkled, and Garrett realized that he was seeing the creation of the world he knew. Mountains were born in an instant, as were the new oceans, rivers and seas.

They tried to destroy everything to shield their escape, said the Gregangel. *But we stopped them.* Garrett stared at the destruction below him.

How could anyone survive that?

We saved as many as we could, said the Gregangel, *along with a few other species...not all, but many...enough so that your race would survive for at least a while. But there was one thing we could not save.* Garrett focused his senses and after a moment, moaned.

The earthsoul is gone, he cried.

Not entirely, said the Gregangel. *But yes, we killed the soul...the consciousness...of your world...the one single power that bound your race together. Since this time, you have been living on a dying world. Worse, your race has grown small and weak and divided. Soon, I fear, it will disappear entirely.* Below them the shattered globe began to spin faster. They were once again moving in time. He watched as the poles formed and weather patterns began to dot the atmosphere.

Here, said the Gregangel as they stopped again. *For one final time, Garrett, cast your senses below.* Numb from what he had witnessed, both in the dead galaxy as well as the destruction of his own paradise, Garrett obeyed. He saw what the Gregangel wanted him to see immediately.

You caught them, he said.

And imprisoned them, said the Gregangel, *using a remnant of what you call Earthsoul.* Garrett could sense the several domes dotting the now reformed Earth. There was the one he knew so well, in what would someday be called Florida. Garrett was not great with geography, but he could sense another in the west, perhaps Nevada. The rest were scattered across the other continents.

How long did it take?

Almost two thousand years to capture them all, said the Gregangel. *By then we were so weakened that we were no longer capable of the level of destruction you have witnessed. I was given the task of guarding what would become the Gamblemonster.*

I don't understand, said Garrett. *I saw your enemy trap Gamble's soul and take his body, but are you telling me that that has never happened before, in all the time you've been here?*

Of course it has happened, said the Gregangel. *Many of those you label conquerors, or murderers or monsters have been possessed by my enemies…not all, but many.*

Because their prisons are getting weaker, said Garrett.

Partially, said the Gregangel.

But there's more, spat Garrett. He snorted in disgust. *There's always more.*

Before we managed to capture them all, said the Gregangel, *They walked hidden among your people. They took bodies at will so that they could corrupt and cajole followers. They raised armies, leveled nations, burned cities…*

And?

And they used those bodies to breed, said the Gregangel. *They had children, and the descendants of those children walk the Earth today.* Garrett stared at the Gregangel, but before he could reply, they made their final time jump.

Chapter 21

Crash Course

*T*his time the shift was much shorter. When Garrett looked down again, he recognized his home. Half the globe was in darkness, alive with thousands of tiny points of artificial light. He was back in the world as he knew it. He stared at his shattered planet, thinking of Eden. Then he broke down, weeping non-existent tears for all that had been lost. The Gregangel said nothing, giving him time to grieve.

What else? he asked at last, turning his attention to the Gregangel. *There's more. I can feel it.*

Only a little, said the Gregangel.

I'm listening, said Garrett. He was beyond weary, but he could feel that the end was near.

You recently were...visited...by someone dear to you...someone you lost.

My daughter, said Garrett. *She was killed by the Gamblemonster.*

And yet she came to you, said the Gregangel.

Twice, said Garrett. *And it was real. I know it.*

Indeed, said the Gregangel. *Her body was destroyed, but she still lived. She moved inward, but because of her great love for you, she managed to pierce the barrier behind her.*

Inward, said Garrett. *To where? Heaven?*

I...I don't know, said the Gregangel, grief lacing his voice. Garrett stared at the old man. The Gregangel nodded. *And now we come to the great tragedy of my race. We have existed in this form from time beyond time. Even we have no memory of our beginnings. We are immortal.* A sarcastic reply popped into Garrett's mind, something along the lines of 'sucks to be you', but suddenly he choked back the words. In a flash of insight, he got it.

You're trapped here, he said, staring at the old man, *just as you were trapped in your own reality.*

Yes, said the Gregangel. *We know, or at least believe, that there is much more to creation than this or any other physical universe. We believe that there are layers, Garrett, uncountable layers. When a mortal sheds his physical shell in this reality, his soul moves inward to a new life. Not only that, but as the soul moves inwards, he finds that each layer is far more wondrous than the last.*

Wait a minute, said Garrett. *I don't have any memories of a previous life. Some of my people claim to have lived before, but...*

You have no prior memories because you...and we...exist on the outermost layer, said the Gregangel. *As to those who think they remember, perhaps they are somehow 'remembering forward' to the next layer. Your daughter is proof that the barriers between layers can be pierced.* He smiled a sad smile. *You are just beginning your journey inward, Garrett. You have no idea how much I envy you. I would give everything I am to be able to journey inward, toward the center.*

And what's at the center? asked Garrett.

The true beginning, said the Gregangel, *the Source of all life. What else could there be?* Garrett pondered that, watching the globe below spin slowly. Then he looked back at the Gregangel.

That's what your war was all about, he said. The Gregangel nodded.

My enemies wanted our race to shed our immortality so that we could move inward en masse. They reasoned that the only way we could accomplish that was to destroy ourselves, and they took it upon themselves to make that happen, he said. *We opposed them. We did not know if we would move inward, or simply cease to exist. Here's a bitter truth about us, Garrett. The only thing we fear more than being trapped for eternity is the emptiness of oblivion.*

But you can die, said Garrett. *In your war, you must have had casualties.*

Yes, said the Gregangel, *although I have no idea whether or not those who were lost moved inward. For all I know, they simply ceased to exist.* Garrett felt a quiver of fear emanate off the Gregangel. It hit him that his companion was truly terrified of dying.

So you're not really immortal, said Garrett.

We can die, said the Gregangel. *But we are extremely hard to kill. It takes a staggering amount of our power and a great deal of time. The backlash alone has already destroyed far too many worlds.*

Your enemies…that's why they took human bodies, said Garrett.

Yes, said the Gregangel. *It allowed them to escape their prison, but there was more. They took on the limitations of their hosts. They suddenly possessed a lifespan that…to us…lasted no longer than a puff of smoke caught in a stiff breeze. They became mortal, and they died.*

Did it work? asked Garrett. *Were they able to move inward?*

Again, I don't know, but I can tell you this. The souls of those whose bodies they stole were utterly destroyed.

No, Garrett groaned. *Melody.*

Now you see the real danger for her, said the Gregangel. *You are not just fighting for your mate's life, but for her very existence.* Garrett's heart surged. He suddenly wanted to charge down to the earth below, reclaim his body, find the Gamblemonster and rip it apart. He would have done so, but he was hindered by the simple fact that he had no idea how to do it. Something the Gregangel said earlier popped into his mind.

When we were watching John Gamble die, he said, *you said that this was where everything changed, but you also said that others had taken human bodies before. What made this different?*

The difference is what you think of as the dark power, said the Gregangel. *Do you know what it is?*

A remnant of the power you used in your war, replied Garrett. *What else could it be?* The Gregangel did not reply. Garrett thought about it. *I've always perceived your power, and the power of the Gamblemonster, as green*, he said slowly. *When it poured through the tear and even back at the canal, when it healed me. Now that I think of it, it was the same color as the power I saw in Melody's eyes.*

Keep going, said the Gregangel. *You're almost there, and I promise you, this is the last.*

The power that nearly destroyed us in the canal, said Garrett. *I saw it as black.* He looked hard at the Gregangel. *It's not the same power, is it? It's not even the same power Gamble used on Melody...or me. It's different.*

Yes, said the Gregangel. *Reach out to your world as it is now, Garrett. You can sense that power. What do you feel?* Garrett opened his senses, focusing them down to where the canal lay. He found a great pool of the dark power immediately. It festered deep below the canal. He flinched. The stuff was vile, but he managed to study it. A moment later, it came to him.

I've felt that before, he said slowly, *or at least something like it, in Eden.* He looked at the Gregangel, and the old man returned his gaze. *It's earthsoul, isn't it?* The Gregangel nodded.

It was earthsoul. Now it is something else. Call it darksoul. That is what the Gamblemonster changed, he said. *He did not just steal Gamble's body. He used a corrupted form of earthsoul to take it. He merged with both Gamble's body and the darksoul. In a very real sense, he became a child of earth...a bastard child, to be sure, but a child of your world nonetheless.* Garrett's mind was spinning. He tried to sort out the magnitude of information he had been fed since leaving his body. An ancient war, a devastated galaxy, a dying world, a bloodline of humanity spawned by powerful ancient beings...he tried to fit the pieces together. For a moment, he despaired. There was too much, and it was too big. Then something clicked in his mind. He grabbed the thought and held on to it.

He's going to destroy the remaining earthsoul, he said at last.

No, said the Gregangel. *He is going to corrupt it using his own power. He will bend it to his will and turn it into darksoul. It has taken him thousands of years, but with the help of his bloodline, he has managed to corrupt a great deal of it already, and it is his intention to corrupt it all.*

Why? asked Garrett. *What can he hope to gain?*

We used earthsoul to construct his prison, said the Gregangel. *He will use the darksoul to destroy that prison. Then he will free his brethren. They will be powerful enough to destroy the few of us that remain. After that…*

A vision flared in Garrett's mind; The Gregangel's enemies freed from their prisons and empowered with darksoul. They would destroy their jailors and then turn their attention to the humanity. Their descendants would flock to them, eagerly offering themselves as living sacrifices. They would invade the bodies and destroy the souls. Then, being mortal, they would set out to end their war once and for all.

They're going to burn my world, gasped Garrett. He could see them with their legions of human followers, mad with darksoul, spreading across the globe, an unstoppable plague.

Yes, said the Gregangel. *They will release the darksoul in one great burst, destroying your world and releasing their bastardized souls to travel inward. At least, that is what they believe. A moment ago I said that you are fighting for your mate's soul, but as you have already seen, you are fighting for much more than that.*

Garrett's mind reeled. Here was something else that was

too big. He could not meet it head on. He tried another tack.

But why has the Gamblemonster kept his hold on Melody's family all these generations? he asked instead. *And why just the women?*

He feeds off their souls, replied the Gregangel. *They are of his bloodline...not just descendants of John Gamble, but descendants of my enemies as well. He can compel them to come to him, but soon he will not need them. Because of his prison, he is trapped in Gamble's body. Once he is free, he will not be bound by that limitation. He will discard Gamble...and his line...once and for all. As to why only the women, there is still some form of Gamble's mind left in the Gamblemonster, and although it is in no way alive, it wields some small influence. From what I understand, John Gamble liked his women.* Garrett was approaching overload again.

You can't put the fate of the world on me, he said softly. *I'm not that big...nobody is.*

No, you are not, said the Gregangel compassionately.

I just want to save my wife, said Garrett.

To do that, you must destroy the Gamblemonster, said the Gregangel. *And if you do that, you will save your world.*

But there are others, said Garrett. *Even if I could somehow destroy the Gamblemonster, it won't stop them.*

The Gamblemonster is the only one of them who has learned to corrupt the earthsoul, said the Gregangel. *You are correct, of course. It will not stop the rest, but it may take thousands of years for them to discover what the Gamblemonster knows. Leave that battle for another generation, Garrett. Destroy the Gamblemonster. That will be enough.*

I can't do it, said Garrett. *Not alone.*

But you are not alone. I will be with you, and you will have the man and woman of faith at your side.

Greg and Andie? But what good can any of us do? I've seen the power of the Gamblemonster. This is your fight.

Reach out to your world Garrett one final time, said the Gregangel. *There you will find your answer. But hurry. Our time grows short.* Garrett had a strong impulse to argue, but instead he focused his senses down to the planet below. He felt the darksoul, throbbing like a malignant tumor deep under the earth. He flinched away, wondering just what the Gregangel wanted him to see.

Look away from the corruption, whispered the Gregangel. *See that all is not lost.* Garrett scanned deeper and deeper, until...

Oh...

You see it, said the Gregangel.

It's still here, cried Garrett. *I guess it had to be...the Gamblemonster couldn't have corrupted it all, but I had no idea that there was so much left.* The earthsoul lay deep within the earth, flowing sluggishly through narrow arteries or pooling in deep, hidden caches that existed both in and out of the physical realm. Garrett thought back to what he had sensed in Eden. Compared to that, this earthsoul was miniscule. But it was there, and it was pure.

Is it enough? Won't Gamble just corrupt it and use it against us?

The Gamblemonster is a usurper, said the Gregangel. *What he uses, he uses by force. The earthsoul is yours by right of birth. You already have a connection to it, even if you are not consciously aware of it. You're experience in the canal has deepened that connection.* It took Garrett a moment to realize what the Gregangel was saying.

The power I used to free Andie and Erica, he said slowly. *That was pure, uncorrupted earthsoul. I knew it was different from your power, but with everything going in, I just assumed that you somehow gave it to me.*

I could not give you my own power, said the Gregangel. *Even in my weakened state, it would have destroyed you. And just as I cannot give you what is mine, neither can I give you what is already yours. I merely acted as a conduit, and even that small act injured me. My power is not meant for you, nor is yours for me. It was you and you alone who wielded it so effectively. You will do so again.*

But you said it yourself ...your people are very hard to kill, and it takes a great deal of time and power, said Garrett. *In case you haven't noticed, I don't have a lot of either.*

But it's your power Garrett, said the Gregangel. *It belongs to you, not the Gamblemonster.* Another memory flared in Garrett's mind. He thought back to the night the Gamblemonster had tortured him...the night he had lost decades of his life.

Gamble said that I didn't know how to use what was mine, he said slowly.

He was right, of course, said the Gregangel. *You did not know how to use the earthsoul, and so you used your own life force. It nearly destroyed you.*

But how did he reach out to me when he's imprisoned?

Through your wife, of course, said the Gregangel. *The two of you share a bond that goes far beyond the physical realm. When the Gamblemonster forced your wife to come to him, he was able to use that bond to warn you to stay away.* Garrett stared hard at the Gregangel.

What happened the night my daughter died? What really happened?

The Gamblemonster attempted to escape, said the Gregangel. *It was not his first attempt, but he came closer than ever before. I barely managed to stop him, but even then, the damage was done. His prison was weakened, and the damage to the physical realm...*

I know what happened, snapped Garrett. *I was there.* The Gregangel nodded.

Your mate acted differently after that, did she not?

She left me, snapped Garrett.

Because of the Gamblemonster's hold on her, said the Gregangel. *She did not have a choice.* The old man smiled a sad smile. *As terrible as that is, you can take some comfort in it. She did not leave you willingly.*

Some comfort, repeated Garrett softly. The old man shook his head.

You've come a long way, Garrett. You have learned a great deal. Believe me when I tell you this; you stand a greater chance of destroying him than I and all of my brethren do. We cannot use the power of your world. The only way the Gamblemonster could use it was to corrupt it with the remnants of his own power. The Gregangel shook his head in honest wonder. *It's amazing, really. Even after all the damage we have caused your race, you still have the ability to bend the earthsoul to your will.* Garrett studied the pure earthsoul below him.

You didn't answer my question, he said. *Will it be enough?*

Garrett, I honestly do not know.

For someone who's lived so long, you seem not to know many things, said Garrett. He was aiming for sarcasm but could only manage wry humor.

Indeed, said the Gregangel in the same tone. *Amazing, isn't it? Are you ready?*

Wait a second. I need to...

We cannot, said the Gregangel. *Our time is gone. If we do not go now, all will be lost.*

But...

The Gregangel grabbed him, and an instant later they were plunging toward the surface. The sky flared from inky black to brilliant blue. The land rushed toward them. Despite everything he had experienced, Garrett felt buttocks that he did not possess clench. Then the Gregangel slowed their descent. The North American continent filled Garrett's vision, then the southeastern United States and finally Florida. The peninsula was bathed in warm sunlight. Garrett remembered that it had been early morning when they had been taken by the men of the Shamrock.

The land went from indistinct mottled greens and browns and blues to recognizable lakes, rivers, fields and forests. He could see cities, although after seeing the city of Eden, he knew that he would never think of them as true cities again. They passed through a thin layer of clouds and were momentarily blinded. When Garrett's vision cleared, he recognized the Aucilla River rushing toward them. There were the Warriors, even more mazelike when seen from above, and there, just emerging from the Warriors was the Shamrock. Garrett could feel the corrupted Earthsoul emanating from it like an acidic heat.

How did that thing make it out? he wondered. *We barely managed to get through in a canoe. For that matter, how did it get in?*

It is a thing only partially bound by time and space, said the Gregangel. *It must respect physical barriers, but it is not limited by them, just as it is not limited by the Gamblemonster's prison. Do you remember how you first tried to leave the canal? Even though you could see the way out, you knew that it was blocked.* Garrett wasted a moment pondering the concept and then shoved it aside as irrelevant. Instead, he turned his attention to the time. He noted that the sun was well up in the sky.

How much time has passed here?

Perhaps an hour, replied the Gregangel. *You must return to your body now. Already your physical life is draining away. The body cannot survive very long without the spirit to drive it.* Garrett grimaced at the memory of the Gregangel separating him from his body.

This is going to hurt, isn't it?

I'm afraid so, said the Gregangel. *Are you ready?*

Please stop asking me that, said Garrett.

No, said the Gregangel. *Come.* They swooped down to the Shamrock. Garrett's body was lying exactly where he had left it. Greg was lying next to him, still unconscious. Garrett could see that the preacher had sustained serious injuries from his beating at the hands of the Shamrock's crew. At the rail, Andie clung to her children, holding them tight. The Gamblemonster's men were scattered about both decks. A handful of them kept a watchful eye on their prisoners while the rest simply waited for the journey to be over. In the pilot house, the

Darksoul writhed and boiled. Garrett looked away and centered his attention on Greg.

Is he... he began.

No, said the Gregangel, anticipating his question. *Neither he nor his mate belongs to Gamble's line. However, I believe that they are not here by accident.*

What do you mean by that?

I mean that despite all of my knowledge, there are things that I do not understand, said the Gregangel. *You know this already. When I entered the man of faith, I felt a power within him that had nothing to do with earthsoul.*

What kind of power?

Somehow, through his faith, he has managed to touch something greater, said the Gregangel. *It is a power that does not recognize barriers or layers. It indwells him and gives his faith power. I believe that, if he is strong enough, this power will merge with the earthsoul and grow even more powerful. It will make him a formidable ally.* Garrett stared at the old man.

Are you talking about God? he asked.

You persist in asking me questions for which I have no answers. Now prepare yourself, Garrett. Garrett felt the Gregangel's arms enfold him. Then he was sinking into his body. He felt something surround him on all sides...another kind of barrier. It formed a sphere and began to shrink. Garrett screamed in pain. He thrashed about, lashing against the sphere, but it continued to push in on him. The Gregangel was not gentle. Garrett understood that the time for gentleness was long past.

The sphere contracted, growing smaller and smaller. Garrett screamed again, this time not only with pain but also with grief and loss. His marvelous senses were disappearing. One by one they grew dim and winked out. He sank into his body, and the Gregangel went to work.

Connections were patched together again, only now it was different. Underneath his agony, Garrett realized that his perception of his body would never be the same again. The Gregangel was a skilled surgeon, but for all his skill, he could not completely restore him. For the rest of his life, Garrett would see his physical shell as no more than a temporary dwelling that could be discarded at will.

And still the sphere closed in on him. He curled into a tiny ball. The sphere conformed itself to his spirit's shape and continued to shrink. He was crushed, compacted. The last of his expanded senses fell away, and darkness descended. The wonderful lightness that had allowed him to soar across the universe was replaced with an unbearable heaviness. He struggled some more, and suddenly he was suffocating.

Breathe, Garrett, said the Gregangel. His voice was faint.

Where are you? The searing pain eased, only to be replaced with an emptiness that was far worse. His intimate connection with the Gregangel was gone. He was truly alone.

Here, said the Gregangel from somewhere impossibly far away. *Breathe, Garrett. You need to breathe.* Garrett's chest heaved, but his lungs were frozen. He tried to gulp in the air, but they would not function.

I'm dying, he cried.

Yes, you are, said the Gregangel. *And if you die, your mate dies as well, only for her, there will be no journey inward. She will cease to exist, and you will have to move on without her. Now breathe, Garrett.*

BREATHE! The Gregangel's shout rang through his mind. Garrett heaved, and heaved again, and suddenly his lungs flared to life. Fire and ice poured into his chest. He choked, exhaled and gulped in another breath. More fire followed more ice, only now Garrett understood that it was ordinary, everyday air. He drew another breath, and another, until gradually it became easier. The air became warm and humid. His hearing returned, bringing with it the dull 'swoosh swoosh swoosh' of the Shamrock's paddlewheel accompanied by regular thrum of her steam engines. The heaviness grew, but now he recognized it as the physical presence of his own body.

His sense of touch returned, and with it, a multitude of aches and pains. He suddenly remembered that he had been shot, as well as soundly beaten by both the un-man and one of the Shamrock's crew. *Roy*, he thought. *His name is Roy.* He felt something flutter in the region of his (head? Yes, head) and understood that he now possessed both eyes and eyelids. It took him a moment to remember how to operate them. When he managed to get them halfway open, he saw that he was still lying on his side on the wooden deck. His right hand was next to his face, and he studied it. It was covered by some kind of vile dark paste, and he remembered that he had been sprayed with both Kyle and Reggie's blood.

The pain intensified. His jaw throbbed from Roy's repeated blows, and his mid-section burned from the un-man's ministrations. He tried to move but could only manage to make two of his fingers wobble. The sun was beating down, but he was freezing. His body had been in the process of shutting down. The Gregangel had pushed their time to the limit.

How am I supposed to get us out of this? he wondered, no longer certain if the Gregangel was listening. *I can barely move.* From somewhere now far away and yet very close, he heard the whisper of an answer.

Reach out to the earthsoul, said the Gregangel. *Do it now!*

Help me!

I cannot, said the Gregangel. *It would weaken me even further, and I have my own part to play in the coming battle.*

I can't feel it, said Garrett. *I'm stuck in this body, with these senses.*

No, you are not, said the Gregangel. *You already know this. I have returned you to your body, but your connection with it is far more tenuous. You still possess those senses that allowed you to see so much. They are filtered through your physical body, and thus considerably weaker, but they are there. Use them now.*

Garrett closed his eyes. He tried to reach out and discovered that he could. The Gregangel was right. All that he had gained while he was out of his body was still there. Those marvelous senses were still functioning, albeit at a greatly reduced level. He sent them out, feeling his way. He felt the dark power…the darksoul…infesting both the crew and the riverboat. It was still vile, and it was still powerful, but after all that he had witnessed, Garrett was no longer impressed. He ignored it and reached out further. There was the canal with the darksoul lurking far below. He edged past it, knowing instinctively that if he studied it too close, the Gamblemonster would sense him. Once it was behind him, he continued on, sending his senses deeper into the Earth.

Hurry.

You be quiet, snapped Garrett. He kept searching, until…

There, he said. It was as he remembered; a pool of uncorrupted power, hidden deep beneath the Earth.

Take it, said the Gregangel, only now his voice was weaker. *Save your mate.* Garrett moved close and reached out to the earthsoul. Amazed, he watched as it began to move toward him. It felt fresh and new, a distant echo of Eden. A threadlike tentacle wove its way through the Earth.

You will need much more, said the Gregangel, his voice even fainter now.

I said be quiet, snapped Garrett. He concentrated on the thread, trying to guide it. It weaved and wobbled. It seemed that the harder he tried, the more it resisted. Frustrated, he focused his will on the thread, but suddenly it sank back into the pool.

This is your heritage, said the Gregangel. *You have both the ability and the right to command it. Do not wish it to be so. Believe it.* Garrett resisted the urge to tell the Gregangel to shut up again. He looked deep into the pool, marveling at its light, strength and purity. Then he thought of Melody, trapped by the monster who was at least partially responsible for destroying countless billions in that distant galaxy; the same creature who had inflicted so much death and misery on his own world. What might humanity have achieved by now if it had not been for the Gamblemonster? Perhaps they would have already left the cradle of their world and discovered the magnitude of life that existed in this galaxy. Maybe they would have even discarded their physical shells and moved inward en masse to the next level. But for the Gamblemonster…

No more, thought Garrett. Suddenly, he was angry. By what right did these beings that had lived for so long destroy his world? *Damn them all to hell. This ends now._*Again Garrett focused his thoughts onto the earthsoul. He reached out again, but this time was different. This time he claimed his birthright. This time he *wanted* it.

The earthsoul moved toward him. In his mind, he saw a wide tentacle shoot through the Earth. He drew his senses back into his body, braced himself and let it come.

There was no hesitation. The shining tentacle of earthsoul slammed into him. He clamped his mouth shut, trapping the scream of rage and joy that threatened to burst out. The earthsoul poured into him. What he had commanded in the canal had been a firecracker. What filled him now was a very big bomb on a short fuse. He let it in, certain that he must be glowing like the sun.

GARRETT! The Gregangel's voice was still far away, but the fear and urgency it conveyed stopped Garrett short. *You must be careful. Take in too much, and it will destroy you.*

It's incredible, said Garrett. *I want it all.*

You must use restraint, said the Gregangel. *You are of no use to your wife and friends dead.* That brought Garrett up short. He backed off, trying to cut off the flow of raw power into his body and was suddenly terrified to find that he could not stop it.

Help me, he cried out.

I told you that the earthsoul is yours to command, said the Gregangel. *Quickly Garrett; you do not have time for this foolishness.* Garrett struggled some more and then calmed down. He took a deep breath and looked deep into his own body and soul. He saw where and how the earthsoul was entering him, and he saw how to shut it off. He imagined turning a valve, shutting down the flow, and to his relief, the earthsoul dwindled. A moment later, it stopped entirely.

Better, said the Gregangel.

Now what? asked Garrett.

Heal yourself, said the Gregangel. *Then heal your friend. As I channeled the earthsoul into you in the canal, you must channel it into him. He will know what to do.* Garrett might have argued that he had no idea how to heal himself, but it would have been useless. He had to learn fast. He looked inside his soul and saw the raging furnace of earthsoul now stored there, demanding to be used.

He used it. As the Shamrock chugged towards its final destination, he channeled the white hot power into his expanded senses. Overjoyed, he felt them spring to life, even though they were still filtered through his physical body. Then he trained his senses on his injuries and directed the Earthsoul to fix what needed to be fixing. He nearly laughed out loud at how easy it was.

Moments later, he was whole. Even the deep purple bruise from the bullet he had taken in the river was gone. He opened his eyes and saw Greg lying next to him.

Your turn, he thought. He grabbed a fistful of Earthsoul and used it to scan Greg's body. He winced at the damage. The beating he had endured had broken several bones and ruptured what Garrett was pretty sure was his spleen. Small wonder the man was still unconscious.

Garrett set about his task with a will. Carefully, he sent tendrils of Earthsoul into Greg's body, probing for any other injuries. Once he was satisfied that he had catalogued them all, he went to work; first the spleen, which was bleeding internally, then the bones, then the deep bruises. He lost track of time as he worked, but he knew that he had to finish before they reached their destination. Finally, he was done. Greg was still unconscious, but he was whole.

One last thing. Feeling like some kind of spiritual voyeur, he looked into Greg's spirit. If Greg was going to fight at his side, he needed ammunition. *And there you are*, he thought. The spark glowed softly. Garrett stared at it, remembering what the Gregangel had said about Greg's faith somehow changing and amplifying the earthsoul. *It is different*, he thought. He felt a thrill of excitement. Maybe they had a chance.

Greg stirred, slowly regaining consciousness. Garrett had to move. He opened that valve inside his spirit and shot a huge portion of earthsoul into Greg's spirit. The tiny spark blazed to life. Greg jerked and groaned. Garrett cracked his eyes open, checking to see if any of the Shamrock's crew had noticed. No one seemed to be heading in their direction. Most of them, in fact, seem to be more interested in Andie and Erica than the two bloody men lying on the deck.

"What…what have you…done to me?" Greg's voice was low, but it was strong. He had rolled over and was now face to face with Garrett.

"I've healed you," he said without moving his mouth. "Look, we don't have time for a crash course." From somewhere far away, he thought he might have heard the Gregangel snicker. "Remember the canal, Greg. Remember the power I used to free Andie and Erica. I've put that same power inside of you." Greg's eyes went wide.

"How?"

"No time," said Garrett. "We need to take this boat. Can you help me?" He saw doubt and uncertainty flash across his friend's face. He waited, knowing that he had gone through the same process. Greg closed his eyes, and Garrett knew that he was both remembering the canal and studying the earthsoul within him. Long minutes passed. Then Greg's eyes opened.

"I'm ready," he whispered. His eyes glowed with unbreakable determination. Garrett nearly fainted with relief. A part of him had believed that it would take the preacher more time than what they had to understand the earthsoul. Then he remembered how the Gregangel had told him that Greg's power was different...enhanced. Probably, Greg had been unconsciously using it for years. It was no doubt what had made him an effective leader. Garrett nodded at his friend.

"Now," he said. Garrett felt Greg's power surge. His shackles flew open and fell to the deck. Then, as one, the man of faith and the man of earth rose to meet the dark power of the enemy.

Chapter 22

The Taking of the Shamrock

By the time they were on their feet, the men watching from the upper deck were in motion. Shotguns, hunting rifles and pistols were leveled at them in almost perfect unison. Garrett harbored no false delusions. Despite the incredible power flowing through him, he was vulnerable. Given time, he might have found a defense, but at that moment, if the men fired, both he and Greg would die. They were going to have to strike first.

There was a loud clatter. Garrett looked toward the bow and saw Roy scrambling down the wooden stairs. Three men followed close on his heels.

"Leave these to me," said Greg, keeping his eyes on Roy. "Maybe you should deal with them." He motioned to the upper deck.

"Are you sure?" said Garrett.

"Heck of a time to ask," muttered Greg. Garrett had to choke back a laugh. Since that terrible night when the

Gamblemonster had shattered his family, he had been thrust into a battle that he was in no way prepared to fight. He did not know the rules, he did not have the means, and he most certainly did not know the stakes. Now, for the first time, he was ready.

The earthsoul flowed through every fiber of his being, demanding to be released. He focused his attention on the eight men on the upper deck. Roy reached the lower deck. His right hand gripping his pistol, his left clenched into a sweaty fist, he swaggered up to Greg.

"You get down now, boy," he spat. His face was twisted into an unnatural rage. Garrett actually flinched at the venom in the man's voice. Here was a hatred that had festered for a lifetime. It had been enhanced by the darksoul infesting the man's spirit, but it had undoubtedly planted by generations of human influence. His eyes were wide, and his upper lip twisted into a thin sneer. "I'll put you down hard, boy, and then go to work on those nigger bitches of yours." Greg said nothing. Roy thrust his face forward until his eyes were less than an inch from Greg's chin. "I said GET DOWN," he screamed. Garrett risked a glance at the confrontation. For the first time, he noticed that Roy was considerably shorter than either of them. Before, he had been a dark, menacing figure. Now he was just a pot-bellied, stoop shouldered middle-aged man, puffed up with his own importance.

"No," said Greg simply. Roy's widened, and his sneer became a snarl. He swung a slow and clumsy fist straight at Greg's temple. Greg could have blocked it with his eyes closed. His open hand came up and caught Roy's punch, stopping it in mid-swing. Roy yelled again. His two friends stepped forward, rifles at the ready. Garrett glanced at the men on the upper deck. Their guns were still pointed in his direction, but he could see that they were more amused than alarmed. *Enjoy the show boys.* He risked a quick glance at Greg.

"Gaaaagh." Roy wrenched his hand away and took a step backward. He hocked at Greg, who did not bother to dodge the spittle. It struck his right cheek and rolled down to his neck. "You're dead, boy," he snarled. He swung his pistol up and made to pull the trigger.

"Roy," shouted one of his friends. "Don't! He'll have our…"

"SHUT UP," screamed Roy. He centered the barrel on Greg's forehead.

Greg moved. Almost casually, he reached out with his left hand and grabbed Roy's gun. He jerked his arm in a savage twist, and suddenly he was in sole possession of the weapon. Garrett looked back at the men on the upper deck and saw that they were no longer amused. Three of them were sighting in with their rifles, ready to fire.

With a single smooth motion, Greg tossed Roy's pistol overboard. Roy was beyond reason now. He lunged at Greg, hands outstretched, ready to grab the preacher by the neck and choke the life out of him.

"That's enough," said Greg in a very low voice. He released his earthsoul. Garrett felt the surge of power leave Greg and slam into Roy and his friends. All four men screamed and fell to their knees. Readying his own attack, he wasted a single moment and reached out. The darksoul infesting the three men fought back, but it was outgunned. An instant later, it was obliterated. Roy fell to his stomach. Whimpering, he started to crawl away. Then he put his hands over his head and sobbed. All of this happened in a matter of seconds. It took the men on the upper deck that long to realize that the balance of power had shifted.

"Take 'em down," shouted one of the men.

Garrett could not afford to be subtle. He had already wasted too much time. He jammed that valve inside of his spirit open, only now the power flowed out, not in. Thinking back to the canal, he focused his mind and spirit.

The earthsoul flew away as what he perceived as a wide, blunt wedge. It struck each man simultaneously, knocking them back. Some of them screamed; others merely crumpled to the deck. All of them dropped their guns. Two of the men tumbled over the rail, falling to the lower deck. One of them landed on his back, knocked unconscious by the fall. The other hit at an angle, and Garrett heard the sickening 'snap' as his neck gave way. There was a deafening CRRRRAAAAK as the shotgun the dead man had been holding went off when it hit the deck. Buckshot tore through the rail. Garrett and Greg swung around in perfect unison, looking for Andie, Sean and Erica. Both men gasped in relief when they saw that they were unharmed. Andie was staring at her husband, her eyes wide.

"Stay there," yelled Greg. There was a sudden movement behind him, and he turned to see Roy staggering to his feet. "Run away," he said, lowering his voice. He took a step toward the smaller man, both hands clenching into fists. "Run away, or as God is my witness, I will pound you into bloody hamburger." Roy's head tried to swivel in every direction at once. The hatred and rage that had been seared into his face was gone, replaced by sheer terror. He saw his three friends still lying on the deck. One of them was shaking as if in the throes of some epileptic fit. The other two were still. He looked up and saw the men on the upper deck struggling to get to their feet.

"What did you do to me?" he screamed, his voice breaking. He whirled to face Greg. "What…what did you put in me?"

"More than you deserve," said Greg, taking another step toward him.

"I'm on fire," cried Roy. "Oh God, I'm burning!"

"Run away now," said Greg. There was no compromise in his voice, and no mercy. He advanced toward the man who had threatened to rape his wife and daughter. Roy looked into Greg's eyes, screamed again, and bolted. He tried to leap over the rail, but his foot caught and he fell headfirst into the river. Garrett could hear his frantic splashing as he dogpaddled away. "Hope there's gators," muttered Greg, staring after him, "Big ones, with sharp teeth." Then he turned and glanced at the upper deck.

"They're getting up," he said casually. Garrett saw that Greg was right. Some of the men were still down, but four of them were struggling to get to their feet. One of them even had the presence of mind to grab his gun. "Do you see him anywhere?" Garrett shook his head. He knew exactly who Greg was asking about.

"He's here," he said. "And I've got a pretty good idea where." Both men looked toward the pilot house.

'We're going to have to face him if we want this boat," said Greg. "We *do* want this boat, don't we?" Garrett thought about it. They could bolt over the side and swim to shore. With their captors down and Kyle dead, they stood a good chance of finding their way back to Kyle's store. Greg and his family could reclaim their car and drive away. Garrett did not have that option. He was not about to leave without Melody.

"Take your family and go," he said, turning to face Greg. He was fairly certain what Greg's response would be, but he had to make the offer. "Get out of here, Greg. You've suffered enough." Greg looked at his family, still huddled against the rail. Andie was staring at the men above her, unaware that they were no longer a threat.

"No," he said, his voice firm. "I won't leave you now, and I don't think that Andie will either, but I've got to get my kids out of here." He gestured toward the men. "Take care of that, will you?" Garrett nodded. Greg clapped him on the shoulder and then trotted over to his family. Garrett headed in the opposite direction. He ran to the bow and bounded up the stairs, reveling in the wholeness of his mended knee. He reached the upper deck just as the man who had managed to retrieve his gun swung to face him. Like Roy, his face was a mask of rage and hatred.

Garrett did not hesitate. He let fly with his earthsoul, only now he willed it into a needle thin beam. It struck the man squarely between the eyes. Garrett's initial attack had damaged but not obliterated the darksoul within the men. He immediately set out finishing the job. The beam plunged into the man with the gun, a deadly missile seeking its target. Once again earthsoul and darksoul collided. Neither could abide the existence of the other, and after a brief, vicious struggle, the earthsoul won. The darksoul dissolved into nothingness.

The man dropped his gun again, staggering backward. His arms flailed about, clawing at something that only he could see. Garrett broke off his attack, turning his attention to the rest of the men. Something tickled the back of his mind. He sensed movement above him and knew that the un-man was stirring. There was a sudden hiss, followed by a loud clank as the Shamrock's engine shut down. Silence fell as the riverboat's forward momentum slowed. A quick glance told him that they were drifting toward the left bank. All of the men were now on their feet. Some of them backed away, sensing the power of the earthsoul.

Given the chance, Garrett might have allowed these men the same choice Greg had given Roy. His time, however, was gone. He could feel the darksoul coalescing above him. Again he focused the earthsoul into a blunt wedge, and again it struck every man full force. No one screamed this time. The target of Garrett's first attack fell to the deck, unconscious. He wasted a moment he did not have and peeked into the man's spirit.

Dear God. The darksoul had fled, leaving behind a vast emptiness. At the center of that emptiness was a dim spark. As Garrett watched, it slowly faded. The dying man opened his eyes. They focused on Garrett. The man opened his mouth, trying to speak. Despite the approaching danger, Garrett moved toward him. The man struggled until he finally managed to whisper two words.

"Thhhhank youuuuuu." The spark within him flickered and winked out. He closed his eyes and died.

There was a loud slam above and behind him. He whirled and saw that a trap door had been flung open in the roof near the bow. It swung downward, extending a ladder that had been built into it. A single work boot appeared on the top run. It was followed immediately by its mate as the un-man began to descend. Darksoul poured through the trap door. With his enhanced senses, Garrett could see it pooling on the deck, spreading out, creeping toward him.

"Greg!" He was under no delusions. The creature coming toward him was far too powerful to handle alone. "Greg, a little help please!" The un-man's waist was visible now. The pool of darksoul continued to spread out, flowing toward him. Garrett flinched but held his ground. The earthsoul still infused him, but he had used a great deal of it on the un-man's henchmen.

The un-man's face came into view, and now Garrett *did* take a step back. Terror and loathing boiled within his spirit. At their first meeting, he had not been able to make sense of the man's features. Individually they were all there, but as a face they simply did not add up. Now he saw the un-man's true face.

There was no life…only darksoul. The physical body was long dead. Inside, where there should have been a heart, lungs and other organs were lumps of decaying tissue that were rotting from the inside out. The blackened skin on his arms, neck and face was peeling away in wide strips. The stench made Garrett want to vomit. Some kind of vile fluid soaked through the un-man's shirt and pants, giving the impression that he had just emerged from the river.

Half of the face was eaten away. Garrett could see light coming through the eye socket and realized that there was another hole in his skull, near the top of the head. There was no hair, only a mottled scalp with patches of exposed skull.

"Now you know," said the un-man. Despite lack of lips or teeth or even tongue, his diction was perfect. He reached the bottom of the ladder. Garrett took another step backward. He nearly tripped over one of the men lying on the deck. He grabbed the rail, steadying himself.

"The amazing thing," continued the un-man, "is that Gideon Reemes is still in here." A rotting finger tapped a rotting cheek. "He was the foreman on Gamble's plantation, and Gamble took him along for the ride." He snickered, and Garrett very nearly screamed. For just an instant, he could hear a human soul trapped within that snicker, one that was dammed beyond damnation. "I offered him eternal life, and he agreed." Garrett managed to shake his head.

"That's not life," he croaked. The un-man laughed.

"Of course not," he said. "I lied. But at least he still exists."

"It's an abomination." Garrett nearly fainted with relief. Greg's voice came from behind the un-man. He saw that the preacher was now on the upper deck.

"Took you long enough," he said. Greg ignored him, his attention focused on the un-man.

"You will release that soul you hold," he said. "I don't care what atrocities he may have committed in life. He doesn't deserve this hell."

"You know nothing of hell," said the un-man.

"Maybe I do," replied Greg, his voice cold steel, "I think you showed me a glimpse of it in the canal, but it makes no difference. I command you in the name of God, release that soul." Garrett waited for the un-man to laugh, but to his amazement, he flinched as if he had been slapped. He hissed and whirled on Greg. Garrett felt the darksoul boil and writhe.

"GREG," he shouted, but it was too late. The un-man lashed out. The darksoul slammed into Greg, driving him to his knees. The preacher screamed.

"Do you understand now?" said the un-man. "I am power incarnate. I am the vessel for the master. I am his eyes, his ears and his mouth. His power flows within me, and his life sustains me." In horror, Garrett watched as the darksoul began to seep through Greg's defenses. He fought back. His earthsoul, enhanced in some way Garrett could not understand, slowed the dark power's advance, but it did not stop it. Greg pitched forward, falling to his stomach. He closed his eyes and fought for his soul. His power flared again, but still the darksoul advanced. His mouth moved, forming a single word.

"Help."

Garrett jerked, as if waking from a nightmare. The sheer viciousness and power of the un-man's attack had nearly overwhelmed his senses. He had hesitated…only for a few seconds…but it had nearly been enough to finish his friend. He shook his head, fighting to bring his mind under control. He called upon his own earthsoul, but before he could strike, the un-man pointed a clawed hand in his direction.

"None of that, now," he said. Thick strands of darksoul lashed out. Garrett tried to form his earthsoul into some kind of shield, but he had neither knowledge nor time. The darksoul reached him, but instead of slamming into him, the strands wrapped themselves around his face, chest and arms. The un-man jerked them tight, and Garrett's body went rigid. "I'll get to you soon enough," said the un-man. He turned his attention back to Greg. Garrett struggled against the bonds, but they held him tight.

Think, you idiot. He tried to attack, but his earthsoul seemed to be bound as well. He could only watch as the un-man tore into Greg. His darksoul surged, penetrating the preacher's spirit, sinking deeper and deeper toward the core of Greg's being. Garrett could feel that irreplaceable spark of life within him growing dimmer by the second. *Help us,* he screamed in his mind, but if the Gregangel was listening, he was either unwilling or unable to help.

The deck lurched, and Garrett fell back, arms flailing. The Shamrock had swung to port and run aground. Garrett tried to grab onto the rail, but he could not move. He fell backward, hitting the deck hard. Sparks flared behind his eyes. The un-man staggered also, and for an instant, his attack was interrupted. Greg cried out and tried to crawl away, but again the un-man struck.

This time Greg could not even scream. His spark was fading fast. In seconds, it would be snuffed out. Garrett focused his attention on the un-man, searching desperately for any weakness, but there was nothing. He did not merely channel the darksoul. He *was* the darksoul.

Remember his words. The Gregangel's voice was faint, but it was there.

Help us, Garrett cried out in his mind.

His words, Garrett…remember his words.

Help… The plea choked in his throat. Suddenly the un-man whirled on him. His attack on Greg lessened, although it did not stop entirely. In the same instant, the Gregangel's voice went silent.

"What are you doing?" he demanded. Still on his back, Garrett stared at the abomination, unable to answer. The un-man lifted a hand, pointing a skeletal finger. Garrett's darksoul bonds tightened, squeezing both his body and spirit. His chest began to heave. "Stay down," said the un-man and turned his attention back to Greg. The bonds flexed back to their former strength.

Garrett reached out, trying to find the Gregangel, but there was nothing. *Remember his words.* Garrett tried to feel betrayed, but on some level he knew that it was not yet the time for the Gregangel to intervene. He was saving himself for the Gamblemonster. The battle with the un-man had to be fought and won by Garrett Webb and Greg Powell.

What did he say? Garrett closed his eyes. *I am the vessel for the master. I am power incarnate. I am his eyes, his ears and his mouth.* Garrett suddenly understood. *Not a mouth,* he thought. *A mouthpiece.* Keeping his eyes closed, he reached out with enhanced senses. The darksoul radiating off the un-man burned him, but he forced himself to study it. Finally, he saw it.

Gotcha. Darksoul infused the un-man, but now Garrett could see that it did not originate within him. It flowed into him from a thick, writhing tentacle fastened at the base of his neck. The tentacle…an obscene opposite of the beam that had given Garrett his earthsoul, stretched away from the Shamrock. It plunged into the river and Garrett knew that it ran straight to Gamble's Run. *He's just a puppet,* he thought. *A really disgusting meat puppet, but still just a puppet.*

Greg was almost gone, and still the un-man poured darksoul into the preacher. Garrett could feel the bonds holding him tight, just as he could feel the bonds trapping his earthsoul. He had to break free, and he had to do it now. He reached deep into his spirit and grabbed onto his earthsoul. The darksoul bond resisted and pushed him away. *No.* Again he reached down. He felt the un-man turn his attention back to him and opened his eyes.

"I said be still," he snapped. Again the bonds tightened. Garrett felt darkness closing in on all sides. He was losing consciousness.

Not like this, he cried silently, flailing against his bonds. His earthsoul remained trapped. He could not force his way past the un-man's barrier. He thought back to when he was lying on the deck. He remembered how he had brought the earthsoul from deep under the earth, not by forcing it but by *wanting* it.

And he understood.

This time he did not fight against the darksoul binding him. This time he simply wanted what was his. The earthsoul seemed to sense this and began to swell, pressing against the darksoul. His darksoul bonds tightened. The un-man broke off his attack on Greg and turned his full attention on Garrett.

"Fine," he said. The darksoul lunged at Garrett. Now, it did not bind him. It penetrated him, sinking deep into his spirit, but Garrett ignored the attack. Even at full strength, he could not have resisted the un-man's sheer power. Instead he focused on his own earthsoul as it continued to swell. It strained against the darksoul, and for a timeless instant, they were perfectly matched. Then the darksoul gave way. Garrett's earthsoul shattered its bonds and soared free. Gasping, he scrambled to his feet.

"Come at me, then," said the un-man. Garrett marshaled his power. He felt the un-man form some kind of barrier between them…a shield of sorts. He took a split second to study it and understood that he could form one as well. That might help later, but now, he only had one chance to end this fight. He formed his earthsoul into a thick beam and let it fly. It struck the un-man's shield and was immediately deflected.

"Try harder," said the un-man. Garrett clenched his teeth and attacked again.

"Pathetic," said the un-man, easily deflecting the attack. "I got a better fight from the preacher." He lowered his shield, reforming the darksoul. Garrett perceived it as a thousand razor sharp spears ready to plunge into him. The un-man made to launch them, but then Garrett used his single chance. He formed his last bit of earthsoul into a single blade, just a little wider than the tentacle fixed on the un-man's neck.

With no time left, he aimed and let fly. It lanced out, making straight for its target. The un-man sensed the attack, but he could see that this single beam of earthsoul was far weaker than the darksoul he possessed. He raised a withered hand to deflect it, but Garrett was ready. The blade swerved, arcing around the un-man and making straight for the tentacle. Too late, the un-man saw Garrett's strategy. Before he could counter it, the blade severed the tentacle. It snapped away from the un-man, writhing along the deck and flopping into the river.

The un-man did not scream. He did not make a sound of any kind. Garrett saw the darksoul infesting him drain away, dissipating through the deck. The un-man began to crumble. He did not fall forward or backward but rather sank to the deck. Garrett heard a sound like the crumpling of stiff paper and knew that it was the sound of a soul long confined freeing itself. He tried to see it with his enhanced senses, but there was nothing to see. He got the barest hint of something rise from the decayed flesh, hover for a moment and then dissolve into nothingness.

Garrett was still reeling from the vicious assault, but there was no time to waste. The Gamblemonster would know, of course. It had been his voice coming from the un-man's empty skull, and his power animating his corrupted body. He staggered over to the remains of the un-man, trying not to gag at the stench. All that was left was a sagging pile of decaying flesh. Even the bones had dissolved. Something shuffled against the deck. Garrett turned and was relieved to see that Greg was alive and on his feet.

"Are you all right?" he asked and then winced. It was a stupid question.

"No," said Greg. "I think I understand what happened to Andie in the canal now." His haunted eyes met Garrett's. "I don't think I'll ever be all right again." He looked down at the un-man's remains. "You beat him," he said. "I thought it was all over. I thought..." His voice broke.

"Get your family and get out of here," said Garrett softly. "They need you now."

"I know," said Greg. "I'm sorry, Garrett. I was going to stay with you to the end, but..."

"Go," said Garrett. He held out a hand. "I hope that someday you'll forgive me for what I brought upon you and your family." Greg took his hand in a firm grip.

"I've already forgiven you," he said. Then he stepped forward and wrapped Garrett in a tight hug. "God be with you," he whispered. He broke away, turned and took the steps down to the lower deck. Garrett gave the lump of flesh at his feet another glance. He wanted to throw it overboard, but he could not bring himself to touch it. He looked behind him and saw that the un-man's henchmen...those left alive...were still out cold.

I should probably toss them overboard as well, he thought. It was a good idea, but he lacked the physical strength. The only other option would be to kill them as they lay there, but no matter what their crimes, he would not become their executioner. The first man's dying words haunted him. Garrett could not help but wonder if he had been conscripted against his will, and if that was true, how many others were like him? It was an uncomfortable thought.

He grabbed the ladder the un-man had used and climbed up to the pilot house. The door was standing open. Garrett hesitated, but there was no hint of darksoul. The un-man was gone, and with it, the Gamblemonster's hold on the Shamrock. He stepped inside.

The controls looked straightforward enough. He was fairly certain that he could make the riverboat go where he needed it to go. He peered through the dirty glass to the lower deck. The bow was still resting against the riverbank. He would wait for Greg to get his family off and then fire up the engines.

Hang on, Mel, he sent, hoping against hope that his wife could hear him. He thought of the un-man. *And if you can hear me,* he sent to the Gamblemonster, *then know this. I don't care how strong you are. I don't care what kind of hold you have on my wife. I'm coming for you, and before this day is over, you are going to learn how to die.*

Chapter 23

Return to Gamble's Run

*G*arrett ran his hands across the Shamrock's controls. There was no wheel. Instead, three thick brass pipes rose from the deck, each ending about waist high. The left and right pipes were about four inches wide, while the center pipe was twice that size. Bolted onto either side of the center pipe were two devices; a standard compass and the engine telegraph. A large lever on the telegraph allowed the pilot to order reverse, slow, half or full speeds.

The left and right pipes each ended in a single brass lever. Both levers were about a foot long and extended away from the center. Garrett moved them back and forth and felt the ship rock gently. *Rudder controls*, he thought. A thin chain dangled down from overhead, and he realized that it was the ship's whistle. He shuddered, remembering its damned shriek, and decided that he would never pull it.

Next to the chain was another brass pipe, about three inches in diameter and extending from the ceiling. It ended a few feet above and to the right of the telegraph. The end twisted ninety degrees and flared out, giving it the appearance of a tiny, old fashioned gramophone. It took Garrett a moment to identify it as a speaking tube, no doubt connecting the pilot house to the engine room.

Definitely low tech, he thought. Examining the telegraph, he realized something.

"Crap," he muttered. There was no way to control the Shamrock's engines from the wheelhouse. All the telegraph did was relay messages to the engine room.

I'll find a way, he thought grimly. He glanced down at the bow again, wondering why it was taking Greg so long to get his family off. Suddenly, a shadow fell across the door. He whirled, his earthsoul surging. For an instant, he was certain that the Gamblemonster had resurrected the un-man and had sent him to the pilot house for Round Two. He was both relieved and irritated to see Greg framed in the doorway. The preacher held up both hands, palms out.

"Whoa Garrett, take it easy," he said.

"Why are you here?" said Garrett.

"It's good to see you too," replied Greg dryly.

"I mean it, Greg. Why are you still on this thing?"

"We're coming with you," said Greg evenly. "All of us."

"No way," growled Garrett. "I won't have your blood…"

"Garrett," said Greg.

"…on my hands," continued Garrett. "I want you…"

"Garrett," said Greg again.

"…off this boat," finished Garrett. Greg shook his head.

"Garrett, shut up." Garrett started to object, but a stern look from the preacher silenced him. "We're coming with you," said Greg. "We both know that you can't do this alone. It took the two of us to bring down that abomination."

"You were out of the fight," retorted Garrett. He was starting to get angry. "*I* took him down."

"Do you really believe that?" asked Greg softly. Garrett opened his mouth but shut it again. He looked away and shook his head. "Let me tell you why we're coming," Greg continued. "Do you think that any of the men who tried to take us at Nutall Rise are on this boat?" That caught Garrett by surprise.

"I have no idea," he said.

"Me neither," said Greg. "And if they're not here, then they're still out there somewhere." Garrett looked at Greg, meeting his eyes.

"I hadn't thought of that," he admitted.

"It gets worse," said Greg. "Thanks to you, I'm not exactly defenseless, but the poison that the Gamblemonster has been leaking into this place runs deep. I think that it's infested most if not all of the locals, which means that they could all be a part of this. There's no way I'm going to go plowing through what amounts to a jungle knowing that they're out there. Add to that the fact that I have no idea how to get to back Kyle's store. Do you?" Garrett shook his head.

"So what do you want?" he asked, his anger draining away.

"I think that the only way any of us are getting out of here is to finish this fight once and for all," said Greg. He stared hard into Garrett's eyes. "I don't want to do this. What I want to do is call down the fire of God on this place. I want to take my family home and forget that this ever happened. I want us to be safe, but I honestly believe that the only way for that to happen is for the Gamblemonster to die."

"That's not going to be easy," said Garrett. "It may, in fact, be impossible."

"Judging from that pile of rotting flesh lying on the deck below, you may be right," said Greg. "Are we going to have help?"

"I hope so," he said, wondering if the Gregangel would indeed join the fight. "Where's your family?" asked Garrett.

"Finding a better use for their shackles, along with some rope we found coiled up near the bow," said Greg. "They're making sure none of those punks causes us any more trouble. They threw the guns overboard."

"Good idea," said Garrett. Greg glanced at the controls.

"Can you drive this thing?" he asked. Garrett thought about it for a second.

"Not alone," he said finally. "I think that it's going to take both of us; one to steer, the other to make it go." He shrugged. "Your choice."

"In my teens I worked in the furnace room of a hospital," said Greg. "I had to maintain some good-sized boilers there. This thing can't be too different. I'll check on my family and then take the engine room."

"Try not to blow us up," said Garrett as Greg left the pilot house.

"Just drive. I'll push," retorted Greg over his shoulder. He dropped down through the trap door, leaving Garrett to study the controls. He played with the levers, getting a feel of the boat. He was just about to yank the lever of the telegraph when he felt a surge of earthsoul.

"Garrett? Garrett, are you there?" Greg's voice was coming from the speaking tube.

"Yeah, I'm here," he shouted back. Then he realized that he needed to be closer. He brought his mouth to within inches of the tube. "Greg? I'm here. Are you all right?"

"I'm fine," said Greg, his voice low and muffled through the tube. "One of Roy's playmates was hiding in the engine room. He might recover. Andie's seeing to him."

"What about the engine?" said Garrett. "Can you make it work?"

"I think so," said Greg. "Hang on." Garrett waited, counting off the seconds. Finally Greg called back. "Okay, got it. Send down a command."

Garrett grabbed the lever on the telegraph. Then, remembering a dozen old movies, he pushed it all the way forward and then brought it back to read reverse. A bell rang out, followed a few seconds later by another. The dial on the telegraph moved to read reverse.

"Here we go," said Greg. The engines coughed to life, and the Shamrock shuddered. Garrett looked out the back window and saw the paddle wheel begin to turn, slowly at first and then picking up speed. The ship vibrated as it fought to get clear of the muddy bank. Seconds later, it broke free.

"Okay," said Garrett aloud, "I can do this." He grabbed the levers, pulling one and pushing the other. The Shamrock's bow began to swerve into the riverbank, and he realized that he had it backwards. He reversed the levers. Seconds later, they were pointed in the right direction. Garrett rang for full speed ahead. The paddle wheel reversed, and soon they were chugging up the river.

"Not bad," said a voice from behind him. Startled, Garrett jumped.

"Thanks," he said. Andie moved into the pilot house, peering through the glass at the river.

"I blamed all of this on you," she said, keeping her eyes forward.

"You were right to do that," said Garrett. Andie shook her head.

"No, I wasn't," she said, turning to face Garrett. "I want you to understand that. Maybe if you hadn't come with us, this would never have happened." She shrugged. "Maybe it would have. Do you know for certain either way?"

"No," said Garrett.

"Judging from the way those men at Nutall Rise talked, they would have taken us whether you were here or not," said Andie. "Either way, I was wrong. I just wanted you to know."

"I appreciate it," said Garrett. "I really do, but why?" Andie pointed at the river.

"We're going to go up against something that shouldn't exist," she said. "I want things to be right between us. I think that it's important." Garrett nodded. He felt the sting of tears in his eyes and quickly wiped them away.

"Consider them right," he said.

"I'm still not sure I even believe any of this," said Andie softly. "Even after all that's happened, how could something like John Gamble still exist? Better yet, *why* does he exist?" Garrett realized that he needed to share the knowledge he had gained from his travels with the Gregangel.

"You definitely need to know," he muttered.

"Excuse me?" asked Andie.

"Hang on a sec," said Garrett. Keeping his eyes on the river, he called on his earthsoul, feeding it into his enhanced senses. Almost immediately, his perception changed. The sunlight seemed to dim, and the water went from brownish green to jet black. Garrett focused his senses forward and found exactly what he was looking for.

Just ahead, darkness that had nothing to do with storm clouds reared high above him like a mighty fortress. Black beyond black, it seemed to be burning a cavity into the sky. He could feel the raw, rancid darksoul radiating out of it. It dwarfed the Shamrock, not to mention its rookie pilot. He grabbed the telegraph and ordered one-quarter speed.

"Garrett," called Greg. "What's wrong?"

"I need to see everyone in the pilot house," Garrett said.

"But I've got to be here," said Greg. "What if we need to stop fast?"

"The river's clear," said Garrett. "And as far as I can tell, we're a good fifteen minutes away from the canal. Please Greg, it's important."

"On my way," called Greg. The Shamrock's engine throttled back. Soon after, Greg, Sean and Erica crowed into the pilot house. "Okay," said Greg. "What is it?" Quickly, Garrett told them what the Gregangel had revealed to him, from beginning to end. With the canal drawing closer, he managed to boil it down to a ten-minute tale. By the time he was finished, the writhing darkness that hung over Gamble's Run was almost on top of them.

"That's…the most incredible thing I've ever heard," said Greg at last.

"I know what I saw," said Garrett defensively. Greg held up a hand.

"I believe you," said Greg. "And when this is all over, I'm going to have to find a way to reconcile what you've told me with what I've believed all these years."

"Sorry about that," said Garrett. Greg laughed.

"I'll manage," he said, clapping Garrett on the shoulder. "More importantly, faith manages."

"There's something else," said Garrett. He quickly told Greg about his enhanced earthsoul. Greg stared at Garrett.

"Prayer," he said simply. "Or meditation, if you want. I've always believed that I've been speaking to someone when I prayed, but more importantly, I've always felt that I've *touched* someone…or something." He looked out at the river. "We're getting close," he said, his voice low.

"We're about to get a lot closer," said Garrett.

"Then I'd better get back to the engine room," said Greg. "Sean, give me a hand?"

"Yeah," said Sean. Garrett heard fear in the youth's voice, but he also heard determination. He glanced at Erica and Andie and saw the same determination etched into their faces. Greg and Sean left.

"We'd better check on our guests," said Andie over her shoulder as she and Erica started toward the door. "We wouldn't want them getting loose at the wrong time."

"Maybe you should pitch them overboard," said Garrett.

"Believe me, I thought about it," said Andie. "But somehow it doesn't feel right. Don't worry, they won't be getting loose."

"The Gamblemonster could use them against us," said Garrett.

"If it comes to that, I'll take care of them," said Andie. Garrett gulped and managed a nod.

"Could you at least take care of that mess we made?" he asked, meaning the un-man.

"Already done," said Erica. Her voice reeked of disgust. "He…it…is feeding the fish."

"I doubt the fish would have him," muttered Andie as she left. Erica followed her mother out of the pilot house while Garrett fixed his attention on the approaching darkness.

Can you hear me, you son of a bitch? I'm coming for you. He grabbed the telegraph and wrenched it hard, ordering full speed. A moment later, the riverboat surged forward.

"Garrett." It was Greg.

"We're almost there," he said.

"I know," said Greg. "I can feel it. We all can. Are you ready?"

"Hell of a time to ask," he said, mimicking Greg's earlier comment.

"I'm serious, Garrett. Are you…powered up? At full strength, I mean." Garrett froze. His breath caught in his throat. Without answering, he closed his eyes and looked. His earthsoul was still there, and it was still powerful, but his battle with the un-man as well as the Shamrock's crew had depleted it. He guessed that he was barely at half the strength that he had been before taking the riverboat. His hands started to shake, and he grabbed the steering levers tightly.

"No," he managed to croak.

"Then do it," said Greg. There was an edge in the preacher's voice. Garrett could not blame him. He had been heading into the fight of his life at nowhere near full strength. The Gamblemonster would have slaughtered him.

"I'm on it," he managed to get out.

"You'll have to share," said Greg. "I need to know what you did and how you did it."

"Watch," said Garrett. "You'll see."

"On my way," said Greg.

"Stay where you are," said Garrett. "You can sense what I do from down there. Just watch." Greg gave a muffled 'okay', and Garrett set about fixing a near fatal blunder. He closed his eyes and reached out, searching for that tendril of earthsoul. To his relief, it was still there, floating in the water. In fact, it seemed to be following them. Garrett reached out and was gratified to see it streak toward him.

The instant it entered him, Garrett sank to his knees, still gripping the steering levers. Raw power flooded into him. He soaked it up and then turned his internal valve. The flow lessened. He wanted more, but he had not forgotten the Gregangel's warning.

His spirit sizzled. It thrashed about in his body, demanding to be set free from its prison of flesh. Garrett could barely control it. The Gregangel's spiritual surgery had been effective, but he was no longer tightly bound to his physical shell. All he had to do was let go, and he would go soaring out of his world. With his eyes closed, he reached out and easily found Greg.

Do you see? There was no answer. Garrett focused his attention on the preacher. *Greg, we can communicate through the earthsoul.*

Dear God. Both wonder and terror laced Greg's mental voice.

Take it, said Garret. *It's your birthright.*

I don't...

GREG!

Yeah, said Greg. *Okay.* His effort was clumsy but effective. Garrett felt Greg's gasp as the earthsoul filled him. Then he showed him how to shut it off. A moment later, it was done.

You'll need to show your family, said Garrett. *It's going to take all of us.*

I know, said Greg. *Garrett, I had no idea...*

Just make sure you keep doing whatever it is you do that enhances your earthsoul, said Garrett. Greg did not answer. Garrett felt him reach out to his family. With his enhanced senses, he saw them catch fire, blazing with a power that most of humanity had forgotten. He felt both fierce joy and deep sorrow as they flared up one by one. The happy, carefree family he had met by the river was long gone. They were forever changed, drafted to fight a battle that they were only beginning to understand.

We're ready, sent Greg. Garrett gave a mental nod. The hulking darkness was now on top of them, soaring overhead. Just ahead was the gentle bend that hid both Nutall Rise and the canal's entrance. Garrett did not wonder how the Shamrock would get through an opening that their canoes could barely traverse, just as he no longer bothered to wonder how the riverboat had navigated the Warriors or made it past the bridge they had hidden beneath. It did not matter. The Shamrock belonged to them now. It would take them where they needed to go.

They rounded the bend, and Nutall Rise came into view. Directly across from it was the opening that led to Gamble's Run. He yanked the telegraph forward and then brought it back to one-quarter speed. Greg answered, and Garrett gently tugged the steering levers until the bow was pointed straight at the opening.

If he had been in a speedboat, he would have zipped past it without another glance. Even knowing what to look for, the physical opening was hard to spot. It was not as choked as the other end, but it was still hard to see.

His enhanced senses showed him something very different. The darkness seemed to coalesce, forming itself into a mighty wall, thousands of feet high and miles long. It ended on either side of the opening, dwarfing the tiny riverboat. Stretching across the opening was a massive gate.

"Are you seeing what I'm seeing?" Greg's subdued voice was barely audible through the speaking tube.

"If you're seeing a big freakin' wall and an even bigger gate, then yes," he replied.

"Why wasn't it like this before, when we came through the canal?" Garrett considered Greg's question.

"I think the Gamblemonster was playing with us," he said at last. "He thought he had us locked up tight, but he didn't expect the Gregangel to intervene."

"We're going through it, aren't we?" said Greg. It was a statement, not a question.

"Oh yeah," said Garrett. He gathered his earthsoul and felt the Powells do the same. Then, in perfect unison, they lashed out. Their earthsoul streaked toward the gate, but when it hit, it merely dissipated. Garrett frowned and readied another attack.

Wait. This time Greg's voice sounded out in his mind.

Why? he asked.

The Shamrock, said Greg. *That's our way in.* The engines revved up to full speed.

"What the…" Garrett felt Greg release his earthsoul, only this time he sent it into the Shamrock. The entire ship shuddered, but to his amazement, it actually soaked in the power. To his enhanced senses, the riverboat began to glow, softly at first, then with a blazing light that could not be seen with the naked eye.

It's a thing of both worlds, sent Greg. *The Gamblemonster has used it for years. It's ours now, but it's still a part of both worlds. Do you see?* Garrett did and in fact was slightly embarrassed not to have figured it out first. He followed Greg's example and sent his own earthsoul into the Shamrock. Andie, Sean and Erica joined in. Garrett gripped the levers as the black gate drew closer. He reached out to the earthsoul tendril, letting it fill him even as he filled the Shamrock.

CRAAAAAK! The riverboat shuddered from stem to stern. A few seconds later, he heard the trap door slam open. Erica popped through and stumbled into the pilot house.

"The lower deck has a huge crack in it," she said, breathing hard. "It can't take much more of this." Something tickled the back of his memory. A second later, he made a connection. Suddenly, the absurdity of the situation got to him.

"Captain, the engines are overloadin'," he said, mimicking a thick Scottish brogue. "They're canna take much more!" Erica stared at him.

"You are certifiable," she said, shaking her head. Garrett laughed again.

"We're in a riverboat built in the 1800s, heading toward a stronghold that holds the ghost of a man who built the canal, who was in turn trapped by a being that came from somewhere beyond the stars." He grinned at

Erica. "Please explain to me exactly what certifiable is." Erica did not hesitate. She pointed at the black gate.

"That," she said. Her voice trembled. "That is certifiable." Garrett's wild humor vanished as quickly as it had appeared.

"Sorry," he muttered. They were seconds away from the gate. He could see the natural opening with his physical eyes. It was far too small for the Shamrock, but that did not worry him. The black gate was the true barrier. Something creaked as they channeled even more earthsoul into the riverboat. Garrett could hear the sound of wood splintering.

"You'd better get back to your mom," he said, "and both of you get inside the engine room. This is going to be rough." Erica left without bothering to reply.

"Hang on," he yelled at the speaking tube. The Shamrock lunged forward. Garrett sent another jolt of earthsoul into aging riverboat.

The bow rammed the black gate. Garrett was flung backward, hitting the wall and falling to the deck. He heard the sound of wood disintegrating and felt the earthsoul filling the riverboat quiver and recoil. He scrambled to his feet and grabbed the steering levers.

At first, he thought that they had been stopped cold, but when he looked out, he saw that they were still moving forward. The gate was bowing under the assault, but it was holding. He felt a surge of earthsoul and knew that Greg was still conscious. He followed suit, pouring power into the fragile riverboat, heedless of how much he was using. If they could not break this barrier, nothing else mattered.

The Shamrock's bow had shattered down to the waterline. Black water sloshed into the hull. The damage was catastrophic. The riverboat was on its final voyage.

They ground to a halt. The paddlewheel kept spinning, and the riverboat struggled to move forward. The black gate bowed even more. For long seconds, two opposing forces matched each other strength for strength.

The gate gave way. To Garrett, it sounded like an ocean-sized sheet of ice colliding with a massive blast of steam. The roar screamed through his mind, and again he sank to the deck. He channeled more earthsoul into his already enhanced senses.

The gate splintered into millions of tiny shards, many of them striking the Shamrock. Even though they were not entirely of the physical realm, they still had an impact. The glass in the pilot house shattered. If he had been standing, he would have been blinded and probably killed. There was a loud 'pop' below, and he knew that the crack in the hull had expanded. The Shamrock did not have long to live.

Garrett scrambled to his feet. The engines were still running at full speed. He gripped the levers, trying to keep the riverboat centered in the canal. Despite its damage, the Shamrock valiantly struggled forward.

Melody! Can you hear me? Are you there? He mentally shouted the words as loud as he could, but there was no reply. Ahead, the Gamblemonster waited.

Chapter 24

The Gauntlet of the Damned

*B*ehind them, another darksoul gate formed. It closed quickly, severing the tentacle of earthsoul that was feeding Garrett. Dismayed, he watched it sink into the canal and disappear. The only power they had now was what was stored inside of them, and while it was considerable, it was also finite. He reached out, hoping to touch Melody, but drew his senses in immediately. Concentrated darksoul surrounded him, burning his enhanced senses.

The sun and even the sky had disappeared. They were surrounded by darkness. Garrett could see the water sloshing over the Shamrock's broken bow, but beyond that, nothing. He fed earthsoul into his natural sight, enhancing it. Vague outlines of both canal and land shimmered into view, but the darksoul fought him.

The images faded to mere ghosts. He had to try another way.

Suddenly, the riverboat began to glow. He felt the surge and knew that the Powell family had already figured it out. This time, they were not trying to shatter an impenetrable barrier. They were only trying to light their way. The Shamrock vibrated with the power as they fed earthsoul into its damaged hull. The glow increased until the riverboat was a blazing star in a dark universe.

The trap door flew open, and Andie climbed out. Garrett glanced at her and gasped. To his earthsoul enhanced vision, she was glowing from the inside out. She stepped into the pilot house, no longer an ordinary woman from Tampa. She was a goddess, shining with a power she wore like a second skin. Her face possessed both the stunning beauty of youth and the deep wisdom of the aged.

This is what we were meant to be, he thought, staring at the woman before him. *This is what they stole from us.* Andie regarded him with blazing eyes, a high and holy thing. He had to resist the urge to kneel before her.

"I feel the same way," she said. Garrett frowned, confused for a moment. Then he got it. With a thrill of amazement, he realized that she was seeing the same thing in him. Also, the earthsoul they shared was making it possible for her to pick up on his thoughts and feelings. Garrett fumbled for the words.

"Is everyone…" he began.

"Greg, Erica and Sean are fine," said Andie. She looked toward the canal. Garrett sensed her distress.

"What is it?" he asked. He could probably have seen it in her mind, but it did not feel right to pry.

"Those men are dead," she replied, her voice shaking. "We took cover in the engine room, but they…were unprotected." Garrett remembered how the darksoul gate had shattered, sending shards of raw power into the Shamrock. The prisoners would have been sliced to pieces.

"It's not your fault," he said softly. Andie nodded.

"I know," she said. "It's just…what was that?" Garrett felt it too…a surge of earthsoul.

"Trouble," he said. He focused his senses and saw it immediately. They were under attack. Thick tentacles that he remembered all too well were lunging toward them. Greg, Sean and Erica were fighting back. For the moment they were winning, but they needed help. "You need to get down there," he told Andie. She was already on her way.

Garrett gripped the steering levers, keeping the limping riverboat in the center of a canal that was far too narrow to accommodate it, but nevertheless did. All around them darksoul tentacles streaked out of the darkness. The Powells took up stations at the four corners of the Shamrock. They were learning fast. The tentacles came at them, only to be cut down with blasts of earthsoul. Garrett felt his own power stir, eager to join the fight, but he restrained it. The tentacles were only the opening salvo.

You have to hurry. The voice tickled the back of his mind, and he jumped.

Where the hell have you been?

Hiding, sent the Gregangel. *But that no longer matters. Your mate is dying. He will destroy her soul before he releases her.*

Then you need to…

You must get closer, interrupted the Gregangel. *At the moment, I am still hidden, but that cloak will soon be torn away. When that happens, I will attack.* Garrett felt the Gregangel's terror and understood.

You're going to lose, aren't you?

Most likely, said the Gregangel. *And I fear what will happen to me. I have lived so long that I no longer know how to die.*

You're not dead yet, said Garrett. He grabbed the telegraph and rang for full speed. Then he realized that Greg was standing on the bow, fighting side by side with his daughter.

Suddenly, the tentacles disappeared. Garrett felt them withdraw, seeping back into the darksoul walls. He reached out and saw that all four Powells were still standing. They glowed with earthsoul, but now that glow was slightly diminished.

He's not trying to stop us, he thought, dismayed. *He's wearing us down.* It was a grim but obvious truth. *Save your power*, he sent to Greg.

How? Greg's reply stated the obvious. They had to repel the attacks, no matter how much earthsoul it cost them.

The Shamrock was drifting toward the left bank, and he corrected his course. The riverboat responded sluggishly. Greg had throttled the engines back to a crawl. They were listing to port, and it was clear that they would not stay afloat much longer. Never mind the fact that the natural canal was only a few feet deep and not nearly wide enough for the riverboat to navigate. He could feel the weight and the depth of the dark water beneath him. If they went under, he had a hunch that they would sink for a long time. The sinkhole that had taken Molly flashed through his mind, as well as the underground vision he had shared with his daughter. *The waters run deep*, he thought.

"Look out!" Greg's voice sounded from below. Garrett focused his mind and saw the Gamblemonster's next attack.

"You've got to be kidding," he muttered. He flashed back to the Gamble plantation, remembering how the Gamblemonster had risen from his deathbed and dragged his slaves to their deaths.

The slaves were indeed dead, but that did not slow them down. They came out from the trees along both banks, tentacles of darksoul feeding each and every one of them. They did not shamble, like the zombies of so many George Romero movies. They splashed into the water and charged, as strong and agile in death as they had been in life. The water barely came up to their knees. It seemed that they were able to shift between the physical reality of the shallow canal and its hidden depths.

Garrett could see their faces in his mind. Like the un-man, their skin was blackened and rotting. It hung from their bodies in thick flaps. They were wearing the clothes they had worn when Gamble took them, but the remaining cloth was little more than a few dangling strips. He focused his mind on one of them, a young man who at the time of his death might have been in his early twenties. Pressing against the burning darksoul, he forced his sight deep into the man's center.

"Oh no," he moaned. He could see a dim spark inside the slave. A quick look confirmed that there was one in each and every man, woman and child coming toward them. Their bodies were dead and decaying, but the Gamblemonster had trapped their spirits within the rotting corpses.

Garrett. Greg's voice sounded in his mind. He saw it too.

Yeah, just like Gideon Reemes. Fine. We know how to deal with that.

Yes, we do, sent Greg. The preached attacked. His earthsoul, strengthened by something that not even the Gregangel understood, lanced out. He aimed for the nearest slave, cutting at the darksoul tentacle that fed him. The tentacle was severed immediately, but to Garrett's dismay it quickly reformed and reattached itself to the corpse. The slave did not miss a step.

That's not good, sent Greg.

You're going to have to do it the hard way, said Garrett.

Yeah, said Greg. *It's time to free these people.* Again the preacher's power lashed out, only this time it struck the slave square in the chest. Garrett watched as earthsoul and darksoul contended with each other, but the enhanced earthsoul wielded by Greg Powell was stronger. The darksoul broke apart, leaving the slave's glowing soul free. Garrett waited for it to flee the rotting corpse, but to his horror, it began to fade. *No,* cried Greg. Instinctively, he tried to send his power into it, to save it, but the instant the earthsoul touched the dying essence, the glow winked out. Garrett felt sick.

Greg.

No. Garrett winced at the anguish in Greg's mind voice.

Greg, you know what…

Don't you dare finish that thought.

Greg…we don't have a choice. Whatever we destroy, he'll rebuild…except for them.

I can't, said Greg. *Maybe their bodies, but not their souls. These poor bastards are still human.*

If they stop us now, we lose everything, said Garrett. The slaves continued to advance. The first wave had almost reached the Shamrock.

You know what you have to do, he sent to Greg.

I'm supposed to save souls, not destroy them, cried Greg.

You have to, sent Garrett. *Hurry!* A young girl who might have one have been fifteen reached out and grabbed at the deck, but when she touched the glowing riverboat, she recoiled. She opened her mouth to scream, but she no longer had lungs to make a physical noise. She screamed anyway, a scream that came from her tortured mind. The sound drove deep into Garrett's own mind. He moaned but managed to keep his hands on the steering levers. He saw the girl fall away, but he also saw a little of the darksoul contained within the creature seep into the Shamrock. The riverboat's glow dimmed.

Don't let them touch the boat, cried Garrett silently.

I saw, sent Greg, his mind voice filled with agony. *They're human, Garrett. They have...* Garrett could wait no longer. The rest of the slaves were almost upon them. He sighted in on the girl who had touched the Shamrock, formed his earthsoul into a narrow beam and let it fly. It shot out from the pilot house.

NO! Greg and Andie's mind voices shouted in perfect unison, but Garrett was not listening. The beam smashed into the slave, and again she screamed. As it had with the un-man's now deceased henchmen, the earthsoul burrowed deep into the darksoul, destroying it as it went. This time however, when it reached that dim spark, it snuffed it out. The body crumbled into the water and disappeared.

Garrett, don't do this. This was from Andie.

Help me, he sent, trying to reach all four of them at once, *or this fight ends here.* He sent a beam of Earthsoul into another slave, and once again what Greg Powell had once believed was an immortal soul winked into oblivion. Tears rolled down Garrett's cheeks as he destroyed another soul, then another and another. He was using his earthsoul at a frightening rate, but the slaves kept coming.

They were not mindless zombies. Once they were human, and underneath their rotting flesh, they remained human. The only way to stop them would be to destroy their last remaining bit of humanity. They would not move inward toward the Source. Their journey would end here, in the canal they had dug with backbreaking labor. They had lived and died as property. Now, instead of being released from their bodies and allowed to soar free, they would be obliterated.

He felt a surge beneath him. Greg had entered the fight. The preacher was joined almost immediately by his family. Earthsoul reached out, destroying slave after slave.

The battle raged on. Walking corpses continued to emerge from behind the trees and struggle into the water. While Garrett concentrated on steering, the Powells cut them down. A few reached the riverboat, and each time they touched it, its light dimmed.

Finally, it was over. The last soul of the last slave whiffed out. Garrett scanned his friends. Dismayed, he saw that they had used at least half of their power. He felt their grief and rage at the atrocity they had just committed and left them alone. The Shamrock creaked and groaned.

We are here, whispered the Gregangel. *Put the boat on land over there.* Garrett felt an invisible finger point to the left shore.

The darksoul… he began.

I will make a way, said the Gregangel. *Trust me, Garrett…one final time.* Garrett yanked the steering levers and the Shamrock lumbered slowly to the left.

Hang on everyone, he sent. The list was getting worse by the second now, and for a terrible moment, Garrett thought that they were going to capsize. Then the engines surged. Greg had seen the danger and returned to the engine room. With a final lunge, the Shamrock rammed against the land. There was a loud groan and then a series of harsh pops. Garrett looked and saw that the Shamrock had split in two, its back broken. The stern was sinking slowly into deep water that both did and did not exist. The paddlewheel was already submerged. Garrett scanned for the Powells and was relieved to see that they were all near the bow.

Go…now, said the Gregangel. Garrett felt something rip away, like a fragile veil in a stiff wind.

YOU. With so much darksoul surrounding them, he did not wonder that he could now hear the Gamblemonster. He felt the Gregangel rise from the Shamrock.

Yes, he said as he rose. *It is time to end this.*

It is you who will end, said the Gamblemonster. *Do not force me to destroy you.*

That choice is no longer yours, said the Gregangel. He plunged into the darksoul wall, and to Garrett's amazement, it cracked. An instant later, a wide fissure formed. The Gregangel had forged a path, but Garrett could sense that the encounter had weakened him.

Seconds later, the earth shook. The battle between two ancient foes had been joined.

Hurry. Now there was pain in the Gregangel's voice. *And someday, please try to forgive us.* Garrett staggered out of the pilot house. The entire deck was canted at a severe angle. He barely managed to get through the trap door and down the ladder. When he got to the stairs, he was relieved to see that the Powells were already on land. They were waiting for him just beyond the Shamrock's shattered bow.

There was another long series of creaks and pops. Behind him, the stern continued to sink. Then the stress became more than the Shamrock could handle. The stern broke away completely and disappeared into the depths of the canal. Garrett's leap cleared the bow. He landed on soft mud and fell to his knees. Greg was at his side in an instant, helping him to his feet.

"We've got to move," said Garrett. The glow from the Shamrock was dimming, but it did not matter. Like Andie, Greg was shining from the inside out, as were Sean and Erica.

"Which way?" said Greg. "I can feel the battle, but…"

"There," said Garrett, pointing into the woods.

Quickly they started out, Garrett taking the lead. They could all feel the Gregangel and the Gamblemonster close by, mortal enemies tearing into each other with no quarter asked or given. They tried to hurry, but the heavy underbrush hindered their progress. They had no choice but to follow the path the Gregangel had created. The darksoul walls rose high above them on either side. He could feel the path narrow as they began to repair themselves.

"Faster," he gasped.

"I don't see how…" began Greg, but suddenly they burst into the open. They pulled up, trying to get their bearings. They were standing in the middle of a wide, dirt road. Garrett stared at it, trying to remember where he had seen it before. Then it hit him.

"This is the road to the Gamble Plantation," he said, his voice raw.

"But the plantation wasn't this close to the canal," said Greg. "I know that much."

"Doesn't matter," said Garrett. "I think the Gamblemonster has recreated it here, and he's used darksoul to do it."

"So what do we do?" demanded Andie. "Walk right into it?" Again the Earth shook. All five of them staggered, but they managed to steady each other. Garrett looked hard at his friends.

"Yeah," he said.

"Garrett's right," said Greg. "The Gregangel's getting weaker. I think he's dying." Andie's eyes swiveled back and forth between her husband and Garrett. Then she looked hard at her two children.

"Don't even think it, Mom," warned Erica. "We're going with you." Andie nodded.

"Then let's finish it," she said. "And heaven help that thing if it hurts my children or my husband." She looked hard at Garrett. "Or you."

They followed the dirt road, peering ahead, trying to pierce the cloak of darkness that surrounded the Gamblemonster. The path made by the Gregangel continued to narrow. Darksoul closed in, held at bay only by the glowing earthsoul within each of them. Suddenly, they stopped. The path before them was blocked by a throbbing darksoul barrier.

"Only one way to go," said Greg. He reached out and took Andie's hand. She took Sean's who took Erica's who in turn grabbed Garrett's. Greg's voice echoed in Garrett's mind.

We move together, on three, he said. *One, two...* As one they stepped into the darksoul barrier. Garrett felt the weight of it, crushing him into oblivion. It was far more powerful than their first time in the canal, but this time they were better prepared and armed. Their earthsoul formed into a dome, shielding them. One step, then two, then three; the darksoul lashed at them, demanding that they stop, but no one was in the mood to obey. Four steps, five and then six. Then, just as Garrett could feel their shield begin to crack, they were through.

To their natural eyes, they emerged into a circular clearing perhaps a half a mile in diameter. There were no trees or brush, only hard, sun baked dirt. The clearing was empty.

All of them knew better. They channeled their earthsoul, and partially from Garrett's brief teaching but mostly from ancient memories that were awakening within them, the Powells used it as if they had been born to it. The other reality of the landscape sprang into full clarity.

The Gamble mansion stood in the exact center, glowing green with power from another place and time but also laced with the black of corrupted earthsoul. It was perfect in every detail, right down to the holes in the roof and the rickety front porch. Garrett could even see glowing fields of cotton behind it, along with the barn and stables. There were no slaves though. They were gone forever.

A man stood in front of the mansion, barely ten yards away. He wore the garb of a wealthy land owner from the 1800s. He was tall, well over six feet, and his face was young and handsome. His clothes appeared to be new made.

It was John Gamble's face, the same face Garrett had seen in the picture at Starbucks, but this was no decaying, imprisoned slave, nor was it a tool like Gideon Reemes. Gamble's body regarded them with glowing eyes, whole and perfect. Behind those eyes, the Gamblemonster peered out.

There was a hint of movement to the creature's left. Garrett glanced at it and saw what looked like a cocoon floating in the air, although this cocoon was made entirely of darksoul. Something struggled within it, and he had a sickening feeling that the Gregangel was out of the fight. He turned his attention back to John Gamble's body. The perfect face gave them a charismatic grin.

"What were you expecting?" he asked. He had the pronounced accent of a southern gentleman. "Did you think I would allow this shell to remain old and used up, or decay the way my servants did?"

"Slaves," spat Greg. John Gamble's body shrugged.

"Slaves, servants, their designation is irrelevant. They were my property, boy, just as you should be." He waved a hand. "Just as she is." The double doors to the mansion flew open, and a figure floated through them. It glowed with the green of the mansion. Garrett cried out. He formed a lance of Earthsoul and hurled it straight at the Gamblemonster. The creature did not even move. The lance struck him in the chest and dissolved into nothingness.

"This is my place, Garrett. It belongs to me, as does she." Garrett screamed in both defiance and grief. The figure was Melody, but it was not the Melody he had married, nor was it the Melody from the first visitation.

This version of his wife was a withered old woman, easily eighty or ninety years old. Her skin was wrinkled and dried up, her hair a dull a lifeless white. Her eyes were white with cataracts, and it was obvious that she was blind.

She's not here, he thought desperately. *This is some kind of cruel illusion.* But he was wrong. He knew his wife's face, no matter what her age, just as he knew the scar on her cheek...the scar she had received the night Molly died.

"Here ends your quest," said the Gamblemonster, and the laughter in his voice was terrible. "Do you want her back? I am nearly finished with her." Melody floated over to where the Gamblemonster stood. He reached out a spectral hand, forming it into a scoop and placing it on her chest. The hand sank into her, and when it did, she screamed. Garrett screamed as well. The pain in his wife's voice was unbearable. The Gamblemonster pulled his hand back, and it was glowing with a dull white light. He opened his mouth impossibly wide and ate the glow. "Mmmm," he said, licking his fingers. "She has been so good, but now she is nearly done. You can have the leftovers."

With a wave of his hand, he flung Melody away. She flew straight at Garrett, landing just a few feet in front of him. He heard the snapping of more than one bone. Moaning, he sank to his wife's side. Gently he cradled her head in his arms, brushing back the white hair from her wrinkled face.

"Mel," he whispered. "Mel, it's me. I'm here. Come on, honey. Don't leave me now." For a moment, he feared the worse. Then Melody's blind eyes fluttered and opened.

"Garrett," she whispered in the cracked voice of an old woman.

"I'm sorry," cried Garrett. "I'm so, so sorry."

"He fed off me," whispered Melody. "I tried to fight him, but he was too strong. I tried to reach you. I thought that maybe I did, but I guess he was just playing with me."

"No, it wasn't," said Garrett. "You beat him, hon. You found me, and I found you. It's over now." The old woman shook her head, a barely discernible movement.

"He's still got me," she said. She coughed up dark blood. "Garrett, please…free me."

"I will," cried Garrett. "Just hang on."

"I always loved you," said Melody, and now her voice was a whisper. "Even when…I hated you, I loved you. I should…never have left you." She coughed again. Her breathing was shallow and labored.

"Stay with me," pleaded Garrett. Melody's cracked lips barely moved.

"Freeee meeee," she whispered. And she was gone. Her head slumped in Garrett's arms. Something rattled inside her, and her body began to dissolve. Hands that had once caressed him disintegrated, followed by the arms and legs. The torso and head were last, until all Garrett was holding was a partial skull and a handful of dust.

"No," whispered Garrett, "please don't leave me." But it was too late. After all he had endured, all he had overcome, he had failed. Melody was dead.

Chapter 25

The Gamblemonster

*G*arrett cradled Melody's skull in both hands. He felt a surge of earthsoul and understood that the battle with the Gamblemonster had begun. He knew that Greg needed him at his side, just as he knew that the battle would be lost if he did nothing, but he could not bring himself to abandon Melody's remains.

"Garrett!" Greg's shout barely registered. He ignored it, just as he ignored the powers of light and darkness being hurled back and forth in the clearing. "Garrett, for the love of God, get in the fight!"

Free me. Melody's dying plea echoed back and forth in his mind. *Free me.* Garrett closed his eyes, searching for Melody's soul, terrified of what he would see.

No, he cried silently. *No, no, no.* It was there, still entwined with her remains, but it was far different than those of the slaves. Their souls had been trapped within rotting bodies, weakened beyond hope of salvation but still essentially intact. Melody's soul was weak, dying even, but it was no longer her own. Wrapped around it, and sinking *into* it, were thousands of threadlike tendrils of darksoul. Garrett understood the bitter truth. He could not free her. Even with all he had learned, he was powerless.

"I can't," he sobbed. The battle intensified, but he paid it no mind. Melody was dead, and all his hopes had died with her. He laid her skull gently onto the parched earth.

You can, said a very faint voice in the back of his mind. *You must.*

How? cried Garrett. *We tried to save the slaves. You saw what happened.*

You tried to save souls that had been trapped and tortured for over a hundred and fifty years, said the Gregangel. *Your mate's soul is still young, and despite what you see, it is still strong.*

There's no time!

You do not need time, said the Gregangel. *You can step out of time.*

What are you talking about? Garrett stared at the wreckage of Melody's body. There would be no bringing her back, but he was beginning to realize that the Gregangel was offering hope of a different sort.

You must feel it, said the Gregangel. *When I removed you from your body, bonds were severed that could never be fully repaired. I managed to reconnect you with your physical self, but...*

But those connections can be broken again, finished Garrett.

Not broken, said the Gregangel. *Undone. And when you step out of your body, you can also step out of time. Now hurry. You have much to do.* Garrett was not about to argue. He closed his eyes and focused his mind inward. He found the bonds that connected him to his body immediately. He perceived them as flimsy strings, tied off in small, easily undone knots.

He untied the knots. It took no time at all, and the instant the last knot fell away, he floated free of his body.

With a surge of raw, animalistic joy, he felt the vast senses he had acquired during his journey with the Gregangel return. He rose from his body and turned his attention to the battle. Greg and his family had been beaten back against the barrier they had forced their way through just moments ago. Thanks to their instinctive knowledge of the earthsoul, they had managed to erect a shield, but it was cracking. They huddled together, trying to protect each other.

Now, Garrett, said the Gregangel. *You know what to do.*

I do, said Garrett. *I really do.* With an almost casual shrug, he stepped out of time. The battle stopped. Even the Gamblemonster froze.

He's trapped in time, thought Garrett. *He took Gamble's body, and now he's bound by its rules.*

Yes, said the Gregangel. *As you will be, once you return to your body. You cannot fight this battle here. You can only free your wife.*

Hey, wait a minute, said Garrett. *Why can I still hear you?*

I cannot leave this shell, but for now, I can still send my thoughts out of time and communicate with you, said the Gregangel. *This will not last long. I am growing weaker even as we speak. Save your wife, Garrett. After that...*

After that, we'll see, said Garrett. He sank to the ground and focused his attention on Melody's dying soul. Now that he was free of his body, he could see exactly where and how the darksoul infested it. *He's right*, he thought, *I can do this*. He tried to focus his earthsoul, but nothing happened. *What the…*

Look into your body, Garrett, said the Gregangel. *It is a thing of the Earth, as is the earthsoul. Your spirit is a thing beyond Earth.* Garrett could see that the Gregangel was right. He easily sensed the earthsoul emanating from his body. He tried to call it out, but it resisted.

You are no longer a physical creature, said the Gregangel. *You can still use your power, but it will be much harder, and much more dangerous. Remember the slaves.*

Yeah, I got it, muttered Garrett. He concentrated, willing the earthsoul to come toward him. It strained him nearly beyond his limits. If he had been in his body, he would have been dripping with sweat. Finally, a threadlike strand moved toward him. He reached out to it.

Careful, warned the Gregangel. *You must move slowly.*

Be…quiet, snapped Garrett. He touched his earthsoul and nearly screamed. It burned him, but he managed to keep his hold on it. Then he turned to Melody. Her soul still hovered just above the ground, trapped by the thick strands of darksoul. The snakelike tentacles quivered, and he understood that like the earthsoul, they somehow existed both in and out of time.

Garrett went to work. He sent a narrow beam of earthsoul into one of the tentacles and was gratified to see it shrivel. *Good*, said the Gregangel, but Garrett ignored him. He destroyed another tentacle and then another. Melody's soul flared brighter and brighter, but each passing moment was taking its toll on him.

Wielding the earthsoul in his spirit form was both difficult and painful. He could feel a deep wound growing within his own soul. It was not the same type of wound he had received from the Gamblemonster, but it was just as devastating. He knew that if he did not finish soon, he would be permanently, perhaps fatally, damaged.

He kept going. Oblivion terrified him, but he could not bear the thought of losing what was left of his wife. He had come too far and endured too much. Another tentacle withered and died under his assault. His own power burned him.

Then it was finished. The last thread of darksoul quivered as the earthsoul seared it. Melody's soul flared with the light of a thousand suns. It rose above the ground, a stunningly beautiful, bright thing that was no longer a part of his world. Garrett released his earthsoul, and it sank back into his body. He was weakened, perhaps dying, but he no longer cared.

Free. It was Melody's voice. She started to shimmer, and Garrett realized that she was leaving.

Mel? Is it you? Is it really you? The glowing orb froze.

Garrett? My love, you did it. You freed me.

And now you have to go, cried Garrett. The soul shimmered again and began to change shape. A head formed, followed by a glowing, ephemeral body. Melody's eyes opened, and for the first time since she had walked away from him in that courtroom, Garrett saw the face of his wife. She smiled at him.

And you have to stay, she said. She glanced at the frozen battle. *They need you. That monster must be destroyed.*

I know, said Garrett. *But I don't want to lose you...not again.* Melody shook her shining head and smiled.

I remember everything, Garrett. I'm taking it all with me. I'll never forget you.

That's not enough, cried Garrett. *I want us to be together forever. Promise me that...please.* Melody shook her head.

I can't, she said. *Something is calling me. I have to go. I think that there's an incredible journey ahead of me.* She smiled gently at Garrett. *Your time will come, and when it does, we may meet again.*

Then let me go with you, begged Garrett. Melody's eyes bored into his.

No, Garrett, she said. *Your soul is growing weaker. Please my love. You still have much to do, and I cannot stay.*

No, said Garrett. *I want to go with you.* Melody frowned and shook her head.

This is not your time. Her voice was hard and unyielding. *Go back, Garrett. Finish the fight.* Garrett wanted to argue, but he could not bear the stern look on Melody's face. It burned him nearly as much as the earthsoul. Swallowing his grief, he nodded.

Goodbye, my husband, said Melody. *I love you.* She shimmered, and suddenly she was gone.

Wait, cried Garrett, but it was too late. He bowed his head. A dull pain washed over him, and he knew that even though he was outside of time, his time was gone. He focused his mind on his body and set about re-entering it. Like before, it was painful, almost beyond endurance. Once again his marvelous senses dulled. He sank into his body, reestablishing the fragile ties, and as he did, he stepped back into time.

What? The voice of the Gamblemonster echoed in his head. His body had fallen to the ground, face down. *What have…what have you done, Garrett Webb?* Garrett could hear both rage and disbelief in the Gamblemonster's voice. *That soul was mine.*

"She was never yours," gasped Garrett. The Gamblemonster snarled, but Garrett barely noticed. He was back in his body, and the only good thing about that was that he was able to use his earthsoul. Now that it was filtered through his physical body, it was no longer a danger to his soul. He called it forth, bathing his wounded essence in it. It did not heal him, but it gave him strength. It also used a great deal of his power. He managed to stand and face the Gamblemonster.

Nothing had changed. The Powells were standing with their backs to the darksoul wall. Their earthsoul shield was flickering. The Gamblemonster had nearly destroyed it. Andie and Sean were both on their knees. Greg stood in front of them with Erica at his side. The Gamblemonster glared at Garrett. The mask of John Gamble's face was contorted with rage.

"Fine," it spat. "You freed your wife. On your head be it. I claim another in her place." Garrett focused his earthsoul, preparing to attack, but stopped short. The Gamblemonster's words froze him.

"What?" he cried. "Wait!" He looked at Greg. "NO!" It was too late. Darksoul, laced with another, far more ancient power lashed out from the Gamblemonster. It crashed into Greg's dying shield, obliterating it. Greg screamed and tried to fight back, but he was overwhelmed. He went down, but he was not the Gamblemonster's target.

Thick tentacles, black mixed with green, streaked toward Erica. Andie tried to throw herself between her daughter and the Gamblemonster, but he was too fast. The tentacles smashed into Erica, sinking deep into her body. She went rigid. Then her eyes glazed over, and she fell to the ground. Even from where he was standing, Garrett could see that she was dead. Andie screamed, as did Greg. Sean simply stared at his sister's body, unwilling to believe that she was gone. Andie fell forward, covering her daughter. She kept on screaming.

Greg struggled to his feet. How he was able to even move after the Gamblemonster's assault was a miracle in itself. His face burned with rage and grief. He lashed out, but now even his enhanced earthsoul was weakened to the point of uselessness. The Gamblemonster shrugged off the attack.

"This is my place," said the Gamblemonster, "the center of my power. No one, not even those who wield this world's power, can touch me here." With an almost casual wave of his hand, he attacked again. Greg did not even have time to scream. He went down, although the remainder of his earthsoul managed to protect him. The Gamblemonster turned to Garrett.

"I think I'll save the woman for later," he said, smiling cruelly. "She might not be of my bloodline, but I really don't care. She's a fine little blackbird!" He drew out the word fine, making it sound like 'faaaahn'. "But you, Garrett Webb, you took what was mine, and now I will..." Garrett struck. He focused his Earthsoul into a needle thin lance. It flashed out, stopping the Gamblemonster in mid-sentence. Still smiling, he raised a hand to block the attack. Then his smile disappeared. For the second time, Garrett managed to surprise him.

"FOOL!" He whirled to meet his enemy. Garrett had aimed straight at the tentacles feeding the Gregangel's darksoul prison. His precision attack severed them, but as with the slaves, they reformed immediately. The prison barely flickered, but it was enough. He felt the Gregangel step out of time and then step back in, only this time he was on the outside of his prison.

Thank you, my friend, said the Gregangel. Then he charged.

The two foes met, and the force of the crash hurled Garrett to the ground. His earthsoul barely shielded him. Both Andie and Sean were knocked unconscious. In a flash of insight, Garrett understood that both the Gregangel and the Gamblemonster were drastically weakened. If they had been at full strength, the resulting collision might very well have destroyed the entire planet. Even so, he could see that the Gamblemonster was stronger. The Gregangel was being pushed back, and this time Garrett knew that he would not be trapped within a darksoul prison. This time the Gamblemonster would stop at nothing short of the death of his enemy.

Garrett attacked the Gamblemonster, trying to distract it, but the darksoul permeating the creature deflected the blow. The Gamblemonster roared in rage but kept his attention focused on his ancient enemy. He pounded the Gregangel, who now was so weak that he no longer had the ability to attack. He still managed to shield himself, but his defenses were crumbling.

Help me, Garrett cried out, painfully aware that his ally could not even help himself. *What can I do?* The Gregangel could not answer. His life force was being crushed out of existence. *Leave,* urged Garrett. *You can step out of time again. Get away from here.*

Can't. Trapped.

Then Garrett felt something give. The Gregangel's defenses shattered, and he was left open and vulnerable. Once again, Garrett saw the frail old man who had shown him so much. He stood before his enemy, waiting. With a roar, the Gamblemonster attacked. Garrett closed his eyes, but it did no good. He felt the Gregangel die. He felt his agony as darksoul tore into him, but far worse, Garrett felt his despair as he looked out into eternity and understood a single, devastating fact.

Not for me. Not for me. It was the Gregangel's last message. Garrett heard a final scream of terror. Then, a creature that had lived for billions upon billions of years died. He merely ceased to exist, the wonders of the next layer of creation denied to him. Garrett would have wept at the loss, but the Gamblemonster turned back to face him.

"My jailor is dead," he said. "Now it is your turn." He attacked. There were no more taunting words, no more gloating. Darksoul, laced with a power from beyond the universe, smashed into Garrett. He managed to gather his own power and form a shield. To his amazement, it held, but it was weakening by the second. He reached out to Greg or Andie, but both of them were still out. He tried to form some kind of counterattack but could barely hold off the Gamblemonster.

"Your power is nearly gone, and your allies have fallen," said the Gamblemonster. "Your time is over." Suddenly, Garrett had the insane desire to slap his forehead and let out a Homer Simpson 'doh!'

Time, he thought and acted immediately. The Gamblemonster had managed to trap the Gregangel in time. *But you don't know that he gave me that ability as well.* He did not hesitate. He stepped out of his body and then stepped out of time.

Once again, the Gamblemonster froze. Garrett floated above his body, studying the scenario below him. He glanced over at the Powells, taking a moment to study Erica. She was indeed dead, but her soul was intact. It was trapped in her body, surrounded by a shell of Darksoul, but it lived. It could still be freed and allowed to move inward, but only if he could find a way to destroy the Gamblemonster.

He reached out with senses that could now perceive the cosmos and took a good, hard look at the creature who at one time had been a man named John Gamble. He could see that the same type of tentacles that fed the slaves and the un-man also fed the Gamblemonster, only these seemed to sink deep into the earth. He traced their path, and as he did, he began to understand the sheer enormity of his task.

The tentacles grew wider and wider, burrowing downward and intertwining with each other. By the time they reached the festering pool of darksoul, they were massive. Garrett perceived them as the trunks of huge, malignant trees, each hundreds of yards wide. They sank into the darksoul pool, gulping in the power.

Worse, the unnatural power contained within the Gamblemonster, the same power that had shredded galaxies, was still there, mixing with the darksoul. It enhanced it, but it also seemed to fight it.

We were fools, thought Garrett, despairing. *Even at full strength...even if we were an army...we couldn't beat him.* He snapped his vision back to his own body, frozen behind its hastily erected shield. His earthsoul was not even a fraction of what the Gamblemonster wielded.

He looked outward again. Free of his body, he was able to pierce the barrier that surrounded the canal, the same barrier that had cut him off from the tentacle of earthsoul. Again he sent his vision plunging into the earth. He found the pool of pure earthsoul he had used before, but even that, when set against the power of the darksoul wielded by the Gamblemonster, was miniscule. He drew in his senses and covered an imaginary face with equally imaginary hands.

Dear God, what now? He was not praying. Despite all that he had learned, he still was not sure that he believed in an actual, intelligent, omnipotent being. He knew that there were layers upon layers of creation beyond his own, just as he knew that at the center of it all was the Source...the beginning of all life...but to believe that the Source was actually God was a leap that he was not prepared to make. So it is understandable that he did not expect an answer to his semi-prayer.

He got one anyway.

You will fight, my love...and you will win. Suddenly, the air shimmered. He looked up, and there, in front of him, was a shining door. Gaping, Garrett watched it open. Behind it was a light that could only be described with a single word...*pure.* A shining form stepped through, followed immediately by another. Garrett cringed away from the glow, but unlike the earthsoul, it did not burn him. Rather, it bathed him in a warm, healing embrace. He stared at the blazing figure in front, not daring to hope.

M-m-m-m-Melody?

Once, said the glowing form. It quivered and then coalesced into a recognizable human shape...Melody Webb.

I was Melody, said the image. *But I have lived so many lives since then.*

As have I, said the second figure. The very recognizable features of an adult Molly Webb took shape.

I don't understand, gasped Garrett.

I left this life, said Melody. *I traveled inward, through layer after layer of creation. I lived a thousand, thousand lives, each more wondrous than the last, until I came to the Source. I touched the Source, and now I...we...have been sent back to this time and place.*

But how...? He looked at Molly. *You came to me in my dream, but this is different.* Molly smiled, and suddenly she was his daughter again.

Really, Dad, you should have figured this out, she said. *Time is irrelevant.* Melody nodded and held out a shining hand. Garrett took it, aware that he was also glowing. The warmth of his wife's touch flowed over him, and he held her hand to his cheek. He felt her soul and knew that it was truly his wife.

I still don't understand, he said, basking in his wife's glow, *but right now I don't care.* Melody gently pulled away.

I traveled the layers, she said. *Because that is what we all must do. We all seek the source, Garrett. I had to go, but as Molly says, we are no longer bound by time. When it is your time to travel inward, you will understand. You will find the source yourself, and you will touch it, but before that...* Melody pointed at the Gamblemonster. *This abomination must be destroyed.*

What are you saying, Mel?

Listen to me, Garrett, said Melody. *There is the Source. It is truly the beginning of all life, but there is another power set against it. It lurks outside all of creation, waiting. You could call it the Anti-source.*

You mean the devil? Satan? Garrett stared at the image of his wife.

You have reached beyond the limits of your body, my love, said Melody. *Now you must reach beyond the limits of your mind. You cannot name this thing, just as you cannot name the Source. Both are simply too big.*

It was the Anti-source that began the war between the peoples of the Gamblemonster and the Gregangel, said Molly. *It fueled it, goading both sides on until the conflict split reality itself.*

These beings should never have entered into this level of your universe, said Melody.

So you are here to help me, said Garrett. He could not help grinning. The fight was not over. *Will the three of us be enough?* Melody shook her head.

Not the three of us...just you. We cannot fight this fight. Even though we can speak with you, we are not truly here. We both moved on so long ago. Garrett's sudden hope vanished into nothingness.

I can't do it, he said. *Not alone. I don't have the power. You must know this.*

That's why we're here, Dad, said Molly. *We touched the Source, and we've carried that power back to you.* She glanced over at the prostrate form of Greg Powell. *He's managed to use it*, she said, *or at least a very small part of it. Think of him as a firecracker. We're here to give you a nuke.*

How...

The same way you channel the power of this world, said Melody. *As your body understands the power of the earthsoul, your spirit understands the power of the Source. Take it, Garrett. Use it.*

Do it, Dad, said Molly. *Take what we give you and end this thing.* Garrett stared at the two women he loved more than life itself. He could give only one answer.

Yes, he said softly. Molly and Melody smiled in perfect unison.

Do not go back into your body until this fight is over, said Melody. *The Source Power would destroy it. You will have to give it up when you are done.*

I understand, said Garrett.

Then receive, said Melody. Her eyes burned with the fire of Creation itself. The power flowed through her, but it did not come from her. She was merely a conduit. Garrett reached out to it, and when it entered him, he exploded.

Chapter 26

Powers of Light and Dark

*G*arrett exploded outward and upward, outracing time and thought. He flew out of his universe, and then out of reality itself. In a space of time too small to be measured, he found himself looking down on creation in its entirety. By comparison, his journey with the Gregangel had been little more than a stroll around the block.

His senses grew until they became nearly infinite. He perceived the creation as a great contradiction…a marvelous orb that somehow grew larger as he peered inward. He could see every layer, beginning with the outermost…his own. Each layer had countless levels of its own, different realities that were both separate from each other and yet somehow connected. He marveled at its infinite complexity and could only laugh at those who insisted that it had come into existence by accident.

He concentrated on his own layer, peering into the countless realities. One stood out from the others. He knew when he saw it that it was the former home of both the Gregangel and the Gamblemonster.

You were wrong, he thought sadly, knowing that the Gregangel would never hear him again. *The war didn't end when you came here.* It was empty, devoid of life, but not of power. Poisonous green lightening still permeated the reality, flickering in and out of existence. *You never knew. Your entire reality was destroyed and you never knew.* He tore his eyes away from the dead reality and focused his attention inward. Further and further in, he followed the layers, until...

He saw the Source. It blazed out from the center, a beacon for all who had the desire to see. Its power permeated every layer, imparting life and light.

Stretching out from the Source was a glowing ribbon. Somehow it seemed not to pass through the layers, but rather wound *around* them. Like him, it also existed outside of time and space. It was the power Melody and Molly had channeled into him. It reached out all the way from the source, connecting him to it in a way that even in his disembodied state, he could not begin to describe. That connection not only empowered him, it healed him.

He could not take his eyes off the Source. It had no discernible shape or size. It simply *was.* He wanted to rush into it and be engulfed by its living light. He reached out with arms that did not exist and willed his spirit forward, but something barred his way. Reaching out, he discerned an invisible barrier. He pressed against it, trying to force his way through, but it was impenetrable.

Please, he cried out, *let me come to you.*

STAY.

It was not a voice. It was not even a thought. It was power incarnate. Garrett screamed and curled his soul into a tiny ball. The sheer weight of that single command threatened to crush him out of existence. The echoes reverberated, growing stronger instead of weaker. They assaulted him from every side. He tried to hang on, but it was like trying to ride out a hurricane in a rowboat.

Mercy, he cried.

LOOK. UNDERSTAND. Again Garrett cried out. He was terrified that the Voice would pound him into non-existence. Then, the same barrier that blocked his way reached around him, encompassing his soul with an unbreakable grip. He was opened and turned away from the Source. *LOOK.* It was impossible to disobey. He looked…and saw.

Beyond the outermost layer of Creation was something…and nothing. Even in his expanded state Garrett could not comprehend what his senses were trying to show him. It was not emptiness. It was not blackness.

It was never-ending madness.

Anti-source, he whispered. It was an eternal void, empty and yet not empty. It writhed and churned, as if trying to tear itself apart. It was not alive, but it was aware, and in its never-ending chaos, he could sense purpose. *No,* he thought, resisting the urge to avert his gaze, *not purpose…anti-purpose.* He saw something else as well. The anti-source was not only raging against itself, it was raging against Creation. It surrounded the great orb, lashing at it, trying to get into the outer layer.

If he had not been protected, his soul would have burned away, leaving only an empty shell that still knelt on the hard ground near Gamble's Run. The earthsoul he wielded in his body was nothing more than a flickering candle when set against the gale force of the Anti-source.

But he was protected by something far greater than earthsoul. The force that bound him also shielded him. He was able to look into the Anti-source and not go mad. He could feel the madness peeking in around the edges of his protective shield, but he had to see. He had to understand.

He saw it; a tentacle protruding from the Anti-source, worming its way into Creation. It was the polar opposite of the ribbon of power that connected him to the Source. Garrett followed the tentacle and saw that it had found its way in through the Gregangel's reality. Now, it was using that reality to invade others. His own reality was already under siege.

That's the real damage they did, he said, staring at the invading tentacle. *The power they threw at each other not only ripped a hole into our own reality, it gave the Anti-source a way in.* He felt agreement and approval. He focused his thoughts and took it further. *The Gregangel told me that his power could destroy my reality, but this is far worse than that. The Anti-source won't just destroy the layers. It will obliterate them. It will make them as if they never existed. It will eat its way through each and every layer until...*

And his mind finally shied away. Two all powerful forces, colliding in a way that he could not begin to comprehend...it was just too big. He scurried back to safe ground. *The Anti-source has got to be stopped here, in my layer.* Again he felt agreement. *I'm going to have to win that battle, but it doesn't stop there, does it? There are others like the Gamblemonster.* The Voice spoke again. This time however, it was still, small, and very close.

There are others like you.

And he was sent hurtling downward. Creation rushed toward him. It engulfed him, and suddenly he was back. He sank into his world, and it felt like coming home after a long trip. In the space of time between the 'tick' and 'tock' of an old fashioned clock, he returned to the canal. The power of the Source burned within him. It was time, he knew, to end the battle with the Gamblemonster once and for all.

He was still outside of time, and he knew that he was going to have to stay that way. If he reclaimed his body now, the power of the Source would burn it to ashes. He was going to have to drag the Gamblemonster out of time and face him in spirit form.

Melody? Molly? There was no answer. They had come and gone, and he could only hope that in some distant future, he would find them again. He put them out of his mind and focused on the Gamblemonster.

The creature was a raging contradiction. He was infused with the power of his own reality mixed equally with darksoul. But there was a third power, one of which even the Gamblemonster was not aware...one which Garrett was finally able to perceive. The power of the Anti-source was there, creating ties that forced the two lesser powers to work together. Without that power, the other two would have flown apart.

The fool, thought Garrett. *He actually thinks he's in control.*

It was going to be an ugly fight, but for the first time since he had come face to face with the Gamblemonster, he had a real chance.

First things first, he thought. He called upon the power of the Source. It thrashed inside his soul, ready and willing to obey his commands. *Do it*, he commanded.

The raw power of creation flew away, a blunt force trauma heading straight toward the Gamblemonster. Garrett concentrated on the ties that bound the Gamblemonster to John Gamble's body. Thanks to his recent out-and-in-and-out-of-body experiences, they were easy to target.

The Source Power smashed into the Gamblemonster, and instantly the ties were obliterated. The Gamblemonster screamed in pain as it was ripped out of the body it had stolen so long ago.

But Garrett was not yet ready to meet it head on. Again he released the Source power, only this time it had a very different target. He sent it hurtling deep into the earth. He could still see the massive trunk-like tentacles that fed darksoul to his enemy. Before, they had nearly driven him to despair. Now, with the power of the Source permeating him, they did not seem all that threatening.

Darksoul met Source Power. Garrett grinned as the darksoul burned. The trunks were severed. They withered into nothingness, falling away from the Gamblemonster. The Source Power dove deep into the cache of darksoul, searing it into oblivion. In moments, it was gone. He had effectively destroyed a third of the Gamblemonster's power.

YOU! His enemy's voice reverberated inside his mind.

Yeah, said Garrett, calling on the Source Power again. *It's time for you to die.* He could not give the Gamblemonster a chance to regroup. Now free of both body and time, it towered above him, a shapeless, writhing mass still infused with the power of its own reality. That power, mixed with the power of the Anti-source, was still formidable. Garrett's first attack had merely been a stinging slap to the cheek.

The Source Power lashed at the Gamblemonster, beating it back. Garrett pressed his attack, trying to rip his enemy apart. He could feel the creature's pain, but he could feel something else as well…fear. Encouraged, he fought harder.

But the Gamblemonster was still strong. It wielded great power, and it had survived countless battles over billions of years. It weathered Garrett's assault behind a thick, impenetrable shield. Garrett struck at the shield but could not get past it. He broke off his attack. The Gamblemonster rose again. Now it took the shimmering form of a twenty-foot high John Gamble.

My turn, it hissed. Garrett reacted without thinking. Using the Source Power was not unlike using earthsoul. The only real difference was scale. He threw up a shield just in time to deflect the Gamblemonster's assault.

If it had been just the Gamblemonster's own power, he would have shrugged off the attack and retaliated. The battle would have ended then and there. But the power of the Anti-Source would not be denied. It crashed into his shield, driving him back. He channeled more and more Source Power. He could still feel the ribbon feeding him, but he was beginning to realize that it would not be enough.

Did you really think that it would be that easy? laughed the Gamblemonster. Its fear was gone now. *You might have hurt me, but you will never destroy me. My power…*

Idiot, screamed Garrett. *That's not your power. It belongs to something else, and it's using you…*

JUST LIKE YOU USED GAMBLE.

The Gamblemonster hissed and doubled its assault. Garrett's shield began to waver and crack. He could feel the power of the Anti-source seeping through, burning him. He had nowhere to run.

Mel, help me. There was no answer. *Molly?* Nothing. He called out one last time. *If you're there…if you're listening…please help me.* This was not directed to his wife and daughter. It was a plea directly to the Source. He reached out along the ribbon, desperately trying to make contact.

The vision sprang full blown into his mind. Garrett gasped. The Source had literally given him a blueprint for victory.

Of course, he thought. *It's not for me, it's for him.* His shield was buckling. The only way to firm it up was to pour more power into it, but the only way he could win would be to cut himself off from the source of that power. The instant he did that, his shield would fail. He was going to have to take the full force of the Gamblemonster's attack. His soul would simply wink out, just like those of the slaves.

For an instant, he wavered. He cast about in his mind for an alternative, but there was nothing. He was out of options. He did not want to end. He wanted to be with his wife and daughter. He thought of Melody.

I saved you, he said, sending his thoughts out to her, hoping that she might somehow hear him. *And no matter what else, it was worth it. Live forever, wife. Live for the both of us.* And there was nothing left for him to say. He grabbed on to the Source Ribbon with his mind. Then, throwing a final surge of power into his shield, he severed his connection with the ribbon. It was no different that severing his connections with his body. The ribbon came loose, and an instant later, his shield collapsed. He could see it all happen as if in slow motion. The power of the Gamblemonster came crashing through, ready to crush him into oblivion.

It never reached him. There was a flash of pure white light, and the Gamblemonster's attack was deflected. For just an instant, Garrett stood free. Unhurt, the Gamblemonster screamed and readied another attack, but that instant was all Garrett needed. He flung the ribbon straight at his enemy. It streaked away, moving with the speed of thought.

The Gamblemonster saw the attack and formed another shield, but the ribbon was not just Source Power. It was a direct link to the Source itself. It sliced through the shield as if it did not exist. It struck the Gamblemonster in the chest, sinking deep into the ephemeral body. Garrett fell back, trying to digest the fact that he was still alive. He stared at the Gamblemonster.

The ribbon anchored itself deep in the creature. Garrett could see it putting out smaller ribbons, tiny threads of light. They spread to every part of the Gamblemonster's body, and as the spread, they grew. The shape of John Gamble shimmered and disappeared, replaced by the shapeless cloud.

The threads continued to grow, and now Garrett saw that it was seeking out the power of the Anti-source. The two powers, opposites in every conceivable way, tore at each other. Neither could abide the existence of the other. But the Source Power was not striving to destroy its enemy. It struck at the ties that bound it to the Gamblemonster's own power.

The Gamblemonster fought back, or rather the Anti-source fought back, using the Gamblemonster as a host. Garrett could feel the Gamblemonster's rage at the invasion, but he could also feel its fear and disbelief. The Gamblemonster was beginning to understand.

WHAT ARE YOU? it screamed, and the ties were severed. *DON'T...NO, DON'T...* The last tie broke and the power of the Anti-source exploded. Garrett still possessed some of the Source Power and managed to form a flimsy shield. If the blast had been directed at him, he would have been obliterated, but the power flew upward, fading into nothingness.

The Gamblemonster was still there, but it was a pale shade of its former self. All it had left was its own power, and now power that was greatly diminished. Both Anti-source and darksoul had been ripped away. It wavered and then drove back into the motionless body of John Gamble.

No, thought Garrett. *There's no way you get out of this.* He could not reclaim his own body while he still held the Source Power, but he could step back into time. Maybe...

It's okay, Garrett, said a familiar voice. *It's my turn.* Startled, Garrett turned and saw Andie standing above her body.

How...

A beautiful young woman named Molly helped me, she said. *She said that you would need me.* Garrett thought back to the blast of power that had deflected the Gamblemonster's final attack.

That was you, he gasped. *How?*

When I left my body, I could see what was feeding you your power, said Andie. *I recognized it. I think I've been touching it for a long time, just like Greg. I was able to use a part of it to give you the time you needed.* She looked at John Gamble and then at her daughter's body.

Let me finish this, she said, and the pain in her voice was unbearable. *Please.* Garrett was inclined to argue. He owed the Gamblemonster just as much if not more than Andie Powell. He wanted retribution for Molly and Melody. He wanted to end it, but when he looked at Andie and saw her grief and torment, he could only nod. He watched as she sank back into her body and froze.

It's time for you to release the power, said a much loved voice from behind him. He turned to see both Melody and Molly standing in the doorway. *Your friend will deal with the one you call the Gamblemonster.* She smiled. *You won, my love.* Garrett glanced over at the all too still form of Erica Powell.

And paid a terrible price for that victory, he said.

Garrett, you must release the Source Power, said Melody. *You cannot return to your body until you do, and you must return to your body. Your work is not yet finished.* Garrett let his senses dwell on the power still shining within him. It made him feel, well, godlike.

It's amazing, he said. *It's the power if life.*

It IS life, said Melody. Garrett nodded. He looked at Andie. Her body was still frozen in time. The instant Garrett returned to his own body, the battle would end.

Life, he repeated. Without thinking, he moved toward Erica.

Garrett, what are you doing?

Fixing something that should never have happened, said Garrett. He glanced at Melody. *Are you going to stop me?* Smiling, Melody shook her head. Garrett turned and focused his senses on Erica. He could see her soul. It was still bound by threads of Darksoul. With a casual shrug, he destroyed those threads. The soul rose, free. *No,* he said softly. *You will make that journey eventually, but for now, your family needs you.* He peered into her ravaged body. With the Source Power flowing through him, he could discern every atom of every cell and could easily trace the path of destruction caused by the Gamblemonster.

How fragile we are, he thought, *and how easily repaired.* He set to it. He marveled at how easy she was to fix. When he was done, he gently took her soul. Holding it the way he used to hold Molly when he gave her a bath, he eased it back into her body, reforming the bonds that held the two together. The Gregangel's surgery had been both hasty and clumsy. Garrett's was measured and precise. When he was finished, Erica was restored both physically and spiritually. He looked back at Melody.

She is special, said his wife. *Protect her, Garrett. She has a great role to play.* Garrett nodded, staring at Melody.

Are you really Mel? he asked. Melody smiled, and it was the smile he knew and loved.

Yes, she said, *and no. I remember everything about her, and her life with you, but I have grown so much since then.* Garrett eased over to her, standing as close as he dared. She reached out and put a warm, real hand against his cheek. *You will understand when your time comes. Trust me, it will be all right.*

I've really missed you, whispered Garrett. Melody nodded. *Will we ever be together?* he asked.

There is so much I cannot tell you, said Melody. *But know this...our journey together is not over yet.* She held a hand in farewell. Molly moved to stand next to her mother. *Be well, Garrett. Live well, and love well.*

We left a gift for you, Dad, said Molly.

A gift? asked Garrett.

You'll know it when you see it, said Melody, and an instant later, they were gone. Garrett stared at the empty space, weeping non-existent tears.

Goodbye, he said softly. Then, remembering that the battle was not quite over, he slowly released the Source Power. He expected to feel alone and empty once it was gone, but was surprised to find that he felt healed and whole. Quickly, he slipped back into his body. This time there was no pain or discomfort. It was like slipping on a favorite pair of jeans. Time swirled around him, and an instant later, he was back in his physical world.

Several things happened at once. John Gamble's body came to life. With a look of utter terror, it turned and began to run. Earthsoul flashed, and suddenly that body fell to the ground. Garrett looked at Andie and flinched at the look of raw hatred on her face.

"NO!" The scream ripped out of John Gamble's throat, but it was the Gamblemonster doing the screaming.

"Yes," said Andie in a low, deadly voice.

"You want help?" asked Garrett. The look Andie gave him said in no uncertain terms, *Back off.* Garrett considered telling her that her daughter was no longer dead but decided against it. He could see Erica beginning to stir. Neither Greg nor Sean had noticed yet, and Andie did not need to know. There was no place here for mercy.

Andie poured on the earthsoul. White fought with green, but now the white was stronger. It annihilated the green one piece at a time. Garrett was fairly sure that Andie could have destroyed the Gamblemonster in one fatal blast, but she was taking her time. She wanted to *hurt* it. Garrett thought the countless people who had been corrupted by the Gamblemonster. He thought of Melody and Molly, and he thought of Eden. He kept his mouth shut.

The fight was over in seconds. The Gamblemonster's power flickered and then went out. An instant later, John Gamble's body exploded into dust. The tiny particles flew in every direction but then disappeared as if it they never existed.

Please. The voice sounded in his mind, weak and fading. Even with his earthsoul enhanced senses, he could barely perceive the Gamblemonster as a weak, ephemeral cloud. *Please, no.* Then like the Gregangel, it faded from existence. Andie fell to the ground, weeping uncontrollably.

"Mom? Dad?" Erica sounded as if she had just awakened from a long, deep sleep. Garrett saw that she was getting slowly to her feet. She looked troubled but very much alive.

"Erica? Baby?" Andie rose, her face a mixture of disbelief and heartbreaking hope. Erica reached out to her mother, and the two women fell into each other's arms. It took a moment for the commotion to register with Greg. He turned, and when he saw his daughter alive and whole, he got up, stumbled across the short distance and sank to his knees again. Both Andie and Erica met him there. The three of them threw their arms around each other and held on for dear life.

Sean watched his reunited family, his brow furrowed. He did not quite seem to grasp the fact that his sister was alive. Then Greg reached up and pulled him into the family embrace. Garrett looked away, giving them their space. He let his eyes wander around the clearing. The glowing mansion was long gone, as was the barrier.

This place is clean, he thought, shaking his head at the wonder of it all. *I wonder if it will make a difference to the people who have lived here for so long?* He thought of Melinda Chance. He would have to tell her what had happened, but he doubted that she would believe him. *The waters run deep. I guess they always will. People have to choose to change.*

"Garrett?" Greg's voice came from close behind him. He turned and was suddenly swept into a massive bear hug. Seconds later, Greg was joined by his family. As Garrett stood in the middle of the hug, he suddenly realized that for the first time since he lost Melody and Molly, he had a family.

"Garrett, what's happened to you?" Andie broke away, staring hard at him. Considering recent events, Garrett had to throttle the urge to break out in a fit of uncontrollable laughter.

"What do you mean?" he asked instead. Greg was now looking at him as well, as were Sean and Erica. They shared a single look of amazement.

"You're...you're..." began Sean.

"You're young," whispered Andie. "Your face, your body...you could be in your twenties." Garrett's heart thudded. He broke off the hug and stared at his hands. They were a young man's hands. He felt his face, but the wrinkles that had been there since the Gamblemonster had stolen his life force were gone.

"I'll know it when I see it," he whispered.

"Garrett, what's happened?" asked Greg. "It's over, isn't it? Garrett nodded.

"Yes…and no." Greg understood.

"The others," he said, and Garrett nodded.

"That's a battle for another day," said Greg. He slid one arm around Andie and another around Erica. "Let's go home."

"How?" said Andie, sniffing a little. She really was not all that concerned.

"We'll find our way," said Greg. "We'll follow the river and get back to Kyle's store. Our cars should still be there."

"What about his friends?" asked Sean. Garrett felt Greg's Earthsoul stir.

"Do you really think that they'll be a problem?" He smiled. It was not a nice smile. Sean shook his head. Greg took a last look around. Then, his arms still around his wife and daughter, he started off. Sean fell in beside his mother, who pulled him close. Garrett followed behind.

"You coming with us?" Greg asked. Garrett nodded, thinking of Melody's command to watch over Erica.

"All the way," he said.

Epilogue

They followed the canal to the river and followed the river to the landing. From there, it was easy to get to the store. They encountered no one along the way. By the time they arrived, they were all filthy and exhausted. It was late in the day, and they wanted nothing more than to put as many miles between them and the canal as possible.

"What about the bodies?" Garrett had asked as they trudged along the river bank. He was thinking about Kyle and Reggie, as well as the men on the Shamrock.

"I honestly don't know," said Greg. "Sooner or later, someone will notice that they're missing. They'll find

Kyle and Reggie eventually. I doubt that anyone will ever see the men on the Shamrock again."

"Could we be…" Garrett let the question hang.

"We'll see," said Greg. Garrett did not find his answer at all comforting. Desperate battles of light and dark aside, there were a dozen missing men, not to mention two bodies lying somewhere not far away, their faces shattered thanks to the un-man's shotgun. The barrier, the Gamblemonster's former prison, was gone. It had faded with the death of the Gregangel. Sooner or later, those bodies would be found.

They walked in silence. After a while, Erica fell back to walk next to Garrett. She looked troubled.

"You okay?" asked Garrett. She nodded. "How do you feel?" She thought about it for long seconds. Then she said a single word that chilled him to his core.

"Reborn." She looked at Garrett, and for just a moment, he thought he could see just a glint of the Source Power shining out of her eyes. Then she moved back to her mother, leaving Garrett alone to ponder the implications.

They came up behind the store. As soon as they rounded the corner, Sean gave a shout of glee. Both cars were still there. He started to rush forward, then stopped.

"Kyle took our keys," he said. Greg laughed.

"We'll search the store," he said. "But even if we can't find them; well, I wasn't always a preacher. I can get them started." Garrett laughed at the look on Sean's face.

They came around front and stopped. Sitting on the front step was a man. He was young, maybe in his thirties, with a thin, pale face. He wore filthy jeans and blue work shirt. Garrett did not recognize him, but he had no doubt that he was a part of the gang that had been waiting for them at Nutall Rise. Four Powells and a Webb focused their earthsoul, but the instant they saw the confused, empty look on his face, they relaxed. This man was no danger.

"Who are you?" he asked. There was no malice in his voice, and no recognition. Greg stood before him.

"We're just passing through," he said. "Are you all right?" The man shook his head.

"I think…something's gone. I…can't remember." He looked up at Greg, his eyes pleading. "I can't find it. Do you know where it is?"

"Yeah," said Greg softly, "and trust me on this. It's not coming back." The man stared at Greg a moment longer and then looked away. A single tear rolled down his cheek. "About what you asked before, Garrett," said Greg in a low voice, "about Kyle and the rest. I don't think that it's going to be a problem."

"I think you're right," said Garrett. They searched Kyle's store and were thrilled to find both sets of keys lying next to the register. Greg grabbed them and handed Garrett his.

"Where are you going?" he asked.

"That depends," said Garrett. "What are you going to do?" Greg thought about it.

"Heal," he said. "Go home and try to get my life back." He looked at his family. "*Our* life back." He cocked an eye at Garrett. "You want to tag along?"

"Yeah," said Garrett, "If you'll have me."

"You know the answer," said Andie. "You're a part of us now." They went outside. The man was still sitting on the steps, his face blank. Greg unlocked his car, all the while staring at him.

"I know that look," said Andie. "What are you planning?" Greg bit his lip.

"You won't like it," he said.

"I never do," said Andie. "Spill it, Powell."

"I'm thinking that we have men and women in our church that can take over for us," said Greg. "I'm thinking that we destroyed the evil that has possessed this place for generations. I'm thinking that some of the people here are going to need a lot of help." He looked at Andie, unapologetic. "And I'm thinking that a new church might be exactly what they need." Andie stared at her husband for a moment and then shook her head.

"Yeah, I figured it was something like that." Greg looked at Garrett.

"You in?" he asked.

"I've never really been into the whole church thing," said Garrett, "but yeah, I'm in."

"Come on, Greg," said Andie. "Take us home. We have a lot to talk about." They got into their car, and Garrett got into his. After all that had happened, starting the engine and pulling out to follow Greg seemed ridiculously mundane.

They followed the dirt road to the main highway and turned toward the interstate. Greg had assured Garrett that once there, they would be in Tampa in a few hours.

As they drove, Garrett tried to wrap his mind around everything that had happened. The memories of the wonders and terrors he had witnessed when he was out of his body were fading. His physical brain simply could not contain them. He was grateful for that. He felt strongly that no human should have to live with that kind of knowledge.

He had become a part of something much bigger than he could ever have imagined. There would be other battles. He was certain of that, just as he was certain that there were others like him…and Erica, especially Erica.

He still grieved over Melody's death, but his grief was tempered by the knowledge that both she and Molly were alive and well. He had an eternal perspective now, and it would serve him well in the coming years.

He squared his shoulders, feeling the strong firm muscles in his back, arms and legs. He was healthy again, and whole. Possibly better than whole. Thanks to Melody and Molly's gift, he felt more alive than he ever had before, and while he was not sure, he had a sneaking feeling that his lifespan was now quite a bit longer than normal. Melody had restored him with the power of the Source, and that kind of power left a lasting mark.

He drove on, following the Powell's to his new, albeit temporary home. Sooner or later, they would return to Gamble's Run, but his journey would not end there. He had a new life, a new family and a new mission. It was not what he wanted…not by a long shot.

But it would be enough.

The End

David F. Gray is an award winning television producer and director although his first love has always been writing. He wrote his first short story at age 10 based on the television show Lost In Space and featuring his boyhood crush, Penny Robinson. Three years later he abandoned poor Penny in favor of the more worldly Judy.

He is older and heavier than he would like to be and possesses a sense of humor that has gotten him into trouble on more than one occasion. Contrary to the opinions of his friends and his two adult offspring, he is NOT insane. He is currently working on the sequel to Gamble's Run entitled Darksoul Rising as well as a handful of short stories. He and Heidi, his wife of thirty-four years, live happily in Sulphur Springs, Florida, an older Tampa neighborhood where rumors of ghosts are common.

<u>Other HellBound Books Titles</u>
<u>Available at: www.hellboundbookspublishing.com</u>

Blood in The Woods

Based upon true events...

For Jody, growing up in the late eighties and early nineties in the small Louisiana town of Hammond with his best friend Jack was filled with wonderful childhood memories.

Time spent playing in the woods, shooting pellet guns, blowing up mailboxes, fighting at school and upon the dawning of interest in the fairer sex, their carefree lives typical of children with few responsibilities and no worries beyond the next pop-quiz or getting to second base. As they grow older together and experience the joys and pains of life, love, family and friendship, they uncover a grim secret that their home town has kept, and through little more than an innocent, idle curiosity, Jody and Jack stumble upon something horrific in the woods and their lives quickly take a most sinister and dangerous turn as they find themselves hunted by an unspeakable evil...

Them

Ray Sanders returns home from Florida to bury his mother.

Soon, the supernatural evidence behind his mother's demise begins to surface in the form of dreams and mysterious happenings.

During all of the madness, Sanders must face his destiny and vanquish the generations-old evil that has plagued his family since the 1800's...

In 1854, Louis Sanders, with the help of Elias Atkins, dug a well to provide water to the family farm. What they did not anticipate was the water to be infested with Odomulites - ancient sins. These malevolent beings - were trapped in our world on their way to the spirit world - formed a pact of protection with both Sanders and Atkins; the families would serve as guardians of the Odomulite nests and in return, a blind eye would be cast when the Odomulites took host bodies to inhabit and feed upon. It was this pact, which in 2016 would propel Sanders and Julie Fontaine - a young woman with a special connection to the Spirit World - into the heart of the last active nest to rid the town of its insidious Odomulite population.

Southern House

"Move over Slenderman, there's a whole new reason to be afraid of the dark!"

There are some places that lie where the barrier between worlds is thin and growing thinner. These corridors are as old as the Earth itself, hidden in dark and forgotten places, waiting to be found. There is a being who stalks these places and travels between those worlds. He was given the name Mr. Shift by generations of children and madmen. Just as Hickory Grimble hits rock bottom, he inherits his grandparents' farm and believes his luck is changing. He soon finds he inherited more than money and land. Haunted by his own inner demons, now he has new problems. He begins to see strange creatures on the dark, sprawling acreage, animals that have no business living in middle Tennessee. He also discovers a decrepit, abandoned house in the forest that never seems to be in the same place twice. Balanced on a razor's edge between, addiction and fate, Hick is now face to face with an ancient evil that has returned once more to claim more of the town's children.

Worship Me

Something is listening to the prayers of St. Paul's United Church, but it's not the god they asked for; it's something much, much older.

A quiet Sunday service turns into a living hell when this ancient entity descends upon the house of worship and claims the congregation for its own.

The terrified churchgoers must now prove their loyalty to their new god by giving it one of their children or in two days time it will return and destroy them all.

As fear rips the congregation apart, it becomes clear that if they're to survive this untold horror, the faithful must become the faithless and enter into a battle against God itself.

But as time runs out, they discover that true monsters come not from heaven or hell...
...they come from within.

David F. Gray

These Walls Don't Talk, They Scream

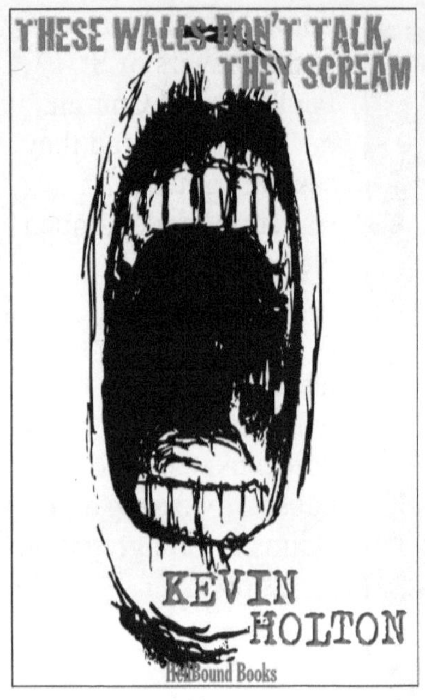

When three-year-old Charlotte witnessed her mother's death and was left alone with the body, she began hearing the voice of a person living in the walls of her house.

This voice comforted her as best it could, guiding her to call 9-1-1. Twenty five years later, Charlotte has returned with her own family to reconnect with this presence.

The recent death of her son leaves her distracted and mourning, though, so she doesn't realize her daughter can hear this entity too.

The Children of Hydesville

When the malevolent entity that Maggie and Katie Fox unleashed in Hydesville in 1848 returns in 2018, it must be stopped - at all costs.

Manhattanites Derek David and his wife Edith receive an invitation to visit the Keilgarden Colony, a secluded community located five hours north of the city in the village of Hydesville.

Dedicated to nurturing children with psychic abilities, the colony was built in 1948 on land that includes the cottage where Maggie and Katie Fox first heard the ghostly rappings in 1848 - which started the Spiritualist movement.

But what begins as a late-summer respite swiftly turns into a confusing and terrifying ordeal as Derek and Edith experience increasingly bizarre and disturbing events, which drives Derek to set fire to the Fox house.

Months later, New York Times reporter Sheila Irving and her boyfriend, Kevin Jackson, visit Hydesville to investigate Derek's motivation. If those gathered in the village succumb to the powerful entity that controls the area, they will partake in the creation of union children - psychically gifted offspring whose malevolent powers will reach far beyond the confines of the small township.

Schlock! Horror!

An anthology of short stories based upon/inspired by and in loving homage to all of those great gorefest movies and books of the 1980's - that golden age when horror well and truly came kicking, screaming and spraying blood, gore & body parts out from the shadows...

It was the decade that brought us everything in the cinema and on VHS from the Italian 'nasties' to *Elm Street, The Lost Boys, Hellraiser, The Thing, Day of the Dead, Reanimator, Return of the Living Dead, My Bloody Valentine, Henry: Portrait of a Serial Killer, Cannibal Holocaust*....and superlative directors such as David Cronenburg, John Waters, Roger Corman and - of course - Clive Barker.

All of this was, naturally, reflected in the books we devoured - Guy N Smith, Clive Barker's *Books of Blood*, James Herbert, Jack Ketchum, Gary Brandner and Richard Laymon, to name but a mere handful.

This 80's themed/inspired tales of terror is compiled by one Mr. **Bret McCormick**, himself a writer, producer and director of many a schlock classic, including *Bio-Tech Warrior, Time Tracers, The Abomination, Ozone: The Attack of the Redneck Mutants* and the inimitable *Repligator*.

A HellBound Books LLC Publication

http://www.hellboundbookspublishing.com